Praise for *Firebrand*

"A fantastically violent, utterly thrilling tale . . .
Philip's clear prose is as fiery as whiskey."
—*The Sunday Times* (London)

"The immortal (though not invincible) Sithe world
of the brothers and the all-too-familiar human
world come alive with expertly drawn details."
—*RT Book Reviews*

"Philip has created a compelling tale with
top-notch world-building and characterization.
Readers will thrill to her creations and eagerly
await the next offering in her Rebel Angels series."
—*VOYA*

"Add in murder, betrayal, and the politics of
queens and warrior factions and you have
a powerful fantasy filled with satisfying mystery
and challenges. Perfect for fantasy and
even mystery collections."
—*Midwest Book Review*

Tor Books by Gillian Philip

Firebrand

Bloodstone

BLOODSTONE

REBEL ANGELS
BOOK TWO

GILLIAN PHILIP

TOR®
fantasy

A TOM DOHERTY ASSOCIATES BOOK • NEW YORK

This is a work of fiction. All of the characters, organizations, and events portrayed in this novel are either products of the author's imagination or are used fictitiously.

BLOODSTONE

Copyright © 2011 by Gillian Philip

Originally published in Great Britain in 2011 by Strident Publishing Ltd.

A Tor Book
Published by Tom Doherty Associates, LLC
175 Fifth Avenue
New York, NY 10010

www.tor-forge.com

Tor® is a registered trademark of Tom Doherty Associates, LLC.

ISBN 978-0-7653-6942-0

Tor books may be purchased for educational, business, or promotional use. For information on bulk purchases, please contact Macmillan Corporate and Premium Sales Department at 1-800-221-7945, extension 5442, or write specialmarkets@macmillan.com.

First U.S. Edition: November 2013
First U.S. Mass Market Edition: June 2014

Printed in the United States of America

0 9 8 7 6 5 4 3 2 1

This one's for my Lost Boy

ACKNOWLEDGEMENTS

Bloodstone had a long and convoluted birth, and I have lost count of the people who helped me drag it kicking and screaming into respectable form. Hilary Johnson and Chris Curran beat those truculent Sithe into shape, and I send them huge thanks – which also go to my terrific agent, Sarah Molloy, to Derek Allsopp, Michael Malone, Pam Fraser, Tanya Wright, and Fiona Cruickshank. An early draft stretched the admirable patience of Brian Keaney and Jon Appleton of the Literary Consultancy.

Seth had an extra outing for this edition. For taking him to a war zone and keeping him right, I'm enormously grateful to Hugh Fulton: ex-soldier, OSCE election observer, and human cannonball.

I madly love everyone at Tor Books, especially Whitney Ross, Eliani Torres, Amy Saxon, and Alexis Nixon, for their enthusiasm at taking Seth stateside, and for their endless patience with me and my last-minute rewrites. Thanks, too, to Alison Stroak and

Keith Charters at Strident, who cut and polished the *Bloodstone* for its UK outing.

Graham Watson and Jennie Hood – I couldn't have done this without you. Thanks to you both, and to the ferocious Martin Bowes of the Glasgow Company of Duellists, for showing me the proper way to resolve a dispute about semicolons. Longswords at dawn, guys, anytime.

Endless gratitude to Katherine Langrish for allowing me to use a quote from her haunting Tam Lin poem "Janet Speaks."

All the mistakes and omissions are, as always, mine. Except when the Sithe mess around with their Gaelic, because that's what they're like.

And as always, much love and humble thanks to Ian, Lucy, and Jamie, who put up with an awful lot of door-slamming, head-banging, and burnt pizzas. *Twice*.

Oh Queen of Fays –
If I had known of this day's deed –
I would have let your knight, Tam Lin, ride down
    to Hell on his milk-white steed.

– Katherine Langrish, "Janet Speaks"

THE SITHE

(WITH TRUE NAMES WHERE KNOWN)

Kate NicNiven: Queen of the Sithe, by consent. Queen of the Full-Mortals, in her dreams.

Leonora Shiach: Witch. Mother of Conal and bound lover of Griogair.

Conal MacGregor (Cù Chaorach): Rebel clann Captain; son of Griogair MacLorcan [Fitheach; assassinated].

Seth MacGregor (Murlainn): Half brother to Conal; bastard son of Griogair and Lilith [Kate's counsellor and friend; died voluntarily at Kate's hands].

Stella Shiach (Reultan): Sister to Conal; daughter of Leonora, and former courtier to Kate NicNiven.

Aonghas MacSorley: Rebel fighter; bound lover of Stella (Reultan).

Finn MacAngus: Daughter to Stella and Aonghas.

Eili MacNeil: Daughter of Neil Mor MacIain; lover to Conal.

Sionnach MacNeil: Eili's twin brother; Seth's best friend since childhood.

Torc Marksson: Fighter; formerly of Kate's clann, now of Conal's.

Cluaran MacSeumas: A captain of Kate's clann.

Gocaman: Watcher at the Fairy Loch–Dubh Loch watergate.

Cuthag, Feorag, Gealach, Iolaire, Easag, Lus-nan-Leac, Bradan & Alainn: Fighters of Kate's clann.

Grian: Healer; fighter of Conal's clann.

Fearna, Carraig: Fighters of Conal's clann.

Orach: Fighter of Conal's clann; occasional lover of Seth.

Skinshanks, Slinkbone & Slakespittle: Lammyr: corrupt cousins to the Sithe.

PROLOGUE

The man I was going to kill had strikingly beautiful eyes. I could see them in the magnified sight, warm and honey brown, reflecting the flames from the blaze in the mini-mart.

My shoulder was hard against a parapet: not stone this time, but pockmarked concrete, the dust of it hanging in the air from the last artillery bombardment. Down below me on the pitted road lay a bloated red dog, legs stuck out rigid, like a toy some child had knocked over. Beyond the high-rise flats, half-eaten by shell fire, rose dry golden hills, hovering in the haze of summer warmth, pretty and distant.

I barely noticed the smell anymore. *Animals. Muck. Human waste.*

Wasted humans.

He isn't the first to die here, and he won't be the last.

Something cold trickled through my veins and

nerves, stiffening my muscles, and my finger trembled on the trigger. *Witless reflex.* I clenched and unclenched my fist, relaxed. I tweaked grit out of my eye and blinked into the sight once more.

He'd moved. He'd jumped down from the personnel carrier and walked behind it, snapping an uncooperative plastic lighter at his cigarette. A militiaman shifted between us, an RPG launcher slung over his shoulders. That one was human.

The one who followed him down from the cab, the one with the Zippo lighter? It wasn't.

Bloody hell, had four centuries turned me into a full-mortal? The thing was as human as I was. I was a twenty-first-century Sithe; at least, I was these days. What should I call it, then? *Differently evolved.*

I swallowed. This didn't explain everything about the man in my sights, but it explained a lot. It wasn't as if full-mortals needed a personal Lammyr to encourage them – but, hey, carnage could always be worse if a man used his telepathically enhanced imagination. The Lammyr's stained and punctured beret, scavenged off some corpse, was tilted at a rakish angle. This one had style. I watched it flick its scrawny thumb on the lighter wheel and offer up a dancing flame to its titular captain.

I wondered if the man with the beautiful eyes had a brother who loved him: a brother with a head for heights and a good shooting eye. A spot between my shoulder blades started to itch.

Get out from behind that truck, you inconsiderate sod, and give me a chance.

I mean, it's nothing personal.

He'd got his cigarette lit, at least. I was happy for him. He sucked on it and blew smoke into the afternoon air. It dispersed, drifting with the dust of shattered buildings.

It's nothing personal.

I wondered if the old woman in the headscarf had been something personal. I hadn't looked at her for a while, but I knew she lay on the edge of my vision, spraddled without dignity in the middle of the road, face lost in a dark stain of blood, hand still outstretched to her fallen shopping trolley. No, I doubted it was personal.

Another Jeep rumbled into the deserted street, kicking up dust clouds, and militiamen climbed out of it, swinging weapons like they were designer bags. The man with the cigarette laughed, shouted to a colleague, pointed at the far hills.

Come out, then. Or somebody move the truck. I want to go home.

You can't go home, whispered the voice of reality. *If you could go home, you wouldn't be here.*

I drew a breath, sighed it out. More than a decade since I'd been to my real home. Centuries since I'd had a chance to live there. This was not my war. My war had been on hold for a long time. It waited for me beyond the Veil, with my lover and my friends and my best of enemies. It waited in a world beyond a Veil that hadn't died yet, but that grew more shabby and threadbare with the years. My queen had sent us into exile, me and my brother and my beloathed family, and if we didn't find her precious

Bloodstone in the next couple of decades – the one that would determine the Veil's fate – I could see Kate getting her way without it. I could see the Veil dying of its own accord, and my own world dying with it; I could see this wretched otherworld having to be mine forever.

Maybe I liked this war better. Maybe that went for all my full-mortal wars. Because they were nothing personal.

Anyway, at least the old girl with the headscarf had gone fast, with a sniper's bullet to the head. In my sixteenth-century day, she'd have been toasting on that fire in the mini-mart.

The captain was striding towards a group of his fighters now, throwing down his cigarette half-smoked and grinding it thoroughly with the toe of his boot. Which struck me as hilarious, given that half the town was in flames. I brought the stock back to my shoulder and found the sweet spot between his beautiful eyes.

'Are you out of your *mind*?'

It was said on a strangled rasp, right behind my shoulder. I cocked my head round and lifted an eyebrow at O'Dowd.

'No, Sergeant. Right inside it, Sergeant.' *And yours, if you only knew it.*

'How did you get here? I didn't even notice you were bloody missing.'

You shouldn't even have noticed now. Who was your great-great-grandfather, Tam fecking Lin? 'I, uh . . .'

'Bloody well back off, MacGregor. Unless you want to cause an international incident.'

'You'll have to give me a minute to think about that.'

'No, I won't. You have rules of engagement, and this doesn't fall into them. Back off. Now.'

'He's a mercenary psycho. And he's hanging out with a – a . . .' *Right. Explain that to the sergeant.* 'Another psycho,' I finished lamely.

'Let me spell this out for you, seeing as I've had my ear bent right off by the lieutenant. That bastard down there? His best mate is the future PM's favourite warlord. And the future PM is going to sign that cease-fire agreement on Thursday.'

'I'm dead impressed with your grasp of current affairs, Sergeant.'

'It's irrelevant, MacGregor. This is the relevant bit, right? We are *not here to get involved in firefights*. Now, *back* the *feck off.*'

My finger itched, but I couldn't do it now. I'd blown my chance. I turned back to gaze longingly at my target, standing in full view now in his dust- and blood-spattered fatigues, the sun on his red blond hair and the crinkle of laughter round his warm burnt-sugar eyes.

I'd met him before, of course. I'd crossed bullets with him in other wars. I hadn't liked him even before he met the thing with the Zippo lighter, so it was probably just as well he didn't catch sight of me. But the thing with the Zippo did.

It pulled off the beret, ran skinny fingers through

its strands of hair. Lazily it tilted its head up, to the sun and to me.

Its yellow eyes creased and it smiled. I knew I'd lost, this time. So I smiled back.

I wished I could have killed Laszlo. But even though I didn't like him, it wasn't as if it was personal.

Not in this world. Never personal.

PART ONE

Seth

'We shouldn't be here,' said Aonghas.

There were so many replies to that one, I didn't know where to start. I kept my mouth shut, and my opinions to myself. My brother wouldn't thank me for starting a squabble. Conal wasn't looking at either me or Aonghas as he pressed his hand to the wet salt-crusted rock face, but I'd seen his shoulders tense with irritation, and I wasn't in a mood to push it.

The cliff face had unnerved him too: he never was good with heights. I'd found the way down and he'd climbed after me, but he hadn't liked it and his edgy temper lingered. I'd thought that being with Eili MacNeil last night would have softened his rough edges, but leaving her yet again had only made things worse.

So what? I missed Orach, as much as I was capable of missing anyone. It didn't mean I couldn't soak up the light and the landscape of home, storing it away in my cells for the next long exile. In my head I knew the silver sheen on the water was no different on this side of the Veil, or the shatter of waves on rock, or the clamour of gulls. My heart knew it was a different world: a whisper's breadth and a whole universe away. I'd never stopped missing it and I never would. I'd make the most of it on the chances I got.

Find me the Stone, Kate had said. *Don't come back till you have it.*

We shouldn't be here. But it had never been any other way. We'd stopped short of swearing that we'd never cross the Veil, would never come home till we found the Stone. We'd told Kate we'd stay away, but we'd given no oath.

So we lied. So what? As if we could live without breathing our own air once a decade.

Kate NicNiven must know that as well as we did. And she must suspect that we sneaked through the watergate like thieves now and again, as if we were skulking Lammyr and not the sons of Griogair Dubh. But if our queen wanted to kill us, she'd have to find us first.

It was a game, that was all. It had become our life's game. We risked death every time we played, but if we didn't play, we'd go mad. Anyway, what's life without an adrenaline kick?

I think I liked it better than Conal, though. And Aonghas liked it least of all, especially now.

'I'm serious,' he went on. 'We've been here too long this time.'

'I know that,' snapped Conal.

I gave Aonghas an I-told-you-so look, and he rolled his eyes. They seemed even greener than usual because of the khaki green of his T-shirt. He also wore ripped jeans, and his sword in a scabbard on his back, and despite his claims to seriousness, a broad irrepressible grin.

He had that wistful look too gods help us. I knew what was coming.

'You know,' he said, 'we could just stay over there. With the full-mortals. Settle in.'

'Gods' sake. You sound like Reultan.' And who'd have ever thought that proud bitch would become such a convert to the otherworld?

'She likes it over there. And know what? Maybe she's right. Maybe we should just – you know – adapt. It's all right. When's a full-mortal ever tried to harm us?'

I laughed in disbelief. 'Since May last year, you mean?'

'That was your own fault. I'd have got my mates to beat the shit out of you too if she'd been my girl-friend.'

'So what are you saying? We should leave the Veil to Kate's mercies? Let it die?'

'Course not. But maybe . . . we could let things lie. Keep our heads down. Just for a bit.' He glanced out to sea, embarrassed. 'Till Finn's grown up?'

'Oh, right. It's your baby brain again. Wars don't wait for you to stop breeding, you know.'

'Shut it, you two.' Conal laid his head against the

rock, as if he was listening to its voice. 'Sorry,' he muttered. 'But we've come this far. We might as well—
Ah!'

Four hundred years on and his sudden smile could
still catch me by surprise, could still turn my surli-
ness to a matching grin.

'You found it,' I said, and laughed.

'I found it.'

'Knowledge is power, so it is,' I said as we rode eastwards. 'And Leonora wouldn't want me having that.'

'Ah, get over it. You know now.' Conal looked distracted, but I was angry. The tunnel in the rock could
have saved me a lot of hassle, a long time ago. It
would have saved me a desperate run across the
machair under a too-bright moon, and a climb that
nearly killed me, and all to get Conal and me back
into our own dun.

'She could have made it easier. It's not like anyone
else knows about it.' The Veil had been woven tight,
dense, thick as rope around the tunnel entrance, and
that was a witch's work. No wonder it had been hard
to find.

'And nobody ever should. You can both start
working on a block right now. Put it to the back of
your minds.'

'Why did you show us now?' Aonghas looked happier, now we were on our way home, but that was
understandable.

'She's only just told me about it,' said Conal. 'Believe it or not.'

'And,' I interrupted. 'He's worried about the old bat. *Ow.*' I should have learned by now that if I was going to insult Conal's mother, I should make sure I was more than an arm's length away.

But, 'Seth's right.' My brother's voice was all gloom. 'Kate keeps her hands off the dun only because she's scared of Leonora. If anything happens to her—'

'And there's no reason anything should,' pointed out Aonghas.

'Want to bet? She's got that look in her eye.'

Yeah. I'd seen it myself, and I had mixed feelings. Leonora's death was to be dreaded, and she'd already stayed in life three and a half centuries longer than anyone else I'd ever heard of, after the death of a bound lover. It was a hell of an achievement, what with her soul being dragged in Griogair's wake every minute of every day. Didn't make me like her any better, but it *was* an achievement.

All the same, if she gave in and went to her death, our exile would be over, and I wanted it to be over. How long since I'd stopped believing in the Stone? I'd lost count of the decades, if I'd ever believed in it at all. Prophecy, fate, talismans? Horseshit. Leonora and Kate might be the most powerful witches the Sithe had ever known, but they were both in thrall to some mad old soothsayer, and I expect the ancient loon was squawking even crazier nonsense by the time Kate's Lammyr finally killed her. I'd heard what she said about me – try forgetting it, when you live with a superstitious old Sithe-witch – and I shoved it to the back of my mind with the bad grief and the worse jokes and the old guilt, all the other detritus of life. No demented half-dead lunatic was dictating my life choices. Not anymore. She'd sent me into a four-hundred-year exile in search of a nonexistent Stone, and that was more than enough.

No bit of rock was going to save the Veil, defeat the queen and return Conal and me to our dun and our people. I knew what was going to do that: fighters and good blades, and the sooner we abandoned the hocus-pocus and pitched into a proper fight, the better it would be.

I was glad to see Conal in a better mood as we rode back towards the watergate. Maybe he was thinking the same as me, at last. Or maybe he was just baby-headed, like his brother-by-binding. When Aonghas actually started to whistle, I couldn't take the surfeit of happiness anymore.

'Do shut up,' I said. 'That's bad luck. And wipe that stupid smile off your face.'

'Ah, leave him alone, Seth. He's soft in the head. It's his hormones.'

'Wasn't him that was pregnant.'

'You'd have thought it was. I swear to the gods, he threw up every morning.'

'And he put on a belly. Still got it, actually.'

'The pair of you can hide up your own arses,' said Aonghas cheerfully, patting his stomach, which to be honest was as thin and hard as mine. Well, maybe I was a little jealous. But he had a right to be happy. They'd waited long enough, him and Reultan.

It was one of those days of intense slanting sunshine and black rain. When the sudden spattering showers lifted, the light would come under the clouds like a torch-beam, bronzing the fields and making the sodden trees glitter. It was pretty. We were home, for now. None of us minded getting wet. We rode with the sun's rays, and I suppose that their dazzle was harsh looking the other way.

Which must have been why the child didn't see us.

It was under Conal's hooves before it realised its danger, but its impetus carried it stumbling beneath the black horse and safely to the other side, where it tripped and crashed into the bracken. It was already scrambling to its feet, sobbing with terror, and I had to haul on the blue roan's bit to keep it from lunging for the boy. It *was* a boy, though in that state, to the blue roan, it was nothing but prey. Conal's black was showing a hungry interest now, and I could see a food fight coming.

'Don't run!' I shouted, furious. 'Don't run, you stupid little—'

I might as well have yelled at the rain not to fall. The boy – seven or eight, I'd guess – had bolted again; luckily for him, he ran straight towards Aonghas, who simply leaned down and scooped him off his feet and onto his rather more biddable horse, holding him tight in front of him.

'You're fine. Jaysus, child, you're fine, this is a horse, not a—'

Aonghas's words had no more effect than mine; already the boy was hammering him with his fists, biting at his bare arms, struggling and kicking. Aonghas swore and slapped him; the boy slapped him back and gave as good a mouthful of abuse, and Aonghas finally lost his temper and seized the child's forehead with one strong hand. 'Sleep, brat.'

The boy fought him for maybe two seconds, but he was too young to block well, and his body slumped, limp. Well, at least an unconscious child wasn't such a provocation to the black and the blue roan. As the two horses snorted and stamped and calmed a little, Conal stared at Aonghas, and the child, and me.

'What in the name of the gods? Doesn't he know a frigging kelpie when he sees one? Don't his parents—?'

I looked beyond him, and nodded. 'Wasn't us he was scared of.'

We fell silent as we watched the smoke curl beyond the brow of the hill. Now we could hear screams, the thwack and chunk of blades hitting flesh, the hungry crackle of building flame.

Conal lifted his thumb and forefinger, maybe an inch between them.

'This close,' he said through gritted teeth. 'We are *this close* to the dun lands.'

'But not within them.' Aonghas eyed him.

'Chancers,' hissed Conal. 'How feckin' *dare they.*'

Aonghas said, 'We can take the child. Get him away. More sensible.'

I stayed out of it. It was Aonghas's place to counsel him, not mine. But hell, I was hoping he'd lose the argument.

Actually, I think he was too. A bit.

'Aonghas, listen to it.'

Aonghas cocked his head. 'Three of them. Four, maximum.'

'And they're not expecting us.' Conal was seething.

The roan was behaving now. It had forgotten the
boy, and was yearning and tossing its head towards
the sounds and smells of a fight. I patted its pearly
neck.

'And famously,' I said, 'I'm a one-man army, me.'

Aonghas rolled his eyes. 'I had to try.'

Conal grinned, or rather he bared his teeth. 'Yes,
you did. But you stay here with the child. Me and the
one-man army'll do this.'

'Aw, come on—'

'An order.' Conal winked. 'I'm not half as scared
of you as I am of my sister.'

Aonghas looked down at the unconscious boy
in his arms, a smile tugging his mouth. Yup: baby-
brained. 'Well, do it fast. I don't want to have to come
in and save your arse, not with a child on board.'

They were not expecting us. They were expecting
nothing but poorly armed farmers, who must have
refused to give up tithes to Kate or one of her captains. The crofter was dead already, but the captain
of the raiding party hadn't yet put his sword through
an older boy; he was still gripping him by the neck
while the youth kicked for air.

'Put him down,' barked Conal, and made him do it.

The leader's death left us only one each, and a
spare, and Conal was in enough of a rage not to
share nicely. He was flinging himself off the black
and slamming the third one to the ground, his teeth
grinding in the man's ear, while I was still chasing
down the last panicking horseman and trying not to

harm the even smaller child screaming under his arm.

The fighter backed his horse into a corner by a burning shed, and as if that wasn't stupid enough, he dropped the child. I didn't bother with my blade after that, or only to strike his sword out of his hand. He was so scared of the roan, he was barely watching me, so I grabbed the neck of his shirt, pulled him to me and punched him as hard as I could. And again. And again.

I was still punching when Conal yanked my other sleeve. 'Wasting time,' he said, and spat out another bit of ear. 'Get that child. Its mother's alive.'

Its mother was half-blind with blood and grief and rage, but she was indeed alive and she had enough wits about her to know she shouldn't have been. And she didn't have a choice now, and anyway her croft was gone and her beasts slaughtered along with her lover. She took the smallest infant from my arms, and the middle boy from Aonghas's, and she and the older boy scraped up weapons from the raiders' bodies and limped in the direction Conal showed them. Our dun was two days' walk at most, and they wouldn't be safe outside it.

I was sucking on my bruised and skinned fist by now, and sulking at my own stupidity.

'Stings?' Conal winked. 'Eejit.'

'Don't listen to him,' Aonghas told me. 'You've got style.'

'I know I have. He's jealous.'

'You've got style, and he's stuck with morals. Course he's jealous.'

I laughed. 'You say morals, I say politics.'

'Cynic.'

I was still grinning at Aonghas as his laughter died. He wasn't looking at me anymore; he'd raised his head to stare across the burning croft. I felt my heart shrink.

'Conal!' he yelled.

Conal rode to our side, staring with us at the distant riders. They were coming on fast; perhaps the remainder of this patrol. I'd wondered why there were so few of them. 'Damn. Let's go.'

'It's okay. They haven't seen us.'

'No, but they'll have to. We'll have to draw them off. *Shit.*'

Well, of course we would. We knew what would happen if this new patrol caught up with that woman and her children. I swore through my teeth, just to relieve my feelings, and then we put our heels to our horses' flanks and rode for it.

We crossed their line of sight in the full flare of that late sun and the burning buildings. They couldn't miss us, and we couldn't miss their shouts of shock and triumph.

'Cù Chaorach! Cù Chaorach, you rebel bastard!'

It wasn't a chance they'd pass up. Every one of them came after us, and I had time to be glad the crofting family were out of it, and to regret my brother's suicidal altruism for maybe the five hundredth time. Then there was only time to draw breath and ride.

There were trees ahead, and that made it easy for us. The roan leaped a fallen log and we plunged in among birks and thick undergrowth, Conal to my right and Aonghas to my left. I saw them only as blurred movement broken by silver trunks, and I could hear only my pounding blood, and the roan's hooves, and the yells and the thunder of pursuit.

It was fine. As I risked a glance over my shoulder, I knew it really was fine. Relief hurtled through me on a giddy high and I let myself whoop. We'd been far enough ahead and we'd taken them by surprise; we were going to outpace them with ease. I knew this land and I knew where Conal was heading as I swerved the roan around a slalom of birk trunks. He'd taken a wide arc round but we were almost on the northeast edge of the dun lands now, back on our own territory, and Kate's patrol would never follow there.

As we broke from the trees and galloped headlong onto the high moor, I almost laughed. Luck had held solid for Conal again. Beyond the saddleback hill I knew I would see the first boundary stone of the dun lands. Thank the gods for fast horses and stupid enemies.

Their frustrated yells were growing more distant, and as I saw the boundary stone flash past my left foot, I knew that one by one, the pursuing riders were drawing up. There was a strange note to their shouts, though; a funny mixture of disappointment and triumph. I didn't have time to think about it. I goaded the roan down a rocky slope and into the next belt of trees, Conal a neck ahead of me and Aonghas at my heels.

A few hundred yards on, Conal reined in the black

horse and spun to face me, laughing. The roan danced to a stop at his side and we turned to meet Aonghas, grinning.

He was upright on the horse's back, so for a moment I thought I was seeing things. He was playing some stupid joke. Typical, but a bit inappropriate in the circumstances. My grin froze, and I felt it die.

Aonghas was looking at Conal with regret and aching grief. A smile trembled at the corner of his mouth, and a bead of blood. His khaki T-shirt was stained wet, and the stain was spreading onto his jeans. Everything was so vivid in that slanting light, and I'll never forget the colours: the green of Aonghas's T-shirt and the brighter green of his eyes, the dark mud red of the spreading stain, and the inch of quivering silver that stuck out from his ribs.

'Aonghas,' I said.

He said nothing. His voice was already gone, and his life went as Conal hauled him off his horse and into his arms, weeping and screaming his name.

I wanted to say something: I wanted to tell Conal that the jutting point of the blade was hacking at his chest, mingling his blood with Aonghas's, but I don't think he'd have cared. I think, just then, he'd have taken the whole foul thing in his own heart, if it would only bring Aonghas back.

I had to hand it to those women: they were tough. Hard as permafrost. What were their souls made of, Reultan and Leonora? Steel in the genes.

It wasn't that Reultan didn't want to follow Aonghas. It was just like her mother when Griogair was killed: she made herself stay. And she did have a choice. Whatever any full-mortal thinks, she had a choice. We'd have taken the child and raised it; not my vocation, I grant you, but we'd have done it. I reckon we'd have made a better job of it.

Maybe if it had been Conal alone, she'd have left the child with him. But she had to factor me into the equation, and I knew that was what she did that day at Tornashee, in that drawing room flooded with summer sunlight.

Her eyes were bloodshot and she clutched the infant against her like some sort of lifeline. It was an ugly little thing, black-haired with startled eyes, but it was endearing when it wasn't squalling. It fascinated me. I could imagine growing to love it, the way you do with babies. The rest of the prediction was inconceivable, but Reultan must have feared it anyway. She couldn't look at me, but she was glaring at Conal with inextinguishable rage and grief.

'She'll stay here,' she hissed. 'Fionnuala stays here, where she's safe. Forever, Conal. Do you hear me?'

'I hear you, Reultan. I—'

'Don't call me that! *Ever again.*'

'Reul – Stella, don't make decisions now. Please. It's not the time.'

'Yes. It is. And you will never tell Finn about that – other place. Never. She's what's left of Aonghas, and she's staying with me. *Shut up, Seth!*'

I held up my hands. 'I never—'

'It's none of your business. Stay away from my child. She's nothing to do with you.'

'I know that. I—'

My block was down and it was a cheap shot, but she took it, knocking me physically backward with the force of her contempt. I rubbed my temples, trying not to curse out loud, to make allowance for her grief. But I was afraid of her, now; afraid of what she might do.

'Get it through your stupid heads,' she snarled. 'Kate cannot be beaten. I was her friend and adviser for seven decades, and you *will not beat her*. And I? I've betrayed her for love, and my lover is dead. She has half her vengeance. If I go back there, she'll take the other half, and it isn't me she'll kill. I know her better than any of you. She's too cruel to kill me.'

'Stella, we'll protect the baby. You know it—'

'Damn right you will, and this is how. Listen to me, Conal.' The baby's head was tucked so tightly against her throat I thought she might suffocate it. 'All of you. I swear on my life. You are my witnesses, and I *swear* I will never go back there.'

I stared at her. ~ *Don't. Please.*

Me, begging Reultan. For the first time, and the last.

Deliberately, coldly, she turned her back on me. 'I will never cross the Veil again. On my oath, Conal. On my *life*.'

In the silence, I heard the unaccustomed sound of Leonora weeping.

'Stella,' whispered Conal. 'What have you done?'

Ah, the lies that child was told for the next sixteen years. Still, it was nothing to do with me.

She grew up alone. How could it be otherwise, with a mother who was cold even by Sithe standards? She lived in the shadow of the Veil and she never knew it, so there was no question of even trying to get herself noticed. She wouldn't have known where to start. Of course, she couldn't be told anything. Leonora would have liked to tell her; Conal even more so. But nobody could argue with Stella.

And the child was nothing to do with me. I certainly wasn't going to argue with that.

A surly little thing with pale protuberant eyes, she reminded me of a deepwater fish. The older she grew, the more I thought of a moray eel, lurking in darkness, shy and alone, hiding lethal teeth. And let me tell you, you haven't felt native hatred till you've seen it in the eyes of a six-year-old.

She detested me because I ignored her, because I kept my distance, because I made no secret of my distaste. She wasn't loveable, but then that suited her mother, who seemed satisfied with our mutual stand-off. Sometimes I could feel sorry for the fatherless child with the distant mother; sometimes I recognised the desperation in her eyes and hesitated, thinking I could defy Stella. It wouldn't be the first time.

And then I'd see Finn chewing a lank strand of her black hair, watching me with wary loathing. That was when I'd have liked to know what she was thinking, but I didn't dare try. Well as I blocked, if I pried, Stella would have known; and if she hadn't, the child might well have sensed it herself. And over the years I'd made myself not care.

If Aonghas had lived, it would have been so different; Stella wouldn't have feared me so much, feared the prophet's stupid ramblings. But he hadn't lived, and everything changed for all of us, and most of all for Finn. I wanted her to question her false life, and I daresay it wasn't her fault that she didn't, but it was easier to shrug my shoulders and blame her obtuseness than to discuss anything with Reultan: Reultan, who was so bitter and grief-eaten, she denied even her name.

You'd think the child would have the inborn wit to know what was being kept from her, especially when things went wrong, or far too right. I suppose little Fionnuala thought she had no friends because she was boring. I suppose she thought no-one took any notice of her because she wasn't worth the effort, and I suppose she thought her teachers forgot her because she was too stupid to bother remembering.

But you'd think she'd have asked herself about the other things: the chemistry teacher who fried his hand on a Bunsen burner when she so dearly wished he would; the uncongenial classmate who sliced off the tip of her thumb with a craft knife at Finn MacAngus's whim. The child could have willed a gullible acolyte into its own death, that's what I thought. Finn could have used her Sithe blood even though – quite literally – she didn't know she had it in her. She could have used it to kill: it wouldn't be the first time Sithe blood had done that, in an otherworld with no guard up, and children can be ruthless. The gods know that, and so do I.

Conal watched her, and worried. Conal virtually brought her up, Stella being as useless a mother as any Sithe woman despite her impulsive hysterical oath. I was glad the child had Conal, and was reassured, and I thought that despite everything, not much harm could come to her when he was around. For all her ugly charmlessness, he adored her. To be fair, that was not an unprecedented reaction for him, the insufferable saint.

'When she grows, she'll look like Stella,' he used to say, and Leonora agreed with him. I thought it outrageously unlikely, but I wasn't about to say so.

Leonora doted on Finn just as Conal did, and tried to teach her silversmithing, and jewellery work, and the imagined traits of stones. The girl had a feeling for the stones – or so Leonora said; to me they were geological trash, tumours hacked from pure rock – but at the rest of it, apparently, she failed dreadfully. Too clumsy, too impatient, breaking a hundred saw blades and burning her fingers on the blowtorch. It didn't stop her spending hours in the old woman's workshop, watching Leonora work or playing with her evil raven-familiar (which was fond of her).

But it was Conal who took her down to the river and taught her to swim; he let her climb trees, and stuck plasters on her knees and ice packs on her head when she fell out of them. Conal knew a thousand crap jokes to make the surly girl laugh; and he consoled her when she came home crying from the bullies. He taught Finn to drive his precious Jeep, and didn't even slap her when she drove it into a ditch. He bossed her around, kept her under some sort of control, told her where to get off when she threw her many tantrums.

I was irked that he was so patient with her, rarely losing his temper and never whacking her soundly on the ear (as she so often deserved). Conal was that child's father, in all but biological reality, and sometimes I wished – for Finn's sake and for his – that Stella would disappear up her own arse and let him get on with it.

I fought with Conal about Finn. I told him his sister was wrong, but it's not as if I had to: he knew it.

So, as was always the way of things, he got angry with me instead.

'It's Stella's decision!' he would yell at me, point of

a blunt sword at my throat. The cellar below the old barn was empty and echoing, a fine place to practise swordplay and settle quarrels. 'Her choice! Her child!'

~ *Her fatheaded stupidity,* I would tell him, rolling away before he could blacken my eye.

But as time went by, I learned it was a waste of time to argue. I didn't interfere anymore. The girl was nothing to do with me. Prophecies were the wild woven fantasies of charlatans, nothing more.

If I had got involved more, if I'd focused on my life and my family in the otherworld, it's strange to think what might have happened instead, and what might not have happened. Strange to think how different things would have been, had I not come over homesick again, had I not gone to the watergate that early spring night.

Maybe they wouldn't. Maybe it would all have happened, but in another way, in another time. Who knows? It can drive you mad, wondering. I did go, though. I did go to that watergate, the dank kettle loch in the small wood by the main road. If I hadn't, I'd never have seen the boy.

So it might have happened another way, but it didn't. It went like this.

The black water reeked of weed and rot, and in the trees the dusk had thickened to night. The boy stood still, listening to nothing, and fearing it, and wishing he hadn't come.

I knew all that. I crouched in the darkness and watched the boy and I knew it.

No distant traffic rumble; barely a streetlight glow. He shouldn't be here, stupid child. What was he likely to find that was worth stealing? Because that could be his only motive.

I had my own business, and I wanted to get on with it. I wanted to smell the air and taste the water of home; I wanted my horse and my wolf and the woman I sometimes loved. I itched with lust of many kinds: a ferocious homesickness, unbearable impatience, and the most ordinary lust of all.

I couldn't go through the loch till this skulking little thief was out of the way. I didn't trust the boy not to notice me; he was too close, too antsy, too suspicious. His nerves almost crackled inside his skin. I looked longingly at the watergate, glassy, inky with shadows and night. He was polluting it with his fear.

What had driven him here? Mischief? Boredom? Desperation? I wondered once more what he imagined he could thieve from the ramshackle hut, the one hardly anyone noticed, the one that blended into the wood as if it had grown there.

Any shine had long rusted off its tin roof. A faint sky was visible beyond it, a patch of black cloud tinged with orange, but the sickly urban twilight didn't penetrate the trees. That unnerved the boy. Good.

The old tramp had left earlier; I knew that. I'd watched him myself, striding away from his shack, shrouded in his long filthy leather coat, the plank door swinging shut behind him and bouncing off its rotting frame. His hard arrogant face was half-hidden as always, by the brim of a water-stained hat, by thick-lensed glasses taped at the hinges.

I'd waited, silent and patient, till I knew he'd gone. I wasn't scared of the old bastard, but I didn't want him to see me go through the Veil to the other side. I didn't like other people knowing my business, never have.

And then I'd spotted the boy, sidling through the murk, an eye to the main chance. I'd almost laughed out loud. The idiot child.

Now he slunk closer to the shack, holding his hand over his nostrils against the loch-stench. It was so alien to him. He wanted exhaust fumes and concrete, that boy. He needed more shops than could ever get to know his face; a big, swarming jungle to hide in.

I blinked. How would I know that? I wasn't even interested. It was as if there was so much of him, it spilled over and leached into me; a strong mind but an ill-controlled one.

All right, now I was curious. And arrogant, of course, arrogant as I ever was. And there was time to kill, and another human mind to invade, and trouble to forestall or to provoke. Could I help it if, centuries into my erratic exile, I still got bored?

Oh, to hell with honour and privacy and my brother's moral scruples. Like pulling on a coat that was only a little too small, I slipped inside the boy's mind.

He shoved open the plank door, grabbing it to stop it banging, and had to stifle a yelp when a splinter pierced the base of his thumb. That hurt me as it hurt him; give me a hand of my own and I'd have slapped him.

But I wasn't him. I could feel him, hear him, I was tangled up in him, but I wasn't . . . him. I was still separate, somehow, as if I was hanging on to the side of a speeding car and I'd fall off if I lost my grip. Something was wrong. Gods, I was confused.

Still arrogant, though. Still too nosy to leave.

He eased out the splinter with his teeth, tasting blood. Smelling it too, and suddenly he was ambushed by a sense that the loch too was all black

blood, clotted and still and stinking. I felt his cold
fear, his hatred of the water, and I didn't like it.

Stop that, child.

He obeyed without knowing it. Shaking off a
tremor, he searched the shack. Nothing. He wanted
to spit at the waste of time, and I felt much the same.
Nothing but a plastic-and-steel chair that looked
like it had come off a landfill, and a rickety Formica
table, and a couple of empty beer cans, and half a
supermarket loaf, and a few grey blankets. And that
pile of rags in the corner.

As he reached to unravel those, his hand was shaking, and he growled under his breath. Stupid, to be
scared of shadow and silence. There were worse
things in the world; I knew he knew it. Annoyed
enough to be careless, he lifted the rag-bundle and
shook it, and something clattered dully to the floor.

It glinted. Through his eyes I stared at it, mildly
curious, while he began to panic.

His thoughts were quick enough, I grant him: The
loaf was ready-sliced, and the blade was long, too
long for gutting fish. Its honed edge caught all the
light there was, a lethal intense glow. The handle was
mottled with thick dark stains and when he touched
it, a sensation shivered up his arm.

This was a boy who knew what bloodstains looked
like.

The thought of the police flitted through his head
as he turned the knife with a fingertip. It only flitted,
though, and was gone. *Forget it.* He couldn't tell the
police; he couldn't tell anyone. He'd forget he'd seen
this, forget he'd ever come in here—

Something behind us creaked. His heart stuttered in my chest. Both of us knew the door had opened, even before the cold night air hit his shoulder blades.

He didn't want to turn.

Oh, Jesus.

But he had to. I made him do it. Very slowly, he turned.

His breathing was the only sound in the place. He couldn't seem to do it silently. He sucked it in as a high whine and it came out the same way.

The blade's light bounced off the tramp's glasses, obscuring his eyes. But fleetingly, the man looked stupefied.

We each took our chance: I was out of his head like a bolt of lightning, back to watching from the darkness; the boy just bolted. Shouting with terror, he barged full-on into the tramp, making him stagger aside. Shoving, scrabbling away, he stumbled out into the dank air and ran.

He blundered through the trees, unable to find a path. I should have stayed with him, helped; but I couldn't. Not now the tramp was back. I had my own agenda; the boy was on his own. Clumsy and hopeless, he slipped, stumbled up through twining grass and sucking water.

And all the time, he knew it was coming

I froze. *What?* I wasn't in his head, but I knew what he was thinking.

Any moment now: the clutch of a hand and the bite of a blade

Gods, I'd got too close, I knew his mind. I put my hands over my ears and tried to block him out.

He wouldn't hear the tramp coming

There's nothing to be afraid of, I wanted to scream. Leave me alone. Run and be safe. Get out of my sight and my life and my head. . . .

He wouldn't hear the tramp—

He did, though. As he fell against the wire, tore his flesh on the barbs, he heard the roar of the tramp's laughter, as loud as I did. When he dragged himself over the fence and fell hard to the roadside, the boy picked himself up and ran again, and ran, just like I told him.

And I knew, because I heard it too. For far too long, it rang in my eardrums. Until the boy stumbled, crying, to his own home, the laughter echoed in his head like the last thing he or I would ever hear.

Was I scared, or fascinated, or both? I hated to think it was the former, but I'd never felt a full-mortal mind like that one: all random aggression and fear, spiking like bolts of static, untamed, and so out of control, it could leak into mine without permission. I wanted to know where that mind came from. And not being one to fight my urges, I decided to postpone my trip through the watergate, and find out.

Nothing changes, especially not me.

He'd walked a long way from home, and he ran much of the way back. I didn't know if that was an achievement or not, because it was hard to tell his age. He had the face and the frame of a child, no more than twelve or thirteen; but his eyes were ancient and wary, and his mouth was a tight line. I wondered which of the peaceniks at the disused base had fathered him.

They put the air base there for the big open skies and the clear northern weather. I knew it during a war, when Shackleton bombers lumbered nightly into the sky. Later, when the country grew fatter and more complacent and less fond of wars, the base acquired its own peace camp. The hippies must have liked it better than the air force did, because when the base closed and the planes were decommissioned, they bought their piece of land from an apathetic Ministry of Defence and turned it into a ramshackle settlement: the kind of place where they grew their own lentil casseroles and knitted their clothes out of cat hair.

It wasn't much to look at: some caravans, some eco-homes with grass roofs; a tiny pottery studio; children's swings and a climbing frame. They got their power from small wind turbines and solar panels, and that was interesting enough for me to make mental notes, though not so interesting as the people. They sold driftwood sculptures and dreamcatchers and tai chi classes, but they lived mostly off money brought in by discontented rich kids in search of fun and meaning. That was all I knew about the place when I followed the boy there in the darkness.

In theory, the community members were equals, but you could spot the first among them straightaway. He was a big man, broad as well as tall, with wild dark hair and a greying beard and high colour on his prominent cheekbones. His physical presence wasn't all that gave him away; most of them that warm night were clustered round an open barbecue, drinking beer, and it was the big man who sat at the apex of the semicircle. He was first to help himself to bottles from the crate, and the others glanced at him constantly, smiled for his approval, deferred to him.

I thought the boy was heading towards him, at first, but no: there was a woman at the big man's side, and he sat down on the sandy ground beside her. I liked her immediately: a mischievous face, a wide smile, and long blond hair that reminded me nostalgically of Orach. The big guy wasn't touching her, but she leaned towards him, and his arm lay proprietorially across the back of her low canvas chair.

Never let it be said that I walked away from a challenge.

On the surface at least, the group was famously easygoing, and its membership changed and moved on constantly. That made it easy enough to sidle into the semicircle of drinkers and act like I'd been invited, like I'd always been there. Anyway, I wasn't noticeable. I didn't stand out. It was the big advantage of the Veil, or one of them. It made people like me inconspicuous.

So I had to wonder why the big man's brilliant eyes fixed on me straightaway.

I blinked, smiled, laughed at a joke from the girl on my left as if I'd known her for at least a dozen years. I raised my bottle in deferential salute to the big guy. He didn't react, but went on watching me for long seconds, then turned casually back to the blonde.

I didn't like him.

He seemed reluctant to detach himself from her. Still, he can't have thought me much a threat, or he wouldn't have stood up to take a walkabout through his people like some bulletproof autocrat, and he wouldn't have let himself be distracted by a conversation with a tall skinny man whose face I couldn't see. But by that time I was on my third beer:

just enough to give me an even bigger sense of entitlement.

The boy took no notice of me as I sat at his mother's side, and I didn't encourage him. There was still something intriguingly strong about his mind, but he was tired, and he didn't know what he was up against. His perceptions were easy to deflect, and not many minutes later, he got to his feet and went off with some other kids to do what kids do. Take drugs, break windows, whatever. The blonde blew him a kiss as he left, laughing when he blushed and tried not to grin back. Such an effortless mother–child bond.

I leaned across and chinked my bottle against hers. 'Hi.'

She smiled as she turned, a little startled. 'Oh! I didn't see you there.'

'I know,' I said. 'I get that all the time.'

'Can't think why,' she said, and bit her lip, and grinned.

So I knew I was in like Flynn.

We were last to leave the fire, or nearly. Opposite us a couple snogged heartily, but we might as well have been alone, and the boy hadn't returned. Jed, his name was. It was one of the first things she told me. I suppose I faked an interest, though I was far more fascinated now by his mother.

'You can't have no family,' I said.

'I haven't got one *now*. They don't approve of me, and I don't approve of them.'

I could relate to that, so I don't know why it made me sad. 'What about Jed?'

'I'm enough for him. He's more than enough for me.'

'Really?' I did the slow grin that worked on Orach.

Mila slapped my arm. 'You're all the same. I mean, Jed's the only one I want around all the time. The rest of you, you're too much trouble.'

'You have no idea.' I leaned back on my elbows. I liked her sudden smile. 'What about the big guy?'

'Who, Mack? He's all right. He doesn't own me. That's not how we are here.'

'So he's not – y'know. Your boy's father?'

Mila shrugged. 'No.' Yawning, she reached back to scratch between her shoulder blades. I took my chance, sat up: scratched the spot for her, quite idly. Her tiny shiver was barely perceptible.

My thumbnail went on scratching lightly. 'He looks like he thinks he owns you. Your man Mack.'

'No. He's okay. You don't know him.'

Behind me a voice said, 'I know your type, though.'

Mila and I both looked round. I'd known Mack was there, and the skinny sidekick in the darkness beyond him, but I tried to look surprised. I raised an eyebrow, wondering what made the big guy stare at me like that. Besides the obvious, I mean. I was shamelessly hitting on his favourite blonde, but still.

'Who's this, Mila?'

'This is Seth.' She smiled openly up at him, and I decided her judgement was a little erratic. The man owned her whether she knew it or not.

'Is it, so? I've seen your kind before.'

A little trip-trap trip-trap down my spine: an echo from the past. So long ago, I couldn't remember.

'You're Mack, right?' I wasn't going to stand up. Not that the height difference would threaten me, but scrambling to my feet would feel undignified. 'Mack who?'

'Mack nothing.' He was confused that I still sprawled there, vulnerable and kickable, or apparently so. 'John MacLeod.'

'Oh,' I said.

There were a lot of them about – MacLeods – but that was beside the point. I could see the family resemblance now. Physical resemblance, anyway. Centuries must have diluted the memories to nothing, and he wasn't about to remember any ancestral vows, least of all a promise of protection. But no wonder he could see me.

They say he has the blood himself. Old Ma Sinclair about the MacLeod I'd known, and both of them long dead. Not his bloodline, though. That wasn't dead.

I wasn't entirely foolish; I'd been long enough in the otherworld. Besides, beer on an empty stomach had made me feel slightly sick. I got to my feet.

'I'll be going,' I said.

'I think that's a good idea,' he said.

I wanted to punch his smug face, and slap away the skinny pal's twitching smirk, but I didn't have to. I'd seen the disappointment in Mila's eyes.

Live to love another day, I always say.

It was never easy, tugging the Veil aside, keeping a full-mortal's focus and fascination, but Mila made it as straightforward as it could ever be. She wanted to see me, after all. Hell, within a day or two, she wanted to see me all the time.

It was mutual. I liked her. The boy was a nuisance, but we didn't see much of him. He didn't go to school, and I wondered how he got away with that, but he seemed to have plenty to occupy him. Robbing shops, probably, while we lazed in the sand and watched rig supply ships move eastwards on the horizon.

'I homeschool him,' said Mila.

'That so? I'm surprised they haven't arrested you.'

She giggled. '*They* don't know he exists. I never registered his birth.'

'How about his grandparents?'

'Don't know he exists either. They disowned me. Fine by me; I don't need their money anymore, do I? I've got this place. We help each other here.'

I was uneasy in the role of Voice of Reason, so I didn't comment, but I didn't think giving all her money into Mack's keeping was altogether smart. To stop myself lecturing her, I put my arm over my eyes to shield them from the sun, and pretended to be asleep.

Her lips touched mine, making me smile. She tasted of sea; her skin was still damp and seawater-cool. By contrast I felt sunburnt and sweaty, but I didn't want to move to go swimming again. I laced my free hand into her hair and pulled her face back to mine, muffling her giggle. Her foot, gritty with sand, hooked round my leg and rubbed my calf muscle.

'Gods' sake, woman,' I mumbled. 'I just got dressed.'

'It's not like you're wearing much.'

'Fair point. And you'll catch your death. Let's get you out of that wet shirt.'

'MIL-AAA.'

We both jolted up. Her eyes widened with horror.

'Shit,' I said.

'MILA!'

'He'll kill you.' She crawled on hands and knees to the edge of the sandhill, peering through the grass.

'I'd like to see him try.' But there was a time and a place, and this was neither. I grabbed her hand, and we scarpered.

Funny how we'd given up the pretence that he didn't own her, I thought as we scrambled up the dunes, dodged into the trees, and ran. All the same, we were both laughing, which made it harder to catch our breath. As we skidded down a rough grassy slope between pines, we paused, hearts thudding. Her eyes on mine were wild and excited more than scared.

'I can handle him, you know,' I said. 'If you want.'

She shook her head. 'No, no, no. Please. No trouble.'

'Bit late for that.' I grinned.

She sucked in a gasping laugh. 'He's coming!'

'Down to the sea. Round the rocks. We'll lose him.'

We ran again. It might have been smarter to head deeper into the woods, make our way round the base and come back to the camp by the main road, all innocence and ice cream. But I wasn't thinking straight, and there was something else anyway: more sounds of pursuit, and coming from the trees. There was something odd about it; I knew that even at the time. But I didn't stop to think. I was having too much fun.

Where the sand ended, we plunged through water and up onto the black rocks, slowing to edge round the crags. Mack was in sight now, running across the hard sand beneath the dunes. It hadn't been him in the trees, then. I sprang from one slab to another, skidding on weed but not falling, catching Mila as she leaped to join me. Mack was barely ten yards behind us, flushed with fury and humiliation. I grabbed a spur of rock, swung up to balance on a narrow ledge, reached down a hand for Mila.

She lost her footing, slipped back. Mack snatched her ankle.

I roared at the same time he did, Mila caught between us, but my hands and feet had had centuries of practice clinging to rock. I released her hand to seize her armpit, and when I tugged hard, her foot slipped like a fish from his grip. She gave a yelp as she reached the ledge, half fear and half hysteria, and I caught her in my arms to stop her falling back.

No-one stopped Mack. His feet could find no purchase on the green wet rocks, and he was sliding, slipping, flailing crazily. Hopeless. His backward tumble into the water below was almost graceful, but the splash was gigantic as a wave swallowed him.

I stiffened, fearful and guilty just for an instant. Mila's hands were over her mouth.

Then he was staggering to his feet, soaked, coughing and spitting salt water, his beard full of sand. The water was only up to his thighs, till another wave hit him, and he was knocked forward onto all fours again. Once more he hauled himself up and dragged himself back through the rocks and onto the beach, cursing us with every choked gasp.

I didn't shout back. I was still trying to control my hilarity, though Mila had suddenly stopped laughing and was trembling in my arms. Mack was still shouting something at us, something I was glad I couldn't hear; but I wasn't watching him anyway. I was watching his skinny friend, who was striding nonchalantly across the sand, hands in pockets, hailing Mack. He came from the direction of the trees.

It came from the trees.

I wondered why I hadn't recognised it before. It grinned up at me and winked one yellow eye, then gave me a little wave before turning back to console the incandescent Mack, laying a calming arm on his huge shoulders.

I squeezed Mila's waist.

'He'll be livid,' she said, biting her lip.

'So we'll stay clear for a bit.' I started to climb across the rocks, drawing her with me, trying not to look back at Mack and his parasitic pal. When had he attracted that?

I shuddered. I'd stopped laughing now. 'Let's get out of here.'

A city: they belonged in a city, not some rank small town where they couldn't vanish when they needed to. I remember thinking that as I left Mila and her son, as I shut the car boot and handed over her pathetically small bag of belongings. She smiled at me.

'We'll be fine,' she said. 'We're always fine. It's not the first time I've been kicked out of a place.'

'Hasn't been my fault before.'

'It wasn't your fault.' She kissed me, but I didn't move, just leaned against the car door, watching her eyes. 'And thanks for finding us this place.'

Arms folded, I looked up at it: dank concrete and unwashed windows, an overgrown yard, the smell of piss, the thud of bass from a ground-floor flat vibrating my bones. I should have been able to do better, but landlords can be fussy about a tenant with no bank account and no utility bills, just a scrawny teenage son with the eyes of a thief. Speaking of whom, he was already casing the place, peering in a neighbour's filthy window. I almost felt sorry for him, with his sunken sleepless eyes and his twitching fingers. But there was a limit to my sympathy, and he'd reached it.

Mila would be fine. I was pretty sure of that. I'd never indented for a lifetime's support and she'd never expected it. I wasn't abandoning them, but it

wasn't as if I could move the pair of them into Leonora's house at Tornashee.

'I'll see you tomorrow?'

'Maybe wait till Jed's gone out?' She tried again,
nervously touched my arm. This time I laced my fingers into hers.

'Yeah,' I said. I was never sure how much he took
in, but I felt easier when he wasn't around. I let her
kiss me. I kissed her back.

I'd intended to go straight home, after that, so the
gods knew why I detoured by the base once more. I
felt guilty, I suppose, and guilt gave me an unfocused
sense of injustice and resentment. It's not as if I knew
exactly what I was going to do when I confronted
Mack, but it wouldn't have ended well. So it's just as
well I was intercepted before I found him.

It was waiting in the dirty copse of trees beside the
traffic lights, and it moved a little out of the shadows
as I turned down the road to the base. I stopped.
Glanced at the ground beneath its feet, and the nonexistent shadow.

'Long time no see,' I told the Lammyr.

'Where you off to, Murlainn?' It lit a cigarette.

'You know fine.'

It took a deep drag, tilted its head back, blew
smoke at the sky.

'Those are bad for your health,' I said.

It grinned. 'Women are awful bad for yours.'

'Thanks a feckin' bunch,' I said. 'You tipped him
off, didn't you?'

'You shouldn't have interfered.'

'Interfered with what?'

It examined the tip of its cigarette, sucked on it again to stop it going out. 'Stay away from my protégé.'

'Oh. I see. I must say, you're getting on fine.'

'That I am, and I don't want Griogair's runt in the way.'

'In the way?' I was trying to be civilised, but I couldn't stop my lip curling. 'Listen, pal, you're welcome to Mack. Feel absolutely free. I wish you joy of him. Just keep your scrawny hands off Mila.'

It shut one eye, tapped ash off its fag, half smiled. 'I'm not interested in the woman.'

'That's not what I said. Stay away from her.'

It shrugged. 'Don't warn Mack about me.'

'Like he'd believe me.' I laughed. 'Even if I wanted to warn him.'

'We understand each other.' It crushed the cigarette under one foot. 'You're a civilised man, Murlainn.'

'One of us has to be.' I paused as I turned on my heel. 'A man.'

'Cheeky.' It wagged a finger. 'Stay away.'

'Same to you.'

I turned one last time at the traffic lights, ready to shout back at it, but as hard as I stared into the copse of trees, I couldn't see the Lammyr. Gone to its protégé.

And I'd only just realised it had given me no promise.

PART TWO

FOUR YEARS LATER

Jed

He was running for his life, and his brother's life, and getting caught was not an option. He wasn't about to break the habit of a lifetime for one bloody-minded mark.

Not that this one was playing the victim; the blond bastard was actually gaining. Oh, Jed attracted bad things, bad luck, bad karma. He pulled foul worlds into his orbit like a great black hole. But he sensed he'd never attracted anything as bad as this.

Jed had a perfectly good excuse for taking the guy's wallet, but he wasn't about to explain himself, not with the blond on his heels, not when the nape of his neck tingled with the closeness of capture. It wasn't like he'd get any sympathy. A good kicking, that's what he'd get.

He sprang up and over a car bonnet as it braked with a screech on the bypass. Risking a glance back, he felt the stirrings of real terror. If the blond had taken it as personally as it seemed, you'd never know it from his face: cold, grim and not a sign of strain. He wasn't even tired.

But, Jed, now: he was tired.

Air rasped in his throat, hurting his lungs. Off the bypass, then, and into the station. As the automatic glass doors slid open, too slowly, a fist snatched a handful of his jacket, but he wrenched away. Give the blond his due, thought Jed, he could swear with style.

Jed bounded up onto the railway bridge, feet clanging, briefcases and bags banging his shins, but commuters dodged back as he shoved through, and nobody was enough of a chancer to have a go. That held up the blond. By the time Jed leaped the stunted hedge into the superstore car park, he was fifteen metres ahead.

Across the stagnant ditch – almost tripping on the tangle of abandoned wire trolleys – and he sprinted down the side of the next warehouse. *Oh, God, let him be gone.*

It was a warren, back here among the wire fences and the broken glass and the sickly grass that cracked ancient concrete. No way would the man know where he'd gone. No way.

Not unless those were running steps, now, behind—

Shit. He ran again, sucking in a gasp like a sob. *So help me I'll never steal again.*

Shaking sweat from his eyes. *I'll never steal from* him *again* –

Left, and left again. Over a low wall and round the back. Down the gut of a narrow alley, cut both hands on broken glass but he was there, he'd done it—

– from him, on a Monday –

Piece of piss. Lost him!

NO!

He slammed into the wire fence he hadn't seen coming, almost bouncing back off it. Clutched and tried to rip it in rage. *Oh, stupid, stupid. Climb, you wanker—*

He'd barely gripped the wire when hands seized his wrists. He was torn down from the fence with such ease, he knew right away there was no point fighting.

Go limp. Relax, it won't hurt so much—

His face slammed hard against the wire. Jed felt its diamond pattern branding his cheek, cutting into his skin, but he was afraid only of the grip on his neck, strong enough to snap vertebrae, and the burning, blinding pain between his temples. He twitched, blinked, fought the need to struggle, his lashes butting against a strand of wire. The blond's breath was hard and furious at his ear as he took back his wallet.

Not the polis. Not the polis. Just give us a kicking and go—

Dropped abruptly, Jed fell in a curled-up heap to the ground, waiting for a foot to slam into his rib cage. That always hurt, but that was okay, so long as his head didn't get kicked—

Nothing. Above him the man was still and silent, and he was suddenly so afraid, he thought he might wet himself. The headache hadn't gone; it was worse, searing his brain. *Can't even think—*

He didn't hear them at first, the footsteps. By the time he did, they were retreating calmly up the alley. They faded, and as he blinked and dared to look, so did the pain in his head. Slowly he took his arms away from his skull, and looked up.

Gone.

Jed blinked hard. No, he really had gone. No police, and despite the headache, it seemed his skull was in one piece.

He was shaking, and he was still afraid. Two industrial-sized wheelie bins were jammed against the warehouse wall; he shuffled backwards till he was squeezed between them, forced himself not to cry. It wasn't so much the fear of a kicking as its absence. *Useless wanker. Run faster next time, or fight like a proper ned. Or pick the pocket properly, so the bastard doesn't notice.*

Jed sat hugging his knees in the cold, drowning in misery, aching with rage, but he didn't cry. At least he didn't cry.

Not till he felt something strange in his inside pocket. It scared him before he even saw what it was, before he dragged out a bundle of paper and fumbled through it. His hands shook and he dropped it, but he snatched it up again before it could gust away. Rubbing away hot maddening tears, Jed shoved the bundle of banknotes back in his pocket.

Then he got up, and ran again.

He propped his head against the peeling doorframe, stilling his trembling muscles as he listened to his mother's voice through thin plywood. She was reading to Rory for once, and Jed recognised the story: Creatures of Hostile Intent. Winnie-the-Pooh so afraid, and desperate to bump into Christopher Robin, but quite accidentally, and only because he liked him so much.

Jed shut his eyes, inhaling the stench of the stairwell. A heavy bass line from the neighbour's flat thrummed up through the soles of his shoes and into the back of his skull. Sometimes Jed wanted to break that door down and choke the life out of the woman. Sometimes he wanted it so badly, he had to bite his knuckles till they bled.

He shoved away from the wall and into his own flat, slamming the flimsy door. His mother's singsong voice fell silent.

'Jed?'

'Yes. Course.' He kicked the lounge door strategically in one corner, where the split veneer fanned out from the damp plywood. If you didn't kick it, it didn't open.

'Jed, baby!' Her eyes were huge and sparky. She almost rose, almost dropped Winnie-the-Pooh and Rory with it, but he held her down, finger to his lips. All startled shock, she looked down blankly at the baby on her lap.

Jed prised the book from her fingers and lifted Rory, who half woke, smiling sleepily and grabbing his nose. 'Ed!' he said.

'Hi, angel.' Jed stroked his tiny sunken temple with a thumb.

Right till the moment of its birth he'd hated the

baby, but as soon as the bug-eyed bloody creature slithered into his hands, he'd fallen in love with it. Mila hadn't. Jed had known that straightaway, though the slimy runt couldn't have been that hard to push out. When it was done, she'd lain and cried like a lost soul, but Jed went to his room and pulled a pillow over his head, and it was soon over.

'Jed . . .'

'What?'

She bit her lip. 'You've been to that loch again?'

Abruptly he stood up. It wasn't like he wanted to go there himself, not after that first time. But he couldn't do without the shortcut. He had to rob the supermarket in the next town because his face was getting too familiar at the local one, and that was more her fault than his.

'What loch?'

'The Fairy Loch,' she said. 'It's deep, Jed. So deep. And there's that tramp. I don't like that place.'

'I don't go near it,' he lied.

The luminous glare was gone from her hollow eyes. Fingers trembling, she tore a nail with her teeth. 'Be careful, Jed?'

'Aye. Like always.'

'I love you, Jed.'

'Uh-huh.' His toe had scuffed a hole in the threadbare carpet. Glancing up, he forced a smile. 'I know.'

The knock on the door was a dull tremor on plywood. He started. 'Who's that?'

She smiled. 'It's okay.'

'It's not okay.' His guts went cold. 'If you're feeling flush, why don't you give me the money?'

'Jed. I don't . . .'

'No.' He lifted Rory into his arms. It had taken him a while to work out how she afforded the drugs. It had come to him in the middle of one night like a kick in the midriff, jolting him out of his half sleep and sending him tumbling into the bathroom to throw up. 'You don't pay him, do you?'

'Don't ask me, Jed. Please.' She bit a knuckle. 'What are you doing with Rory?'

'I'm taking him with me. He's not staying here while that tosser's in the flat.'

She grabbed his wrist. 'Jed. What else am I going to do?'

He shook her off. 'You suit yourself.'

Clutching Rory, he flung the door wide and stared at the dealer. Yellow eyeballs, nicotine fingers, amazingly white teeth. The man was so thin, it was hard to believe his heart was beating, but Jed never felt sorry for him. It was like he was made out of lengths of wire, twisted together until you'd need a bolt cutter to make a dent in him. Bits of him were so thin, they were nearly translucent, but there wasn't any weakness there. No weakness, no pain, no pity.

The dealer smirked. 'Jed.' A whispered sigh, like a death rattle.

Jed tightened his grip on Rory as he jerked his head. 'She's in there.'

The man went on smiling, thin-lipped. A shudder rippled down Jed's backbone.

'You're a good boy, Jed. Let me know if I can ever . . . help you.'

The dealer always made him want to be sick, but

this time the urge was so violent Jed had to barge past and stagger down the stairwell. Above him he heard a bone-dry laugh, just as he made it to the concrete courtyard and threw up. Clutching Rory in one arm, he leaned on the wall.

He flung a last look of hate up at the windows of the flat. No point going back for a while. Spitting out the evil aftertaste, he tightened his arms around his brother.

He needed to steal; he needed to take something from someone; he needed to hurt another human being. Jed headed for town.

Seth

Stella, who once was Reultan, did her best to be civil. It was important to her self-image. I knew her motives were mixed, and were bound up in our complicated games of provocation and reaction, but at least home life was frostily calm. Her civility, though, was brittle as glass. Most of the time, she'd have liked to slap me, and I loved to see how close I could get.

Like I said, I was bored. And that late September afternoon, I knew Finn was at the door, eavesdropping. Furtive little minx. How could I resist?

I poured a whisky for myself, handed one to Stella. 'Your mother's losing her grip.'

'Is that so, Seth?' Chilly, like snow. 'What do you plan to do about it?'

'Me? She's your mother. Don't you care?' I sighed. 'Course, caring's not really your thing, is it?'

She ignored that. 'What do you suggest? Locking her up in Calderwood House?'

'Ha! Death's waiting room? Aye, she'd love that.'

'But don't think it hasn't occurred to me,' she said. 'I know what the alternative is.'

'Oh, I see. Place of safety and all that? Sometimes your funny new instincts seem quite rational.'

'I'm well aware you're thinking of yourself, Seth.' Her voice was a breath of winter. 'But for once in your life, you're right.'

Which was when the door slammed open. Finn stood there, beetroot with rage, no longer able to contain herself.

'Oh dear, Stella.' I smiled. 'We had company.'

Stella glanced at me, then at Finn for a long assessing moment.

'Finn,' she said, turning her glass in her fingers. Stella didn't need ice in her whisky. You could practically see the frost flaking off her fingertips.

'Mum.' Finn fisted her hands at her sides. 'Are you putting Granny in a home?'

'Best place for her.' Oh, I loved baiting that girl. 'Plastic cups. Plastic seats.'

'How dare you!'

'You're going to listen at doors, you're going to hear stuff you don't like.' I shrugged and swallowed the last of my whisky.

'She's not senile! She's not even old!'

Gods, I thought. *If you only knew.*

I knew fine that Finn watched Leonora, just as I did. I saw the child's curtain twitch at night like a Morningside matron's, saw her watch the old woman stride down the gravel drive. Saw her return, an hour or two later, silk trousers soaked to the knees with mud from the reedy fringes of the Fairy Loch. Finn knew as well as I did where her grandmother went, in the smallest darkest hours of the night.

What she didn't know, of course, was how Leonora hankered for home, ached after it, fought the drag of it that was worse for her than for anyone. So Finn must have worried, despite all her protests, that the old bat was losing her mind, that she was going to tumble into the dark water and drown. Finn couldn't know it wasn't ultimately the Fairy Loch Leonora longed for, but another water altogether.

Leonora could look decrepit enough when she wanted to, seeing as she cast such a fine glamour. And there was always an aura of age about her, like a patina on beautiful wood. Her face remained uncreased, except for the laughter lines, the gazing-into-space lines, the marks left by peering at a thousand stones through a loupe. But old she did not look, unless it was the look of an especially lovely velociraptor.

So I understood Finn's frustration. It's just that I didn't feel like indulging it.

'If you put Granny in Calderwood House,' she said through her teeth, 'she'll throw herself out the window.'

'No worries, Dorsal.' I reached for the whisky. 'We'll put her on the ground floor.'

The rage and the hate struck me like a dart. Amateur, unschooled, but she had the raw witchy ability, that was for sure. My head jerked with the lance of pain, and she smirked.

I gritted my teeth, partly to stifle the pain, partly to stop myself retaliating. It was a tantrum, nothing more. Giving her tit for tat would be a bit of a give-away. Besides, Conal would kill me.

Instead I gave her an indulgent, beatific smile. 'Clever girl.'

'Did you get out the wrong side of your coffin?' Her look was full of malice. 'Away back while I get my stake.'

'Finn, shut up.' Stella glared at both of us. 'And you, Seth. You're supposed to be a *little* older than her.'

Genuinely tickled, I laughed. 'Maybe Finn should be in on the discussion anyway, Stella. I mean, for such a little smart-arse, there's so much she doesn't know.'

Livid colour crept up Stella's neck. 'I said *shut up*!'

Abruptly her glass slipped through her fingers, crashing to the tabletop. Crystal popped, snapping the air, and whisky went everywhere.

Recoiling, Stella clutched her temple, staring at Finn in shock. She wasn't the only one. Bloody hell, I was impressed.

But it was me Stella turned on. 'Leave Finn out of this!'

'She's Leonora's granddaughter,' I murmured, not entirely shit-stirring now.

'She's my daughter,' said Stella, 'and she will leave the room now. *Now*, Finn.'

Stella's eyes were about fifteen below zero. Finn marched out of the room, with what dignity she had left, and I decided it was time for a strategic retreat. I couldn't resist turning back for a last shot, though.

'Chip off a very old block, that girl.'

Stella's reply was so high-pitched, it was incoherent.

At least one member of the family was a grown-up: Conal always seemed to slide quite naturally into responsible jobs. I shouldn't have been surprised, and I did eventually stop doing a double-take when I saw him in a business suit. He was quiet, unobtrusive, devastatingly effective, and never attracted the kind of notice that would have brought out the corporate knives. If I got a proper steady job like his, he told me (till I was sick of hearing it), instead of being little better than a mercenary in the worst trouble spots I could stick a map-pin into, he wouldn't expect me to spend so much of my time nursemaiding Finn.

No wonder the brat eavesdropped; no wonder she hated knowing nothing. The child still had no friends, attracting only the nastiest kind of attention, but that didn't mean she was content to hang around Tornashee keeping her head down and learning how to be a good full-mortal citizen. She wandered.

Conal drew the line at the Fairy Loch: for obvious reasons it was strictly out of bounds, no questions, no deals; and because it was the only place forbidden to her, she quite reasonably stuck to that rule. As for the rest, we kept an occasional eye on her, as far as we could. And because I couldn't hold down a job for any length of time, I got stuck with it more often than the people who actually cared about her.

Conal's theory was that I was looking after the girl. Me, I reckoned I was looking after the people she met – especially given the filthy mood she was in that autumn when she turned sixteen.

I told them. So many times. There are many things that are my fault, but that isn't one of them.

Speaking of things that were my fault, I saw Jed again that day. Even if he'd seen me, he wouldn't have recognised me – I'd had time and leisure enough to get into that wild mind of his and rearrange the dark fog of the Veil for my convenience – but I couldn't help a vestige of curiosity about him. Guilt too. Their life wasn't what it had been before, but then I wasn't the one who'd signed her worldly possessions over to Mack. It gave me only a little satisfaction now to know he'd died in some fatal drunken brawl: too drug-addled for Skinshanks to bother with anymore, and swapped, presumably, for a new and more promising protégé.

Not that that helped Mila and her sons. To be honest I didn't know how the younger one survived; the sickliest thing I ever saw, he was. It would be easier for Mila and Jed if he got it over with and died. You only had to look at him to know he wasn't destined to stay in the world for long, but Jed was attached to him. Jed was clearly not so good as I was at distancing himself from those he should love.

I'm not saying I'm proud of that. But I am good at it.

Don't get me wrong. I saw Mila a lot, in the early days. It's not as if I simply abandoned her; not immediately. I couldn't have: truth be told, I couldn't stay away. I didn't care that the stairwell stank of piss and stale sweat and rancid fast food; Mila's skin smelt of oranges and cheap white musk. I didn't care that the walls were so thin, I could hear the suck of her neighbour's lips on a cigarette, the rattle of phlegm in her throat, the ping of her microwave. All we had to do was turn the music up.

When he was there at all, Jed took no notice of me. That was what I wanted. He stayed away more often, slept rough sometimes. I'd done the same in my youth, many times, so it didn't seem to me like a sacrifice. And she never stopped adoring him, after all. She seemed to me a paragon of motherhood, but it's true I didn't have much to compare her with.

Perhaps that's why I didn't worry when I finally left them both. They had each other, and I knew he'd look after her. Jed knew her better than I did, and I couldn't handle her addiction. At four hundred and something, I wasn't grown up enough. I didn't want to leave her. I had to. She'd do better with Jed.

It didn't seem like such a bad deal for Mila, who'd looked after him so well, and anyway, she'd stopped needing me by then. She'd stopped needing anything but dreams and nightmares and high oblivion.

The last time I saw her was Guy Fawkes Night, fireworks in the town park. The smell of gunpowder, and the smell of Mila; my arms round her and my face bent into her hair. Stars in her eyes, all right. Rockets exploding onto the night like a million flung jewels, spangled for an instant on the cushion of black sky, flowers of spark. When the crowd blinked and clapped, she kept looking up at the emptiness. That was when she saw the cloud spiders. When a firework dies, you see its ghost, she said, so long as you keep your eyes open: spiders made of smoke in the sky.

She watched them with such wistfulness. And I was no better, because I wasn't taking notice of the fireworks either; I was looking only at Mila.

Sentiment is one thing, but I felt no responsibility for any of them. It was her choice to be permanently off her face: hers alone.

But I did go by the house now and again. It wasn't on my way anywhere, but it wasn't a huge detour. I just liked to know the place hadn't burned down.

Not that what I found that day was much better.

As Jed came storming out of the communal door with the infant brother in his arms, I ducked quickly out of sight; no point taking silly chances. Then he faltered, and bent over, and threw up.

Cold horror in my spine, and a slow sickening recognition that perhaps Mila's choice hadn't been an entirely free one. I waited till Jed spat, and recovered his dignity, and trudged off towards town. He was going to find it awkward nicking stuff with a baby in tow.

I needed to confirm my suspicions, and I didn't have long to wait. Mila's dealer came out of the flat not ten minutes later. When it turned the corner, I lunged, slammed it into the wall with my arm against its throat, and whispered in its papery face.

'I told you, Skinshanks. Leave her alone.'

It blinked, gave me a strangled grin of recognition, and went limp, pointing at its own throat. Reluctantly I eased the pressure. It coughed delicately and pushed my arm away with distaste, then adjusted its collar.

'Could be worse, Murlainn. Don't interfere, or it will be.'

'You said you weren't interested in her!' Desperation and humiliation wormed in my gut.

'I'm not.'

'So – who—?' My throat dried.

'I've never been interested in the woman, I told you. She's a means to an end.'

'I'm warning you—'

'Don't come between me and a protégé.' It tutted, pulled out a packet of cigarettes and lit one. 'You know better than that.'

I did know better. I knew better even as the picture cleared, nauseatingly, in my head. 'The boy.'

'Bingo! And you didn't even have to phone a friend.'

I could only stare at it. Jed was doomed if I interfered, doomed if I didn't. I thought I could see his attraction for the Lammyr. That feral intelligence, that devotion underscored with ruthlessness: all that would amuse a Lammyr. He was a game to it. Or perhaps just – game.

'Don't worry, Murlainn. He won't come to a sticky end like dear Mack. He's very promising.'

'What went wrong with Nils Laszlo?'

'Wrong? Nothing went wrong. He's doing grand. Barely needs little old me anymore.'

'Skinshanks, you're a bastard.'

It grinned. 'Funny insult for you to toss around.'

'Don't hurt Mila.'

'Don't interfere.'

I locked my gaze with its livery yellow eyes. Stalemate.

'I'll kill you.' Useless threat.

It shrugged. 'Sure. And Slinkbone will take over from me. That Gocaman's getting careless in his old age; your watergate needs a new Watcher. There's plenty of us around, you know.'

I shook my head, beaten. The truth was, I didn't want to involve myself. It would only make things worse for Jed and Mila both; after all, I knew Skinshanks from way back.

And the boy – let's face it – was more expendable than Mila or an innocent baby. He might even do well with a Lammyr mentor. Lots of people did.

Lots of people did, and still loved their mothers.

I didn't know what else to do, so I followed Jed into the town centre; besides, I was meant to be keeping an eye on Finn. It would help if I actually went looking for her.

It didn't take me long to find her, but I kept being distracted by the boy and the baby. The infant didn't seem to be cramping his big brother's style after all. Through plate glass beside a cafe counter I watched Jed sweet-talk an old lady with a tartan shopping trolley, but she went soppy over his baby brother, and he stopped short of sliding a hand into her bag. That attitude wouldn't last long, not with Skinshanks on his case.

The mother with the sleek off-road buggy didn't get the same soft treatment; I watched him pick up the toy-overboard, make her screaming toddler giggle, and help himself to her purse. Who could blame him? It was in full view. And the boy had style.

Mila was fine, with him around. *Fine.*

'OY! FIONN*UUUUUUUU*ALA!'

Ah, lift a small-town rock, and there was always entertainment. Remembering why I was here, I picked up my coffee and went outside.

The screecher was on my side of the road, a beautiful, cocky girl with glossed hair and lips and four clones at her high heels. Shania Rooney, endless font of torment for Finn. Finn herself was on the far side of the road, all limp black hair and hunched shoulders and shame, trying to blend into the pavement like a grey chameleon. She wasn't far off. I rolled my eyes and wondered if I could get a job on the rigs.

'MacAngus!' Shania cupped her hands to her mouth to up the volume. '*BUGFACE.*'

Shania was perceptive. Truth was, Finn did have bug eyes, almost too big for her skull. And like a scared beetle, she was trying to scuttle through the crowds now, lose herself under some stone. *Gods,* I thought, *here we go again.* The trick was always to intervene without Finn noticing you were doing it.

Shania hovered on the kerb, jabbing the air with a polished fingernail. 'I'm *talking to you,* MacAngus!'

I wandered closer, propping myself beside the *Big Issue* seller to pretend I was talking to his dog, and watched Finn out of the side of my eye. She'd paused, looked over her shoulder. The humiliated loathing in her face was striking. I wondered if Shania was sharp enough to see that.

Obviously not, because her voice rose above the shrieks of her gang. 'Her mum must have shagged a beetle. I mean, her dad took one look at her in the delivery ward and dropped dead.'

Holy shit. That one took even my breath away. The girls were hooting with horrified delight, and one of them shrieked, 'Sha*NIA*!'

Still, at least Finn had got her head up, and her expression wasn't scared or humiliated anymore. That was naked hatred shining out of her silver eyes.

No, Dorsal Finn, I thought. *No you don't.*

Somebody stopped to buy a magazine, obscuring my view. I dodged round him, trying to keep track of Finn, alarm making my heart trip faster. Now, if I was Shania, if someone was looking at me like that from the opposite pavement, the last thing I'd be doing right now was crossing the road.

Finn was expressionless as Shania reached the traffic island. That's when my attention was caught by Jed once more. He was watching Finn, very intent, clearly fascinated. He should be watching Shania; he should be riveted by her beauty and her cruelty and her sheer obviousness. Unease tickled my spine. That bloody boy and his chaotic mind. Unintended consequences, they called it: and all my fault.

Finn didn't look remotely scared now. She glanced to her left and then back at Shania, and her face was twitching. For a couple of seconds I thought she was going to cry, till I realised she was trying not to laugh.

I thought, *Uh-oh,* and I shoved through the shoppers. Jed was between me and the little scene, and he was pushing forward himself as if he feared what was going to happen, as if he was about to get involved. I couldn't see. I cursed, dumped my coffee in a bin so my hands were free. . . .

Too late. Shania stepped off the island, and Jed's free hand clutched empty air. She glanced down, wobbled, and tripped. There wasn't anything there; nothing. But she tripped on it anyway.

I swear I nearly laughed too. It was funny, watching that gorgeous creature trip on nothing and stagger, arms flailing, mouth gaping, as Jed stumbled back to keep his balance with the infant.

Then it stopped being funny. Shania pitched headfirst into the road, shedding her makeup along with a layer of skin as her face skidded on the tarmac. Her hands scrabbled bloodily, almost as if she was trying not to break a nail. It looked undignified and downright painful, but it wouldn't have been life-threatening. Not if the Land Cruiser hadn't been roaring up to the traffic calmers, not if its driver hadn't looked up too late, phone frozen at her ear, mouth opening in a great comical O.

Already running, I heard the squeal of a bystander, saw the Land Cruiser driver shut her eyes. If Shania was making a sound, it was drowned out by the shriek of brakes and tarmac, but I don't think she was. She just lay there, eyes huge, watching her death coming straight towards her in a colossal four-by-four. I skidded to a standstill.

Luckily, so did Death.

My heart thudded in the eerie silence. The huge tyre was kissing Shania's scalp, but she didn't move her head. She just opened her mouth, and started to scream.

There were people crowding round the scene, goggling at the girl on the tarmac and yammering into mobile phones, and some of them – Jed included – were trying to haul her to her feet. Finn hadn't moved; clearly didn't feel the need. She loitered, the quicksilver glint lingering in her eyes, only one emotion flitting across her face: a tiny twitch of disappointment. Licking her lips, she cocked her head and listened hungrily to Shania's screams.

Gods, she was her mother's daughter.

It was time for me to slink away. I'd been sloppy, and it was a near miss; but no harm done, not this time. There was no reason to stay; there was plenty of reason to go for a stiff drink. There was no threat to her, not now; Finn might as well have been invisible. No-one was interested, no-one watched her.

Except for Jed.

I frowned. I wasn't mistaken: he'd drawn back from the mob, his skin pale, and his eyes darted from Finn to the Land Cruiser driver, who was sobbing on her knees in the road beside Shania. The woman's car door hung wide open; the strap of her bag lay visible on the passenger seat.

~ *Whoa, no. That's enough for one day, boy.*

I'm not sure he reacted to me; maybe he made the decision all on his own. I hope so, because I regretted what I did next; I regretted it for a good proportion of the rest of my life.

I walked away. It was just that Finn had too: bored now, she was slouching towards the park. It was all over. I didn't imagine Jed would be interested anymore. If I thought at all, I thought he'd stay around beautiful, frightened Shania.

I didn't take account of bolshiness, and seething curiosity, and a feral uncontrolled mind that had been meddled with once too often.

Jed

He hated the woodland tracks that wound up the edge of the park: straggly oaks and untrimmed firs; dark paths that were always ankle deep in dogshit. Hampered by an armful of Rory, watching his feet, Jed almost fell over the girl when she stopped.

'Hello,' she said, but she didn't look round.

'Uh,' he said.

'Why are you following me?'

'I'm not.'

She turned, then, and Jed felt heat flood his face. She wasn't the prettiest Barbie in the box, but here in the dimness she looked more in her element, and her bug-eyes made her look like a sinister fish.

'You were watching me. In town.'

There didn't seem any point denying it. Jed shrugged.

'You weren't watching Shania. You were watching *me*. Why would you do that?'

He shrugged again. 'That was amazing, what you did.'

She tensed. Now he was reminded of those snakes that bunched up their muscles before they bit. 'What did I do?'

'You nearly fecking killed her, that's what you did.'

'I wasn't anywhere near her,' she said.

'Yeah. That's why it was amazing.'

The girl tilted her head, thoughtful. 'Shania the slapper can't walk in her own stupid heels, so don't blame me.'

She turned and strode on, then halted on the edge of the old quarry. Exposed slabs of pink rock fell away vertically, forty feet towards the football pitch.

Following, Jed hitched Rory higher in his arms. 'The *slapper* didn't look to me like she can't walk in heels. You tried to kill her.'

Abruptly the girl turned to meet his eyes, and he took an involuntary step back. He felt like making the sign of the cross.

Her voice was silky. 'It was a good try, wasn't it?'

Jed felt a sudden tingling awareness of the cliff, and vertigo flipped his stomach. He'd never registered the height of it before. Now he saw how easy it would be to slip and fall. If he fell, he wouldn't stop till he hit the scrubby littered grass on the edge of the football pitch. The edge beneath his feet was nothing but packed earth and scraggy grass, crumbly after a hot summer, and he could almost feel it moving. Reality tilted. He took a sharp step away from the cliff.

'Give us the wee boy,' she said.

Why did he do it, he wondered later? Because he thought he really might fall, simple as that. And hers wasn't the kind of voice you'd argue with, not without a long moment to gather your thoughts. So he shoved Rory at her, squeezed his eyes shut, and fought to get his balance back.

'Sun's got to you.' She lifted Rory and studied the boy's face, breaking into a grin. 'Who is he?'

'My brother.' Jed ducked his head, trying to get the blood flow back.

She kissed Rory's hair fondly. 'Hello, sweetie. Your big brother's a fruitcake.'

'Why do your eyes glaze over like that?'

'Maybe you're boring me.'

'They glaze over and go *silver*.' Jed wanted to hit her. 'What you did to that Shania? You just did it to me and all.'

Scornfully she tapped her temple. 'That was your own stupid head.'

Gotcha. 'What was my head?'

She froze. 'I dunno.'

'Liar.'

Her hand strayed to her face.

As the silence lengthened, Jed said: 'I won't tell anybody.'

'Nobody would listen if you did.' She nuzzled the back of Rory's head so that her eyes were hidden.

'Would if you'd killed her.'

'Nah.' She gave him an assessing glance. 'It's you they'd lock up, mad boy. Nobody even notices me, except Shania. And I dunno why she does.'

'Smells your fear,' he suggested, cheekily.

'She can't. Not anymore.' Finn hitched Rory onto her hip and set off down the tree-shadowed path towards the park. 'But I'm getting a distinct whiff of hers.'

Jed actually laughed; couldn't help it. She was an odd kid, and a scary one, but in the end Shania hadn't been flattened, and he hadn't fallen over the cliff. It was okay. No worries. No harm done.

The scummy lake between the sports pitches and the playground was meant to be a duck pond, but most of the ducks had long ago been evicted by a gang of antisocial gulls. Rory screeched at the sight of them, laughed and pointed. The girl settled herself on the grass, snuggling Rory against her neck, looking as if warm butter wouldn't melt in her mouth.

Jed reached for his brother. 'Give us him.'

For long silent seconds she teased Rory's hair, making his dry fringe stick straight up. She kissed his nose, and he chortled. 'Shania *should* be scared, wee man, shouldn't she?'

Rory giggled again.

'Stop it,' barked Jed. 'And give him to me.'

Reluctantly she handed him over, and Rory snuggled into Jed's throat, his blinking lashes tickling his skin. Jed held him tighter, an echo of vertigo lingering in his head.

'Can you do that stuff?' she asked him.

'What?'

'The stuff I do. Can you do it too?'

'Don't be stupid.'

'Oh.' She folded her arms round her knees and

chewed her sleeve. 'Figures. I never met anybody who could. I thought maybe you might. Because you noticed. Oh well.'

The silence was awkward. 'I should go,' said Jed.

'Yes.' But she didn't look at him.

'Where do you stay?' he asked.

'Tornashee. It's a house,' she said. 'Outside town. It belongs to my grandmother.' She picked a stone out of the lumpy grass and flung it at the water, sending gulls bleating into chaos. 'Till she gets put in a care home by the demon relatives.'

'Er. Your gran's house had a name, not a number? Big, is it? Her house?'

She hesitated. 'It's pretty big, yeah.'

Jed watched her out of the corner of his eye. Her cool sulky face. Her expensive enamelled earrings. The thick chain round her neck, dangling a couple of hundred quids' worth of elaborate Orkney silver. He nibbled his lip.

'Gonnae show us it, then?'

'You weren't kidding,' he said. 'About the size of it.'

Jed did remember this house now, lurking away among trees and laurels, overlooking a steep gorge. You couldn't see it from the road but he'd known it was there; how could he not? He just hadn't remembered.

At first sight of it he was ashamed, and then he was ashamed of being ashamed. Rory had been exhausted, he'd needed a nap, so they'd taken him home first (Jed praying his mother wouldn't be lying underneath the pile of bones with the bad smile) and tucked him in, and that meant the girl Finn had seen where he lived. He'd thought he hadn't minded. He'd decided she could take him as he was. But he felt very small when they turned the corner round overgrown laurels and her house smacked him in the face with its beautiful immensity.

Jed's inferiority complex dissolved fast, overwhelmed by a sense of sheer good luck. He was well in, he knew it. If he played it right, his days of nicking crisps out of Poundland were over. For a month or two, anyway. People this wealthy didn't know what they had, and sometimes they didn't even miss it.

'It'll be a hell of an old folks' home they're putting your grandmother in.' He couldn't help saying it.

Finn shrugged as she led him up the mossy drive. 'They won't get the chance. She'd sooner top herself than go in a home. I've heard her say so.'

'Nah.'

'You don't know her.' And she did sound absolutely calm and absolutely sure. 'She gets up in the middle of the night, goes out walking. I've seen her. Comes back with her clothes soaking wet. She's getting up the nerve, that's what I think.'

'Yeah? What for?'

'Drowning herself in the Fairy Loch. That's where she goes.'

He balked, and said without thinking, 'More likely to get her throat cut, then.'

'What?' She raised her eyebrows.

'Nothing,' he said quickly. 'Kidding.' And even if the old bat did get her throat cut by that psychotic old tramp, at least it would be quicker than drowning.

'They're a bunch of liars,' she said. 'My family. They lie all the time. Even Conal. His chest's covered in scars and he says he was in an accident, but he's never crashed a car in his life. And he says he was drunk when he got this huge tattoo on his shoulder. That's a lie too.' She brightened. 'Look, Granny's in her workshop. Come on up.'

Finn's easy mood-slips and subject-changes were unnerving, as if none of them were real or true. Or, if some of them were, even she didn't know which. And something about this whole place made him shiver. Like Finn's moods and Finn's stories, he wasn't sure whether to believe it was real.

Jed followed her up a broad flight of stairs, two at a time to an upstairs corridor and an open door. The woman inside didn't turn: she was intent on something in her fingers, rubbing it between her thumb and forefinger, her silk sleeves pushed up. Across the workbench in front of her were scattered stones, silver fixings, pliers, wire, a blowtorch; a long embroidered coat was folded over her chairback.

The grandmother didn't look like one; her tawny hair had only a few silver streaks. Or maybe that was just the way the light slanted in, because it did create strange effects. Jed almost imagined he saw a stone move on the workbench, hover by the old woman's hand. He hesitated in the doorway, waiting for the illusion to vanish; when he blinked, it did. The stone was firmly between the old woman's fingers: an uneven shard of dull glassy mineral.

She pulled a loupe from her eye socket. 'You had so much promise,' she told the stone, 'but you're not what I'm looking for.'

Uh-huh. So even if Finn didn't want to admit it, her demon relatives had the right idea.

'Hello, Finn.' The old woman still didn't look round. 'Who's this?'

'Eyes in the back of your head, Granny. This is Jed. Friend of mine. Jed, this is Leonie. What's that?'

'Nothing spectacular. Here. It'll fit that necklace you made.' The woman turned at last to pass the stone to Finn. 'Hello, Jed.'

'Hello,' he said. He smiled his best old-lady-killing smile but he had the horrible feeling Leonie could see right past it, right through his skin and down to his bones and his marrow. It wasn't unlike the feeling he got from the skinny dealer.

'How kind of you to walk Finn home.' The old woman's eyes were bluer than the stones on her workbench, and three times as hard. 'Has she been in trouble again?'

Startled, he shook his head.

'Granny,' Finn scolded her, fondly. She held out the stone to Jed. 'It's an emerald, look.'

Was it? To him it was a cloudy lump of green crystal. It might as well have been a bit of glass salvaged off the beach. 'Very nice.'

Finn's grandmother opened a drawer, drew out a chain and a rough half-finished necklace. 'Go on, Finn, you have that stone. Time you finished this. You sweated over it long enough.'

'It's crap,' said Finn as she took the necklace, but she was pink with pleasure.

She was right, the pendant wasn't very lovely. It was a primitive-looking thing, a jagged claw. Jed could have bought a better one at any street market, but Finn seemed pleased with herself, and the claw was obviously made to clasp a stone.

'That'll look great,' he mumbled, unconvinced.

'No, it won't.' Finn laughed. 'But it'll be mine. Where's Faramach?'

The old woman threaded a thin metal blade into a saw frame. 'He went on ahead.'

Finn gave a little mystified laugh. 'What?'

'Who's he?' Jed asked.

'Leonie's pet raven. The necklace is meant to be his claw. What did you say, Granny?'

She blinked. 'I said I reckon he's dead.'

'You didn't—'

'Everything dies. Can't be helped.' The old woman laid down the saw frame, took off her glasses and studied Finn's face. 'Something's upset you? Apart from the usual.'

Finn forced a smile. 'Just the usual.'

'Conal wants what's best for me. Your mother means well.' Leonie leaned over her workbench again. 'And Seth's . . . such a dear boy.'

Finn looked about to ignite and burn herself to a crisp. Uncomfortable, Jed stared at her grandmother's hands: the mottled papery skin, the swollen knuckles. He couldn't think what Finn's objection was to the care home, because the old girl must be a hundred and three in the shade.

'Seth's straight from Hell. Conal ought to know better. And my mother could sink the *Titanic* on a warm night.'

'Ah. That shard of ice in your mother's heart. She needs it, you know. It's how she kept her heart in one solid piece. It would have broken in two otherwise.'

'It was Dad that had the heart problem,' spat Finn. 'Hers still works. In theory.'

Leonie's hand shook, and the thin blade snapped.

Sighing, she threaded another blade into the frame. 'For heaven's sake, Finn. My future is my own affair.'

'Yeah? The family werewolf thinks it's his. Like your house.'

'You know, dearie, I'm fond of Seth. Cut him some slack. He's a troubled man, your uncle.'

'Not nearly troubled enough,' she muttered. 'And he isn't my uncle.'

'Your cousin, then.'

'He's certainly a stroppy adolescent.'

Leonie sighed heavily. 'Dear. I have plenty of saw blades, but they are fiddly things for old fingers, so take that mood of yours elsewhere.'

Jed was already backing towards the door – he hadn't let himself in for a family domestic – but Leonie stood up and grabbed his wrist, and Finn's too.

'Leave me alone, dears.' The voice quavered, the brilliant eyes were suddenly pale and watery, and her skin was creased like crumpled tissue. Her grip had a creepy feebleness, like the touch of a mummified corpse. Recoiling, Jed tugged his hands free, not worrying how it looked. He didn't need to, anyway. Finn had gone white; she slapped her grandmother's hand away and dashed from the workshop.

She rubbed her hands against her jeans, rattled her wrist on the banisters as she ran downstairs. Jed knew how she felt; death had run a dry finger down his spine as soon as the old woman touched him.

At the doorstep, Finn stopped, tossing the grubby emerald up and down. If he hadn't been so unnerved, Jed might have snatched it right then, and made a run for it.

But then he only had her word for it that the stone was valuable at all. For all he knew, she was delusional. Demented. Maybe it ran in the family.

'Bloody Seth,' she said, but she was grinning. 'He doesn't fool *me*. Let's see if he likes somebody messing with *his* stuff.'

Seth

'And the latest news flash: Finn thinks we're trying to put your mother in a home.'

Stripping off his shirt Conal shrugged, avoiding my eyes. 'Let her think it.'

'That's a bad idea. You know how fond she is of the old bat.'

He scowled at me and raised his sword.

'Just saying.' I lifted mine, gave him a mocking salute. He lowered the blade again, turned and clicked on the iPod dock. Full volume, drowning me out. And he went for me.

We were both dripping sweat when we staggered apart. I grinned at him.

'That got a bit personal,' I panted. 'It's the truth that stings—'

'Yes,' he bit out.

I stretched my shoulders. Even I sometimes knew when to stop. I did wonder, though, if Finn's child-hood curiosity would abate with age, or if it would only sharpen till we all cut ourselves on it. It was only a matter of time till Finn explored too far. There was rowanwood in the panelled walls of this vast cellar, but not an impenetrable quantity; neither of us liked to be entirely blind to what was going on above us.

I grabbed a towel, rubbed my neck, gave Conal a conciliatory grin. 'Enough for today?'

He hesitated, then smiled back. 'Wore you out, did I?'

'Funny.' I tugged my T-shirt over my head, then eyed the timber ceiling. 'Finn's brought a friend home.'

'Gods. Not another one.' He rubbed his face with a hand. 'So soon after the last girl?'

'The last girl was three months ago.' I couldn't help the edge in my voice. 'Don't worry, this one'll forget she exists and all.'

'Exactly. I don't know if I can stand the fallout.'

I smirked, and climbed the stairs in the silence of self-righteousness, Conal at my heels. The evening was lovely; sunlight dipped and shifted across the front of the house, dappled with the drifting shadows of dead birch leaves. Give Leonora her due, she wove a fine glamour, and the Veil around Tornashee was dense. The double front door stood wide open and the leaf-shadows spilled over into the hall, and that just made the whole place seem even more like a phantom outline in empty land.

It was like us. People didn't notice it, much, which is why it drove me crazy when Finn imperilled that by bringing her temporary friends home. Not that she knew any better, I had to keep reminding myself.

I stopped short when I saw who it was.

Mila's boy?

Unease tickled the nape of my neck; no, worse than unease: dread. The recognition was horrible: I was trying to hold too many spinning threads, and they were tangling and knotting in unforeseen ways. For more than one reason, I didn't want Jed getting involved with Finn. I didn't want him around me, around Conal, around any of us.

I glanced into his labyrinthine, resistant mind; difficult, but I was familiar with it now. My, but he was growing hard to handle. I hoped Skinshanks was finding the same. I hoped he unnerved Skinshanks as much as he did me.

Jed and Finn made a right pair: him in his over-sized army-surplus jacket with the deep pockets, with his sleep-deprived eyes and his shaven head; her with her sulky rich-girl attitude. It almost made me smile.

But not quite.

The two of them were engrossed in something, but Jed glanced up as we walked into his field of vision, and his face froze. For an instant I felt sick, thinking he'd recognised me; but before I could open my mouth and give myself away, I realised it wasn't me he was looking at. I don't think he could see anything except Conal. His mouth opened in frightened horror, his eyes widened; then he ducked his head and feigned a vast interest in my bike. My beautiful, black, brand-new motorbike.

Which was when I realised what was going on.

'You bloody little *cat*!'

I snatched the stone out of Finn's fingers, stared at the scored chassis, at the jagged lettering.

COMPENSATING.

Conal caught my raised hand before it could connect with her face. 'At least she can spell it,' he murmured.

In disbelief I stared at what I'd assumed was a chunk of gravel. The raw stone was as green as sea over white northern sand. You could almost see the skin of water, the stir of something deep within it, something ancient that you might not want to see when it surfaced. The nearby burn gurgled over smooth stones, a light breeze whispered in the dying birches, a door slammed somewhere in the outbuildings. Tornashee was suddenly so solid, I could almost hear it living and breathing.

'This is an emerald,' I said savagely, closing my fist round it. 'Did your boyfriend nick it?'

She snatched at it, furious. 'No, he did not, you arse.'

Conal seized her wrist before she could hit me, and pulled her round to face my damaged bike. 'That's coming out of your allowance, kiddo. Apologise to Seth.'

'Like hell I will.'

'I don't want her fecking apology, I want her *head*.'

'Finn, apologise.'

Jed still wasn't looking at any of us. His face was white. He was clearly afraid of Conal, but when I glared at my brother, I saw no flicker of recognition. His face was hard and expressionless.

Finn shrugged. 'I don't know what the big deal is. Seth can afford a respray. When he gets Granny committed. When he gets the house.'

'That's enough. Apologise to Seth or be grounded for a month.'

Well, she managed. Through teeth grinding like tectonic plates, but she did manage. 'Sorry, *Seth*.'

Despite the snarky tone, that had cost her. Good. I gave her my worst smirk.

'Seth, get a quote for a respray. Finn, quit showing off.' Conal glanced at Jed, who was inching backwards, but still he showed no flicker of recognition. If I hadn't been so angry, my heart would have been in my mouth. 'And by the way, leave your grandmother out of it. We do not discuss family in public.'

Finn snorted with contempt. 'Does public include me, then?'

'We're only looking out for her.'

'Like she needs looking after,' Finn sneered.

He took her stone from my hand, examined it, and gave it back to her. 'Leonie didn't give you this so you could make havoc. Have some respect for her yourself. And remember you don't know everything, you little smart-arse.'

'I don't know anything.' Her voice was chilly. 'It might help if you trusted me once in a while. I do have a functioning brain, unlike my demented *grandmother*.'

'Finn, it's me. Don't bite my head off.' He sighed. 'School bad, was it? Want me to talk to the teachers?'

'No!'

'Don't panic,' he said, winding his fingers into hers. 'What do you expect me to do about it, then? I'm not your father, Finn. It's up to your mother.'

She squeezed his hand. 'Well, I wish you were my father, and I wish she wasn't my mother.'

I inhaled a dramatic lungful of air, let it out in an I-told-you-so sigh. Conal said sharply, 'Stop it, Finn.'

She looked away. 'Sorry.'

'You're getting better,' I said. 'That even sounded sincere.'

'Shut up, Seth.' A moment's silence. 'Ach, Finn. It's me that's sorry.'

'How is it your fault?' She head-butted Conal's arm, all affection.

He grabbed her head and shook it playfully. 'It isn't yours either, toots. Remember.'

I thought I might throw up soon. 'I'm glad we got that clear at last.'

Finn took it for sarcasm, but Conal glowered at me anyway, grabbed my arm and started to turn away. He still hadn't taken a blind bit of notice of Jed, and I'm sure Jed was as relieved about that as I was.

And then Finn called after him, the silly cow. I could have cut out her tongue.

'Oy, Conal. How did you know Granny gave me that stone?'

'I'm a mind reader.'

'Ha bleeding ha. Oh, I never introduced you.' She turned to the boy with pride, and snatched his arm. 'This is Jed.'

I shut my eyes. If Conal knew Jed, he knew Mila,

surely – and that was meant to be my business. Mine only. I didn't fancy explaining the whole sordid story to Captain Morality.

When I opened my eyes, Conal was standing in front of Jed, studying his face. I'd bet it was the longest thirty seconds of Jed's life. It was pretty long for me.

Then Conal said, 'I know.'

Jed didn't hesitate. He didn't even say good-bye. Give that boy his due, he could run like a roach when the lights go on.

Jed

He wouldn't see Finn again; Jed was sure of that. So he was taken aback when she sat down beside him on the war memorial steps two days later. He was even more surprised when she invited him back to her place again. None of that was as surprising as the fact that he agreed, but maybe he talked himself into that.

'I didn't *run away*,' he said indignantly.

'You so did. What happened? Conal thought you were out of your mind.'

Aye, right. 'I had to get back to Rory, is all. I hadn't fed him.'

'What's your mother for?'

'You may well ask.'

She opened her mouth, hesitated, then obviously decided to let it go. 'You have to get back to him now?'

'Well, no, I—' He wished he could take that back, say Rory needed him. But the fact was that the baby was already asleep, and he'd dumped a bagful of stolen baby food jars in his mother's lap just half an hour ago.

Can you not just feed him on time? It's not difficult!

Jed, don't shout. I forgot. I'm sorry, I won't forget again—

No, you won't. I'm away out.

Jed, please don't go by that loch—

Where's your skinny pal? You're more likely to die of him than I am from some old tramp. Now I'm going. FEED RORY.

He shivered at the memory of his high enraged dudgeon. Mila would be okay. It was just that he hated leaving her on a bad note. He worried about her. Thing was, he worried about Rory more.

'No,' he admitted to Finn. 'Rory's fine for a while.'

'So come on up to Tornashee. I want to show you something.'

'Oh, no.' Jed stepped back.

'Don't worry, Conal's not home.' She gave him a little smile, with a touch of what he thought was evil mischief. 'Thought you didn't run away? Ha! *Are* you scared of Conal?'

'Don't be stupid,' he said. 'Why would I be scared of Conal? I never met him before.'

Which may have been a touch too much protesting, but that was him committed.

'Listen, Jed. If Conal does show up, don't mention that thing with Shania, 'kay?'

He wanted to shout, *I thought you said he wouldn't be there.* Instead he managed to say, 'What, you nearly killing her?'

'Yeah. He'd give me hell. He'll ground me again.'

'How would he know that was your fault?'

'He just would. He knows about stuff like that. Don't ask me how. I assume he was there when I got bitten by the radioactive spider.'

Jed snorted, and she gave him one of those anxious sideways smiles, like she was happy just to have someone to laugh at her jokes.

'What d'you want to show me, anyway?' He glanced nervously at the outbuildings as they walked up Tornashee's drive. He didn't like the shadows and the darkness between the pines and the oaks and the laurels. He didn't like the breezy rustle of their leaves, loud enough to obscure footsteps or voices. He didn't even like the smell of the place, all leaf mould and wet earth.

'It's that stone she gave me.' She climbed the curving granite steps so he had to follow, and eased open the huge door as if she was scared of being heard. 'It's weird. I want you to *feel* it.'

'Feel what? You are seven kinds of nutjob.'

She looked hurt. 'Just come upstairs and see.'

'No. I am *not* going into your grandmother's workshop.' He could see it all now. Him in a silver workshop; Conal catching him there. This time the man would call the police. This time he would, and then it would all be over. Rory in care. Jed on a chain gang with the other Young Offenders. His mother in rehab. *Aye, right.*

'I'm not going,' he said again.

'Yes. You have to.' She seized his wrist.

Not only was she unexpectedly strong, he realised that fighting her would be the worst option. Even if Conal wasn't in, somebody would be. He needed to get in and out of there fast.

Besides, if Finn was stupid enough to put him in arm's reach of pocketable jewellery, who was he to argue?

'Granny's watching *Newsnight* at the other end of the house. She always watches to the end. Has the hots for Paxman.' She giggled. 'C'mon.'

Up in the studio, Finn parked herself at the workbench, screwed her raven's claw into the vice and sat back. She pulled open a drawer, lifted out the stone and balanced it thoughtfully on her palm.

'This stone,' she said, 'tells me stuff.'

For an instant Jed was back in the commune, humouring some skunked-out posh girl with delusions of depth. Rolling his eyes while her back was turned, he examined the room. There were some nice pieces lying loose – practically on free offer – on two shelves behind him. Easing towards them, he slid his hand back, finding cool metal and warmer stone.

It was in his hand. Jed glanced at it as he slid it into his pocket: gold. He'd lucked out at last. Three stones in the brooch, bloodred like rubies. He grinned, felt behind him for another one.

Finn turned abruptly. He jolted.

'Here! Feel it.'

His heart thrashed so hard, he was afraid she'd

hear it. He put out a shaking hand for her rough green stone, and she dropped it into his palm.

'What?' He'd flinched as it touched his skin, and he was annoyed with himself. 'There's nothing wrong with it.'

'You wait. That was just to prove I haven't had it in the fridge, okay?' She took it back, pushed the emerald awkwardly into the grip of the claw, and pliered the talons down over it. 'Ow.'

'What?'

'Pricked my finger.' She sucked it.

'Can you file it down?'

'Can't be arsed.' She wiggled the stone, forced the setting down harder with the pliers. 'Seems tight enough anyway. That won't fall out.'

Jed thought it was loose. He also thought she should file the vicious points off the talons, since she was actually sucking blood off her finger, but he wanted out of there, and he didn't want to get into any kind of a conversation. The brooch in his pocket felt heavy and obvious.

Her head jerked up. 'There!'

Jed's heart pounded. Once he was out of here, he *never* wanted to see her or her demented relatives again. He backed away as she stood up and came towards him.

'Hold it! Hold it!'

He realised at the last moment before he took to his heels: she meant the stone. Jed stuck his hand out, almost from relief. And Finn dropped the whole coarsely set pendant into his waiting palm.

His fingers curled tightly, out of pure shock. It was freezing cold: so cold, it burned. He wanted to let it go but he had to force open his fist and shake it loose. 'What th—?'

As Finn stared up at him, he realised she was as shocked as he was. 'It's never been *that* cold—'

They gaped at each other for a few interminable seconds.

So it was very easy to hear the front door clunk quietly shut.

Seth

Funny how I always knew it was a dream. In some part of my head, anyway. I was never truly tempted to believe it was real when I dreamed about Mila, but when it happened, I liked it. At the time I did. The moment of waking was cruel, but I deserved that. I always tried to delay waking, and of course as soon as you think that, you wake.

Despite the bitterness of the memories, I did miss her. I didn't miss watching her play hunt-the-vein; I didn't miss wiping spatters of her blood off the wall so her son didn't see them, but I missed her old dead self, I missed her skin and hair and smell.

This time, though, I swear I could smell her hair. Not like it was the last time I left her: burnt-sugar and scalp-sweat and dust. In my dream the glossy strands of it between my fingers smelled of orange blossom and grass, of the supermarket shampoo the boy Jed used to steal for her. I closed my eyes, pressed my face into the back of her head. I put both arms round her to hug her body tighter against mine, scared suddenly of letting her go.

'It's all right,' she murmured.

'But I want to be sure.'

Her arms closed round mine, holding me holding her.

Desire stirred in me along with sadness. As I ran my palm down her arm, the sadness left me altogether, and I kissed her shoulder, smiling. I licked her skin to taste it better: citrus and salt, like a margarita. She wriggled with pleasure, and I sensed her smile. She lifted one languid hand to pull her long hair aside, letting me nip her ear, and my hand slid down across her belly, and this time plain hot lust surged through me. I clutched her hair, trying to turn her, and opened my eyes to her soft laughter.

Wrong, this was wrong. The hair wound round my fingers was chestnut red. I blinked, trying to draw back, but she twisted, caught my face in her hands and laughed silently, her bright eyes holding my stare.

'*Kate?*' My world tip-tilted.

I could have pulled away, I know I could. Even though it was a dream, I could have shoved my queen away from me, but I didn't: just pressed even closer against her. Well, my body did; my mind recoiled, but my mind wasn't in charge. Beneath the sheets her fingers closed round me and I sucked in a breath.

'Oh, shush,' she said, and kissed me, her tongue flickering into my mouth.

I still had hold of her hair, and I tightened my grip. So real, so vivid that I knew I could break her slender neck if I tried.

I couldn't even try. Wanted to. Couldn't. I wound my fingers tighter in her hair till she gasped.

She nipped my lip as I forced myself to pull away; it hurt. But in a good way. My heartbeat tripped and raced.

'No,' I said. More of a hoarse croak, really.

'Oh, don't be silly. It's a dream.'

'I know. . . .' Didn't I?

'So relax.'

'Uh . . .'

'Not too much, though.' She winked.

I kissed her, tugged on her hair to pull her back from me again. I said, 'No.' I thought about my mother. My father. More to the point, my brother. 'Conal would—'

'Have your balls on a platter, dear one. But even he can't object to a dream shag.'

She'd made me laugh. I slid my hands down her back, pulled her hips tight against me.

'Some dream shag,' I said. 'I don't even like you.' Which proved it was a dream, because I doubt I'd dare say that in real life.

'But I like *you*, Murlainn.'

Must have been the way she said my name. That got me, right on the inside. And why get wound up? My dreams were my own, at least. Conal could hardly be hurt by some subconscious fantasy I hadn't even known existed.

I hooked her leg over mine, stroked her thigh.

Expecting to wake at the crucial frustrating moment, I was pleased that for once I didn't.

I was too old for this, I thought as I finally blinked awake, limbs weak with spent lust, heart twisted with shame. Too old, too experienced, too cynical. But what the hell.

No harm in it.

No harm in it, so I put it out of my mind; I put Kate out of my mind. It took more effort than I thought it should, so I was short-tempered by the time I crouched on Dennis Sacranie's roof that night, cold and irritable. The night above us was black velvet, beautiful with stars, and the moonlight was strong.

What a stupid night to pick. Trouble was, we were both losing patience with Leonora, and that made us impetuous. Conal had wanted to get it done and over with, so here we were.

Poor sod. Like me he was homesick, but he was lovesick too. He didn't want to be here any more than I did; he wanted to be gentling half-wild horses on the machair, he wanted to be building walls and digging ditches in the dun lands, or swimming in the bay. He wanted to be getting mildly drunk under a summer night sky, making music that was by turns wild and racing, then brain-achingly sad. He didn't like Sacranie any more than I did, but he didn't want to be in his house, taking what belonged to him. And he wanted badly to be with Eili again.

With all that sympathy in my head, the gods only knew why I wanted to pick a fight with him.

'Your mother's closer to doing something,' I said.

'And?' There was an edge to Conal's voice as he looped his rope through a carabiner and tugged it firm.

'Just saying. In case you haven't been watching.'

'Of course I've been watching.'

I waited for a few beats. 'As for your goddaughter—'

Carefully he ignored that. 'My mother won't go over. I trust her.'

I said nothing. Not aloud.

'I heard that, Murlainn.'

'Dorsal knows something's up. She may be a royal pain in the arse, but she's not stupid.'

'Her name's Finn.'

'Hardly matters what I call her. She's going to be trouble whatever her name is. And she won't get a true name if things go on like this.'

'Aw, Seth, not now.' Conal rolled his balaclava down over his face. 'I'm busy.'

'You're always busy. You're avoiding the issue.'

'All of them. Too right I am.' Silently he lifted the loosened pane of glass out of the roof. ~ *Now shut up. Please?*

I lay on my stomach and watched him lower himself headfirst, slithering down the rope, legs hooked securely round it. The floor was alarmed, touch-sensitive, but he wasn't going to fall. He never did. He wouldn't even wear a climbing harness, despite his dislike of heights, and that was pure pride. I was the better climber, but I hadn't the patience for this job. The figure below us, sprawled in tangled

sheets, stirred and grunted; I turned my mind on
him, almost bored.

~ *Hurry up,* said Conal.

Sighing, I tried to focus. Dennis snored, mumbled
and rolled over, making us both freeze, but there
was no way Conal could touch him to drain him of
more consciousness. Besides, through a deeper sleep
I might never find the code in his head. Conal had
plied him with too much lunchtime booze as it was,
hence his insanely early night.

I reached out my mind to Dennis's. It had been
hard the first time I did this, finding the pathways
and the sparking connections that led me where I
needed to go. But I'd got the hang of it alarmingly
quickly, and now I'd done it so often, it was a breeze.
I don't think Conal truly appreciated how good I
was. He retained his old distaste for this kind of
theft, though it made no difference to his moral pro-
bity that I did the dirty work for him.

Still, it was no effort these days. Who'd put a lock on
their innermost thoughts anyway? No-one but a Sithe.

Dennis was dreaming of a Bond girl. *Aye,* I thought,
and only in your dreams. In passing I couldn't help
amusing myself with his indignation at his ex-wife,
his plans to shaft his co-directors – Conal included;
now that was interesting – but most of it was none
of my business. I probed an interchange, a tribu-
tary and then – *bingo* – locked onto the sequence
of numbers.

I forwarded them to Conal, waiting upside down
with thinning patience, and he keyed in the numbers
with one gloved hand.

He stilled, waiting as Dennis moaned lightly and turned again. I couldn't blame Dennis. She was lovely, his dream-woman: crop-haired, delicate, as lovely as a Sithe. She reminded me of Eili, a little. And what Dennis was up to with her reminded me suddenly, sharply, of Kate.

I slapped the thought away, freeing myself instantly from Dennis's mind, shivering. I didn't understand myself. I hated the woman, but already desire stirred in my groin. Bloody hell.

~ *You finished yet?* I snapped.

~ *What's with you?* Conal slid a broad square box from the safe, but though the fiery ruby pendant was a stunner, it wasn't what we were after. He replaced it and a folder of financial documents – Mr Integrity, he didn't even glance at those – and drew out a narrower velvet box.

He flipped it briefly open then, satisfied, tucked it inside his jumper. Closing the safe, he twisted upright and shinned back up the rope, slick as a snake.

On the roof, the glass pane replaced, he shook his head to clear the blood-rush headache as I opened the box. Diamonds glittered, pretty in the moonlight, but the stone Leonora was after was the unassuming pink sapphire on the clasp.

'Ridiculous,' he muttered. 'I'll only have to put the bloody thing back.'

'Oh, you don't think this is the One?' I couldn't repress the sarcasm, even if I did feel sorry for him.

'Not this one, not the last six fecking thousand. Or whatever. I've lost count. There's no such thing as this Bloodstone. Why can't she face it?'

'There's no such thing as us,' I remarked. 'Oh, of course the Bloodstone doesn't exist. What matters is keeping your mother interested. She needs a hobby.'

He gave a dry laugh. 'She'll be suspect number one if Dennis remembers how she was ogling that on his girlfriend's wrist. I have to stop letting her come to company functions.'

'So? Even better. They lock her up, she can't go back over the Veil. Better than Finn's mad guess. You know, Calderwood Rest Home for the terminally stroppy.' I slithered down the sloping roof and dropped lightly to the ground after him.

~ *I've heard worse ideas,* he told me glumly. ~ *There's got to be some way of delaying her. Just a few more years . . .*

I felt the Rottweilers before we heard them: they raced round the corner of the house, running silent. Not barking was, I reckoned, a bad sign. I sighed.

~ *You might have put some sleep on those.*

Conal hunkered down, waiting for them, smiling as they skidded and cocked their ears, hesitant.

~ *Hey. Me Alpha Wolf. Show us your belly, Omegas.*

He peeled off a glove and stretched out his hand to the first of them. It sniffed, unsure, the echo of a growl in its throat. Then it rolled over, tongue lolling, and within a second the other one did the same.

I rubbed its tummy with a foot, glanced at my watch as it whimpered happily. 'Pub?'

Conal straightened, pulling affectionately at the bigger dog's ear.

'Pub.'

Jed

Wealthy old women did not throw themselves into lochs. Jed was 99 percent certain that Finn was being a complete drama queen. Decrepitude was easy to bear, he reckoned, if the finest nurses money could buy were mushing your food and wiping your arse. It wasn't what his mother would get. As for Jed, he didn't expect to get that old anyway.

The dusk was pink and very fleeting, and he didn't like how fast darkness fell on the country road. The closing night sucked all the spirit out of him. Headlights swept past, but their brilliance was dazzling, and no comfort, and they spoilt his night vision. Jed did not want to do this. He didn't want to follow Finn, he didn't want to go back to the Fairy Loch and he kept up with her only because he couldn't be alone in this darkness. The fear would freeze his feet to the ground.

A mile out of town Finn stopped, and Jed felt the

loch to his left, brooding and malign. He couldn't
see it yet – only the blackness of its trees against the
stars – but he could smell that weed-choked water,
that stink that was almost like a living thing, except
that it was part dead thing.

He flung his jacket onto the barbed wire, gave Finn
a leg up, then climbed up after her. As she dropped to
the ground on the loch side, hordes of rooks went
clattering and yammering into the sky.

He listened to the silence with a thumping heart,
but there was no sign of the tramp. By the time he
caught up with Finn, she was a shadow among shadows, pressed against the trunk of a huge pine.

'Any sign of Leonie?'

'Shut up,' she whispered. 'Yeah, there. See?'

Jed peered into the oppressive darkness. Beyond
the trees, far and faint, was a shadow stiller than the
pines. It wasn't possible, of course, and Finn was kidding herself, because how would an eighty-year-old
shin over the gate and the barbed wire?

God knew. But there the old woman was, silhou-
etted at the water's edge against reflected stars. Half-
turning, she peered suspiciously over her shoulder.
Jed took a step back – couldn't help himself – but
Leonie stared for a breathless age without seeing
them, then turned back to the loch. The reeds were
still, the water starred with pinpricks of light like a
piece of fallen night sky. The old woman looked
calm. She looked as if she might fade with the trees
into blackness as night fell, and simply disappear.

She moved.

As Leonie waded into the water, a ripple doubled, multiplied, and the star reflections shattered. When it reached her waist she stopped, her coat floating around her.

Then she was gone, and the water closed over her head.

The silence disintegrated. Finn shrieked something unintelligible and plunged forward too, ignoring Jed's shout. She stumbled into the water, instantly sinking into soft unseen mud. She gasped, and Jed thought of how cold the water must be, and the stupid girl was up to her waist, and she wouldn't know the depth. She was fumbling desperately in weeds and silt.

'Finn, don't be stupid!'

She shook him off and waded farther, staggering abruptly. How deep *was* this water? The thought must have struck her at the same time as it hit Jed, because she was suddenly panicking, arms flailing for something solid.

Oh, for feck's sake.

He should leave her. It was her own fault if they drowned together, her and her mad granny. He thought about turning, walking away.

No. Too used to thinking ahead, too aware of how it would be to live with it. Jed swore again and plunged down through the soft ground and into the water – like knives in his flesh, it was so cold – and snatched at Finn's wrist.

Her head whipped round, and there was sheer terror in her eyes.

'It's pulling. Help me!'

He caught her wrist, shouted, tugged hard and stumbled. Then the world was sucked away from him, and the bottom was no longer there, and black water swallowed them both.

Seth

The girl behind the bar was a rangy redhead, hair pulled back to show off her cheekbones. I liked the athletic look of her, and there was a faint hint of sweat on the sharp line of her collarbone that begged to be licked. Leaving my pint untouched, I felt for the Veil. It was fragile, so frail, and still it stood between us.

I focused on the right half of her brain, reached out all my senses. There was the shadow of the Veil, lying like dark matter across her perceptions; easy enough to twitch it like the finest silk. She saw me. Smiled at me. I smiled right back as her left hemisphere clicked in to process the information. I liked the way she was thinking.

'Hi,' she said.

'Hi.'

'Can I get you anything?'

I glanced with amusement at my untouched pint. 'Not yet. Busy night?'

She shrugged. 'Makes the time go faster.'

'Why? What time d'you finish?'

'Soon.' She gave me a very direct, intense grin; then her gaze flicked up over my shoulder. Her grin grew just that little bit broader.

I rolled my eyes as Conal sat on the stool next to me, smiling nervously at the redhead. One of these days he'd come back from the loos at what wasn't exactly the wrong moment.

'Give us some peanuts, love? Please.'

'Salted,' I added, with my warmest smile.

As she turned her back to get them, he shot me a glower. 'I wish you wouldn't do that.'

'Do what?'

'You played with her head.'

'Look who's talking.' I nodded towards the end of the long bar, where she was chatting up a roughneck. She'd forgotten not only the peanuts, but the pair of us as well.

'All I did was take her mind off you. Put things back to normal. Don't make me have to do that.'

'I hate going out drinking with you.'

'Aye, right.' He grinned suddenly and clinked his glass against mine. 'Here's to the Bloodstone. Which this one *undoubtedly* is.'

'Ha ha.' I took a long swallow. The beer tasted faintly of sun-toasted heather. Hell, these days anything could make me homesick. 'And I can't believe you're having a go at me, given what your goddaughter gets up to.'

His eyes hardened, but they slewed away from mine. 'Leave her be.'

'Leave her be? I told you what she did to that Rooney girl.'

'Shush.' He glanced at the nearest group of drinkers. 'That was a one-off.'

'No, Conal. No, it wasn't. You know what it was? It was a *start*.'

'She'll settle down.'

'No. Not until she understands what she is and why she can do what she does. If it's not explained to her, she'll do it again. And again. She can't control herself, and though it pains me to admit it, that's *not her fault*. She doesn't know what to control. Or why. She'll turn out a witch, Conal.'

'They don't burn those anymore.'

'No indeed. She's more likely to hurt somebody else.'

'No. No, she wouldn't. It's not in her.'

I could only gape at him.

He set his glass down so carefully, I knew he was trying not to fling it at me. 'Look, for the fifty-hundredth time, it's not up to me. She has a mother and it's Stella's decision. I can't go against that.'

'You're her Captain!'

He gave me a wry look. 'As if Stella recognises that anymore. Listen, Finn's got a friend now. That boy sees her better than most. I don't know why, but he does.'

'That boy's a feral thug. And a thief.'

'No. He's a thief, but he's not a thug. He's got a good heart. He'll be good for Finn.'

And how could he be so sure? I sighed, but I left it. 'You remember what you always told me? We're inconspicuous, not invisible. We'll slip from their minds, but only if we keep our heads down.' I nodded at the drinkers again. 'Finn won't slip from anybody's mind if she kills somebody.'

'She couldn't,' he said stubbornly. 'It won't come to that.'

I found I couldn't look at him. Whose child was she, for gods' sake? Her whole ancestral gene pool was muddied with the blood of enemies. And he didn't think she was capable of killing?

Hell's teeth. My brother's faith in humanity. To stop myself yelling at him, I turned away. I was about to take another drink but I paused with the glass at my lips. 'Gocaman,' I said.

Conal started. 'What?'

The tramp had come in through the front door on a gust of cold breeze, stopping to tip his leather hat back from his eyes and squint at us through his Sellotaped glasses. He came straight to the bar and stood between us.

We watched him, a little wary. It wasn't like him to leave his post in the woods, and he didn't look happy. Mind you, he never did. Surly bugger.

'Gocaman,' said Conal. 'Drink?'

He shook his head, almost dislodging his glasses, and readjusted them irritably. 'You'd better be leaving yours.' His voice was croaky from disuse. 'Someone has breached the watergate.'

Conal shut one eye. 'That's bad. But isn't it your problem?'

'Certainly your problem if you let one through,' I added. 'What's it to do with us?'

'Everything.' Gocaman cracked a smile. 'Wasn't no Lammyr. And I wasn't about to stop *her*.'

I swear it took a few seconds to sink in, while we stared at each other in dawning horror.

'Shit,' said Conal, standing up so suddenly, he swayed.

I got two more swallows out of my beer. And then I was at his heels, and running for our weapons and our home.

Jed

Jed swore, so creatively that Finn shot him a look of naked admiration.

Staggering out of shallow water, he half crawled half stumbled to her side, trying to catch his breath. Finn already had hers. Jed was shaking water out of his hair and eyes when he realised he didn't have to: he was bone-dry.

'We're dead. Are we dead?'

She took a calm look round. 'Dunno. Don't think so.'

His pride stung. '*You* were the one that panicked.'

'Why didn't you let go?' There was a trace of gratitude in her eyes. 'You should've let go.'

'I couldn't,' he said. 'Believe me, I tried.'

The strip of beach was empty and wind-smoothed. No footprints, no people, no cars in the middle distance. Nothing at all. Certainly no suicidal old madwoman. Jed wondered if that had occurred to Finn yet, because he wasn't going back in the bloody water to look again.

He turned a full circle to watch small waves rippling, cloud shadows chasing sun-glitter across the water. Daylight? Jed fished his phone out of his pocket to check the time.

'No signal,' he remarked. Typical. If he'd paid for the thing, he'd be livid.

'Maybe it got knackered in the water?'

'Why would it? We didn't. Anyway, it's working fine. Just no signal.'

On the far side of the loch the ruined walls of a castle rose from a jutting tongue of land. 'Castle,' said Jed, a little pointlessly.

Finn screwed up her eyes. 'Which one, though?'

'Dunno. Why's it the middle of the sodding day? Who *cares*?' Well, he did, to be honest, because he wasn't a hundred percent certain he wasn't dead. Surreptitiously he checked his wrist for a pulse.

The sun was low in the sky, the air fresh with a bite of chill. Jed waded into dense heather in search of a path, but there was only a maze of animal tracks. He jumped back down onto the crescent of gritty sand, and that was when he saw it, tucked under a rock and a fringe of heather.

'Hey.'

He crouched down, poked tentatively at the plastic wrappings. Thick, and firmly taped, but what was inside was clearly visible. He picked at the plastic, peeled away the tape, and drew out the gun.

Wondering, he lifted it by the trigger guard with one finger. He had never touched a firearm and it felt ridiculously dangerous, like it might blow up in his hand. It was heavier than he'd expected too: a blunt ugly pistol with a silky sheen of menace. He felt a shiver go through him, then realised Finn was eyeing him. Jed straightened, balanced the gun more confidently in his palm, stroked its barrel with a forefinger.

'What's that?' she said.

'Is that you being funny or have you had a very sheltered upbringing?'

She glared at him, then at the gun. 'Why would somebody dump that? I don't like it. Leave it where it is.'

He'd been considering that, but not now he'd been given an order. 'That tramp. He's a killer if ever I saw one.' Not that he had. 'I bet it's his and he had to throw it in the loch.' Avoiding the trigger, he turned the pistol from side to side, thumbing a little switch back and forth, peering into the muzzle. The torn plastic bag blustered away in a sudden gust, bouncing across the heather, trailing its torn tape like a kite-tail.

'So *that* gun would be in the *Fairy* Loch, then.' Her tone was withering.

'Like us,' he said. 'Theoretically.'

She gave him a sulky look. 'Okay. But just leave it.'

'No way. I can sell it. Or if we get hungry, I can shoot us a tourist.'

Straightaway he wished he hadn't said that: something about the look of the gun made the joke turn to dust on his tongue.

'Boys' toys.' Finn shrugged contemptuously. 'So take it. If it makes you happy.'

He tucked it into his jeans and pretended he hadn't

heard her. If they'd somehow lost consciousness and a whole night, he had to think about getting back to Rory, but he was damned if he knew which way.

The only rational direction was towards the castle ruins, towards tourists and cars and presumably a tarred road, but it wasn't that easy. Every track petered out, and the heather had a nasty habit of growing across the path at ankle height.

They stumbled on, Jed's language growing steadily worse. Across the silvered bays, the castle looked aggravatingly close, but somehow never any closer. Even in the afternoon chill, sweat tickled his spine, and Jed's mood grew blacker with every tangled step. Part of him hoped the old bat Leonie was dead in the mud at the bottom of the Fairy Loch. This was all her doing, and if she crawled out of the water right now, he'd throw her back in.

'Sh!' Finn stopped.

'I didn't say anything. What?'

'*Sh!* There it is again.'

This time he heard it, an eerie cry on the breeze.

'Wind in the stones,' he said.

'Big animal,' countered Finn.

The howl came again, then a high scream with an unearthly pitch, and the thrum of the ground underfoot.

Finn said, 'Should we walk a bit faster?'

'Run,' said Jed.

They took to their heels and fled. They ran until the path was lost altogether. Jed wasn't looking for the castle, not anymore. He could think only as far as the next footfall, and the next, as he crashed through the heather, stumbling on bumps and hollows, keeping his feet only because there was no question of falling. Finn was behind him, struggling but keeping up – he could hear her rasping frightened gasps – so he plunged on. He couldn't hear his own running feet for the subterranean echo of hooves and the snarling snorts of something lethal.

Finn cried out and he turned to see her sprawl. Doubling back, he seized her hand, dragged her up and hauled her inside the castle walls. A moment's triumph evaporated.

They'd made it, finally, desperately, to a heap of old stones. There wasn't a tourist in sight, and not a square foot of civilised tarmac. Nothing. And then Jed realised the ground was still vibrating, but not so violently. The sound of hoofbeats stopped.

Silence.

Something about the silence Jed didn't like.

'You know what that sounded like?' panted Finn. 'A wolf.'

'Don't be stupid,' he said.

'Haven't seen Leonie. Where *is* she?'

'She'll be around here. We're fine, aren't we? She'll be fine.'

'Wolves,' she pointed out darkly. '*Grandmothers.*'

No. Never a good combination. To avoid the heavy silence, Jed scrambled up onto a broken wall to check their surroundings. Civilisation seemed a ridiculously long way off. The pale sun was rolling lower on the horizon, but the view was clear. He blinked and pinched grit out of his eyes.

'I know where we are.' His heart slowed and thudded. 'We're on Linn Moor.'

'Oh! Good. So we—'

'Finn,' he said. 'Where's the town?'

She climbed up beside him. There was the wooded hollow of the Fairy Loch; there was the floodplain where shortsighted early citizens had built the town, and beyond that, the notch in the distant coast where the harbour should be. Only it wasn't.

'That doesn't make any sense,' said Finn redundantly.

Jed said nothing. He spread his hands, focusing on the veins. He wasn't dead. He couldn't be dead while the blood made blue channels through his bones. He wasn't a ghost, not yet, though this was the kind of place and the kind of night that made you believe quite strongly in ghosts.

And that was why the sound of a hoof-fall almost gave him heart failure.

Jed let out a single girlish scream as he spun round, then a nervous laugh. A horse: only a horse, and not a rider in sight. In the twilight its coat gleamed, pearly and indistinct, but its head and mane and tail were black, and its silky-feathered legs, and its strangely lightless eyes.

'You beauty!' Finn was in instant raptures. 'Jed, it's just a *horse*!'

It snorted playfully, shaking its neck and pawing the peat. Jed could see what Finn meant: it really was a beautiful thing. Its blank eyes were unnerving, but its solid warm presence made Jed aware of his own blood again, made him certain he was as real as the horse.

'You're gorgeous,' Finn told the horse. 'Jed, isn't he *gorgeous*?'

The horse blew into her hair, nibbled on her jumper, then glanced meaningfully at its own back.

Jed frowned, watching its eyes. 'Don't get on it.'

She shot him an amused frown as she gripped its wither. 'What?'

'Finn, don't. It's – ah – I dunno. Stealing.'

That, unsurprisingly, made her hoot. 'So it's lost. I'll take it to the police. No harm us riding it in the meantime.'

He wasn't sure why he disliked the look of the brute. 'It's too big for you.'

'Now, there you might have a point.' Finn eyed the height of it, chewing her lip. She grasped its back and tried to spring up, but her legs flailed and she dropped back.

Thank God for *that,* thought Jed.

Obligingly the creature dropped forward to its knees like a circus horse.

'See? No problem!' Hoisting herself onto it, Finn caressed its neck and cooed, 'You're so *clever.*'

It whickered as it got to its feet. Ridiculous to imagine it was having a laugh at his expense, but Jed still didn't like its shark-eyes, especially now they'd developed a shimmering greenish glow. But that was stupid. It was the dark, and the strangeness, and being lost, that was all.

The horse ripped idly at the grass, darting Jed an occasional mocking eye. He felt incredibly stupid now, but he still didn't like that animal.

'Come on, I'll give you a hand up,' said Finn.

He stepped back. 'Oh no. No way.'

'Don't be daft, it's huge. It'll take both of us. We'll find town a lot faster.'

'You can go on your own, then.'

'Oh, now you're being ridiculous.'

Jed had the feeling the horse thought so too, but he wasn't changing his plans. 'Fine. I'll find my own way back.'

'Oh, come on. I can't leave you.'

'No, you really can. It's fine.'

A glint of white flared from the twilit grass, making him jump, making Finn glance sideways.

Only a rabbit-scut, but the horse lunged for it. Its shoulder struck Jed, knocking him to his knees, and Finn was flung sideways, but she didn't fall. As Jed scrambled to his feet, he reached for her.

'Get off. *Now.*'

She tugged her fingers, tangled in the black mane. 'I can't.'

'I'll catch you. Just – fall!'

'I *can't*!'

The horse's jaws snapped on the rabbit's spine and tossed it skywards, head high. Small bones crunched, the horse's throat convulsed, and the rabbit disappeared in three gulps down its throat. When it looked at Jed, it was grinning.

He grabbed for its mane, but the horse's jaw slammed into his skull, stunning him. Rolling, panicking, he fumbled at his belt, tugging out the pistol, then aimed wildly, shut his eyes and jerked the trigger.

It made a dry *click*. Jed swore, threw it aside and stumbled to his feet. But by then the horse was gone with Finn, racing insanely towards the dimming horizon.

Seth

My whole being knew I was back where I belonged.
The air crowded into my lungs, crackled against my
skin. Bubbles of it hit my brain and raced into my
blood, and home howled and bayed inside me as it
always did: *What took you so long?*

Conal looked too preoccupied to enjoy it. 'Where's
your horse got to?'

I shrugged, slapped the glossy flank of his black.
'Killing something, I expect. Where's your mother?
More to the point, where's your goddaughter?'

As soon as we were inside Tornashee, we'd known
there was more wrong than we'd realised. Leonora
was gone, and that we'd expected, but Finn too was
gone from the otherworld. Not a trace of her left,
not even her mind, though Conal had hunted wildly
for that when he could ransack the house and grounds
no more. Nothing. She was dead, or she was with
Leonora, and Conal refused to contemplate either
option.

'It's a coincidence,' he said. 'It has to be.'

'She wasn't on that side, Conal. At. All.'

'She could have been blocking—'

'She doesn't know how.' I left the criticism hanging unsaid; he looked tormented enough.

'But Seth,' he flailed. 'Gocaman would know if she'd gone through.'

'Gocaman came to the pub for us as soon as Leonora went past him. And you know as well as I do Finn used to spy on your mother. She watched her going out at night. Wasn't hard to work out where she'd been, with all that mud on her breeks. Finn's followed the old bat. She's gone, Conal.'

He was too unhappy even to rise to *old bat*. 'Finn's forbidden to go there. It's out of bounds and she knows it.'

I rolled my eyes. 'Yep, that always works. Always did it for me. Listen, why don't you go on?'

'I'll have to, if the roan doesn't show soon.'

'That's okay.' I wasn't too pleased myself, but I wasn't about to admit that in front of Conal. If the roan was a delinquent, he was my delinquent.

We'd delayed enough by going back to Tornashee to collect our weapons and packs. The gods knew where Leonora was by now. It looked to me like a lost cause, trying to talk her out of returning and staying in the otherworld; I wouldn't let anyone do it to me, not once home was back in my bloodstream. Besides, even Leonora didn't have the willpower to stay alive forever. But Conal was desperate. I couldn't blame him.

'Go ahead, then,' I told him. 'It might be better if we split up anyway. We can rendezvous later.'

'Don't block, then. Keep in touch.' He tapped his temple, then flicked the black's reins to turn it. 'You've been kind of obstructive lately.'

I winked at him. 'Shouldn't be so nosy.'

He grinned, and nudged the black to a gallop.

I watched him for a few seconds, a worm of guilt gnawing at my gut. There had always been things we kept from each other. It would be odd if there weren't. And I didn't think he'd see the joke where my adolescent Kate-dreams were concerned. Not that I did, either. I wished I didn't look forward to them, and I wished I felt more remorse afterwards.

And I very much wished I could stop worrying about it. For gods' sake, it wasn't *serious*.

I forgot Kate, and dreams of Kate, when something prickled in the nape of my neck, something that might have been familiar or perhaps just opaquely threatening. A few seconds later, I felt distant hoofbeats.

I didn't like to test the unseen riders' minds with my own; that would have been a dead giveaway. I'd just have to wait and see, so I drew back into the copse of wizened rowans, trusting them to shield my mind while I unsheathed my sword. Gods, it was good to see it back in its proper world again. It glowed and quivered like a live thing, catching the last twilight, as if it too was happy to be home.

I was so busy admiring it, I didn't realise the sound of horses had not only drawn closer, but one of them had stopped as well. I didn't like horses that could be so silent. Well, I liked it that mine could, but this one wasn't the roan. Its partner had galloped on, but this horse, or its rider, had sensed me. Uneasily I edged closer to the brink of the rowans.

Steel whispered past my ear. My mind was open in an instant, luckily for the big English git. I spun round, batting his sword away from my face.

'Torc, you bloody lout! Nearly had my head off.'

Torc's blade trailed an arc in front of him, as lazy as his grin. 'Shouldn't sneak up, Murlainn.'

'I'm not the one who – oh, what the hell.' I returned his grin, then stepped clear of the rowans. Sionnach had swerved and ridden back fast; he was off the grey before it had clattered to a standstill, and giving me a happy ferocious hug.

'Murlainn, you infidel hound!'

I had to submit to a hug from Torc too, though it nearly crushed my lungs. I slapped his rib cage as I drew away, and in return he whacked my skull fondly.

I rubbed my ringing head. 'Sight for sore eyes, the pair of youse. What are you doing this far over?'

Sionnach shrugged. 'The usual.'

'Kate's boys and girls have been misbehaving,' added Torc. 'And last night we get a summons from Her Ladyship Leonora. It's a long way to the dun from this gate and she wants an escort, she says. I assume that's why you're here, shortarse? She got away?' He winked.

I shot him a glower, but my heart wasn't in it. I was too happy to see them. 'Yes, damn her eyes. We go out for one lousy drink, which we richly deserve, and the old bat sneaks through the watergate.'

'Well, she's with Eili now.' Sionnach raised his eyes heavenwards.

Torc grinned. 'Yeah, and they're giving each other an earful. We came out to look for you guys. Not that we were worried. Just wanted some peace, y'know?'

'Oh gods, do I know.'

'And where's Conal?' Torc peered round me as if he thought I was hiding him in my back pocket.

'Went to look for his mother,' I said. 'He's probably caught up with her and Eili by now.'

Sionnach's version of a dirty smirk was distorted by his scars. 'At least that'll shut my sister up.'

I raised an eyebrow and grinned. 'Not in front of the child, I hope.'

And Sionnach said, 'What child?'

If I'd been blood-related to Finn, I could have found traces of her mind and I'd have known roughly which direction to take, but I wasn't, and I didn't. Since she hadn't found her grandmother, she could be anywhere. The only thing we could do was ride hard to where Eili was waiting, and hope for the best.

I knew that baby would be trouble from her first bloodcurdling squall.

I rode behind Sionnach on his horse; it wasn't the size of Torc's huge iron grey, but it was big enough. When I'd gripped Sionnach's arm and swung up behind him, the creature had plunged and bucked for four or five paces, but then gathered its dignity and raced on. It knew me, and its acquiescence made me even more resentful of the roan. What was the beast playing at? It had been a few years, for sure, but there were times when I regretted the independence of that horse's mind. Imagine making such a strenuous effort to dodge me, even when it was drawn relentlessly by my calling.

~ *I suspect,* Sionnach pointed out dryly, ~ *that it has prey.*

~ *Still and all. It's an ill-schooled disobedient brat.*

~ *Ah, your brother was so right about that horse and you. You're made for each other.*

He didn't turn, but I knew he was laughing. I couldn't help grinning too. ~ *I'll let that one go. What's with the detour?*

He'd nudged his grey to the east and south; we were skirting the edge of a pinewood and cutting down a rough track. This wasn't the way to the rendezvous he'd mentioned.

~ *Dughall Reid. If anyone's seen anything of your Finn, it'll be him.*

'Might even have taken her in!' shouted Torc cheerfully from behind.

'Gods help him. And she isn't my Finn.'

Sionnach reined in his horse hard, and it plunged and whinnied. 'What – ?'

'I said she isn't my Finn. Gods forbid.'

But I saw straightaway that wasn't Sionnach's point.

. . .

Sionnach's grey picked its delicate way through a black wasteland. What had once been a farm was a desolation. I drew my sword, but there wasn't any point.

Where beasts should have huddled in a field, steam rising off their hides in the cold air, smoke rose instead from butchered corpses. Whoever had done it wasn't interested in stealing the cattle, so we knew what we'd find before we got to the steading yard.

Timber smouldered underfoot, the smell of charring catching the back of our throats. Burnt wood, burnt stone, burnt meat; and not only beef. A roof beam and its last precarious slates creaked, then collapsed.

Sionnach reined in his horse before a heap of smoking logs. It backed and snorted, bared its canines. The smell of burning meat was stronger now, and beneath it a deadlier stench. The logs had limbs, or the stumpy remains of them.

I slid off Sionnach's horse, crouched over the pyre and poked at black shreds of fabric. I'd smelt burnt human more than once; it never got any sweeter. Once it was in your nostrils, you couldn't ever get the reek of it out.

I stood up, sheathed my blade, waited for the sting of a hundred memories to fade.

'This is Reid?' I asked.

'And his family.' Torc brushed his arm once, hard, across his face.

Sionnach said nothing. He was absolutely still on his horse, reins in one hand, staring at the steading: the only building left half-standing, and only because the fire hadn't caught so well.

'There's someone alive,' he said, and his tone was deadly.

Torc nodded. His colossal horse made barely a sound as he swung its head and rode it round to the back of the barn. Sionnach stayed on guard at the front, both swords drawn.

The collapsed steading walls were scalable, but not easily; if the skulker tried to escape sideways, we'd catch him, no problem. Once again I drew my sword, and trod carefully across charred rubble into the half-roofed ruins.

'Come out or I'll cut you out,' I called pleasantly.

The fear, the staccato aggression: they felt so familiar, my spine rippled with apprehension.

It couldn't be. . . .

A movement in the remnants of shadow. He must have known he was rumbled. A deep and audible groan of gathering courage, and then the boy staggered up abruptly, fists clenched, skin filthy, teeth bared in nothing like a smile.

No. He was the last person I'd expected or wanted. It couldn't be, but it was.

Mila's boy was coiled like a snake, every muscle taut for a fight. I'd have liked to tell him to for gods' sake at least unclench his teeth, because in that state he couldn't fight a lapdog for more than two minutes. But something in his eyes stopped me: a diamond ferocity.

I should get him back to his mother. Lammyr or no Lammyr, she'd be fine with him.

For a few seconds he stared at me. There was a high edge of panic in his voice. 'Where am I?'

'That's original.' I rolled my eyes. 'Keep your feckin' voice down.'

He gave me a look of such hatred, I almost flinched. Almost. But I couldn't afford that.

Jed looked from me to Sionnach and behind him to Torc. From Torc to me. And on me his gaze stayed.

'I know you,' he said.

'I don't know what you're talking about,' I lied.

'Oh yeah. I saw you at Tornashee with the idiot Finn. Where is she?'

'No, that's not – who are—? where—?'

'Where are you?' I broke in quickly. 'Nowhere you know. Where's Finn?'

Sionnach shot me a frown, half confusion and half disapproval. 'Finn?'

'Finn's gone,' Jed blurted.

I took two steps towards him and grabbed him by the collar. 'She's gone? Where?'

He flinched, but the loathing didn't leave his eyes. 'A horse. There was a horse. It was tame and we were tired and she got on it and—'

'She *what*?'

'Are you frigging deaf? She got on it! It ran off!'

Oh, gods. No matter what I thought of Finn, she wouldn't abandon Jed voluntarily. Friends, for her, were too hard to come by. 'What colour was the horse?'

'Feckin' *weird*. It was blue.'

. . .

We shouldn't have caught up with the roan as fast as we did, though I called it with a savage insistence and Sionnach knew better than to distract me. All the same, the fool on its back must have fought like a demon all the way for it not to have reached the Dubh Loch by now.

Wind pummelling my face and cold singeing my lips; ah, I could almost enjoy the wild ride if I wasn't imagining what Conal would have to say about my horse eating his goddaughter. Torc had stayed at the farm with the boy; I was glad I didn't have to be part of that conversation, but I wasn't enchanted by this job.

When we first caught sight of her, she was a blur on the crystalline air close to the horizon, but no way was that as fast as the roan could run. As we drew closer, I made out Finn clearly: a thin figure crouched on the roan's back, all tangled black hair and terror mixed up with a raging dark resentment. She was unmistakable: I knew that hair. I knew that temper. No wonder the roan was having problems.

I banged my head between Sionnach's shoulder blades in lieu of the nearest wall, but he was still all concerned with catching up. And thanks to the girl on its back we were, finally, abreast of it, both horses racing across the moor as the Dubh Loch's shining shore grew closer, and broader, and brighter: so close now, I could hear the song of its waves.

Dorsal wasn't paying us any attention. She crouched low across the horse's neck, straining to bite at her hands. Instinct, I thought: born instinct. The horse threw her off balance and her head jolted crazily but when she leaned forward and snapped her teeth again, she caught the base of a finger and sank her teeth into the skin.

We were so close, I could nearly touch her, and spattered blood from her hand hit my face like rain.

Oh, great. The smell of blood was going to make this *so* much easier.

'Don't do it!' yelled Sionnach.

I was more concerned with the roan. ~ *So help me, you brute, you are in SO MUCH TROUBLE—*

Through her raggedly billowing hair, Finn flicked a look at us, but she took as much notice of Sionnach as the horse did of me. Her jaws tore savagely at her forefinger.

'Stop!' bellowed Sionnach.

She spat blood and skin, looking more frustrated than afraid. 'I'd love to!' she screamed.

'He ISN'T TALKING TO YOU,' I yelled, and then, 'YOU *DISOBEDIENT BAG OF WOLFMEAT*!'

I'll be honest, that wasn't aimed entirely at the roan. But I was furious.

As Sionnach nudged us closer still, I reached out an arm and grabbed the girl by the waist, buffeted by her rage and confusion. She thought I was trying to pull her off, and she fought me as well as the horse: livid at my interference, obviously willing to lose her fingers but not both arms. She'd never have all three trapped fingers off in time, but give her credit, she was trying. She gnawed determinedly at her own flesh.

'For gods' SAKE.' I let go of her. Then I got my balance on Sionnach's horse and made the leap to my own, with a lot less grace than I'd have liked.

As Sionnach veered his grey away, I reached round the struggling girl to grab the roan's mane, but now I was astride it, it was already slowing. A fast canter eased to a playful bouncy trot, and then it stood stock-still, flinging her forward to bang her face against its arched neck. It angled its head back for a last look. There was mischievous disappointment in the black eyes as her fingers slipped smoothly loose from its mane.

If Conal had heard the language that came out of her, she'd have been grounded for a week. I sat there with my arms folded and waited till she'd finished, because I knew instinct and adrenaline would have only a limited life. Sure enough, her cool dissolved as soon as she ran out of curses, and she started to shake.

I swung her by the waist down from the horse and into Sionnach's arms, and because he always was more human than me, he held on to her till the shaking stopped.

Only that long, though. Releasing her, he seized her bleeding hand and turned it one way and the other. His own horse swivelled its eyes and stamped at the scent of blood. 'Don't you know any better?'

'No,' she said, and stared at her mangled finger, the ripped work of her own teeth. She'd got to the bone. She gave a tiny involuntary whimper of pain, but then pressed her lips together and shut her eyes tight. Her face had whitened and she swayed a little, but shook off Sionnach's reassuring hand.

He glared at the roan. 'As for you—'

'I'll deal with it,' I said quickly, and slapped its

muzzle quite hard. 'Naughty, naughty. Come when you're called.'

It snorted and gave a derisive toss of its black mane.

'Never grown up,' muttered Sionnach, unspecifically.

Yet again I didn't pursue it, because Finn had turned slowly to face me. The look on her face was part horror, part shock, and a large and recognisable part disgust. I didn't know what to say, so for once in my life I had the sense to keep my mouth shut.

'Well,' she said at last, and her voice trembled only a little. 'Isn't there a *lot* you bastards haven't told me.'

Night had fallen completely by the time we were anywhere near the original rendezvous. We rode in an awkward silence, in the light of a blurred three-quarters moon. Finn and Jed, riding behind Sionnach and Torc respectively, could hardly chat, and I had no intention of explaining anything to Finn. It wasn't my job; it wasn't my fault; and it would have killed my mood – which despite everything was lighter than in ages. Branndair was back; the wolf had flung himself at me so hard, the pair of us had ended up in the mud. I had my horse back too; I was riding him through moorland and hills and wooded gullies and moon-frosted trees. Already I didn't want to go back to the otherworld.

There's no countering the strength of belonging; there's no fighting it. It's a memory in your bones and it sucks at the marrow of them. You can fight it for as long as you like – and the gods know I did, and for a lot longer than that – but there's no beating it. You can only keep your face above the water, trying to breathe, while belonging drags on your scalp.

I'd been starting to drown. I knew that now.

I was grinning as I dismounted and led the roan and Branndair into the copse of rowans between two hills. Me grinning was not a sight beloved of everyone, so I wasn't too surprised when the flat of a blade tilted my chin up. Its quivering edge tickled my throat.

'What's so funny, Murlainn?'

'Eili.' I put a finger between the blade and my jugular and eased it away. 'It's nice to see you too.'

'Well, you can't expect me to recognise you. It's been that long.'

'Ha ha. Where's Conal?'

Sionnach came to my side silently, and with a reproachful sidelong glance at me, he took his sister's hand and pressed it to his forehead. Formalities over, she hugged him, then extended the same hand to me. Absolutely impassive.

Bloody hell. I greeted her properly, but with a very bad grace.

Now she was smiling. Her dark red hair was still cropped short, and it still looked as if she cut it herself, in the dark, with one of the two swords on her back; but even in a filthy mood, she was as beautiful as she always was. She looked beyond us, to where Torc was holding the horses.

Finn and Jed had dismounted with wildly different degrees of grace. Jed positively thudded to the ground, his knees nearly buckling. He wore a thuggishly murderous scowl: in other words, he looked terrified.

'First things first,' I said. 'Do something about her hand, will you? I'm in enough trouble as it is.'

Eili seized Finn's wrist and examined the bloodily torn skin. 'You're not kidding, Murlainn. Your horse had her, did it? Cù Chaorach's going to love that.'

Torc gave Finn a bewildered look. 'Eili, you know this one?'

'I know who she is.' Eili smiled, not very pleasantly. 'I've had the pants bored off me looking at photographs.'

'Oh no.' Torc paled.

Eili's grip looked light, but I could see Finn trying and failing to wrench her hand away, panic starting to spark in her eyes. I was about to object – honestly, I was – when Eili rubbed her thumb hard across the ugly half-congealed wound, splitting it open.

Finn's eyes widened as the blood flowed, but she was clearly too shocked even to squeak – until Eili pinched the gaping rip hard with her fingertips. Then she gave a howl of pain.

I winced in sympathy. True healing hurt, and Eili's bedside manner did leave a lot to be desired. Finn recovered fast though, clamping her lips together, blinking back tears, staring at the sealed wound. 'Thanks,' she muttered shakily. 'I think.'

'Don't mention it,' said Eili. 'That was easy enough. Well, Seth, I'll leave you to explain this one to your brother. She's your Finn.'

'She bloody is not,' I retorted automatically.

I regretted my tactlessness, but 'Too right I'm not,' Finn muttered, snatching her hand out of Eili's.

Eili folded her arms and nodded at Jed, who was goggling in disbelief at Finn's hand. 'What are we going to do with him?'

'Take him along.' Sionnach shrugged.

'You feckin' will not.' Jed's head jerked up, as if he'd woken for the first time since the Reids' steading. He backed off a step, then two, shaking off Torc's steadying hand. 'What is this place? I need to go home. Show me how *now*.'

'Not possible,' I told him silkily. 'Maybe later. If you're good.'

Even in the darkness, I saw him pale. 'I saw that farm. I saw what was there!'

'Your powers of observation slay me.'

'Shut up, you snake.' Protectively, Finn shoved forward to Jed's side. 'I was there too. There were *bodies*.'

'Oh, the horse wouldn't have eaten those. He doesn't go for carrion.'

'You sick bastard. Call the police!'

I just laughed.

She flushed red. 'The authorities. Whoever. We'll tell them if you don't!'

Sionnach said quietly, 'The authorities did it.'

She blinked at him, silenced. I had to learn that trick of his. Anyway, I had no business provoking the girl in these circumstances. Of course she was shocked.

'Reid and his family are dead,' Sionnach told Eili.

'We know. Kate will pay for that, or her filthy patrol will. I mean, where d'you think Cù Chaorach's gone?'

'Oh, don't tell me.' I shoved my hands through my hair, glad of a distraction from the quarrel with Finn. 'He's not at it already.'

'What do you expect? They were his people. They're dead only because they sheltered the three of us last night. I'd have gone out with him, but I had to babysit the old woman.' She twisted her lip.

'I'd love you to say that to Leonora's face.' I grinned, and for the first time got a proper smile back.

'And of course he had to go looking for the girl,' said Eili.

'My brother the sheepdog.'

'What's she doing here, anyway?'

'Came through the watergate by accident,' I said. 'I warned them all. It was out of bounds but, hey—'

'Not her.' Eili shook her head impatiently. 'Not the girl. I mean Leonora.'

I hesitated, frowning. There was a light of expectation in Eili's eyes. 'She hasn't said anything?'

'She's said plenty. Just not what she's doing here.' The expectation faded to fear, then transformed again to fragile hope. 'You found it? The Stone?'

I licked my lips. I hadn't expected to have to explain this part. 'Did we hell.'

'Then what's she . . .'

Sionnach was staring at me too, now.

'Is anyone going to tell me what's going on?' Finn butted in.

'Likewise,' retorted Eili in a deadly tone that silenced the girl.

A cool voice said, 'I'm going to have to tell you sooner or later, aren't I?'

Leonora. She stood in splintered moonlight and tree-shadows; her blue irises glittered, and so did the black marble eyes of the raven on her arm, riveted on Finn. Its screech of disapproval shattered the silence.

The girl didn't respond. She studied the bird intently; I could almost see the pieces of her whole life coming together in her head, and straightaway dissolving in the acid of lies. I thought I saw tears glitter on her lashes. Then, fiercely, she said, 'Shut up, Faramach.'

Somebody had to say something, and it might as well be me. 'Leonora's come back for good. It's all over.'

Eili stared at me, then at Leonora in naked disbelief. She licked her lips.

'Leonora, no. Not now. We've given up too much.'

'I know, Eili.' Leonora touched her arm. 'I'm sorry.'

'We did this for you! You!'

Leonora didn't answer. Instead she reached up to her coiled hair and unpinned it, letting the tawny mass of it fall to her shoulders. It had always been streaked with gold; now strands of it glinted silver.

Ah. Thought so.

Eili recovered her voice. 'You have a few months,' she gritted. 'A few months may be all it takes. You could find the Stone tomorrow. You've no right to give up.'

Finn's confusion was obvious, because it was keeping her quiet. Jed had sidled closer to her, but he too said nothing. Smart boy.

'I will not stay longer,' said Leonora. 'I *will not.*'

'You have to! Give Conal a chance. Kate will invade the dun lands if you—'

'I value my mind, Eili. Conal can't keep me over there and I can't stay, whatever they think. I want the Selkyr. I don't have a choice.'

Eili's pupils were like dirty ice. 'You took him from us. You took him from *me*.'

'Eili. You know how to fight, so go on fighting. If you lose, at least you tried your best. And,' Leonora pointed out with a slight smile, 'Kate doesn't have the Stone either.'

Her coolness was an insult; I knew just how Eili felt. I gave a high bitter laugh. 'Stones, Dorsal! There's a lot of them about! Ah, the things I saw, the things I did, all for the sake of some dead soothsayer your granny once knew! The inconsiderate old lunatic wasn't even vaguely specific. A *Stone*!' I jerked my thumb at Leonora. 'And now this old lunatic's cutting and running!'

Leonora put a hand on Finn's arm before the girl could slap me, and Faramach took a flapping hop onto her shoulder.

'Seth, Seth.' The old witch gave me a surprisingly affectionate smile. 'You've spent too long on the other side. So much rage has seeped into you, you barely know where to aim it.'

Her pity burned. I snarled, 'That's your doing. You've wasted our lives, and now you're telling us to forget spells and prophecies and use our wits like we always should have. If my brother had any, he'd never have talked me into this!'

'Don't you dare, Seth!' barked Eili. 'Conal gave up

as much of his life for the Stone as you did.' Her eyes blazed. 'And so did I!'

'Get over it, Eili.'

'Shut up, the lot of you.' Torc sounded disgusted, as well he might. A pissed-off Torc was such a rare beast, it did shut us up. Good for him. I felt I'd been shocked into momentary sanity.

Finn was pale and contained, and I didn't like it. I knew she was working things out in her head. I thought again of all those pieces falling into place, her life making a picture at last: one that she could recognize, one that finally made sense. Or not.

She moved closer to Jed: closer than he liked, I reckoned, by the way he stiffened. Her voice was clear and filled with venom. 'Jed? Watch what you think. Because they know.'

'Know what?'

'What you're thinking. They see what's in your head. All of them.'

Leonora sighed, and closed her eyes.

The boy was blinking at Finn. He nearly laughed, but the smile died on his lips. He stood up, met my gaze, then glanced sharply away into Eili's.

She made a face. 'Don't overdramatise, Fionnuala. That's not how we work.'

Jed stepped back so fast, he almost stumbled backwards over a log. 'Get out. *Get out.*'

He shook his head violently. Scratched, then tore at his scalp. So he felt it, did he?

'Gods' sake,' said Eili with a touch of impatience. 'It was only a moment's check. You were panicking.'

'I said don't. *Don't* do that again!'

She shrugged. 'Fine.'

I found myself regretting what I'd done to him, but only because I resented the result. I shrugged, drew the sword off my back, and began to sharpen it.

'Extraordinary,' murmured Leonie, studying Jed like a sample on a slide. She turned to Finn, taking hold of something at her throat.

I noticed it for the first time. It was the emerald chunk she'd used to vandalise my motorbike: set now in a crude silver talon with sharply spiked claws. It was the pendant she'd made as her first silversmithing project, and it was crap, because she had no feel for metal. But it held that stone just fine.

Leonora turned the pendant in her fingers, ignoring Finn's deadly stare. 'I shouldn't have given you a shield stone. Not that I knew what it was. Not then.'

Just as well Jed had Finn's hand; otherwise, I think she'd have slapped the old woman's away. 'What is it?'

'It protects your mind. It's how you followed me to the loch without me knowing you were there.' She gave Finn a cutting look. 'Some things are private, Fionnuala.'

Finn spoke through her teeth. 'Private.'

Ignoring Finn's frigid tone, Leonora shook the emerald crossly. 'Deceitful rock. And your setting isn't secure. It wiggles.' She wiggled it to demonstrate, and the stone turned a millimetre in its setting.

'I didn't have long.' Finn fiddled with the stone herself, frowning. 'Rush job.'

'Of course, of course. You sneaked into my workshop! You're cunning, that's good.' She hugged Finn proudly. 'Just like Seth!'

Bitch, I thought as Finn went rigid in Leonora's embrace, eyes icing over. *How to get at both of us at once.*

'You know,' I murmured as silence fell, 'that child just got taken by my horse. She dealt with it well. She dealt with it like a Sithe, because that's what she is.' I met Finn's frozen stare. 'She'd have had that finger off within a minute. To hell with Reultan. You owe the girl an explanation.'

Leonora curled her lip as if she wanted to kill me herself. Eili gave me a small smile. But most satisfying of all, Finn's glacial hatred cracked, dazing her for maybe a second and a half. I laughed inwardly.

'She can get an explanation later.' Sionnach's head jerked up as he listened to the night. 'Something's out there.'

Sionnach's antennae were second to none, so we weren't about to ignore that. As Torc drew his sword with the rest of us, Jed dodged. 'Watch where you're putting that.'

'He'll put it in you if you don't shut up,' growled Eili, sniffing the wind.

'How many?' asked Torc.

'Sionnach, go investigate,' Eili told him. 'And find Cù Chaorach, while you're at it.'

'Doesn't matter how many there are.' I shrugged as Sionnach and his horse melted into the darkness. 'It's not like we can get into any scraps. Not with the babies on board. Let's go.'

Jed, clearly longing to kick my head in, edged towards Torc. The big man only slapped him cheerfully between the shoulder blades, making him reel back towards me. 'No, lad. Murlainn'll take you.'

I raised my eyes skywards as I scrambled onto the roan's back. 'Feckin' nursemaid, me.'

I leaned down and seized the boy. His legs flailed uselessly in midair, and before he had his limbs or his head organized, he was on the roan behind me. I didn't give him time to get back off, or I'm sure he'd have tried. We broke out of the trees, and the horse sprang forward, and all he could do was shriek, and grab my waist, and hang on.

The night was gusty and cold; outlined against starlight, black pines swayed and bannered in the chilling wind, blustering strands of hair across my eyes. As we slowed, the others overtook us, Finn clinging to Eili's back. Eili gave me a snarl for riding ahead, but I was preoccupied with the trees, with the slash of gullies and gathering darkness. I realised the boy behind me was shivering with the cold.

'You okay?'

'I'm fine.'

Nice one. He'd barely got the words out for his chattering teeth.

'You got—' I hesitated. '—people at home?'

'Just my mum. And a little brother.'

'Oh.' I rode on in silence for a couple of hundred yards. 'And this . . . mum. Will she be okay?'

He snorted. 'She's always okay. She can always get off her face. It's my baby brother I'm worried about.'

I tensed. 'She'll worry about you.'

'She'll think I'm sleeping rough. Probably won't notice I'm not there.'

His dismissive tone annoyed me, and it unnerved me too. The thing was, I knew he didn't mean it. I hadn't been a worm in his head for nothing. But if he told himself something often enough, he might start to believe it. That she should depend on him less. Love the baby more.

No, no. It was down to him. All of it. If he hardened his heart, Mila was lost.

He needed perspective. He needed a lesson. 'Get down,' I said.

He hesitated, thinking he'd heard me wrong, so I half turned and swung him bodily off the horse. He stumbled, speechless, giving me time to ride away without a backward glance. The roan picked up its pace a little, and in seconds he had faded into the dusk.

Another couple of hundred yards, and I reined in the horse. The others were ahead, I knew, but I couldn't see them. I wondered, if I left him, how long it would take them to realise he was gone. And . . . whether they'd think it was worth turning back.

The gloom closed in like a wet shroud. I looked back over my shoulder. Jed wasn't visible, not even as a blur in the mist.

Branndair sat down on the boggy ground and looked up at me, quizzical. I watched his troubled eyes, brushed his mind almost casually with my own.

~ It's all right, you know.

He made a small whimper in his throat, tilted his head. He was confused.

So was I. I wondered when teaching the brat a lesson had morphed into the temptation to leave him here to his fate and the Lammyr.

Shit. What was I thinking?

I turned the horse abruptly and rode back into the mist and darkness, trying not to hurry, trying not to let myself believe I was too late. I'd left Jed only minutes ago. I couldn't have lost him. Not yet.

All the same, my heart turned over in my chest when I saw his forlorn shape, shivering worse than ever as he stumbled over the rough ground. A devil made me ride a wide circle, approaching him from behind, so that when I spoke from above him, he yelped with terror.

'Are you afraid now?'

He halted, shivering. Branndair slunk to his other side and watched him expectantly while the roan swung its neck and grinned at him.

'Yes,' he spat.

'Good,' I muttered. 'I'm glad you know how it feels. Now get back on.'

'Thanks. I'll walk.'

I took an angry breath. 'Walk till you drop dead as far as I care, but you're holding me up.' Reaching down, I grabbed him by the arm and yanked him back onto the horse.

'Aw. You've a heart of gold,' he grunted as he thudded onto its back. 'You're the one who kicked me off.'

Torn between laughing and hitting him, I bared

my teeth. 'The horse doesn't like strangers. Except when he's hungry.'

'Ha ha.' He glared at me. 'What did I say, anyway?'

'Nothing. Not a damn thing. Now, can you keep it that way?'

To be fair, he tried. The surly silence wasn't sustainable, though, since he had to hug me tightly to get warmth into his bones. And I had to admit I'd nearly fallen off the horse with relief when I hadn't lost him. And anyway, the curiosity was clearly killing him.

'Who are you people, anyway?'

'Sithe.' I chewed the inside of my cheek. Then I turned so I could glare right at him. 'Faeries.'

His whole body shuddered with the effort of swallowing his hoot of laughter. 'Mmph' was all he could safely get out.

'So welcome to Fairyland, sunshine.' I didn't take my furious eyes off him. It wasn't the first time I'd had this conversation, and I never stopped loathing it. '*My* world. Which is why I wonder why you're in it.'

'And Finn.'

'Nah, Finn belongs here.' I nearly added *So there!* but I managed to restrain my inner five-year-old. 'She belongs with us. You don't.'

'You're telling me.' He suppressed a snigger. 'Anyway, it was an accident.'

'Right. We get those accidents a lot.' I muttered, half to myself: 'And the non-accidents, like Laszlo.'

Jed grunted again.

Kate's full-mortals, I thought with a sigh, were

probably more articulate than this one. She was always coaxing them through the Veil, for better and for worse. There was a time the queen had gone in for poets, kings, knights-at-arms; lately it had been mercenaries with good pecs and a way with a sword. Fickle bitch.

Even as I thought it, a memory of dream-lust rippled through my guts, and I shuddered.

'Who?' asked Jed at last.

Me and my big mouth. 'Who who?'

'Laszlo. Who's he?'

To buy time, I combed the roan's mane with my fingers, and it whickered affectionately. 'Someone like you' was what I settled for at last. It was true in more ways than one. 'That sodding Fairy Loch, it's like Piccadilly Circus these days.'

'I think I know who you mean,' he mumbled.

'I doubt it. And now your little girlfriend's at the same game.'

'Feck off. How's it Finn's fault?'

'Because, *Cuilean,* you can't get through the watergate without her.'

That shut us both up, for different reasons. He was considering the implications, I guess. Meanwhile my entire brain had seized up. I couldn't look at Jed, could only stare ahead in a sort of mild panic, desperate now to catch up with the others. That had been no casually coined nickname. How had it happened?

The moon was rising higher, gigantic. The light made the darkness deeper, and when I glanced behind me again, I saw that Jed had shut his eyes tight, afraid to look too deeply into the moon shadows. It wasn't those he should fear, I thought, and for a few seconds he was in mortal danger again.

He was the unwitting protégé of a Lammyr. He was a complication, he was a bad omen, he was trouble. I had a very bad feeling about his presence here. And if he held on a little less tightly, if I kicked the roan into a sudden gallop, he'd fall.

Not my fault the city ned couldn't hang on. . . .

'Are we there yet?' he asked, his eyes still tight shut.

'No.' Exasperated, I tugged at his arm. 'Can you loosen your grip? It's kind of hard to breathe.'

He untangled his fingers, tried to sit back, but his entire body had seized up, from the motion of the horse and from sheer terror. He opened one eye, looked around at the blackness, then down at the ground. Branndair was smiling up at him, so he flung his arms back round my waist and locked them tight.

I growled. 'I find this affection extremely touching.'

'Just you wait till I get off this horse.' He hesitated, but clearly couldn't help himself. 'Bibbidi-bobbidi-boo.'

'Like I haven't heard that one before.' I gritted my teeth.

He leaned forward to my ear. 'I don't believe in faeries.'

I reined the horse abruptly, sighed, folded my fingers round his and yanked them off. When I turned to face him he was chewing his lip and watching me warily out of one eye.

'Oops,' he said.

'S'okay, Lost Boy, I won't eat you,' I said. 'Actually, that line's always pretty funny.'

Looking away, he muttered, 'It was worth a try.'

I stifled a laugh. 'Homicidal, but funny.'

'Hello?' he said sarcastically. 'Am I the one with a sword on my back?'

'No, you cretin, you're the one with a semiautomatic pistol in your belt.'

The satisfaction of springing that on him put a smile on my face and a bounce in the roan's step. He still couldn't keep things from me, and that knowledge made me feel a whole lot better. I confess it made Jed a little safer too.

'So,' I said smugly, 'where did you get it?'

'Loch,' he muttered. 'The Fairy Loch. On this side. It was wrapped up in plastic. Under the reeds.'

I thought that over for a few seconds. 'It's Laszlo's. Has to be. What a stupid place to leave it.'

'Not that stupid. I only put my hand on it by chance. We were fumbling around a bit.'

A chill tickled my spine. 'You should have left it.'

Behind me he shrugged. 'It's empty anyway.'

I reached back and took the gun from his hands, watery moonlight gleaming on the barrel like a silken skin. Dropping the reins I loosed the magazine from the pistol grip and glanced inside. Then I held it over my shoulder so that he could see the gleam of live rounds in the moonlight.

He swallowed. Said hoarsely, 'It's jammed, then.'

I snapped the magazine back into place, slid back the action, pressed the muzzle to my own temple and squeezed the trigger.

A dry click.

I heard him start to breathe again as I thumbed the switch on the side and dangled the useless weapon over my shoulder by its trigger guard. 'Won't work this side of the Veil. Probably that's why Laszlo left it there. So it was handy if he ever wants to go back.'

'Won't work . . .'

'That's right. Just as well, really, since some dick-wit released the safety catch.'

He almost dropped the pistol as he retrieved it from my finger.

'If Laszlo doesn't know you're here already, he'll know soon enough. Only a full-mortal would steal that thing. You've dumped yourself in pigshit, Cuilean.' I was winding him up again, but in my defence, I'd say I was warning him too.

Just as well guns didn't work on this side. Give the Sithe guns, and we'd have been extinct four centuries ago. Of course, Laszlo must have wanted easy access to the gun if he ever went back to the otherworld, however unwise that would be at his parallel age. Sometimes he must get nostalgic for death and destruction in his true home.

Maybe Laszlo and I had more in common than I liked to think.

I don't exactly remember the first time our paths crossed, ten or more years ago. Some shit-hole of a war zone, where we both felt at home (though I liked to think it was in different ways). I'd certainly seen the man's work in half a dozen villages, arriving too late as peacekeepers always did. I'd had him in my sights that one time, and politics hadn't let me kill him, and I'd paid for politics in guilt when I found what he was capable of, which was basically anything.

And of course he'd attracted the Lammyr Skinshanks; of course he had. And when Kate crossed over to find a new lover, a new distraction, a new game, of course Laszlo had taken one look at her and followed her into her own world. That was perfectly understandable, especially if you weren't fussy about the company you kept, or the governments you propped up, the throats you slit and the villages you burned.

And there was something else Laszlo and I had in common: prophecies. Nonsense that hung over your head like a dirty great boulder on a fishing line. The soothsayer who put her gnarled fingers round my life and twisted it may have been dead and gone, but her breed survived to poison new minds, new timelines.

Splinter-heart, winter-heart, that's what she called me. I was tired of listening to that witch tell me how my life would go: dead all these centuries, the old charlatan, and still dictating to me. Knowing who I'd love, and sometimes who I'd kill; knowing who'd watch me die. Knowing much more than me – though she never met me – because I couldn't know what mattered and what was important; I didn't know what to do for the best, not ever. She never told me the important bits, did she? Oh, how Kate NicNiven must have loved that moment in the dun: holding my dead mother in her arms as she passed on a lifetime's useless information.

Not that I believed a word of it anyway.

The boy at my back was very quiet now. I stared into the darkness, listening to the eerie weeping sigh of the wind. I wondered if he knew what might be stalking us all in the smothering night, and suddenly the nape of my neck felt far colder than the bite of the wind.

'This Laszlo,' he said. 'You're scared of him.'

Get out of my head. Get out.

I sighed deeply. 'Lost Boy, I'm kind of bored with you now. And if you fall off, I won't be turning back for you.' I hissed a word to the roan and it sprang forward. 'So you better hang on.'

It's just as well he did. I think I meant it.

Eili let her horse pace the clearing, searching the shadows though she must have known she was wasting her time. Lovesick, I decided. Her eyes were brilliant as a deer's in the night and she was so tense, she looked as if she would spring away at the crack of a twig.

'Damn it. He isn't here.'

I folded my arms. 'No shit, Sherlock.'

'Not the end of the world,' said Torc cheerfully, though Eili visibly thought it was. 'We'll wait.'

'No.' Leonora was riding at Torc's back. 'We'll move on. I want to be closer to the sea.'

Eili stared at her. 'We'll wait for Cù Chaorach and Sionnach.'

Oh, this was going to be good. I perked up.

'No, no, no.' Leonora tickled Faramach's throat, and the raven crooned fondly. 'No, we won't. Cù Chaorach is taking his blessed time as ever, and I've got better things to do than hang around. You're only his lieutenant, Eili. I'm giving you an order.'

She smiled sweetly. 'And you haven't the right to overrule it.'

The wind had dropped. Nothing moved. Interested, I glanced from one to the other; Torc seemed more fascinated by the leaf litter on the ground.

Recovering, her cheekbones darkening, Eili took a breath to argue; I decided I should intervene. 'He won't come here now. Fall back to the next rendezvous.'

'Oh, brilliant,' muttered Torc.

'Good,' said Leonora. 'Let's go. Cù Chaorach can look after himself, Eili.'

Eili bristled. 'In that case, we'll split up. That patrol's still about. Torc, take Leonora. She can confuse them.'

'Gladly, dear,' said Leonora. 'You only have to ask.'

I loved female politics. Torc's choice, of course, didn't come into it. He grinned at me.

Eili clenched her teeth, but 'Be careful' was all she said. Flirtatiously, Leonora squeezed Torc's torso, and they and the horse melted into the trees like ghosts.

'Seth, take the lead.' Eili turned to Finn, holding a vicious knife by its sheathed blade. 'Can you throw this?'

Finn shrugged. 'I could throw it. But it wouldn't hit anything.'

'Oh, what has your mother been playing at? Take it. Anybody follows us, make like you know what to do with it. Okay?'

'Um . . .' Finn slid the blade a little out from its sheath and examined her reflection.

'I'd rather just take you two back to the watergate,' Eili grumbled.

'Not while Laszlo's between us and it,' I said.

A tremor went through the boy; I felt it. I half turned, not quite looking at him. 'You're scared, Cuilean?'

'No.'

Shoplifted pants on fire.

Eili had chosen her route for the dark denseness of the rhododendrons overrunning the rock-strewn gully, which was fine so long as we were trying to stay out of sight. But I didn't like the tight closeness of them, and the way the straggling branches tangled and clung to fissures in the rock. They'd be impenetrable on horseback, and the confused shapes were humanoid enough in the dark to make the skin crawl, even with my eyesight.

The roan's muscles bunched under me, and its head came up, nostrils flaring wide and lips peeling back. At its high snarl, I whipped my sword off my back.

Ah. Rhododendrons were not the problem.

A brief thunder of hooves, and Eili's horse galloped up alongside mine. Both her swords were naked in her hands; she'd left her reins lying loose. I gave Finn one backward glance to see she'd already slid her knife out of its sheath. I wasn't sure what I saw in her pale eyes: not all fear, anyway.

Ahead, shapes were dappled in leaf-patterned starlight: three horses, one rider.

No, two riders; but one of them was off his horse and on the ground. As he rose awkwardly to his feet, I saw him clearly, and he wasn't alone. His arm was wrapped round the neck of another man, limp in his grip.

'Cuthag,' I murmured.

He stood up straighter, arm still locked round the neck of his victim.

'That's no fighter,' said Eili at last.

Teeth flashed in a grin. 'A waste of time, is what he was.' Cuthag hitched his captive a little higher, slid a blood-streaked blade out from beneath the man's breastbone, and let him collapse lifeless to the ground. There were deep vicious cuts on the corpse's neck and his staring face, and on his bound arms. But those cuts hadn't killed him; it was the final blade in his breast that had done that. Cuthag's favourite methods didn't have much sophistication, and they probably weren't even efficient, but gods, he enjoyed them.

Something chilled my blood as he smiled up at me.

I willed Finn not to drop the knife: she'd be dead in a heartbeat if she did. But flicking a glance back at her, I realised there wasn't a chance of it. It fitted her hand, which wasn't trembling anymore. She looked like she might even have known how to use it, in another life. Another world.

'Bad timing on your part, Eili.' The killer sighed. 'I was only asking him if he'd seen you around. You could have saved the poor man a lot of pain.'

I barked a laugh. 'Still a fighter's fighter, aren't you, Cuthag? Why'd you tie his wrists? Scared he might scratch your pretty face?'

'He was a bit of a wriggler.' Cuthag grinned.

'He was a farmer.' Rage brimmed in Eili's voice.

'He was a very stubborn farmer. I knew he must have seen you.'

'Well, there we are. What are we going to do

now?' I glanced from Cuthag to the man behind him on horseback, who was pointing a sword at us. 'Where's the rest of your gang? Where's your captain? Hey!' My grin broadened. 'Did they leave you two to dig the latrines?'

The rider gave a low growl, and Cuthag's smile tightened. 'They're just killing Eili's brother. They'll be along in a minute.'

Eili tipped back her head and gave a hoot of genuine laughter. 'In your dreams, you dirty big waste of a blade.'

Cuthag still wore a grin, but it had lost some of its glee and taken on an edge of anger. 'Watch your mouth, bitch.'

'And you,' I put in, 'bitch. So why aren't you with your captain? Oh, yeah, that's right. Sionnach doesn't let you tie his hands first.'

Eili shot me a cross look, but her mouth twitched. Cuthag's grin was gone.

'Well,' said Eili. 'I can't see Laszlo making it back anytime soon. Shall we just agree to differ? I won't tell him you let us get away.'

Cuthag smirked. 'You won't have to.'

Eili jerked her head in Finn's direction. 'This one's handy with a throwing blade.'

Finn was managing to smile, her blade catching the starlight prettily.

Cuthag laughed. 'That child? It doesn't even have a name!'

Branndair snarled, and thoughtfully I put my finger to my jaw. 'I gave you the hiding of your life when we were ten. I didn't have a name then.'

Cuthag curled his lip, and jerked his head at Jed. 'That boy, now – he has a name. And he'll be dead by midnight.'

I was on the point of answering when the boy did it himself. 'Says which wanker?'

If I hadn't been focused on Cuthag and his pal, I'd have smiled. I knew that feeling: the anger chasing out the fear. And more fear chasing it straight back in.

'Relax, everybody.' Eili drew the blade of one of her swords slowly along the other, so that they sang a high note. 'One, two, three blades. I think you're outnumbered, Cuthag. That's never suited you, so let us pass.'

The note of Branndair's growl changed abruptly, and I tensed. The shadow to our left might have been no more than rhododendron foliage, so lightly did it move. I sensed the excellent block only at that moment: oh, clever. Flipping my sword, I thrust it backwards.

The blade made a soft scraping sound as it plunged into flesh. I brought it forward again, a steel glint streaked with darkness.

There was a stuttering suck of air; I let myself glance to the side. The woman regarded me with bitter loathing, but the sword in her hand hung useless; she couldn't lift it, not now. As she fell to her knees and then toppled face forward to the ground, her head banged against Jed's foot. He made a strangled sound of horror, but loud enough for only me to hear.

'Okay.' I wiped the bloody blade on the roan's shoulder, making it whicker with hunger, then pointed it at Cuthag. '*Now* you're outnumbered.'

Cuthag exchanged glances with his colleague on the horse.

'We don't want to fight,' said Eili. 'We can all go home tonight if you stand to the side.'

Cuthag gave the farmer's corpse a spiteful kick and backed towards the rocky side of the gully. 'You'd better ride hard, you upstarts.'

'Not a problem. And you can wait here for Cù Chaorach. He's going to love your way with innocent farmers.'

'Aye,' grunted the man on the horse. 'We learned it from him. Isn't that right, Murlainn? From your sainted brother.'

I recognised him, now, too: one of the late unlamented Fearchar's men, from our days as Kate's henchmen. He stared me out and I could say nothing. I was aware of Finn's tension, her still uncomprehending silence, and most of all, of the blade in her grip, steady now and very threatening.

Eili said, 'Get out of the way. I said I didn't want to fight. I didn't say I wouldn't. Back. Farther.'

'Run then, little deer. Run along home.'

Without the horses, we might have had it, for all our arrogant bluff. But the dapple grey and the blue roan paced carefully between the two men, snaking their heads and baring teeth; the men's horses shied and snorted and backed, afraid. This time Eili rode ahead, watching Cuthag with loathing; so I had leisure to notice how he looked at Finn.

His pallid glittering gaze stayed on her, all hate and contempt and something else more frightening. I saw her suppress a shudder; Cuthag saw it too, because that little smile of his was back. I studied his face as I rode. When we were five yards, ten yards past, he went on eyeing her; I turned to see. His malice was a tangible thing.

Eili sheathed her swords in an easy double arc and spurred her mount away at a swift gallop, Finn at her back. I turned the roan a little, so that it danced sideways for a few paces, and I could still keep my eyes on Cuthag and his pal. Nodding at me, he dropped his block, and I heard his spiteful parting shot.

~ *I can wait.*

Mila's boy was at my back, I reminded myself, so I clenched my jaw and resisted the temptation to ride back at him.

Besides, Cuthag was already pulling himself nimbly onto his horse, and the hoofbeats drummed, and even my pride could be hedged about with prudence. Eili yanked Finn forward to sit in front of her, and that reminded me to do the same for the boy. He yelled, but he was too shocked to fight me.

Something bright flew past us as we burst out of the rhododendron tunnel: a thrown blade that shuddered into a stunted tree. Eili swerved and dodged. The next missile thwicked into the ground a few yards ahead; Cuthag's pal had a bow, then. I swore.

Branndair was a black streak, taking his own route. Trusting his instincts, I let him. Eili's grey swerved, racing for the next belt of trees, and as we followed it I felt the whisper of another arrow past my cheek. As we hit the first trees, side by side and almost touching,

I heard Eili grunt and she lurched forward. Then we were into the copse, faces slapped and slashed by branches.

On the far side we broke out into boggy land before plunging into a river. That gave the horses a new lease of energy, and they wheeled and headed upstream, flying through the water as birds would cut through the air. After that, there was no catching us, and the pursuit fell away.

Eili didn't slow down, though, and I rode hard in her wake. She turned the grey towards the far bank of the river, letting it leap clear in a fan of spray, but it was a long time before she let it ease back to a canter, then a brisk walk. Jed tugged my T-shirt.

'She's hurt,' he whispered.

'She's fine.' I was still seething. 'Sonofa*bitch*, I knew Cuthag was going to do that.'

'No, she's been hit.' Jed whacked my shoulder blade in frustration. Eili was reaching back to tug something from her upper arm, then fling it away: a bloody-tipped arrow.

'She's not okay! Stop!'

Finn was white. 'Eili—'

'He said I'm okay,' she barked. 'Stop fussing.' She lowered Finn from the horse, then jumped to the ground herself, wincing.

'How's the arm?' I asked as Branndair materialized at my side and I rubbed his neck fur.

Eili peeled back the edge of the clean rip in her sleeve. There was a mess of blood, but no hole now. 'I told you, it's fine. Leave it.'

'We should have kept Leonora with us,' I grumbled. 'She'd have sorted the tosser of the millennium, proper and permanently.'

Silkily Finn said, 'Not as decrepit as she looks, my old granny, is she?'

Eili shrugged. 'She puts on an amazing glamour. Old pro that she is. You should be proud of her.'

'She's a con artist, you mean. Her and my mother both. And Conal.'

Eili was nonplussed. 'Well. What they did was for your own—'

'Now, I'm not sure whose good it was for.' Finn's eyes burned. Not with tears, I decided, or not exclusively. 'But I'm pretty sure it wasn't mine.'

'You know what I think,' I said. 'It's a crime, and you've all let Stella get away with it. Spoilt bitch that she is.' I met Finn's eyes. 'Because you're all scared of her.'

'Too right I am,' laughed Eili.

For all her skill, I didn't think Eili quite sensed what she was dealing with. And suddenly I realised that didn't matter, because Finn was too clever to take it out on her. Hurriedly I formed a protective block, because it would be me who got it in the frontal lobes, if she decided to lash out, and from the homicidal look on her face, she was considering it.

But she was in control for the moment. Definitely clever.

'Tell me about my mother.' Finn's voice was perilously calm. She was watching me as she said it, but I wasn't going to rise to that. I'd said enough.

Eili shrugged. 'Your mother used to be fierce. Brave as six hounds. Obviously breeding turns your brain to mush and your heart to a sponge.' Bitterly she murmured, 'I wouldn't know.'

What was it about that Fionnuala child that made me want to hurt her? It wasn't as if she'd ever heard the stupid ramblings of that soothsayer, not even from Leonora, not in the face of Reultan's strictures. All the same, I did hurt her. She was, after all, thinking of doing me actual bodily harm.

'Stella's heart isn't a sponge, is it, Finn? It's stone and cold iron, and she loves nobody living.'

I expected her to go for me, but instead her body sagged. 'Why'd she lie to me? Why did you all *lie* all this time?'

'Nothing to do with me, Dorsal. Neither are you.' I shrugged. *Oh, leave her alone, you bastard.*

Eili laughed. 'Stella wants you to be normal, Fionnuala. A respectable little full-mortal. But thank the gods, blood will out.'

'In more than one sense,' I muttered.

Jed stepped protectively in front of her. 'Back *that* up, you—'

'Whoa, Batman, hold on. That's not what I meant—'

Hooves thudded on the earth behind us, and I spun round as the big iron-grey galloped up to us. Well, thank the gods for Englishmen with good timing. 'You lost them?'

'Yep,' said Torc, grinning. 'We lost them. Piece of piss.'

Holding on to him, Leonora smiled at Finn, but Finn didn't smile back. Maybe she hadn't noticed how tired her grandmother was. Because Leonora did look very, very tired. The old fraud wasn't acting for once. That was unfaked age and exhaustion. Unease tightened my spine.

Eili must have realised it too. 'We're not going much farther.' She nodded at a strip of trees that darkened the paling horizon, tapering out to a glimmer of sea. 'We'll stop there.'

I folded my arms, let the roan paw the earth. 'What does Leonora think?'

Eili's jaw tensed. 'That's where we stop. We don't move again till Cù Chaorach finds us.' Her voice was brittle with anger. 'And to hell with Leonora's orders.'

'You're looking good for a dead man.'

Sionnach laughed and hugged me. 'Murlainn. You don't change.'

'It's part of my charm.' I clapped his scarred cheek lightly.

'Where's Cù Chaorach?' The edge of impatience in Eili's voice was like a honed blade.

'Can't track him.' Sionnach slewed his eyes away, angry and ashamed. He wasn't accustomed to failure.

'Cheer up,' I said. 'Nobody can track in this; the gods know I've been trying. The atmosphere's like a snowstorm for some reason. It's all white noise, Eili knows that.'

'I know that. I don't have to like it.'

I wasn't too happy about it myself. 'Ach, he'll be fine, Eili. Give him a minute. Laszlo's a challenge, even for our hero.'

Eili smiled tightly and turned away. I winked at Sionnach, and he grinned.

~ *It's true, Murlainn. He'll be running rings round Laszlo.*

I knew that. He was my brother, my captain. I trusted him not to die. ~ *Your sister isn't really worried either. We know why she wants him back.*

Sionnach gave a sharp bark of laughter, earning a suspicious glower from his twin.

If Leonora was much closer to the sea, she'd be sleeping on the beach, but at least we'd found a high patch of woodland and Torc had started to build a fire. Jed was watching him, huddled into his thick jacket, but Finn sat apart, staring out at a broad strip of moon-frosted machair and the range of dunes beyond it. After that there was only the sea: I could smell it, and the distant islands, and the woodsmoke of the fire, and the coarse cropped turf of the machair. I could almost smell the moonlight. Hairs rose on my neck, and suddenly I was in love with the world again.

Feeling conciliatory, and even a little sorry for her, I sauntered up to where she was ripping sea-pinks savagely from a rocky outcrop. 'You're okay? You did fine back there.'

She shivered. I resisted the urge to put an arm round her shoulders.

'That man. Cuthag.'

'He scared you?'

Stupid question. She took her time answering it, and fair enough. 'He didn't scare me. He just . . .'

'Walked on your grave?'

'Danced on it. Stamping down the earth, I could feel it.'

I was glad she couldn't see my shiver. 'He's just a thug. Don't sweat the small stuff, Dorsal. Cuthag's very small stuff.'

She wasn't sweating. Very calm, very cool, she was. 'And he's representative, is he? Cuthag?'

'Dorsal, you make my flesh creep. Of some people round here, yes.'

'What are you telling her?' asked a voice behind me.

Gods, Leonora's sudden appearances could still make my blood freeze. I hated that about her, among many other things. But I didn't get a chance to retort, because Finn spoke up, her voice almost menacing.

'What shouldn't he be telling me?'

You know those places where the earth's fire comes close to the surface? You can see the carapace cracking, feel the heat building. That's the image that came into my head, and I knew she would erupt one of these times. I hoped I wouldn't be around when she did.

'I don't trust Seth to tell anything well.' Casting me her witchiest glower, Leonora put an arm round the girl. It was the unthinking ease of love, and it riled the devil inside me.

'I don't trust you to tell *anything*.' I was so snagged in my own long-suppressed frustrations, I suppose, Finn's didn't register with me, though I could sense the pressure building, that compact little ball of fury that starts in the base of your spine and burns as it reaches the nape of your neck. I could feel an echo of it myself. But I was angry too; angry enough to run off at the mouth. 'Looks like I'll have to tell Finn why she's such a nonentity. Nobody else will.'

'Seth!' snapped Leonora with a touch of panic.

'The Veil, Dorsal, isn't just a barrier between the worlds; it's a filter. It's why no full-mortal takes any notice of you. Not only are you so different you're downright weird, you're instantly forgettable. And you always have been.'

I felt Leonora grip my shoulder. She yanked me round and gave me a stinging blow across the face.

Fair enough. I put my hand to the mark of hers, stunned into reason. Damn, the woman had a fierce strength, even now.

I waited to get a slap from Finn too, but she only blinked emptily at her grandmother.

'Don't bother slapping *him*,' she whispered.

'He had no right—'

'Well, I do!' she yelled. 'I thought it was me. I thought I was a pointless person. I thought I was a nobody. I thought it was my fault!'

'Finn, I'm—'

'Don't you dare tell me you're sorry. Because you don't mean it! *Do you?*'

She couldn't contain it anymore. I should have seen it coming, we all should, because her eyes looked about to burn up, like boiling mercury. She let it rip, and the missile of fury struck Leonora smack on the forehead.

Finn blinked and shouted with pain, clapping her hands over her eyes. Leonora stumbled forward to one knee, and I caught her arm to stop her hitting the ground. She looked shocked to her core, but she didn't look scared, and the pain in her eyes wasn't all physical. Jed, Eili, Sionnach and Torc were running to us but they were brought up short, silenced by shock. I watched Finn with fascination.

She'd hurt Leonora, really hurt her. I wondered how she'd deal with that – how Leonora would, for that matter. Finn had lashed out at me before – not quite so effectively, I must admit – but never Leonora.

What was it I'd said to Conal? That the Rooney girl was a start? Finn certainly seemed capable of worse. Right now, though, the cold fire in her eyes was gone: all used up, and she looked too empty even for misery.

Jed grabbed her arm. 'Finn. What did you do?'

'You stay out of it.' She rounded on him. 'Family business.'

His cheekbones burned from her verbal slap. 'You need locking up, you freaks. The lot of you!'

Eili's sudden stillness was a lot more alarming than Jed's fury. Oh, this was all going too far. I touched her arm.

~ Leave him be, Eili. He didn't mean that. He's not thinking straight.

Studying him, she tapped her nails against her arm. She didn't bother keeping her own voice silent. 'Not thinking straight is usually where it starts.'

'I promise you, Eili, he isn't the mob type,' I muttered. 'He's got a mind of his own. Had to grow one when his mother lost hers.'

Whoa shit.

'What?'

Jed's expression froze only for a second. Then he lashed a wild fist at my throat, and I had to arch swiftly backward. Stumbling, Jed was caught and locked in Sionnach's arms, saved from falling but also stopped from taking another shot. He panted, speechless.

Sionnach shook his head at me, bemused. 'Seth, what is *wrong* with you?'

I could tell he really meant it, he really wanted to know.

'Oh, sorry.' I made myself meet Jed's loathing eyes. 'Finn told me about your mother. Sorry.'

Finn blinked. 'But I—'

I turned on Finn and gave her a whiplash of the pain she was so quick to mete out. Not too much, but enough, because she had no idea how to block. She reeled, stunned to silence, but kept her footing. And when she looked at me again, disbelieving, she shut up.

Sionnach's grip loosened, and Jed shook him off. Leonora turned on me, eyes glittering blue. 'This is all your fault. You never could keep your mouth shut. I'll expect you to take Jed and Finn back as soon as the coast is clear.'

'You can expect all you like, *dearie*. The only orders I'll take are Eili's, and I'll only take those till Cù Chaorach gets here.'

'Do me a favour, Finn.' Jed's fists were clenched. 'Don't discuss my mother with Tinker Be—'

I didn't think; my hand shot out of its own accord, seizing him by the throat. It was practically a reflex, but I went with it anyway, and tightened my grip. He kicked and struggled for air, scrabbling at my wrist, but it was no effort to hold him fast.

I looked at my hand. Looked at his blood-suffused face and his bulging eyes and his juddering tongue. Hot damn. I was throttling Mila's boy.

I made myself break my hold. He fell awkwardly back, and I flexed my fingers. I don't know what I was feeling; only that I was on the edge of my temper, all the time; always starting to slide. I felt like an addict who couldn't get his fix. Trouble was, I had no idea what my fix was.

I turned away and spat on the ground. 'Don't. Do it. Again.'

Jed wheezed in oxygen, clutching his throat. 'Right.'

'Because I know you've been dying to say it,' I told him. 'But it's really not worth it. Dying. To say it.'

'I just. Meant. My mother's. Not. Your business.'

'Fair enough. And it's not like Finny can criticise anyone else's.'

'*SETH.*'

Leonora's voice was the terrifying one of her youth and power, and I couldn't repress the involuntary cringe of fear. I shook myself angrily.

'I only said it, witch. The rest of you, go on and think it. You hypocrites.'

'It's Stella's business how she—'

'Stella, if that's what you want to call her, is a reckless fool.' I seized Finn's shoulder and thrust her forward. 'Tell her. Tell her. Everything. You owe her.'

Finn was unsteady on her feet, and not just from my rough handling. Leonora stood for long moments, fists clenched, lips compressed, silver kindling in her pupils. Oh, she'd recovered fast. It crossed my mind to thank my own gods that she was dying, because the light in her eye was a deadly one.

Silently Sionnach came to my side. 'Seth's right,' he said.

Leonora looked from him, to me, to Finn. At last she held out a hand to her granddaughter.

'Come with me, child.'

'I'm not a—'

'I said *come*.' Leonora threw me a last, fleeting, homicidal glare. 'We'll talk about this alone. None of it's any business of your—' She fought for a suitable expression. '—your grandfather's *by-blow*.'

By sheer force of will she led Finn, silent and pale, into the dark line of the trees. The rest of us avoided each other's eyes for a hideously long time.

'Ach.' I stood up sharply. 'The hell with all of it. I'll get us something to eat.' I called the roan silently, grabbed a handful of its mane.

'Want company, Murlainn?' Sionnach gave me a half smile.

'Do I ever? I'll have your crossbow.' Pilfering it, I scrambled onto the roan, which was already breaking into a trot.

Company? I couldn't think of anything I wanted less.

Not in real life, anyway.

Finn

'Sod off, Faramach.' Finn ground her teeth.

Ignoring her, the raven settled on her arm. Fair enough: it wasn't the bird's fault. It was her family she wanted to hate, but that was being undermined by some fierce emotion she didn't like to name. It felt a little like being at home. A lot like belonging. And it still made the grief spark and flare into a ball of white fury in her spine, because it was built on such an enduring lie.

She stared at the spot where Leonie had been, where she'd calmly stood and torn to shreds everything Finn had ever known, everything she'd ever thought she was. A little regretful, but unapologetic, the old woman had left her with an abrupt consoling hug, and since then Finn had simply stood and waited for the world to make sense. Her heart felt cold as stone.

The silence of the wood closed in, Faramach's stare making it even more oppressive. Finn liked him, always had, but he seemed different here: not quite so much of a pet. She wanted human company; no, only one human. She wanted Conal, wanted him desperately.

The raven's head tilted up, making her snatch her hand away. He gave a growling caw. A second later, Conal strode towards her out of the shadow of the trees.

Finn's glower cracked into a reluctant smile. She called – whether she was aware of it or not – and he came. Wasn't that always the way? She understood better now why that was, but she had never in her life been happier to see him. He was wearing that long black cashmere coat she'd always liked. He was beautiful in it. Not, she thought with filial pride, that he wasn't beautiful anyway.

'Conal!'

He didn't smile, not even a little, and that was so unusual, a tremor rattled down her spine. She hesitated.

'You're angry with me?' She took another pace towards him.

Conal smiled at last, but it was the ghost of a smile, and all she could sense in it was a massive emptiness. He glanced over her shoulder, towards the sea, then looked back at her and laid the palm of his hand against her cheek. It felt very, very cool.

For the first time in her life, she wanted to run from him. But that seemed ridiculous, so she held her ground and his intent eyes. They were as black and fathomless as the eyes of Seth's horse.

Absently Conal withdrew his hand from her face,

and touched his own throat. Then he glanced down at Faramach, but the bird only stared back at him.

Finn frowned. 'Conal . . .'

His head jerked up, and he placed his fingers against her lips as he stared towards the camp. Then he smiled at her properly, and winked.

And then he walked away.

'Conal!' She had a strange notion then: that she ought to delay him, that she must at all costs stop him walking on. But there was only movement, light and shade, the dull gleam of fair hair, the flick of a black coat merging into shadow. He was gone.

She blinked, her heart twisting; then she shrugged off the hurt and the niggling fear, and took it out on the bird instead. 'What's your problem, crow?'

Faramach looked thoughtfully skywards, then tilted his head back towards her. And then, strangely, he craned his sinister head forward and pressed it to her cheek. It was an odd combination of sensations, the warm skin and feathers, and the cool black beak.

'Finn!' The call was abrupt.

'Eili. I'm—'

Faramach nipped her forearm, hard, and she yelped with shock. Instinctively, immediately, she shut off her thoughts, remembering Conal's cold fingers against her lips.

'Where have you been, Fionnuala? Come back to the fire. Sionnach says there's something out here.'

'Again?'

'In the trees. Don't you believe me?' Eili chewed her lip thoughtfully. 'Look, you miss Cù Chaorach. When he gets here, you'll feel better. Now, come.'

Finn was suddenly very sick of it. She wanted to yell: *His name is Conal MacGregor. And his brother is Seth MacGregor. They don't have other names. THEY DON'T HAVE NAMES I'VE NEVER HEARD IN MY LIFE.*

'Oy. Calm down, you. The north of England can hear you think.' Eili threw her a dark look as she pushed back a branch. Only metres away was the clearing, and the crackling fire. 'Look, I'm sorry about Seth. He's wound you up. Don't provoke him.'

'Seth's a brat.'

Eili sucked her teeth. 'Seth's seen a lot you haven't. He certainly isn't spoilt.' She paused for a heartbeat. 'Not the way you mean. And Conal loves him.'

Glaring at her, Finn sat down close to Jed. 'Conal loves everybody.'

'But Seth loves Conal. And Seth's love is something you don't see every day. You know what? You need to sleep.' Eili laid her hand casually against the back of Finn's head.

Finn was hit by a heavy wave of drowsiness that washed over her brain, flooding and deadening. *Fine. Kill thoughts, and there was more space for dreams.*

~ *That's good. Good! Finn, come!*

She half started awake again. *Mum?*

~ *Yes! Yes, hurry.*

Arms wide and welcoming, smile loving: a strange sight, but distantly familiar. ~ *Mum, really?*

The smile was warm and eager now, the blue eyes regretful. ~ *The part of me that never left here.*

~ *The part I never knew, you mean.*

~ *That's it. Come on, Finn. Come to me!*

Finn touched her emerald pendant, the coolness of it a bright pebble of awareness in the fog of sleep creeping from Eili's fingers. Couldn't think. Didn't want to.

~ *Don't think. Don't think. Dreams are better.*

Seth

I relaxed into it. Why not? I needed to block out the real world, I needed to get my head round how things had changed, and why. I knew why Leonora had returned, and I couldn't see how Conal was going to stop her, and in truth I didn't want him to. I was sick of the Bloodstone, sick of exile, sicker even than I'd been in the early days.

~ *Hush now. Don't think these things. Don't think.*

She curled down beside me, leaves rustling in the faintest breeze, barely distinguishable from the whisper of her dress as it billowed across my body. Nearby I heard the movement of the roan, the small whimpering sigh of Branndair. I was tired but I didn't want to go back to the others yet, even if they were waiting for my still-warm catch. I could smell the deer's blood. I could hear the drip of it onto dry leaves. I must be half-awake still.

~ *No, don't go back yet. Not yet . . .*

Fine by me. I found her dream-mouth, pushed her red gold hair back from her face. She tasted of hazelnuts. Liking that, I stopped kissing her, licked the corner of her mouth, and she made a small happy sound. I felt her hand run across my thigh, slide between my legs, and I gasped and grinned. Her grin was against mine.

I kissed her again.

~ *How foolish it all is. I like you, young man. I like you very much.*

There was nothing I could answer to that. Instead I pulled her against me and onto me.

~ *I even like your brother, traitor as he is. . . .*

It was Branndair's soft resentful growl that made me open my eyes. My heart thudded. The prickle of leaves beneath me was real against my skin, the drip of deer-blood behind me was clear and real. The cool breeze was no dream either.

Copper hair brushed my face, lips touched my cheek, turned my mouth back to hers.

I jerked back, stumbling.

'Kate. *Gods.*' I snatched behind me, seeking my sword. Couldn't shut my eyes on her quiet smile.

Her altogether *real* smile.

Reaching across me, she held my arm. Surprised by the strength in her fingers, I could only gape at her.

'Am I armed, Murlainn? Am I? I no more wish you harm than I did in dreams.'

'You do.' My voice was a croak. I wondered where her fighters were. I could think only that to die like this was the worst of humiliations. I thought of Conal and shrivelled, inside and out.

'Oh, hush. You think I would bring you here to murder you? That's not my way.'

Why not? I thought. *It always has been.*

She laughed, released my arm. I staggered to my feet, pulling my clothes desperately back on. My heart nearly failed as I struggled into my T-shirt, knowing I couldn't see her for a second, but as I yanked it down over my torso she remained motionless, smiling up at me. She reached out her delicate hand. Not knowing what to do, I took it, raised her to her feet.

'What do you—?'

'Listen to me, Murlainn. That's all I want. For you to listen.'

I glanced down at Branndair, who was watching her with fearful hostility. But he had eyes only for Kate, not for the trees around us or anyone they might be hiding. The blue roan took no notice of us at all, only went on cropping the grass where the deer's blood had fallen. I listened for long seconds to the silence of the forest, then eyed her.

'So talk,' I said.

She stroked my face with the back of her hand. I wanted to flinch; I wanted to lean into her touch. 'I've seen inside your head, Murlainn.'

'You had no business—'

'No. But desperate times make us all desperate. I know what you've seen in the otherworld. Centuries of it. So many years of conflict and death and war. They're not like us, Murlainn.'

I barked out a laugh.

'Oh, we can fight, Murlainn. But their hatred is different. You know it.'

I thought of the things I'd seen, the places I'd been as I fought off the longing for home: the things that only made me long for it more.

'I've seen all that too, Murlainn. You think I don't know that world?'

'If you know it,' I said bitterly, 'why would you want to own it?'

Closing her eyes, she sighed. Her arms snaked round my neck and she pressed her lips to it. Sadness and regret seeped from her, pulling at my own tangled emotions.

'You feel the Veil, Murlainn,' she whispered. 'Don't deny it.'

I was silent. I'd thought that was my own secret. Suddenly, horribly, I knew nothing was.

'Do you?' I asked at last. 'Feel the Veil?'

Her head moved against my neck. ~ *No.*

I tried to push her back. I couldn't think straight. Her touch was like water, filtering through my skin and my skull, soothing my brain, calm and cool.

'Kate, I can't do anything with the Veil. I can feel it, touch it, is all. I can't help you.'

'I know that.' Her voice was barely more than a sigh; I sensed it more than heard it. 'I know, Murlainn. I don't want anything like that. I only want to hear you say what you know: it's dying. What will we do?'

She shivered, and reflexively I held her tighter. 'We'll fix it.'

Her brief laugh was almost a sob. 'We can't, Murlainn. I know you don't believe in the Bloodstone. I do. But Leonora's wrong. It's not for saving the Veil;

it's for protecting us. The Bloodstone can't save a dying thing, but it can save us. It can help us break the Veil. Be in control. You know the full-mortals. Don't you want to have the upper hand? Don't you want us to be in charge of our destinies when the Veil dies?'

I thought of Catriona, I thought of Mila. I thought of all the others. 'They're not all—'

'Enough of them are. Enough of them.'

I thought of the wars; I thought of the camps. The rows and piles of skulls. I thought of grinning children wielding machetes.

And then I remembered Conal, and twisted out of her grasp.

'Get away from me, Kate. I won't betray my brother.'

She set her teeth, raked her hands through her beautiful hair. 'I'm not asking you to! Do you think I'm stupid enough to ask that of *you*?'

'Not stupid. But you'd ask it.'

'Once I would have. It's been a long time, Murlainn. I grow more desperate. I don't want to see my people persecuted and killed.'

'Hah,' I said.

She made a sound of frustration, took a step back from me. That surprised me a little, and so did her grieving glare.

'We've had our differences, the Sithe, haven't we? That will mean nothing when the Veil dies, Murlainn. Nothing! We need to prepare ourselves for that, and far more, we need to prepare the full-mortals. We need to ready their minds.'

In the silence, I swear I could hear the trees grow. 'Conal says—'

'Conal, always Conal! Your brother is a fine man, Murlainn, a noble man. But on this he is wrong. I mean him no harm. Why would I? He's the finest soldier I know. To fight with him is foolishness. I want you both on my side. *At* my side. My Captains.'

'Your henchmen.'

She shook her head; I caught the scent of her hair, and almost reached for it. I clenched my fist.

'Your long, long exile at an end. The sons of Griogair on my right and left hand. The Sithe united. The Sithe surviving, strong and wise and in control. The full-mortals—' She shrugged. '—their minds . . . adjusted. Happier than they are now. Disinclined to kill us all. Utopia, Murlainn.'

'We're not made for Utopia,' I said. 'We're not made for peace.'

'What a ridiculous thing to say.'

'We'd quarrel. The Sithe do. So do the full-mortals. You know it would end in war.'

'And there speaks an addict. You love to fight, Murlainn, don't you?' There was anger in her golden eyes. 'But there are other ways, other lives you could live. Don't you believe a people can change? You've seen yourself change. You've seen . . .' Her voice gentled. 'You've seen a full-mortal change. You've seen a full-mortal come to love a Sithe.'

I couldn't answer her.

She laid her fingers against my lips. Gods help me, I kissed them.

'Ah, Murlainn. I'm not asking you to betray your brother, I'm asking you to talk to him. Persuade him. Bring peace between us. If you can do that, you save us all. And I won't harm Cù Chaorach, you have my word.'

'Your word,' I repeated slowly.

'My word. You know that's something I can't break, even if I want to. And I don't. You have my *word*. What is there to lose, Murlainn?'

It stuck in my throat. So hard to say. But I managed. 'My soul?'

Sighing, she stepped back. I forced my body not to follow.

'Consider what I've said. It's all I ask. Think about your race, Murlainn.' Briefly she touched my forehead once more. 'And think about theirs.'

I watched her as she walked away, calm, her back turned on me in complete trust. By the time my foot knocked against my scabbarded sword, and I glanced down at it in shock, she had vanished into the darkness. My hand trembled as I lifted it. Branndair watched me as I strapped it to my back, and as I stroked his head, my fingers still shook.

I headed straight back, but I'd come too far on my hunt. I had time to think, time for my brain to gnaw constantly, pointlessly at what had happened. At moments I didn't believe she'd been real, and I knew it was all a dream just like the others. And then I'd catch the scent of her on my hands and skin, and I'd know it had happened exactly as I remembered it.

I wouldn't tell them. What would I say? I imagined
Conal's reaction when he heard of the dreams, when
he heard I'd kept so much from him. I imagined Sionnach's incredulity, Eili's scorn and her contemptuous
laughter, and that decided me. Nothing was going to
come of this. If Kate wanted to talk to Conal, she
could go to him, shag *him* in his dreams. I wasn't her
messenger boy. Come to that, I wasn't her fighting
man: I was Conal's.

The roan was skittish, excited by the smell and the
bloody weight of the deer slung across his haunches,
and it took me effort to control him, effort I could
have done without. I found myself in a magnificent
temper. Even Branndair was quiet, cowed by my
mood, so when he pricked his ears and shot ahead, I
knew what it must mean. Peering into the trees, I
saw the white shadow, and my relief was hedged
with dread.

It was just as Sionnach had said. What was *wrong*
with me?

Branndair bounded up to Liath, who made a bossy
swipe at his head. Rolling over like the beta-wolf he
was, he nibbled her furry white throat and whined
with delight; Liath straddled him, playbiting his muzzle. I gave him a disapproving scowl, but he was too
happy, and too submissive, to take any notice.

Conal rode out in the wake of his wolf, grinning.
His old leather jacket was slung across his horse's
withers, his black-hilted sword was strapped to his
back, and his slate blue shirt was dappled in bloodspots.

Drawing his horse alongside the roan, he leaned
over to lock a forearm round my neck, and planted a

huge smacker of a kiss on my cheek. 'Laddie. I missed you! What kept you?'

I wrestled his arm off my throat and dug him in the ribs with an elbow. 'Less of the *laddie,* you big tosser. What d'you mean, what kept me? This buck didn't want to cooperate, funnily enough.'

'Finn?' His voice was tense.

'We've got her. You must have known that?'

'I thought so, but—' He frowned. '—there's a lot of interference in the air. You've felt it?'

I shrugged, not meeting his eyes. 'She can't do that kind of thing. Even Kate—'

'Who knows what she's capable of these days? It's been a long time. If she gets her way and destroys the Veil, she's going to want to be strong enough to take advantage, isn't she?'

'She won't get her way.' I wished I felt as confident as I sounded.

'We've still got time, if my mother sees sense.'

I didn't say a word to that.

'The way back to the watergate's clear for now.' He was all mad optimism. 'If nothing else, she'll surely want to see Finn safely home?'

'And Jed.'

'And who?' He reined in the black and stared at me.

'You heard right. He came with her. And you want to hear the bad news? He found a gun in the loch. It's Laszlo's.'

'Oh, Jaysus.' Even in the darkness, I saw his skin pale.

'I take it you haven't dealt with Laszlo, then.'

'He wasn't with his patrol. It was his lieutenant. That bastard Easag.'

'Uh-huh. But you dealt with *him*?'

'Yeah.'

Drawing up the roan, scowling, I grabbed a fistful of Conal's hair and stared into his eyes. Blood and steel, sweat and death.

'Yow.' I let him go. 'That won't go down too well.'

'He started it.' He gave me a wry grin as we rode on.

'We won't be getting a nice peaceful trot back to the dun.'

He snorted. 'Like Laszlo would leave us alone now anyway. If he knows Jed's here.'

The sheltered glow of a fire was visible through the low branches, so we dismounted and led the horses into the thicker undergrowth. I sensed Finn and Jed; as for the others, they were blocking so determinedly, the first evidence of them was the white double-blur of two blades coming unsheathed a foot from our faces.

'Woman!' Conal grinned. 'You'll have somebody's eye out!'

Eili slung her swords back into their sheaths with thoughtless precision and flung herself at him. Finn lurched forward but Conal wasn't even looking at her. Pushing his long fingers through Eili's spiky hair, Conal was kissing her like he wanted to eat her or, ideally, be eaten. I rolled my eyes and sighed.

'What time of night d'you call this?' asked Sionnach, but Conal wasn't listening and neither was Eili.

'He wouldn't need mouth-to-mouth,' muttered Finn, 'if you let him breathe.'

Laughing, letting go of Eili, Conal hugged her. 'And what,' he asked fondly, 'do you think you're doing here?'

'Kind of an accident.' She pulled back and grinned. It was a little odd, the look in her eye. Happy, relieved, but there was a touch of smugness too, as if she and Conal shared a secret no-one else was privy to. I frowned.

'You can explain yourself later, toots,' he growled.

'You too.' She winked.

His grin was a little puzzled, but he turned to the boy. 'Hello, thief,' he said, and pulled him into a bear hug.

Jed's look of frazzled fear gave way to bewilderment that was almost matched by mine. Seemed I wasn't the only one with secrets. As Conal let him go, Jed stumbled back, disoriented, and scratched absently at Liath's thick-furred neck. She sniffed at him with mild interest and licked his fingers. Jed snatched his hand away, eyes wide, then laid it tentatively back on the wolf's head.

'Don't you rush off again, Cù Chaorach,' said Eili, who couldn't keep the ridiculous toothpasty smile off her face. 'You've been gone too long this time.'

'Tell me about it. Brought you a present, though. Eili, you should come over the Veil once in a while, it's not so bad. The shopping! You're a *wumman*! You'd love it!'

Eili smiled drolly at Finn, but the bonding attempt fell flat. Finn only glowered daggers at her, and Eili switched off her smile in an instant. Oblivious of the female politics – gods help him – Conal kissed Eili's nose and stuck a pair of Ray-Bans on it. I wasn't sure I liked Eili's eyes being invisible; actually, it made my flesh prickle.

'And you sorted the patrol?' she asked him.

'Easag's dead,' I interjected, tired of being irrelevant. 'That'll make the return journey interesting.'

Eili pouted. 'I thought the strategy was to avoid trouble, not go looking for it under stones.'

'The boy,' I said, nodding at Jed. 'He's more than one kind of problem. S'just as well Conal didn't mind getting his shirt dirty.'

Conal scowled at me. 'Shut up, Seth.'

'Huh?' Jed blinked.

What, had it only just occurred to him? I'd told him he was a fool for taking the gun. If he wasn't dead, it was because someone else was dead in his place, and that was Conal's doing. I bared my teeth. 'Look a little more grateful, Cuilean.'

He paled, but before he could react, Conal did a double take. 'What did you call him?'

'Yeah. Funny, eh?'

'No, it bloody isn't.'

'What are you – ?' Jed began.

'Sod that. What's with the true name? I don't like—' Conal paused, frowning, and looked up. 'Where's my mother?'

'There.' Finn jerked a thumb over her shoulder, then gave a little gasp and touched the green stone at her throat, as if it had burned her. She spun round to stare at a flattened patch of grass.

Leonora wasn't there. The shadow of her, that was all.

In the silence, a branch on the dying fire broke and collapsed in a small eruption of sparks. Conal stared first at Leonora's empty space, then at Finn.

'*Where's my mother?*' A voice as cold as the breeze.

Finn turned and raced across the clearing, the rest of us at her heels. Conal overtook me and caught Finn on the edge of the trees, snatching her arm so that she half stumbled. The black horse paced to Conal's side, nuzzling his neck fondly as if to stop him spontaneously combusting. Conal clasped Finn, holding her steady as she peered desperately across the starlit machair, his other hand laced into the white wolf's mane.

'There. She's *there*.'

Damned if I could see her, even on the moonlit plain, but Conal grinned humourlessly. 'She's an old deceiver, Finn. You weren't to know. Stay here, the lot of you.'

He caught the cheekpiece of the black's bridle as it surged forward. As he sprang onto its back, it was already running. He ducked the last branch as it plunged out of the trees.

Finn had the look of a slapped infant, all shock and red delayed pain. I'd thought she wouldn't understand. Now I was fearful, suddenly, that she would.

'Don't worry,' I muttered uselessly.

'Why would I worry?' She threw me a contemptuous glare, as well she might. 'I'm not clever enough to imagine what the *hell* they're up to.'

Her fists were clenched, her whole body trembling. I nipped my lip, and searched the darkness around us as I avoided her hostile, grieving eyes.

Gods, I was going to regret this. I called the roan.

We didn't have far to ride. Beyond the grassy plain of the machair, there were low hills of sharp rough grass, then dunes, hard sand and the vastness of the sea. Finn gripped the roan's mane hard, and her whole body in front of me was tense as a bowstring, but she hadn't hesitated. I could only admire her surly nerve in reaching for my arm when I'd offered it to her, and climbing back on a horse that had just tried to eat her.

The roan wasn't interested in her this time. It slid down a shifting dune almost on its haunches and thundered down onto the beach. The black horse was not thirty yards ahead, Conal trotting it first one way and then the other along the edge of the water.

The silvered bay was maybe a mile long, flanked by bulky headlands that spilled a tumble of rocks to the sea. The black-bellied waves were fringed with phosphorescence, and against their light was a figure: too tall, too lanky to be Leonora, hunched into a long coat with an upturned collar. The coat that was no coat moved and glistened like a wet pelt. The creature wearing it turned, and I sucked in a cold salty breath.

No going back, I thought. Not for us, not for Leonora.

The black pawed the hard sand and whinnied, but Conal only stared at the thing. I'd never seen one in the cold wet flesh before, but I knew well enough what it was. Its long-boned face was covered in a thin layer of sleek grey hair, and its eyes were black from corner to corner, like a seal's. Conal's horse called to it again, familiarly, gills flapping open and shut.

'Mother!' Ignoring the creature at the water's edge, Conal yelled, 'Leonora!'

'Conal, my darling!' The voice floated down from the cliff above us. 'Of course you know you have company?'

We could make out the old woman now, standing quite still, right on the edge, gazing down. In front of me Finn shuddered with vicarious vertigo.

Wheeling the black on its haunches, Conal rode back to us, throwing me a glare. I met it with one of my own, and he could only turn away, to Finn, his face softening. I resisted the urge to put an arm round her waist and hug her. It wasn't that difficult, since she oozed poisonous resentment.

'I'm sorry,' he said.

She was too choked with angry emotion to answer him. Conal seemed to hesitate; then he flicked the reins and turned back to the cliff.

'Mother! Don't do this to us! To her!'

'Conal MacGregor,' Leonora chided. 'I don't expect much from your half brother, but have you no respect?'

Conal glared up at her. 'Seth is my *brother* and he's all I'd ask of one.'

'Of course. I apologise.' Leonora's voice was clear on the still air. Then I saw what was behind her on the rocks: another Selkyr in its silvery rippling coat. Leonora glanced back at it, smiling.

She turned back to Conal and his horse. 'Clever Finn,' she called. 'How talented you are! I should have confiscated that wretched stone.'

In front of me, the girl trembled and clasped her pendant.

'For gods' sake, Mother. The dun's shield, all our protection. It goes with you!'

'All the same, my Conal. You can hardly expect me not to go.'

Finn's head whipped round and she hissed at me, 'What's happening?'

I shrugged, avoiding her glare again. 'Nothing we can stop. Keep your mouth shut. Leave it to Conal.'

He yelled, 'You don't have to do this! You could have stayed on the other side. Lived!'

'What? You'd consign me to madness and rot, darling boy? Just for one last try at the Stone?'

'Why not? It's what you've lived for! It's what you stayed for!'

Leonora gave a deep gurgling laugh. 'That's the difference between us, Conal. I know when I'm beaten. Wait till it's your turn, hm? You won't stay, either.

You'll run back where you belong, as fast as you can. You'll die as you should and where you should. You'd be a fool not to.' She hesitated. 'There comes a time when they all must shift for themselves.'

'Indeed.' Conal's voice hardened, and something cruel crept into it. 'Just so you understand, Mother, I'm not taking Finn home. I'm taking her to the dun.'

For a fleeting instant, Leonora lost her diamond cockiness. 'Conal, you can't . . .'

'I've had enough, Mother. She's here. You brought her, and it isn't my fault, and I'm sick of it. Stella can *shift for herself*. In fact, Stella can go hang.'

I should have swelled with self-righteous satisfaction. Instead I felt cold and unsure.

'That's between you and your sister,' said Leonora sadly. 'I have no say in it anymore.'

'You told me,' Conal shouted, 'you told me the child needed you!'

'She had me.' Leonora gave a complacent shrug. Despite the Selkyr behind her, she didn't look trapped. She looked smug, as if she'd caught up with something she'd been chasing for a long time.

'This isn't right,' whispered Finn to no-one in particular. 'It isn't right.'

'Yes,' I said. 'It is.'

She went rigid as steel, and I realised she was crying. Conal gave a frustrated yell of rage and grief. 'Weren't you going to say good-bye? MOTHER?'

'Ah, Conal, you'd only try to talk me out of it. And that would be terrible for both of us.' As Leonora's breezy voice drifted down from the headland, I had to admire the cool of her. Heedless, I thought. Not innocent, not unfeeling: just very, very heedless, as if Leonora could see the long run, and feelings came to nothing in it. 'Good-bye, then!'

Finn's fingers were twisted so tightly in the roan's mane, it was snorting in irritation. 'This is what it was about? This? The care home was a lie. I can't believe I was so stupid!'

'You weren't stupid,' I muttered. 'You heard what you expected to hear. That's not a magic spell.'

'Conal! Finn!' For the first time there were tears in the old woman's voice. 'I loved you.'

She turned into the arms of the thing behind her. Its shimmering coat coiled around both of them, sheathing them like a pelt, and as one they toppled from the rocks. There was barely a splash as they plunged into the water.

Conal stared at the spot where his mother had vanished. Nothing surfaced. Not even bubbles.

Silence echoed, and then Finn screamed. '*Where's she gone?*'

Slowly, reluctantly, Conal rode back and stopped alongside us. 'I don't know.'

'You don't know!' She lunged and struggled as I gripped her arm.

'No, I don't know, I don't remember.' He was in a daze. 'Back where she came from? Maybe we'll all know it when we get there.'

Finn could hardly speak. 'You let her—'

'It's not a question of letting her. She did it, that's all.' Conal nudged the black away so he wouldn't have to look into her eyes anymore. 'You shouldn't have brought Finn here, Seth.'

I said nothing. Thank the gods, Finn didn't either. I didn't think anything needed saying. Instead I turned the roan after him.

'Wait! Wait!'

Someone was squeezing out from the tumbled mass of rocks at the end of the bay so fast, he ripped his jumper. I watched, jaw wide, as Jed clambered and slithered across.

'Wait!' he yelled, casting nervous glances at the shore and the remaining Selkyr. 'Finn!'

Conal hauled the black's head round, stared at him. 'Jed.'

'Yes! Wait for me!'

Dawning horror on Conal's face, mirroring mine. 'Holy shit, Jed! *Run.*'

He was already galloping towards Jed as he shouted, as if this was a wild homicidal hunt, and from the look on Jed's face, I reckon he thought it was. Then we all saw the first Selkyr, striding fast towards Jed from the sea's edge. For all its speed, it didn't look in any hurry.

Jed backed off, up towards the dunes, but it came on remorselessly. He took another step back, and another, scared to turn his back on it.

'Christ's sake, I said RUN!'

Jed was out of choices. He turned and fled.

Finn's legs were flailing, kicking the roan's flanks, but of course it wouldn't move. I put an arm round her, pinning her arms to her torso, lifting her off the roan's back just enough to deprive her of her leverage.

'Sit still,' I snarled. As she swore and tried to wriggle free, I added: 'And stay on this horse. *Stay on.*'

She went limp very suddenly, giving up, crying audibly this time. I took no notice, just kicked the roan into a gallop after Conal. Jed was still running, sliding and stumbling, his hands sinking in gummy sand, seawater soaking his legs. He fell headlong and scrambled up, all out of strength, staring wildly from the seal-creature to Conal's horse.

The Selkyr was within ten yards of Jed when the black overtook it, and then Conal was off the horse and grabbing Jed into his arms.

'What do you think you're doing?' Conal shouted at him; then he took a bewildered breath. *'How are you blocking me?'*

Jed only shook his head, speechless.

'I will *hang* Sionnach!' yelled Conal. Holding Jed tightly, arms locked around his chest, Conal faced the Selkyr as it strode relentlessly towards them.

Jed's eyes bulged with terror. I pulled the blue roan to a slithering halt as the Selkyr stopped, two arms' lengths from them.

'No,' Conal told it softly. 'Not him.'

The blackwater eyes fastened on Conal. It took a step towards Jed, reaching out long fingers, moonlight gleaming through the membranes of its finned hand.

Jed shrank against my brother.

'I said *no*,' said Conal, more intently.

It lowered its arm and curled its fingers into a loose fist.

'Not yet,' it said.

The voice was wet, liquid, cold as death. It turned

and walked away towards the ocean. There was not another sound from Conal, but in the stark moonlight, as he shoved Jed away, there were tracks of tears on his face.

When we rode back to the camp, we didn't have to say anything. We were without Leonora: that said it all.

Sionnach got his deserved bollocking, but with only half of Conal's heart. He was used to Conal's temper; after half a millennium we all were, and besides, as he pointed out later, fair enough if Conal *had* strung him up. Eili was too preoccupied with the loss of Leonora to defend her brother; she simply crouched to sharpen one of her swords, every sinew screaming furious grief. I knew that wasn't over; there would be more bitterness where that came from. I couldn't blame her. Hard enough to spawn a child; near to impossible when your lover was taken from you for most of your long, long life, and to no point at all.

Jed hovered close to Conal now, a small planet round my brother's sun. That clearly irritated Finn, but it didn't annoy me as much as I thought it would.

The boy worshipped him. I could see it already, in his constantly flickering, sleep-deprived gaze. Poor sod; and poor Eili too. Conal, for the moment, had attention only for Finn.

'Take that necklace off. I want to talk to you. Properly.'

Finn looked like she wanted to slap him. 'I'm not sure I want to take it off.'

'I'm here, aren't I? You think I'd let any harm come to you? Take it *off*.'

He was missing the point, deliberately or not, but she tugged the chain over her head, wincing as it scraped her hand. Taking her fingers in his, Conal frowned. 'What happened to you?'

She let him touch the scar gently. I knew her hand didn't need any more attention, but Finn obviously did. 'Ah.' He shut one eye and grinned. 'You old faker, toots.'

'Eili fixed it,' I said, sliding a whetstone down my blade. 'You should recognize her work.'

He shut his eyes, but he'd spent the last of his anger on Sionnach. Finn stared at the unbuttoned collar of his slate blue shirt, where the white line of a scar started at his collarbone. I knew, as she did, that it went down to his eleventh rib.

'See, this is what hurts,' she told him. 'You calling *me* a faker.'

Sighing, he pulled his shirt collar apart with his fingers and peered down guiltily.

'I'm sorry I hurt you. That's the truth. I didn't want to do it.'

'I knew that car crash was a lie,' she said. 'See you?

Always having a go at me for listening at doors, when you've been eavesdropping on me. Spying on my head. *My whole life.*'

'No,' said Conal. He ran his fingers hard across his skull. 'No. I wouldn't do that.'

She stood up, snapped a dry branch viciously and flung it onto the pile of wood. 'The thing is,' she told him, 'I don't believe a word you say anymore.'

'I don't blame you.'

'Stop being so bloody clever!' she yelled.

I let a sigh hiss out between my teeth. Conal turned a Zippo lighter calmly in his fingers and said, 'Be quiet.'

She was.

He snapped the lighter. His fingers were trembling and the fire was poorly built, in guilt and bad temper, but finally the flames caught and licked up into the bark and kindling.

'Thought you'd be more of a Boy Scout,' she muttered. 'Rub some sticks together.'

Exchanging a glance with me, Conal managed not to laugh. 'Finn, I have a good idea how you're feeling, most of the time. That's not so unusual, is it? And seeing your mind is like looking in a lit window: sometimes I can't help it, but it'd be rude to stare.'

Snarkily I muttered, 'Some of her opinions are deafening.'

'But, Finn. Much as I love you, I've got better things to do than read your mind all day.'

Glowering into the fire, she threw on another stick. 'So does that make you feel better, kiddo?'

'No.' Now even I could see she was fighting a grin. 'What could be more interesting than me?'

This time he did laugh. 'You'll soon be able to control it and block. Like—' He glanced at Jed; then at me. I saw him swallow. 'Anyway. Sorry we ruined your life, toots, but it beats getting burnt at the stake.' He reached out a hand.

She didn't move. 'That doesn't make it okay that you lied to me.'

He lowered his hand. 'Finn. You're not as angry as you think you are.'

'And that,' she muttered savagely, 'means you're doing it again.'

'Okay.' Conal stood up and grabbed his leather jacket and the bridle rolled inside it. 'You need to calm down. And I need to go to Eili.' He walked off without a backward glance.

Finn poked at the fire. She swore softly, and blinked hard.

I didn't want to feel such sympathy for her, but there you go. 'Keep your mouth shut, Dorsal; then you won't have to wish you could take things back.'

Her eyes glittered. Through her teeth she said, 'I hate you.'

'I know,' I said, and my memory jolted; then it was lost again.

Ah, the poor little cow. He was the only one who would have anything to do with her; no wonder she loved him, no wonder she needed him.

Dawn was not far off, the sky paling to grey on the eastern edge of the forest, and as the eerie light grew, the trees revealed themselves, ranked like a silent army. Only Torc slept on, snoring like a badly tuned tractor. Sionnach sat staring into the rebuilt fire as he whetted his hunting knife, his beloved iPod stuck to his ears.

I stood up and stretched, and kicked Jed's ankle. 'Missed your deadline, Cuilean.'

Jed blinked at me, and I nodded at the sky.

'You were going to be dead by midnight.'

Maybe it wasn't the most comforting thing I could have said, but truly, I meant it well.

Finn

Strange how little she felt. The grief was like a blade wrapped under her breastbone, the edge working away at its sheath of silk but not quite touching her, not yet. She'd seen Leonie plunge into the water, but it hadn't happened in real life.

Not yet.

Real life. It wasn't that she had a problem accepting this was it. She wasn't turning her back on it, on her home: not now. But Jed had to go. A friend was a friend, but friends could get in the way. He didn't belong here. She did. Surprising how easy it was to want him gone now.

Finn. Don't let the cold iron in.

So Leonie had taken the time, after all these years, to give her a lecture. Whatever the almighty hurry for her own death, she'd had time for *that*. Finn shivered with resentment.

We're cold, Finn, cold. You have to fight to stay human.

Uh-huh? I notice my mother isn't putting up much of a struggle.

She was worried for Jed; wasn't that reasonable? No, she was *terrified*, after what had happened – almost happened – on the beach. The fear of what might-have-been ate at her heart like a maggot. Finn knew what she needed: an ice-shard like Stella's, one to keep her own heart stitched together, to make it impervious to maggots of fear.

Besides, this place is mine. Not his.

Her dream-mother didn't come again; sleep was too intermittent, disturbed by fluctuating resentment, fear and guilt. When the sun rose between the pine trunks, casting striped golden shadows, Finn was awake to see Eili and Conal return. They weren't touching, but Conal had lost his hunted look, and Eili looked downright smug. Sitting up straight, Finn prised herself away from the sleeping Jed.

'Don't give me the silent treatment, Finn.' Conal sat next to her. 'I had to go away. Sorry.'

'S'all right.'

'No, it isn't. I know it's been a rough night. I'm sorry I didn't stay with you, but I'm not too happy myself.' He glanced away uncomfortably. 'And I haven't seen Eili in a very long time.'

Finn rolled her eyes, stifling laughter. 'How old d'you think I am?'

When she met his eyes again, he wore an insolent grin. Touching her hand, he said, 'Eili did that really well. Won't scar.'

Oh, do shut up about Hotlips. 'It's sleep you need, pal, not romance.'

'Ach, you're a bossy cow.' Conal laughed. 'And Hotlips did you a favour, okay?'

She eyed him darkly. 'And again. When are you planning to sleep?'

'I'm not,' he said lightly. 'So. If you're fed up of your high horse, d'you fancy another shot on mine? For fun this time.' He made her hair into a ponytail with his fist and tugged it, a little too hard to be playful. 'A good run will get death and jealousy out of your head.'

She cocked an eyebrow. 'Is it safe?'

'With me, it is.'

'What's his name?'

'He doesn't have a name. He's not that kind of horse.' He smiled. 'Well?'

She was going to die. She couldn't believe she'd done this again, and voluntarily. Death by water horse, at terminal velocity: it was quite a way to go.

She hung grimly against Conal's back – partly so the wind wouldn't sting her eyes but mostly because she was scared to look – so she could see nothing but the weave of his shirt, and her ear was jammed painfully against his scabbard as terror fired adrenaline into her bloodstream. When the horse slowed to buck and prance in the sand, Conal took her by the waist and hauled her round to sit in front.

'You take him this time. Eyes front, toots.' The horse sprang forward.

As he dropped the reins, she grabbed for them, half-blinded by the whipping silky mane. Conal's arm

was round her waist long enough for her to regain
her balance, long enough for her to clutch the reins
and feel the horse's snarling mouth; then he let her go.

The horse lunged forward and she leaned into its
gallop. Ahead were the rocks at the end of the sand,
slanting up like jutting bones, and she thought, if
she thought at all, that they'd break on them like a
wave.

Then, through the stinging slap of the mane and
the rasping of her lungs, she heard Conal's voice at
her ear. It was no words she understood, but when the
sand ran out, she dug in her heels and the horse took
off, the bank of rocks blurring beneath them. She
howled, and not with fear.

As its hooves cracked down onto stunted grass and
solid earth, the horse rolled its eyes back in its tossing
head to watch her. She'd have sworn it was laughing,
but then she could no more wipe her own grin off her
face than stop breathing.

Once more Conal turned the horse and let it lope
down from the bank. On the beach it snuffed the salt
air. Itching for more speed, tremors running in its
muscles, it planted its hooves in the rippling waves
and stared out to sea. Liath, tongue lolling, flopped
down in the sand.

'Good, eh?'

'Huh-huh,' she said when there was air in her
lungs.

Conal took the reins from her hands and lowered
her off the horse, then dismounted after her. He sat
down in the sand beside his wolf, clasping his hands
behind his neck and tilting his head back to soak up

sun. The horse struck the waves playfully with a hoof.

Finn sat down. Licked her teeth with the tip of her tongue. 'Jed needs to get home,' she said at last.

'Yeah, I know.'

'I'm not going.'

He took a long time to answer that. 'We'll see,' he said at last. 'And I'll take Jed soon as I can.'

'I'm not going and you know it,' she said. 'You're longing to get one over on my mother. I heard what you said to Leonie last night.'

'Finn, I was angry then. It isn't safe for you here.'

'I'm not safe over there,' she pointed out. 'And neither is anyone else.'

'Shania Rooney? You wanted skelping for that.'

She bristled. 'You needn't have a go at me, you with the sword on your back. What would you have done, cut her head off?'

He laughed. But he didn't answer.

'How does Shania even notice me, anyway?'

He shrugged. 'How does Jed notice you, for that matter? I dunno. Maybe they've both got traces of Sithe blood. Lots of people have.'

'Put it about a bit, do you? You devils.'

'Angels, dear.'

'Huh?' She wrinkled her nose.

'Fallen angels. That's the full-mortal legend. Seems their God kicked his rebel angels out of Heaven, when they got stroppy. So the ones that fell in the sea became the seals, and the ones that got caught in the sky became the Northern Lights, and the ones that fell on land became faeries.'

She lay back, and turned to face the clouds so he wouldn't see her smile. In the companionable silence she folded her arms across her face, too comfortable to move. The horse stretched its neck to the thin lapping waves and drank.

'So why are you at war?'

Conal tilted his head a little towards her, a smile playing on his mouth. 'Disapprove?'

'Dunno. You can explain.' She hesitated. 'But yeah. I probably disapprove.'

'Okay. Our queen fancies ruling the full-mortals and she'll sacrifice this whole world to gain that one. And us, while she's at it. Well, there's things I'm willing to die for, Finn, but Kate's political career ain't one of them.'

Finn stared at him. 'Try not to go dying for anything, will you?'

'I don't intend to, toots.'

'Wish you'd stop calling me that.'

'Way too late. Toots.'

She rolled her eyes. 'So who's against you?'

He shrugged awkwardly. 'Kate's clann. Anyone who wants a war with the full-mortals. People who bear a grudge.'

'Like Seth,' muttered Finn.

'No,' said Conal. 'Finn, no. He bears a grudge, but he wouldn't go that far.'

She gave him an arch look.

'I heard that, young lady.' Conal trickled sand through his fingers. 'Seth burnt his boats when I did. The day we rode out of Kate's stronghold and took half her best fighters with us.'

'Ooh, renegades.'

'It's not ooh, it's bloody nerve-racking.'

'And you have to fight, do you? Have you people never heard of compromise?'

'Am I being lectured about compromise by a hormonal sixteen-year-old? Listen, Kate's even worse than the rest of us. She'd start a war for the fun of it on a dull weekend. And she gets along grand with the Lammyr. That's not a good thing, take my word for it.'

Finn curled up to watch the horse at the water's edge. It seemed transfixed by the distant islands. The sea was blue and silken beneath feathers of cloud, but it had probably drowned a hundred men. A thousand. Picturing their bodies drifting and rotting below the surface, she shuddered. She did not like seeing beneath the skin of the world, and she did not want to know what a Lammyr was, or why it filled her head with death.

'I love that scabby old Veil,' he murmured into the quietness. 'It's saved my arse more than once. But Kate wants the Veil dead, and that would be the end of the Sithe.' Conal held up a finger and thumb, shutting an eye to trap the distant sun between them. 'I once came this close to getting burnt at the stake. We can't live in that world, Finn. It always ends in tears, or in flames.'

'Oh.' She grunted. 'Right, I think I've got as much of the gist as I'm going to get. Anything else you've forgotten to tell me?'

'I'm sure there is. It'll all come to me.'

'How about explaining last night, then? Why wouldn't you speak to me?'

'What?' He laughed. 'I spoke to you plenty last night. When you weren't sulking.'

'Yeah, yeah. Not then, before. Hours before. When I was in the wood on my own and you came by.'

He opened his mouth. Shut it again.

'I saw you in the trees. You know I did.'

He'd gone very pale and he wasn't laughing. Liath sat up and fixed yellow eyes on Finn.

'I wasn't there earlier,' he said. 'I had to ride like stink to get there when I did.'

'I know it's a secret.' She glanced around impatiently. 'But we're on our own. Conal. Come on.'

He seemed a little stunned at being caught out. 'I daresay you did, Finn. Tell me what I said to you.'

'I *told* you. You didn't say anything. Trust me now?'

'I see.' His pupils were dilated but there was tumultuous silver light in their depths. 'And what was I wearing?'

'Your long black coat. That dead cool cashmere one. Stop it, okay?'

'My eyes, Finn.' He attempted a smile. 'What colour were my eyes?'

'Grey, you big tube, same as—' Her laughter died quite abruptly. 'Black,' she said. 'Your eyes were black.'

He took hold of the back of her head so suddenly, she flinched, but he only gripped her tighter, staring into her eyes.

'Was it your evil twin or something?' She was angry with him now. 'Let go.'

He did let go, very sharply. 'Two sights,' he whispered. 'Oh, Finn. You have two sights.'

He gave the faintest sigh. Then he tucked a lock of her hair behind her ear, holding it so it didn't spring back out. 'Of course you saw me,' he said, his eyes scarily bright. 'But listen. It's my business. Don't mention it to anyone. All right? *Anyone*.' He hesitated. 'Especially not Seth.'

She nodded, speechless. As Conal got up and helped her to her feet, she leaned forward and laid her hand on his breastbone. Then she snatched it abruptly away.

'You're afraid!'

'Yes,' he said. 'But you don't have to be. The fetch can't harm you.'

She opened her mouth to ask what a fetch was, but he was already striding across the sand, and the black horse was turning and trotting to him. The white wolf followed, but not before she'd given Finn the most reproachful look she'd ever felt in her life.

Back at the camp, bewildered and a little angry, Finn was in no mood to share Conal. It wasn't hard to glare Seth into standing up and walking away from the fire with a long-suffering shrug.

A pity, then, that Jed seemed to be attached to her uncle by an invisible wire. The boy had turned into a stalker since the incident on the beach, which was ironic when it was his bullheaded stupidity that had nearly got Conal killed. And himself, of course, but that was beside the point.

Finn wasn't about to move from her place at

Conal's side, but Jed simply wriggled down between them. 'Sorry about Leonie.'

Finn said curtly, 'Yeah.'

'Cheers. I thought she'd be sorrier to leave us.' Conal bit a thumbnail, then slung an arm round Liath's neck. 'She was so ridiculously happy to go.'

Jed shrugged. 'I guess she'd been around a long time.'

'So have I. And I like it that way. Longer my life, the more I get attached to it.'

Jed fidgeted. 'Yeah, I noticed you've got a lot of respect for human life.'

'What?'

Oh, way to ingratiate yourself with Conal, thought Finn. *Good. Now, go away.*

'You got blood on your shirt. Did you kill somebody?'

Conal started on another fingernail. 'Yes.'

Something cracked behind them. Finn glanced round to see Seth chuck a broken branch over their heads onto the blaze. Sparks exploded, cinders flew and Jed scooted back.

'Someone does your killing for you, Cuilean,' Seth told him silkily. 'You're not morally superior, you're a lucky brat.'

'Oh, give it a rest, Murlainn.' Sionnach yawned.

Conal rubbed his temples. 'Life's precious, Jed, but by an accident of fate and a chain of events, your life is more precious to me than his was.' He leaned his jaw on his hand. 'Laszlo's lieutenant was after you.'

'I don't believe that.'

'Believe what you like,' said Seth. 'Here. Have another vicarious death.' Reaching into the fire, he raked out an old charred chunk of rabbit, still singeingly hot, and tossed it into Jed's lap.

Yelping, Jed swatted it away; Torc caught it, shrugged, and ate it.

Jed sprang up. 'You buggers aren't normal.'

'Don't say that.' Finn too scrambled to her feet. The grief and the perplexity were simmering nicely into an unfocused fury, but she didn't know who deserved it more: Jed, for that remark, or Seth, for being an arse.

'Look who's talking, Cuilean.' Seizing Jed's jaw, Seth tilted his head and examined his eyes. 'You're an aberration in a warped world. You don't even exist, *normal boy*.'

'Get away from me!' Jed shoved him back.

Rising, Conal gave Seth a warning glare. 'Yes. Get away from him, Seth.'

'No, let's play *Trivial Pursuit*.' Seth grinned in Jed's face. 'What's your dad's name? Your mother ever tell you?'

'Why would she bother when I don't care?'

'Why would she bother when *she* didn't care? Mothers, eh?' Seth flicked a grin towards Finn. 'The same all over the worlds.'

Finn beat Jed to it. She flung herself so violently at Seth, she almost knocked him off his feet, hammering at his face with her fists and kicking viciously at his groin. Snaking his torso out of the way, Seth grabbed Finn's wrists, holding her at arm's length.

Eili shook her head in disbelief. 'You bunch of infants. Break it up!'

'Look, Conal, look!' Seth was helpless with laughter as he dodged Finn's flailing feet. 'Finny's gone native! She doesn't give a toss for us abnormals, she's sticking up for the whelp!'

'Get your hands off her!' Conal grabbed his brother's fingers and twisted them savagely. Seth stumbled back, blowing on his knuckles, still laughing, as Conal seized Finn. There were tears of fury on her cheeks.

'Mothers, Dorsal! They'll always break your heart, if you've got one.'

'You bloody haven't!'

'And *that's* why I won't end up like your father!'

Finn gave a shriek of pure rage. 'Don't make fun of my dad's heart condition!'

Seth howled. 'Heart condition? Gods yes! No heart goes on beating with a blade in it!'

Silence. Horrible, thick and dark. Conal's expression was like winter without the beauty.

Finn caught a fleeting look of fear and regret in Seth's eyes, but Conal had already seized the collar of his brother's T-shirt and dragged him in so close, their faces almost touched.

'You *bastard son of a whore*.'

Sionnach took a shocked breath. The blue roan lifted its head, paced from the edge of the clearing and hitched its head over Seth's shoulder; Branndair backed protectively against him, showing Conal his fangs in spite of Liath's warning growl.

Seth ran his fingers into the wolf's mane, drawing him closer. He smiled coldly. 'That's me, big man.'

Conal shut his eyes. 'Murlainn,' he said.

'That temper of yours.' Seth's voice was too mild. 'It'll be the death of you.'

'Seth, man, I'm sorry. I'm so sorry. I didn't mean it.'

'No.'

'You know I didn't. I'm sorry.'

Leaning his head against the roan's neck, Seth gave Conal a reluctant sidelong grin.

Finn would rather have seen him get a proper slapping, not just a verbal one. 'Why are you apologising to him?' she yelled.

'He's reminding me,' Seth told her coldly, 'that lies are sometimes better than the truth.'

She stared at him, then at Conal. 'That explains it, then. You lying to me for sixteen years.'

'Yes, actually it—'

'Seth, *shut it*. Finn, it wasn't like that, I told you. I didn't want to—'

'My dad!' She almost choked on the word. 'You said it was his heart. You lied about my father!'

The silence was hideous. Eili raked a hand across her cropped hair. Sionnach inspected the ground.

'Finn, listen . . .' Jed touched her arm, but she shoved him fiercely away and swore. Turning on her heel, she stumbled towards the trees.

'Where d'you think you're going?' demanded Eili.

'I need to throw up.' She was so pale, she looked green.

'Keep your mind open. We need to know where you are.'

'My mind's an open frigging book. Ask Conal.' Fist at her mouth, Finn turned to give him a filthy glare. She took a step back, then another, shaking her head. 'I loved you, Conal. And I never even knew who you *were*.'

Seth

Nobody met anyone else's eyes for long seconds. The past tense hit me like a delayed ricochet; the gods knew what it was doing for Conal. I wanted to feel remorse for what I'd done, but adrenaline still fizzed through my veins. I was so high on it, I could float. *It's all right,* I told myself. *It's all right. Everybody had a tantrum, and now the air's clear and it's over. Best way. Forget it.*

'Shall I—?' began Sionnach.

'I think – I don't know. Let her cool off.' Conal's jaw was tight. 'Just keep tabs. She doesn't want me near her.'

'She'll get over it,' I said.

'Not if you have anything to do with it,' growled Torc.

That stung. I shrugged, hefted the ripening deer carcass and lugged it out of the clearing. Hard to butcher it in the darkness and the closeness of the trees, but that wasn't why I wanted away from everyone. A little beyond the edge of the wood, just below a sandy land-slip, there was a jumbled outcrop of rock. Slinging the carcass down, I drew my hunting knife, aware that Conal had followed me. He kept staring back into the trees.

I did think, briefly, I should offer to go after her. Apologise to the silly cow. Calm things down. Tell her how she'd hurt him; I knew, even if he didn't, that she'd forgive him in the end, and the sooner the better. I'd give her a little longer. Then if Conal didn't go, I would. I could swallow enough pride, even if I choked on it.

I jerked my knife through the deer's belly and tugged out its entrails, then flung them towards Branndair and the blue roan. The horse beat the wolf to it, but they'd both had quite enough anyway. Conal watched me so intently, I knew he was trying not to think about Finn. Pushing his shirtsleeves up his arms, he stared out at the morning lightening over the sea.

'She's just cooling off,' I said. 'She's all right.'

'I know.'

Maybe we didn't want to think anything else. Me especially. If I opened my mouth now, how would I ever explain myself?

It was a bleak old landscape, and it was already paling into winter. The translucent sky was streaked with great archipelagos of cloud, lit by an unseen sun below a cloud bank on the landward horizon.

'Sunrise already,' I said, not looking up from my bloody hands. 'It's been nearly two days.'

'Gods.'

'You don't need to panic.' I sat back on my

haunches and studied his face. Sometimes I wanted to shake my brother. 'But Jed should be long gone.'

'Jed should, yes.' I'd expected a bollocking, not his sad defeated misery. 'Tell me, Seth. Am I wrong?'

'You're asking the wrong person. You know what I think. Finn should have been brought here a long time ago.'

Rubbing his neck, Conal stared at the dunes in the middle distance. The old deep parallel lines still stood out white and ugly on his left arm. 'I'll take her back. Eventually.'

'Not yet, if you really want my blessing. She's not ready, she needs to be where she belongs. She's been lied to for a long time. Stella's had her way for sixteen years.'

'And I'm as mad as hell at her. That what you want to hear?'

I shrugged. 'Fact is, you don't want Finn to go back either.'

'No, I don't. I have to stay now; I don't have a choice. If Finn goes back, I might never see her again.'

'Give her time, then. Give yourself some, for that matter.'

'If you say so.' He tore off a nail with his teeth. 'I'm not sure how long I can risk it. Never mind Kate, my life won't be worth living anyway. I'm for it.'

I grinned. 'You're safe. Stella can't come back here; now you can't go *there*.'

'Oh, cheers. Thanks a lot.' He punched me amicably.

'So you might as well get Jed.'

'I'll do it right now.' He winked at me, and raised his voice only slightly. 'Jed? Come on out.'

The silence and the stillness lingered for a few moments, but neither of us spoke. At last the boy crawled out from a gap in the grey rock outcrop, dusting scraps of lichen off his jeans.

'Thank Christ you're not a social worker,' he muttered.

Conal grinned at Liath. In her amber eyes Jed's reflection was trapped like a fly. 'It's time we got you home.'

'Past time,' Jed grunted. 'I don't belong here.'

'It's not that,' said Conal, slinging an arm round Liath's shaggy neck, 'though you don't.'

Jed shook his head. 'You're such a tosser.'

'See? You and Seth are of one mind.' Conal lay back to watch the astonishing sky, the wolf slumping beside him to wash his ear with her tongue. 'Hey, Liath, that tickles.'

Rebuffed, Liath turned her mothering instincts on Jed, licking his face till he grabbed her muzzle to scratch behind her ears. While he was distracted, I took a long glance at Conal. The morning light was strong on the angles of his face, his eye sockets and cheekbones hollow, the stubble of a dark blond beard on his jaw and lip. His eyes were haunted and miserable.

I shook off a twinge of anxiety. All he needed was a few hours' sleep.

'Cù Chaorach, you look like shite,' I said. 'You need to—'

'Get going. Right.' Conal stood up, the exhausted sadness gone. Or it would have been, if I hadn't known him better. 'And so do you, Jed. You're getting kind of comfortable here. You want to watch it when that happens.'

'Listen, man, I can't wait to get out of here.'

'Just before you do,' I murmured, 'be a dear and give us back that brooch.'

'What?'

'You know. The one you nicked off Leonora's workbench.'

His face froze, but he staunchly avoided looking guilty as he fished in his inside pocket for the jewel and handed it over. It was even more beautiful in sunlight, and the dazzle made the rubies look huge.

'Nicely done,' said Conal. 'You could have given me a few tips.'

'What?'

'I mean, you're better at it than I ever was.' Conal winked.

Jed's fierce blush faded as he let that sink in. 'You're a thief and all?' He paused. 'People don't notice you, of course.'

'Not much.' Conal rubbed his scalp. 'Sionnach will take you back to the watergate, okay?' He examined the elaborate tangle of gold, then placed it back in Jed's hand and closed his fingers over it. 'Don't sell it for a pittance, right? It's worth a lot. Should keep you going for a while.'

Jed was too shocked to say anything, and I thought better of it too.

Conal couldn't quite meet Jed's eyes. 'It was nice knowing you, okay? I think you'll be fine.'

Jed swallowed. 'Are you all right? Is something bothering you? Can I—?'

'Yes. No. And no. Is that all?' Conal smiled thinly, then turned, irritated. 'What is it, Sionnach?'

Sionnach skidded down the bank of rock. *~ The interference. The white noise. It's worse – we—*

'The hell are you on about? Speak it, man!'

'Cù Chaorach,' Sionnach's face was so white, his scars were more livid than I'd seen them in years. 'She's disappeared. Gone. Finn's gone.'

PART THREE

Jed

Jed let go of the barbed wire, dropped to the ground and stared back into the gloom of the wood. The weather had turned fast; the beaten-metal surface of the Fairy Loch was pale grey and wintry between the black pine trunks, a faint breeze feathering its surface. There was an ache in his gut he hadn't expected.

He was glad he'd got out of that hideous wild place. Hated to think what Conal would be doing by now. Stringing everyone up, if he hadn't found Finn. Stringing her up if he had.

He shook off the memory: Conal's wild grief and fury, his bawled order to Sionnach to get the boy home *now* so he could get his arse back and help with the hunt. Jed wondered what had happened to Finn: why she'd vanished, and where to.

Oh, who cared? There was no reason why he should. The way she'd acted out in the last few hours – self-absorbed and snotty – she'd clearly been desperate to see the back of him. Hell with her, and to hell with Conal. It wasn't Jed's business anymore; never had been, really. With luck, his mother would soon up sticks and move again. *Please, God*, he thought, *this time let her pick a decent-sized city*. Somewhere he wouldn't even get the chance to be tempted to make friends.

Mila would have to get her head together soon, before the authorities latched on to her. For all Jed knew, their number was already up and the social workers had moved in in his absence.

Would that be such a bad thing?

He didn't know where the sneaking whisper came from, but it deserved some consideration. *Freedom*, he thought. No responsibility, no trouble, no love. He could make something of himself, make something of his life. Mila could manage without him; she could certainly manage without Rory, since she'd soon forget he'd ever existed. And Rory? Rory would be better off in care than he would with a junkie dam.

And what kind of a word was *dam*? And how had it got in his head?

And how had *any* of this crap got in his head?

Worst of all, why was he so hideously sure it had all happened already?

Fear iced Jed's spine, and he ran.

He pelted along the tarmac faster than he'd ever run from a security guard, ignoring the speeding traffic, almost stumbling under a braking BMW. But he might have been running in a dream: his legs wouldn't work, the air felt thick as honey, he couldn't go fast enough. His focus narrowed to the town perimeter, to grey streets and bleak concrete. The roads were cluttered now, and he barged through crowds, ignoring the yells. His lungs were rasping when he swung into the alleyway that led to his own back door.

The bloody gate was stuck as usual. He leaped for the top of the fence, caught it, and climbed over, then fumbled in his pocket for the back-door key.

The lanky dealer had his fingers on the handle of the outer shared door, but when he caught sight of Jed, he released it, sighing, and stepped back out of the way. Jed searched more desperately for the door key, trying to ignore that flickering malevolent grin.

'Now, this is an interesting development.'

The dealer smiled again, and nausea gripped Jed's gut. He was almost screaming with frustration by the time his trembling fingers closed on the key, and he could hardly fit it in the door. The cadaverous laugh behind him sounded like a boot stamping on dry twigs, but at least it put steel in his bones. He wrenched the door open.

Taking the stairs two at a time, he closed his mouth against the stench, almost choking on lungfuls of ammonia and piss and ... sickness. Their neighbour stood on the shared landing, and Jed bounced off her as he leaped up the last three stairs, shoving her aside.

She staggered, then bristled. 'I've called the police. That wean ought to be in care.' Her nasal voice rose to a yell. 'It's been screaming all morning!'

Flinging open the flat door, he slammed it in her face.

Jed stood still. There was Rory's echoing screaming, and there was the awful stink of vomit. That was all he could take in: that and his mother, facedown on the floor. Her head was turned so that one brown eye was looking right at him.

'Mila?' He started to crouch down, but hesitated. 'Mum?'

Uncertainty in his head, ice in his heart, denial in his gut. And behind it all, distant sirens.

Only one clear knowledge: There was only one of them he could take care of for now. Snatching up Rory's fleece and yanking it down over his screaming head, he gathered the child into his arms. God, the little bugger was sodden and he stank. Jed stuck a nappy in his pocket.

Rory buried his face in Jed's neck, his screams already fading to hiccuping sobs. Jed hesitated, hand cupping his head. He wanted to check on his mother again, but there was no point looking. No time to look. He wouldn't look.

He ran for it.

The stairs made him dizzy now, Rory making him stumble with every step. The scrawny pusher was gone, but the neighbour was in the yard, peering out of the gate that now swung wide and loose on rusted hinges. Jed barged her aside, ignoring her shouts of fury and then no longer hearing them at all because he was already running, the sirens beating on his eardrums.

He ducked out of the alleyway as the ambulance swerved into the street, but its driver ignored him and he ran behind it. At the corner there were more sirens. They were coming from two directions at the T-junction and he doubled back, half stumbling.

Three emergency vehicles for his mother? Even to Jed it seemed like overkill.

At the opposite end of the street he heard them again, echoing off the concrete pillars of the shopping arcade. He couldn't even tell where they were coming from. People were staring but he didn't know where to go, which way to turn. He gave a ragged yell of frustration.

'Oy, you. *Stop!*'

Ducking under a broken fence, he sprinted across a patch of waste ground. He knew his territory, but it was awkward carrying Rory, his small arms locked so tight around Jed's neck. But he wouldn't, couldn't leave him. Like he'd left Mila . . . *no*. He batted away the image of her, lying there so still and badly angled.

At the end of a narrow strip of waste ground he paused at the main road, heart hammering. Shutting his eyes briefly, he darted from his hole, but they were ahead of him: a policeman, hatless, and two women, one in police uniform and one in a black turtleneck and a cheap red blazer. They walked forward, Red Blazer at the front, and slowed as he halted, gasping. She held her hand towards him, eyes brightly intent.

'Come on, son, cool it.' The policeman's voice was low, authoritative, the kind of voice you instinctively trusted. 'Let us help you and the baby. Come on.'

Jed looked at the cop, and he looked at the woman. Her face was fanatical: hungry, even.

Jed spun and ran again. There was nowhere left to go but out of town. The perimeter seemed far away when he heard the shouts behind him, but he got there faster than he could have hoped, Rory clinging like a throttling vine. Horns blared, tyres screeched, and the speed of the cars made him hesitate, but only for an instant; then he was across the bypass and running hard into the countryside.

The pursuit was still behind: Christ, why did they have to mind so much? He hauled in sobbing breaths that tore at his chest. Sirens again, somewhere ahead, herding him. Why so many? Why would they give such a damn?

His strength failed him at the gate of the Fairy Loch and he leaned against it, his lungs aching. He tilted his head back and stared up, all out of hope. There was no way to get Rory safely across the wire: his baby flesh would catch and tear. Jed rubbed his eyes against his brother's damp blond hair, the fight gone out of him, and slumped against the gate.

It sagged wide open; he only just caught himself from falling.

How stupid. It was so funny, he nearly laughed, hysterically. He'd been shinning over a gate with a broken padlock for months. Well, it didn't matter now. It was a hopeless place to hide, but he barged in anyway, ignoring the inner voice that screamed at him to turn back. It was a place to be cornered, a place to be caught.

Then again, so was the road.

In the shadow of the pines he stopped and waited, hoping the cops were a superstitious lot who'd pass by the Fairy Loch. It was a forlorn hope, but if he pressed farther in, hid in the undergrowth, they might give it only a cursory check. He couldn't stay this close to the fence.

He staggered down the slope and deeper into the wood. The tramp was nowhere in sight, and just as well. Caught between a psychopath and social services, Jed wasn't sure what he'd do.

Above and behind him, the gate rattled.

Heart galloping, he fought the welling terror. He was going to jail, and Rory into care, and he would never see his brother again, and very suddenly that did matter, mattered terribly. Cold wrenching fear drove him on, even though it was pointless; after all, without Finn, the loch was no use to him: nothing but a dank, freezing drowning-pit.

'All right, son. Calm down, now. There's nowhere for you to go. We want to help.'

He couldn't see the man in the murk, but the words felt like a lie, and that reinforced his weakening spine. He backed, searching the trees, and one foot sank up to the ankle in freezing water. Rory whimpered and clutched him tighter.

'Come on, laddie. It's not worth it. Come and have a cuppa and we'll talk.'

Jed backed farther, almost against his will, but he couldn't bear to give in to them, not yet. Up at the gate there were more urgent shouts, the crunch of tyres and the slam of car doors. *So many*.

He was up to his waist without even thinking about it, then to his chest. Feathers and fans of ice had formed on the water's surface, and the cold snatched his breath away. Though Rory was in the water too, he was very quiet, grip tighter than ever. Christ, thought Jed with rising panicked fury: if he had a gun he'd shoot those bast . . .

. . . bastards.

He put numb fingers to the pistol in his belt. It wasn't useless here. There were rounds in the magazine: Seth had shown him. He'd shown him how to cock the gun. He'd shown him how to loose the safety catch and squeeze the trigger. And Jed hadn't even realised.

'Ed,' whispered Rory. He pressed his cheek to Jed's and blew a raspberry at his ear.

Jed shook himself. Madness. He could no more shoot a human being than get through this loch. The bloody gun was probably ruined by the water anyway. He buried his face in Rory's neck and hugged him tightly.

That was when a figure broke out of the trees and stumbled into the weeds. Steel-coloured eyes behind thick glasses widened as the tramp stared at him in shock.

Jed could only stare back, wondering what death would feel like. Then he thought he knew, because something like waterweed snaked up, snagging his legs and waist.

The world receded in a rush of terrible blackness, and he was yanked beneath the surface into a cold and deafening void.

Seth

If Laszlo didn't kill the girl, I was going to do it for him.

Finn was more frightening in her absence than she'd ever been in the flesh. Sionnach and Torc and I were wasting our time persuading Conal she was gone, and there was no point looking further; it took Eili to knock some sense into him, and then she got an earful for her trouble. But after hours of combing the woods, he did, at last, acknowledge it was useless.

'How did they get that close? *How?*'

'I dunno, but Laszlo's got her,' I said. 'Must have.'

'Thanks for that statement of the bleeding obvious,' he gritted.

Sionnach looked devastated. I felt for him. 'I swear to the gods, Conal, she was there. I felt her echo. Right up till—?'

'Sionnach,' I said. 'It's not your fault.' Somebody had to say it, since Conal was so disinclined to forgive.

'Now, let's get to the dun. We can't help her any other way, and we've wasted enough time.'

'It's gonna be hard work getting back to the dun,' pointed out Torc. 'They've had plenty of time to get extra patrols out, and they know where we are.'

'I can't go, not yet.' Conal raked fingers through his hair. 'I can't leave her.'

'You haven't got a choice,' said Eili crisply. 'Sorry. At least the boy's gone; that's one less complication.'

'What does she want with Finn? Finn can't hurt Kate. Can't help her.'

'Took her to spite you?' suggested Eili.

And since that was the honest truth, he couldn't argue. It was the wrong thing to say, though, in so many ways. Conal was too silent, scratching manically at the scars on his arm though they must have stopped itching centuries ago.

'We've wasted too much time,' he said at last.

'Just what I—'

'No. I mean we've wasted too much time in these woods. The dun's two days' ride away; to hell with that. We need to get her back before Laszlo gets her to Kate's caverns; if we can't do that, we'll think of something later. Once she's in there, the entire fecking clann won't be able to get her out.'

'Cù Chaorach, that's—'

'Eili, don't say the next word,' he spat. 'I'm not leaving her. Kate wants me to come and get her; if I don't, she'll hang her.'

'We could at least call for reinforcements. Even at this distance, Torc can call Sulaire. . . .'

'Yeah? Has he tried lately?'

Torc reddened as we stared glumly at him. He didn't even have to reply.

'See?' said Conal bitterly. 'I don't know how Kate's doing this to us, but she is. We're cut off. Get used to it.' He grabbed a handful of the black's mane. 'Now, I'm going to get my goddaughter. Anyone coming?'

I hated that we were split again, but it would have been stupid not to maximize our chances. Eili insisted on riding at Conal's side, and Torc went with them; I was happy to be in the quiet company of Sionnach, who anyway was the best tracker.

'So help me, I wish I'd killed Laszlo when I had the chance,' I said.

Sionnach made a face. 'You'll get another. If your brother doesn't get to him first.'

I wished I felt so optimistic. Gods, how I'd hated having Laszlo in my sights, with trigger-squeezing forbidden by some bureaucrat in a distant office, someone who understood the politics better than I did, but had never watched the man at work. I kicked myself daily for that. I kicked myself almost as hard as I had when I tracked his movements again, when I finally thought I'd run him to earth and found only his seventy-eight hostages from that last village.

Well, not them, not as such. Bits of them, hacked to pulp and jumbled in their mass grave.

I shook my head free of the memory yet again. 'By the way,' I added, 'don't underestimate him. He's better with a blade than he ought to be.'

'Not as good as Conal,' said Sionnach.

'Loyal of you,' I said bitchily, 'but I wouldn't bet on it. He was an Olympian fencer back in the day. And he's taken to longswords like a duck to . . . er . . .'

'Homicidal mania?'

'Yup.'

'Well, at least—' Sionnach reined in his horse very abruptly, sniffing the air.

'What?' I half drew my sword.

He frowned. 'Not close. And I can't track. But something's around that wasn't there before. Something human.'

'Oh, gods.' I slapped my forehead. 'Don't tell me.'

'Fine.' He gave me a rueful grin. ~ *I won't say a word. But something breached the watergate again.*

Jed

The strange sensation was breathing. That was it; and it was strange only because he hadn't expected to be doing it. Jed's fingers scrabbled on slick weed and wet stones as he raised himself to a kneeling position and vomited into the shallow loch. It wasn't water he was throwing up, he noticed. It was his last meal and exhaustion and terror, and once his stomach had finished heaving, he felt a lot better.

Rory. He staggered to his feet.

Thank God. Rory was on the beach, laughing his bright blond head off as he flung handfuls of gritty sand at the water. Bending half-double, Jed waited for the spasms in his gut to fade. The sky was dark grey and menacing, but Rory's lank hair gleamed like sunlit barley. The child – if it was Rory – didn't even seem so scrawny, as if he had plumped up nicely in the water. Suspicion rippled through Jed's innards.

Rory peered up, puzzled. Then a broad grin showed

familiar baby teeth and he clambered upright and
waddled towards his brother. 'Ed!' he shouted.

Jed fell on his knees to hug him. Oh, his backside
was soaking and he stank of piss. Poor brat: it was
Rory, all right.

Swiftly Jed changed the disintegrating nappy;
God knew what he was going to do next time. He
tugged the wet jeans back up over Rory's bottom and
stood up.

Feeling the first spatters of rain on his arms, he
smiled at the infant. 'We have to go, angel.'

Curtains of rain swept across the skyline, blurring
the horizon and shrouding the ruined castle on its
spit of land. For half a minute, Jed could see it; then
it was gone. The weather was closing in, and not just
rain clouds. With them there was something else,
something he could feel in his stomach and bones.

Hazarding a guess at the direction, he climbed up
off the beach and set out through the heather, Rory
on his hip, but even the child's bright mood couldn't
outlast the rain that started to lash them within a
hundred metres of the beach. In seconds, Jed was
soaked through, and Rory cuddled into him, water
running off his head and down Jed's neck. He started
to whimper.

'Hush,' Jed murmured automatically, though he
didn't exactly see why the boy should, since he felt
like whimpering himself. He was alone and friendless
and sorry for himself, and now he was almost sure he
was going the wrong way. Still, no point turning back
now. Tightening his grip on Rory, he ploughed on.

Within minutes, the horizon vanished altogether,

as if a giant thumb had smudged it off a watercolour landscape, and then time ceased to make sense at all. All Jed knew was the squelch of his feet in his shoes and the subdued hiss of the rain. Boredom, exhaustion and drenching cold were his new life: he was completely disoriented and had no idea how many miles he'd covered. An hour, two hours passed, and then he gave up looking at his watch, because its face was misted over by the rain.

He might as well press on: it was better than retracing his steps, and anyway, if he stopped, he knew he might never start walking again. His calf muscles ached from struggling through the heather, but he was shivering violently.

Because of Rory, he couldn't even wipe his eyes clear; water sluiced down his face and the constant blinking had a hypnotic effect. Out of sheer spite, the wind had risen and was lashing the rain straight into him.

What Jed really wanted to do was lie down in the heather and rest. He wanted it so badly, he was on the point of doing it, despite the horrible sensation that crept over him as the day darkened.

He was being stalked. He couldn't see it, but he could feel it. It was something in no particular hurry, something that was happy to wait and mock his efforts. *Hostile Intent,* he thought, remembering Pooh Bear and the Woozles and his mother's slurred voice. *And wanting Christopher Robin, and only because he liked him so much.* Jed wanted to giggle. He wanted to cry. He wanted to go home.

Oh, it didn't matter now. It occurred to him that

whatever the Hostile Thing was, he'd hate to pro-
long its fun at his expense. He might as well stop and
sit down with Rory on the bristly heather and wait.
He didn't even feel so cold anymore.

Just as his feet faltered, Jed heard something familiar. At first it was only a fragment of his imagination; then it was a rhythmic pounding beneath his
feet. He should run, he knew, but running belonged
to another time and place: a place where running
had seemed to matter more.

It lunged out of the dense rain right in front of
him: a snarling monster. In one heart-stopping moment, Jed realised it was a horse, its glaring eye as
black as a shark's.

Only a horse: oh yes, he remembered the horses.
He stopped, almost grateful, and held Rory close as
it cantered a languid circle around them. As it slowed
again to a flying arrogant trot, its circle tightening
like a noose, he had to turn to keep it in view. Rory
watched it too, not remotely bothered, and Jed even
heard the gurgle of his laughter as the horse's white
head snaked out to snuff at him, nostrils flared.

The creature backed onto its haunches with a
screaming whinny as it pawed the earth. Even that
didn't faze Rory, who smiled, reaching out to snatch
at the whipping mane. Shutting his eyes, waiting to
die, Jed turned his back on the horse to shield his
brother.

The hoof-blow never fell. Launching itself skywards, the horse leaped over their heads as Jed ducked
beneath its belly. Then it was gone, racing across the
drenched moorland, vanishing into the drizzle.

Gasping, Jed shivered with bitter cold and fear. But at least he was shivering. The sneaking warmth was gone and his limbs were all energy and pain, moveable again. He'd lost all sense of direction now, but there was nothing for it. He hooked Rory onto his hip and trudged on.

Adrenaline might have given him a boost, but that dark malevolence hadn't left with the horse. Jed's spine tingled. He didn't want to look round. He'd nearly died of fright when the horse came out of nowhere, but it was long gone. What remained was a lot worse.

The blood in his veins was thickening, his heart chilling and slowing. Horror was drawing closer; he couldn't put a name to it, and he thought it would be all right if only he could. But it wasn't possible. All he could think was what he'd thought before: that he should stop right here, deny it its fun. He wouldn't go on. It could have him.

He pulled Rory's face into his neck, feeling tremors of fear in the small body. Jed wished the baby far away, but it couldn't be done. It couldn't be helped. Nothing could.

The wind stopped just as Jed did, but the murky air stirred with something else. The something was circling now, waiting too; hoping for a little more fight, maybe. Nausea lifted Jed's stomach towards his rib cage and he seized the collar of Rory's fleece in his teeth, biting down. Deadening terror fogged his brain.

Something formed on the edge of his vision: blurred, but taking a kind of shape as it came out of the mist. Something like a man, or at least skin over human bones. Yellowish skin as cold and smooth as paper, as if all it could sweat was its suffocating fog of evil.

The thing was so hard to see, half-dissolving in the gloom. Jed screwed up his eyes, desperate to see it and desperate not to. He could make out that it was barefoot and bare-chested, that it wore trousers that hung on it as if on a skeleton, and a long flapping trench coat. It spat as it walked on, and the heather singed and withered where the spittle landed.

He'd seen this thing before. He didn't know how or where, but it didn't matter, because he was dead now. He could see just one part of it clearly: the gaping empty smile that opened in its cadaverous face, promising nothing but darkness and pain and horror.

He was afraid, so afraid. But he couldn't run, couldn't save Rory. He didn't mind what it did to him so long as it left Rory alone, but it wasn't going to; he knew it in his bones. He was going to watch Rory die and then he was going to die too.

'Jed . . .'

A bark-dry voice, desiccated as a long-lost corpse. It smiled at him, like an old and dear friend, and then it drew a curved blade out of its belt.

Seth

We saw the newcomer on the grey horse before we saw anything else, his hoofbeats thundering out of nowhere. Sionnach and I were riding hard, but the grey was coming from the opposite direction and it was a lot closer to the Lammyr, and to the shaven-headed boy trapped beneath its foot. The Lammyr wasn't paying attention to horse, man or youth; it held a small child by the throat as it tapped a blade thoughtfully against its cheek.

I gave a howl of rage, but I was too far away. I could do nothing; all the man on the grey horse could do was ride the Lammyr down, and that's what he did, knocking it flying, so that it lost its grip on the infant. As it flew from the Lammyr's clutches, one sinewy old arm caught the child, clutched it, cuddled it swiftly inside a filthy leather coat.

Springing to its feet, Slinkbone squealed with thwarted fury. It lunged for Jed, but the boy had already scrambled to his feet and was running, too scared and desperate even to scream. Sionnach got to him first, leaning down to seize him by the waist and haul him onto his own horse.

Slinkbone's curses stung my ears like a whip, but he'd dropped his blade and he wasn't so fast with the second one as he was with his mouth. The blue roan was on top of him as I caught the glint of it, but my sword was in my hand already, and I was angry enough to dodge and still be accurate. The Lammyr's neck was easier to slice than a willowherb stem, and its head spun away, farther and faster than I'd intended. I wheeled the roan, ducking reflexively as the thing collided with a boulder and exploded into fragments. Sparks of pale liquid flame erupted past me, but the roan was running hard, and none of it touched him. I reined him in, panting, grinning at Sionnach and then at Gocaman.

'Classy teamwork,' I said, and threw up.

'Ach, you should be used to them by now,' said Sionnach cheerfully, slapping my back.

I wiped my mouth, then pretended to spit at him so that he had to dodge. 'You ever get a bit of one on you, smart-arse?'

'You really want to know? Aye, I have. And I'm glad you weren't around to take the piss out of me.' He winked. 'Didn't get on your horse, did it?'

'Nah.' I checked the roan's shoulder and quarters again, just to be sure. 'If the sodding thing hadn't exploded, I could have kept that head. For a curse.'

Sionnach's face darkened as he scowled at me. 'Don't even joke.'

'Arse that you are, Murlainn.' Even Gocaman gave me a disapproving look. 'And I hope you cleaned your sword in wild running water. You know what will happen if you—'

'Do I look like an amateur? I used the burn.' No sense of humour, old Goc. Just because he was about five hundred years older than the rest of us, he still treated us like teenagers. I kicked the roan into a gallop, and heard the others speed up behind me.

Jed was silent on Sionnach's horse, but his quick frightened eyes hunted the moorland. Well, anything that came and killed us now would be a hundred times better than waiting in the sodden twilight for something vile, while the blood turned black and cold in his veins. I hoped he was grateful.

We went at a fast flying pace. The horses were all of the same kind, and their hooves barely touched down, and despite everything he'd been through, Jed was nearly dozing against Sionnach's back when we finally slackened to a walk. He'd stopped shivering at last, and his little brother was asleep in Gocaman's arms, mouth curled up at the corners. Having good dreams, then: astonishing. Gocaman had removed his glasses, and his eyes were wintry. Occasionally he would glance down at the baby, and his expression would cloud with bewilderment.

'Not much point us looking for Finn now,' I grumbled. 'Baby on board again.'

Sionnach was riding close to me now, and on the

horse's back behind him Jed was starting to look a
little more alive. He kept stealing frightened glances
at Gocaman, ten paces ahead now and crooning to
the baby.

'You okay?' I don't know why I bothered. Every
time I asked, he lied.

This time he didn't even answer the question. 'I
thought he was Laszlo?' he said in a voice like dust.

Ahead of us, Gocaman curbed his horse and turned
in disbelief. 'Laszlo?' He spat it out like a mouthful of
poison.

'Hell's teeth, Cuilean,' I said. 'What made you
think that?'

'I found his gun. In the water near his hut.'

'Oh, so it had to be his. Your train of thought got
derailed at Newtonmore. You'd better apologise to
Gocaman. He's very thin-skinned.'

'You are a lying toad, Murlainn,' sighed Gocaman,
then removed his leather hat, shook pooled rain off
it, and jammed it back on his head. 'But still. Laszlo.'
He humphed and shook his head.

Jed had gone a startling shade of red. 'I thought
you must've killed Mack. . . .'

Exasperated, Gocaman turned and rode back to
him. 'Laszlo killed Mack! Did the Lammyr make you
lose your mind?' A hand in a fingerless glove gripped
Jed's chin and turned his face, searching his eyes.
'No, you're sane. A little stupid but sane. All I do is
guard the watergate.'

'Not that you've been brilliant at that lately,' I
muttered.

Gocaman shot me a killing look. 'I was distracted. That Lammyr Slinkbone.'

Jed rolled his eyes, almost meeting mine. 'I was being chased by about fifty cops and half the social services. You must be easily distracted.'

I snorted, and Gocaman barked, 'Easily? Slinkbone fought me bare-handed! I should have known it was a feint, but I didn't, not till I felt the breach in the watergate. And then it slipped away from me like an eel, and it laughed as it went. And since you are still alive to ask: How did you come through the watergate?'

'I don't know, do I?'

Gocaman's throat rumbled. 'Was it you that sneaked through after Leonora a month ago?'

'Nope,' said Jed.

My blood ran so cold, the roan stopped beneath me. Swiftly I got my composure back and spurred it on. Sionnach raised his eyebrows at me.

'No?' Gocaman frowned. 'Well, two came after her.'

'Aye, we followed her yesterday?' Jed hesitated. 'Okay, two days ago, maybe. But not last month. That was somebody else, pal.'

'Ah, I see!' Gocaman's voice brightened. 'You do know time can flow differently here. It's capricious.'

'What?' The colour drained from Jed's face. And, I suspect, from mine.

Gocaman said airily, 'Oh, the time always evens out. Like water! That's what I thought when they built that great canal through to Ness and the west. The levels changing, up, down, but always you end up at the sea.' He nodded, pleased with his little metaphor. 'That's how the time is. Different on either side of the lock, see, but it always finds its level in the end.'

'The time. The time's different.' Jed's face was desolate. I wondered how long it would take for the actual horror to kick in.

'Yes. And even though I came after you straightaway, I had to call for my horse and ride like the devil. Even then I barely reached you. The Lammyr wanted you through on this side very badly, or its mistress did. She won't be too pleased that Slinkbone pissed away its advantage and got its head cut off.' He laughed. 'Ah, a Lammyr is its own worst enemy. If it hadn't played games, none of us would have caught up. Not before it had the last and best of its fun with you.'

Jed shivered, but despite his white face and drained eyes, I didn't think he was imagining what the Lammyr might have done. I stayed quiet, hoping rather pathetically that he'd forget I was there. I expected him to turn on me any moment now, but surprisingly, that didn't seem to occur to him.

Gocaman tucked his coat tighter around the baby. 'Anyway, why do you think I would have heard the pursuit of you? There was none. Two at the gate in a police car, and too afraid to set foot in the Fairy Wood.'

'They were all over the place. They were everywhere!'

'No, Cuilean, they were nowhere.' Gocaman tipped his hat brim back. 'I think perhaps most of it was in your mind.'

Jed opened his mouth, but shut it again when he couldn't speak.

'Don't be offended,' murmured Sionnach over his

shoulder to the boy. 'If it was all in your mind, that's only because someone put it there.'

Jed stared at Sionnach's back, but as if he couldn't remember who the man was, or how he'd got here with him. I should have looked in his mind, but the fact is I was too afraid to. I didn't want to know.

I kept my mouth shut. Not before time.

The land was wilder and steeper now, but we had left behind the worst of the weather, the darkness drifting sluggishly eastward. The bones of the mountains showed through, white rock scraped sheer by ancient ice. As the hours passed, the rock faces closed in, the passes deepening, and the hills faded to massive blocks of emptiness against a navy blue, starspeckled sky.

Gocaman had fallen back to ride between us, and I'd grown so used to the silence, I almost jumped when his low voice broke it.

'See, boy,' he murmured, 'there are humans who touch a Lammyr's desiccated heart. They fall in something like love. Skinshanks had a protégé, and he tired of him, and the protégé is dead, and that is all that happened with Mack. And he tired of Mack only because he found Nils Laszlo more interesting. And now he is bored even of Laszlo.' He gave a high laugh. 'And you thought I was Laszlo! I wouldn't be coming near you if I was.'

Jed scowled, but his curiosity was a blatant, sparking thing. 'You gonna tell me what that's about?'

'Just that he – ah! Murlainn, there.' Gocaman nodded towards a gash in the hills, a smudge of scrubby woodland made visible by starlight.

I stiffened. We'd found them; I knew they hadn't found Finn, but that wasn't what made my flesh crawl with cold dread. I should warn Conal now. I should tell him what must have happened, what made the boy Jed dark and cold with hatred.

I couldn't. I could barely contemplate it myself.

Not till we were much closer did I smell the damp smoke of a well-concealed fire; and then there was movement in the trees, and low voices, the stamp and snort of horses. The blue roan raised its head, gills rippling, and whinnied softly. Before we'd gone another five paces, the wraithlike shadow of Conal's horse emerged from the trees to greet it.

Jed was squeezing his fists so tightly, the knuckles were bone white. I still didn't want to go near his mind, coward that I was, but it's not as if I had to. A black-hot hatred was swelling inside him, swamping his muscles and blood – so relentless, it leaked from every pore of his skin. Being near him made me queasy, like being spattered in Lammyr blood.

We rode into the scrubby trees, ducking branches, the black horse nipping affectionately at the blue roan's withers. Conal took shape in the darkness, eyeing us with a certain wariness. Eili was at his shoulder, one blade out of its scabbard.

'Cù Chaorach,' called Gocaman softly. 'We've brought your wolf-pup.'

As the horses stamped and blew, Gocaman unfolded Rory from his coat, and Sionnach put an arm round Jed's waist and lowered him.

Jed let himself slide down. But his feet had barely touched the ground before he launched himself forward, slamming into Conal, locking his fingers round his throat. The boy and my brother crashed to the ground together.

'You never told me! *You never told me!*'

Conal's eyes were dilated almost black, his eyelight contracted to a pinprick. Air rasped against his constricted throat. 'Jed,' he croaked.

'Liar! Killer. *You let me stay too long.*'

Conal's fingers tugged at the boy's, but I knew if he wasn't holding back, he could have snapped those fingers and flung Jed off like a puppy. The weakness of it seemed to encourage Jed, and enrage him too. Tears started in his eyes as he crushed his hands tighter round Conal's neck, dug his fingers as hard as he could into flesh. Eili lunged for him with a bare blade, but was flung back by a psychic blow that could only have come from my noble-stupid-arsed brother. She floundered to her feet in soft leaf-mould, rubbing her stinging head as Jed screeched.

'Fight me! Fight me, you filthy *murderer.*'

The tiniest shake of Conal's head was all I saw, and I knew what I'd really known from the start: Conal wasn't going to fight him. The little thug was actually had a chance of killing my brother.

It had lasted mere seconds, and I had my mind back. I seized the boy from behind, twisting my fingers round his, prising them away from my brother's throat. I didn't care that I hurt him. As the last finger finally snapped clear, Jed gave a howl of frustrated fury and fell back. I wrapped my arms around him,

pinning his arms to his sides, holding him still, afraid
to let go. Conal propped himself up, gasping harshly,
rubbing the weals on his neck.

Torc and Sionnach seemed in shock; Eili, staggering forward, was splenetic with anger, while Gocaman, the baby in his arms, looked on with a detached
curiosity.

I growled in Jed's ear. 'Calm down, Cuilean.'

'You let me stay!' Jed snarled through his teeth and
jerked his head at Conal. '*He* knew I had to go back.
But he didn't take me. He didn't come. He stayed out
killing people till it was *TOO LATE.*'

I could have ripped the silence with my fingernails.

'Shut up,' I said. 'That's how it is. It could have happened however quickly you went back.' Still holding
him with one arm, I gripped his face between my fingers
and turned it so that Jed could do nothing but meet
my eyes. 'Whatever *it* is.'

'Let him go.' Conal's voice was hard in his throat.
'He might as well kill me.'

'Whatever it is,' I repeated, still desperately searching Jed's eyes, the fear rising.

My grip on Jed's jaw was so hard, he couldn't
look away, but gods, he could slap away my questioning mind with his burning rage. I could see nothing in his mind and he knew it.

~ *You'll know when I choose to tell you, you
bloody warlock.*

Only Jed heard my hiss of shock.

Testing his resistance, finding none, I let him go. Eili
took a menacing step forward as if daring Jed to touch
Conal again. Gocaman shifted the infant into the arms

of Torc, who looked at the baby, shrugged, and began to rock him with the gentle confidence of an expert.

'It's been a month!' Silent tears coursed down Jed's face, running into his mouth, leaking through his gritted teeth.

'Your mother,' I said.

'She's dead.'

Now the words were out; now it was real; now I could no longer hope or pretend. In that instant our minds collided again. The stench of vomit edged into my nostrils and there was an image in my head, a brown eye meeting mine, unblinking, dry as dust. With a sharp inhalation, I wrenched my brain clear of his.

'Jed.' Conal reached out a hand to him, but he slapped it away.

'She thought I was dead!' yelled Jed. 'She thought I'd been abducted or murdered or drowned in a ditch. She thought it was her fault! You see? You play your stupid war games and you don't care about the time and you see what happens? She thought I was *dead*.' He clawed at his skull. 'She was off her head anyway and you knew it. You sent her so far off it, she *forgot to stay alive*.'

The others stared as if it was Jed who was mad. All except Conal, who couldn't look at him at all. I had to do something, and now, because I should have seen this coming. I should have seen it coming for so long, and in so many ways. I gripped Jed's arm.

'Listen to me, Cuilean. This was always going to happen to your mother.'

Jed ground his teeth, trying to pull away.

'Seth.' Conal's voice was too tired to be a threat. '*Nach ist thu*. Be quiet now.'

'Keep out of it, big man. I was younger than him when I watched our father die on Alasdair Kilrevin's sword. Did I throw a tantrum? I kept my mouth shut and my head down because if I hadn't, I'd be dead too.'

'Murlainn.' There was a warning in Sionnach's voice, and pity too. 'Leave the boy alone.'

I ignored him. 'Listen, whelp,' I murmured. 'They'd have taken you and Rory in the end. At least she got to die a mother.'

'She died. Of you people.' Jed trembled with grief. 'And me.'

Torc got to his feet and put Rory into Jed's arms, then paused and gave Jed one of his rib-cracker hugs.

'Your mother didn't die of anyone but Skinshanks,' I said.

'What – ?'

'The dealer. That thing always enjoyed its work. Certainly enjoyed your mother.'

'You get out of my head!' he screamed.

'Okay.' It hardly seemed the moment to tell him I had no need to be in it.

'You and your Veil and your bloody world,' Jed spat. 'This is a *ghetto*. There's a real world out there where real people live.'

'And die in pools of vomit,' I pointed out.

Jed turned on me a look so filled with malice, I had to take a step backwards. Gripping Rory tight against him, he turned on his heel and strode off into the trees.

Jed

'Leave him. I said *leave him*!' Conal's bark was angry and clear enough for Jed to hear; then the woods thickened and closed in around him and all was silence.

He stumbled on until the glow of the fire faded altogether. To his right he could hear the gurgle of a burn as he scrambled uphill, and in his haste he was dislodging rocks underfoot. He didn't want to fall, not with Rory in his arms. Slowing, trying to control his thrashing heart, he edged away from the water. The darkness was absolute under the canopy of branches, but he trudged on up till he felt the ground level out.

He wanted to be far from them, as far as he could go. He hated the sight of the lot of them; they didn't care. He might vanish as easily and completely as Finn had, but Conal hadn't even enough remorse to send someone after him. Not that he wanted to be followed. *No*.

Hitching Rory up, Jed came to an uncertain halt. In the utter blackness he tuned in reluctantly to the sounds of the night, sounds that grew louder the longer he stood. Rustling. Cracking twigs.

Proper physical fear began to chill him.

Eventually he'd have to go back to them, if they didn't slink into the night and leave him and Rory to whatever fate caught up with them. He wouldn't put it past them, given that Seth didn't give a damn, Finn was probably dead and Conal couldn't even face him.

In the darkness below him, a shadow moved among shadows; a sound detached itself from the other night sounds. Jed froze, staring. Whatever it was, he'd rather see it. But though his stomach churned, the deadening instinctive terror wasn't there. It might be someone to hate and fear, but it wasn't a Lammyr.

Part of the darkness paled to a grey distinct shape. Yellow eyes glowed ghostly, but there was no aggression in that languid approach. Conal's wolf materialised from shadow, padded up to him and licked his hand.

'Liath.' Jed's voice trembled.

Her pale coat seemed to attract any light that was going, so that the wood didn't seem so dark anymore. Exhaustion overwhelmed him and he sat down suddenly, the tiredness a weight on the back of his neck. Liath lay down too, her big body curling around his, and Rory's hand moved convulsively in his sleep, clutching a handful of her fur.

Jed lay unmoving, listening to heartbeats and night sounds while the wolf's warmth seeped into them, and let himself wallow in pity for Rory, for his mother,

for himself. Softly growling, Liath washed his cheeks
with her tongue. Jed nestled Rory between his body
and her soft belly, putting his arm around the sleeping child and reaching for the wolf.

She could eat them in the morning as far as he
cared. That was how grateful he was for her bulk and
her warmth, her beating heart against his palm and
simply her company. His fingers laced into her fur,
clutching as tightly as Rory's, till he fell into a dream-
less sleep.

High hysterical laughter woke him. Jed's eyes opened
straight from sleep to a misty disorienting dawn. His
fingers were still stiffly entwined in Liath's coat, but
as he flexed them loose, he felt horrible emptiness
beneath his arm.

'Rory,' he mumbled. He barked it again, hoarsely.
'Rory!'

The laughter bubbled once more, not a dream
after all but Rory's high-pitched gurgling giggle. Sick
relief swept Jed as he pushed himself up and away
from the wolf, dizzy from the clinging sleep. The trees
seemed sparser than they had last night, and strips of
distant hills and sea were visible among the farthest
trunks. Rory was running through toddler-thigh-high
blaeberry scrub, falling on his face in it and clamber-
ing up again, shrieking with delight. He tripped forward into waiting arms and was swung in a circle.

Jed's gut clenched with anger and he staggered to
his feet. 'Put him down!'

Conal's laughter died as he turned. 'Sorry. Tried to

be quiet. We got carried away.' He winced as Rory
grabbed his cheeks and wrenched with all his baby
strength. 'Ow.'

'Who's we? There is no *we*. That's my brother. I
said *put him down*.'

Conal obeyed, prompting an irate yell from Rory.
'I wouldn't hurt him, Jed.'

'Oh, sure. Not *intentionally*.' Jed opened his arms
for Rory, but the boy screamed with rage. Turning
his back on Jed, he reached up, straining for Conal
with all his small being.

The first tiny dagger of many lodged in Jed's heart.
With an apologetic look, Conal passed Rory to him,
and a little grumpily, Rory hooked his arms around
Jed's neck.

'Faithless brat.' Jed hugged him as Rory gave him a
wet inexpert kiss. 'Let's find some breakfast.' Gloom-
ily he scanned the undergrowth, where a few wizened blaeberries clung on among the dark leaves.

'Does he eat rabbit?' Diffidently Conal held out a
metal tin. 'I don't know much about babies.'

'You don't know anything.'

'No.' Conal looked so humble, Jed's anger almost
wavered. There were livid marks on the man's neck,
already turning to ugly blotches of black and yellow.

Reaching for the tin, Jed let Rory seize fistfuls of
meat. Liath stretched and padded over to Conal, put
her muzzle in his palm and lay down at his side.

Staying angry was harder than Jed had expected,
and he couldn't concentrate on nursing his wrath for
the hunger that bit at his own stomach. 'As for this.'
Jed's face twisted in disgust as he pulled Rory's nappy

away from his backside and sniffed. 'Toilet training for you. Like today.'

'You hungry yourself? 'Cos I've got this,' said Conal, rummaging in the leather jacket that lay crumpled beside Liath.

It was stale supermarket bread, but the hunks of venison stuffed between the slices were very fresh and still warm, if slightly bloody. Hunger overcame Jed's reluctance, and he grabbed it. He'd planned to eat standing up, till Liath gave a commanding gruff, and Jed found himself dropping like an obedient pup to sit against her next to Conal.

Conal was quiet as Jed ate, studying a ragged nail. At last he bit it. 'I'm sorry. I really am.'

Jed stared at the remnants of his sandwich, appetite gone in an instant. 'I don't want your apology, do I? What am I meant to do with it?'

'No. Well, it's there if you ever do want it.' Taking the fingernail between his teeth, Conal ripped it across. 'Ow.'

Jed shook his head. 'You're how old? And you still bite your nails?'

'What I mean is, I'm sorry it happened.' Conal's words spilled out awkwardly. 'I'm sorry she's dead. She didn't deserve it.'

'You wouldn't know if she deserved it or not. Would you? You never knew her.' Jed held out his hands to Rory, who was rubbing his eyes again.

Conal drew his hunting knife and took the tip of it to his ragged nail, but only succeeded in nicking his forefinger. Wincing, he sucked the blood off it.

Jed stroked Rory's temple with his thumb.

'I'm waiting, by the way.'

'What for?' Conal sucked in annoyance at the cut.

'You could make me forget, couldn't you?' snapped Jed. 'Forget she's even dead.' His eyes were hot and stinging.

'I wouldn't do that to you.' There was new shock in Conal's voice, as well as irritation.

'No, you're a saint. Wouldn't hurt a feckin' fly.'

'Fine,' spat Conal. 'Listen, you complicate my life right now. You could give me some credit for not slitting your inconvenient throat.'

'Ha,' said Jed contemptuously.

'Meaning what?'

'Well, you could always try and sound *scary* or something.'

Conal drew an offended breath. 'So I'm not so bad, then? I wouldn't kill you and I wouldn't play about with your head. Okay? I don't like to do it. I almost never do it. Satisfied?'

Jed glowered at the trees.

Conal wiped the knife on a soft rag and sheathed it. 'Excuse my temper.' He rubbed his temples. 'It's my mother I'm angry at. If she wasn't dead already, I'd kill her.'

'You're pretty irrational for an old bastard.' Jed felt irrational that way himself, though, so the words got caught on the tears in his throat. He bit the inside of his lip, furious.

'Yeah.' Conal put an arm round his shoulder, and Jed let himself be pulled against him. Conal wore a soft dark blue jumper that smelt of horse, and Jed pressed his face into the hollow beneath his shoulder.

The arm tightened round him and he huddled into Conal's embrace, shivering. With his own arms around Rory, there was no other way to cover his eyes and save face.

With luck, it would pass for exhaustion and cold. Conal might never notice the tears soaking into his jumper, so long as he ignored the occasional silent but convulsive sob. Which, to give him credit, he seemed willing to do, even when the sobs grew louder and the hiccupping more violent. He was prepared to pretend not to hear Jed weeping for a very long time, and for that, Jed thought, he could forgive Conal pretty much anything.

Seth

If there was any kind of advantage to this colossal screwup, at least Conal had no choice now but to go to the dun. He could hardly go chasing armed horsemen around the countryside with a boy and a baby in tow. I had a bad feeling about Finn's fate, and I wouldn't have been surprised if she was dead already, but the only option was to regroup. However long that took.

I climbed the slope to where the trees thinned out, using the pretext of dunking my sword in a running burn again. Eili was up there on guard, and she had forbidden anyone to follow, and she glowered at me as I ducked under a stunted alder and rinsed the blade – no harm in making sure, though the blade felt strong enough – but even she must know it was time to get moving again. Reluctantly she nodded at the haphazard pile of humanity under one of the pines, and even smiled a little. Her fingers were wound into Liath's white mane.

I grinned, feeling almost paternally indulgent. Jed had a great wet patch on his jumper; the infant had peed on him and slept beatifically on in soaked miniature jeans, sprawled half across Jed's chest and half across Conal. Jed was cushioned against Conal's shoulder. Conal definitely had the worst of it, nothing between him and the peaty earth but flattened blaeberry bushes. All the same he was deeply asleep, his rib cage barely stirring. Jed woke as I watched. He risked a slight turn of his head, wrinkled his nose at his piss-covered clothes and saw me.

I said, 'Did you and my brother make it up, then?'

He made a face. 'I suppose.'

'Good,' murmured Eili with the sweetest of her smiles. 'Because if you try to throttle him again, Cuilean, I'll kill you.'

'They planned for that warp in the time,' I told him.

'True,' said Eili. 'Your mother was doomed. Nothing anyone could have done, not even Conal. It wasn't his fault.'

'Whatever,' Jed whispered fiercely. 'That's between me and him.'

'All right, Cuilean.' Eili averted her eyes, her pride wounded, and perhaps her sense of possession too.

'And by the way, what's wrong with my actual name?'

'Oh. Wouldn't feel—' Drawing one of her swords, Eili took a whetstone from her pocket and smoothed it lovingly along the blade. '—you know. Polite.'

'You'd hate me to call you Jed to your face,' I pointed out. 'Like we know each other or something.'

He gave me a startled look.

Eili tutted at me. 'Who rattled your cage, Murlainn? And don't you like your Sithe name, Cuilean? It suits you. Anyway, you're stuck with it.'

'Puppy,' he sneered in disgust. 'Torc says it means *puppy*.'

'Young Dog,' she said kindly. She turned the blade in the pale light, examining the edge. 'I suppose we should wake the others, hm?'

As if he'd heard her, the infant stirred from his sleep and squalled. Jed pulled him to his chest, hushing him, but Conal started awake and sat up.

Jed eased out of Conal's arms. Conal stared at him, and then at me, and then at Eili.

'Morning, Cù Chaorach.' Eili kissed him languidly on the mouth.

Conal pushed her away and got to his feet. 'I fell asleep,' he said in disbelief.

'Not before time,' said Eili, sheathing her sharpened sword. 'Don't worry, we kept watch.'

He tilted his head to the sky. 'It's late. *Eili*.'

'You needed to sleep.' Eili wore a self-righteous smirk. Conal looked as if he wanted to strike her, but she met his stare coolly, and in the end it was Conal who averted his eyes. His focus fell on Jed, who was pulling off Rory's wet jeans and making him pee again into the heather.

'We've lost another day!' Conal sounded frantic.

'And there's nothing we can do, and you know it,' I said. 'We can go to Kilchoran.'

'Seth's right, lover. Break the journey at the bothy. It's fine, perfectly secure, and then we can get to the dun faster tomorrow. There's nothing we can do for the girl by ourselves. And frankly, you'll think straighter with some sleep under your belt.'

Conal's jaw clenched as he turned to sweep up Rory and settle him on his shoulders. His tightened lips formed the word 'Women,' and I snorted.

Conal put his hand on the back of Jed's head and shook it lightly. 'If you stay with us, I promise I'll look after you both. Even if you don't think that's worth much just now. Okay?'

Jed nodded, not looking at him. 'Fine.'

'You trust him?' I murmured in Jed's ear. 'Because I suggest you do.'

'Yeah, whatever.'

'No. Trust him. I mean it.'

'I trust him, okay?' He set his face hard as he followed Conal.

Conal slung the infant down from his shoulders as soon as we got back to the others, and it instantly made a beeline for the crouching Sionnach, scrambling onto his back. Sionnach grinned and tumbled him off head over heels, but the child took no offence, shinning quickly back up onto his lithe shoulders.

'So what kept you?' asked Sionnach.

'Three hours' sleep,' said Eili in a self-satisfied voice.

'Three hours,' Conal echoed angrily. In small revenge it was Eili's pack he went to, helping himself to her spare jumper and tugging it over the baby's head. The soft blue jersey reached to the ground and then some, making him look like a small happy ghost. The boy giggled and grabbed for Conal's jaw again, eyes widening as he clutched the dark blond stubble.

Conal smiled at him. 'Rory, lad, I know. I'm dying for a shave and now I haven't got time.' He perched the infant on the black's withers, swung easily up behind him, then reached down for Jed. 'Where's Gocaman?'

'Gone back to his loch,' said Torc, shrugging.

I said, 'I asked him to stay, but you know the Watchers. Law unto themselves. Said he'd been gone too long already.'

'Good. He had.'

'He's getting on a bit, the grumpy old fart. He's going to be redundant anyway, if the Veil goes.'

Conal glared at me, and the black bared its teeth in aggressive sympathy. 'Don't even say that.'

I don't imagine I was the only one who noticed the baby's new lease on life. He seemed an awful lot healthier than he had, especially his voice box. As we rode west, he was working himself into a spectacular state. Stuck on the horse between Jed and Conal, he was demanding from one what he couldn't get from the other, and throwing a tantrum when he was thwarted.

'Can someone shut up the brat?' My teeth were gritted so tight, they hurt, and even Torc looked harassed.

'I'll deal with him,' muttered Eili.

'Like hell you will,' said Jed and Conal simultaneously.

'We never behaved like that when we were little,' Eili muttered to Sionnach.

'Oh yes, you did,' said Conal mildly, reining in the horse. 'He needs to run around a bit. And he needs a pee break.' Scooping up the child in one arm, he dismounted.

'He needs a slap,' said Eili. 'If we're being stalked, we're not exactly a challenge.'

'What are the swords for?' demanded Jed.

The growl in Eili's throat verged on laughter. 'Aye, Cuilean, it's that easy.'

Branndair and Liath kept the infant entertained for a while, Liath swatting the boy into the heather, Branndair rolling over to let him scramble across his belly. Even Eili seemed in a kindlier mood now that the squalling had been silenced. She pulled her whetstone from her belt pouch and reached up for her second sword. Her fingers didn't close on it, but clenched into a fist as a shudder went through her.

Conal's head whipped round. 'Eili?'

'Ach.' It was a dry rattle of disgust in her throat. She leaped to her feet, both swords drawn.

'Lammyr.' I drew my own blade off my back.

'Shit,' said Conal, on his feet beside her. 'Sionnach.'

Sionnach was already moving, running fast and low to the ground, leaping up to a low granite outcrop and hunkering down to scan the moor. The wolves, stiff-legged and snarling, were on their feet above the child, who had fallen onto his bottom, a comical expression of shock on his face. Grabbing Jed by the shoulder, Torc pulled him roughly back, and the wolves closed in again at his sides. Stunned, all Jed could do was lift his little brother into his arms.

The air around us was still, as if the entire moor was suspended between life and death. Not a bird or an animal stirred.

Sionnach tensed. 'It's in the rowans.'

'Coming now!' yelled Torc. 'To your left, Cù Chaorach!'

'*It's here.*' A flicker of whiplash motion, and I spun and lunged.

Missed the creep, but I didn't wait to regret it, springing sideways. Three spinning blades sliced the air and thunked into empty ground just beyond where I'd stood. Sionnach flung himself to the earth as a fourth flashed over him, and a lock of his black hair drifted to the ground.

Torc wasn't the world's fastest mover, but at least the bulk of him protected Jed and his brother. Snarling, he didn't even try to dodge when the Lammyr doubled back, whip-wire fast, but Conal intercepted it, his sword deflecting the flung blades. Metal met metal with a rasping ring, and Jed was gaping at three blades sunk half into the earth in front of him. They shimmered, quivering: small, curved and evil.

As the Lammyr leaped to clear Sionnach and reached the apex of its spring, it was clearly visible: a thin, strong, grinning thing, pale-eyed and sleek-haired. Not Skinshanks, I realised, spitting out my disappointment as it leaped clear of my sword again. It loosed a blade at Jed, who ducked, but he was saved by the Lammyr's wild aim, not his own pathetic speed.

Eili raised both her swords, slashing them down so that the Lammyr had to bend backwards almost double to dodge them. Licking colourless lips, it sprang back upright like a hazel twig. It took a running leap, slammed its feet into Eili's chest, then ran up her falling body to take once more to the air.

Conal met it mid-leap, twisting like a cat. The two figures spun off each other, grey light glinting on the edge of blades. Conal dropped to earth, awkwardly but on his feet, sword held high. The Lammyr fell like a stone, deadweight. A rattling sigh trickled from its lips before its bright hard eyes went dead.

Muscles rigid, lungs tight, we gripped our swords in sweating hands. Then Conal lowered his sword, flicking the coat distastefully aside to reveal a long slash the length of the Lammyr's naked torso. The path of the blade was so clean, it was barely discernible, only a line drawn on flesh that seeped a pale fluid, but the Lammyr had been cut almost in half. The edges of the wound sagged apart, the stain spreading fast, and Conal flicked the coat back over it.

Jed stepped forward, trembling. The Lammyr's eyes were open, staring directly at him, and the smile was still on its face.

'See that?' I coughed and spat. 'They love death so much, they even love their own.' There was a long gash on the front of my T-shirt, I realised, and a red line on the flesh beneath. Annoyed, I rubbed the cut with my arm, smearing blood.

Conal pulled Eili to her feet. She was still gasping, winded, but she spat at the corpse. 'Carrion. It was aiming for the child.'

As Torc sheathed his broadsword and held out his arms, Jed gave the baby up to him, shaking too much to hold him any longer. Rory's frozen silence melted into sobs of shock, and Torc handed him on to Conal while Jed leaned forward and hung his head down, retching.

Liath's maternal tongue lashed his face. Wincing, he shoved her away and staggered to his feet, trying to reclaim his dignity. As Conal passed the baby on into his arms, Jed gave him a dry look and spat remnants of bile. 'Get you, flyboy.'

'My lovely gossamer wings are under the shirt.' He laughed, then gestured at Sionnach's arm. 'Sionnach, do something with that, will you?'

Sionnach glanced down at his arm, which was pumping bright scarlet blood. Sitting down suddenly, he let Eili take hold of it and slide her fingers deep into the gash in his flesh. He stared groggily at the infant.

'You know what?' he said. 'It went for the boy, not the baby.'

I ran a finger thoughtfully along the edge of my sword. 'I think you're right.'

'Why? A baby's such easy prey. *Ow.*' Sionnach flinched as Eili's fingers tightened hard inside his arm. Simultaneously, she reached into her pack with her left hand and tossed a wet rag to Conal.

Conal caught it. 'Ach.' He wiped mucal fluid from his sword.

'That won't do your blade any good. I wet the rag in a burn, but it's not the same. Get it into running water as soon as we reach some.' Eili turned Sionn-

ach's arm. The wound was an ugly raised ridge, but
it was closed, the bright blood no longer flowing, and
she pulled his sleeve back down. Sionnach got stiffly
to his feet, and kissed her bloody hand.

Conal was still eyeing his sword with suspicion.
'Um. I don't think it's too bad, Eili. Sionnach, if
you're okay, we shouldn't hang about here.'

'Too late,' said Torc.

'What?'

He nodded towards the dip in the hills. 'It was
only an outrider.'

It wasn't an attack; we could tell from the casual way they ambled down the glen towards us, three of them on horseback, and one Lammyr on foot. Skinshanks kept pace easily with the riders, its coat flapping loose around its yellowish torso, the blades at its belt glinting in the weak winter sun. It grinned and gave me a little wave.

We were on horseback to meet them, blades unsheathed but lowered. Conal's teeth were clenched so hard, it made his stubbled cheeks cadaverous. It occurred to me again that I'd seen my brother look a whole lot better.

Cuthag reined in his grey mare five yards away, the other two riders waiting just behind him. Skinshanks sauntered forward and folded its arms. I bared my teeth at it.

~ *I'll have you,* I told it.

~ *I'll be delighted, Murlainn!*

Cuthag encompassed us all in a broad smile. 'Cù Chaorach. This is a pleasure.'

I blew out a bored breath. 'Oh, get on with it.'

'I believe Slakespittle had a word earlier?' Smugly Cuthag eyed my torn T-shirt.

'About half a word, before Conal severed its voice box.'

Skinshanks pouted at that. 'Murlainn, you can be so uncivil.'

'What do you want, Cuthag?' Conal spoke through his teeth.

'Easy. I'm here to return your goddaughter.'

Conal went pale then, and lifted his blade to point it at Cuthag's throat.

'Alive, of course. Alive and unharmed. Relax.'

I raised my eyes to the sky. 'Aye, right.'

~ *Shut it, Seth.* 'What's the catch?'

'Catch? There isn't one. Kate offers you a straight swap.'

Conal's brow creased. He gave me a glance. My spinal cord filled with ice.

'She wants me, she can have me,' he said in a low voice. 'But I want Finn out of—'

'Oh, get over yourself, Cù Chaorach. It isn't you she wants.'

Cuthag had been *so* looking forward to that line. I smiled at him. 'How long did you practise that one in the mirror?'

A red stain suffused Cuthag's neck; one of the horsemen behind him bit his own cheeks and managed to remain impassive.

'Spit it out, Cuthag.' Conal sheathed his sword with an air of utmost boredom.

Cuthag tilted his chin, swelling with self-importance. He nodded arrogantly at something behind us, and Conal blinked and turned to look. We all did.

Jed stood there, his baby brother in his arms, eyes flickering from one to the other of us. I frowned, glanced back at Cuthag.

'The infant.' He smiled. 'He'll do.'

'What?' Conal stared at Cuthag as if the git had grown cow-horns.

He shrugged. 'The baby. No contest, I'd imagine. That scrawny brat for Aonghas's daughter.'

'Why?' was all Conal said. But it was drowned out by Jed, who took a sharp step backwards, arms tightening round his brother.

'You can go fuck yourself!'

'I imagine he has to,' I murmured.

'You're such a diplomat, Murlainn,' said Eili sweetly. 'But that's diplomacy for you. It's nothing without a little truth.'

She and Sionnach had backed their horses, barely perceptibly, to protect the boys. Conal, on the other hand, nudged the black forward to bring him close to Cuthag. Torc was playing with his broadsword: flip-and-catch, flip-and-catch. I smiled. Cuthag had been in the lines the day Torc took Fearchar's head off, and memory lit his eyes with fear.

'You'd be wise to hand him over,' he gritted. 'We'll take him anyway. This way, you get Aonghas's witch-spawn back in one piece.'

Slowly Conal turned once more to study Jed,

whose forehead was pricked with sweat. He glanced
back at Cuthag, jerked his thumb in the boys'
direction.

'What the boy said.'

Cuthag's features stiffened with rage, but the Lammyr smiled cheerfully. 'Ah, Cù Chaorach! I was hoping that would be your attitude.'

'Quite.' Cuthag recovered his sneer. 'You know
how a Lammyr loves a slow hanging.'

Conal closed his eyes, languidly drew his sword
again, and flicked its point to Cuthag's throat. I saw
the man's flesh convulse as a tiny bead of blood welled
up. Conal's eyes snapped open.

'You touch her,' he said quietly, 'I'll skin you from
the feet up.'

I nodded, examining Cuthag from head to trembling toe. 'He'd look much better as a bridle.'

'Several bridles,' said Eili, shutting an eye to measure him.

Cuthag spat, kicked his mare hastily into reverse.
His dignity took a blow when the startled animal
brushed against the Lammyr and shied violently.

Recovering his balance, he snarled. 'I wouldn't
touch her with a spear-shaft. I'll get somebody else
to put the noose on her neck. I'm shocked, mind you.
That you'd let the girl die for the want of a half-
breed runt.'

My head jolted round so abruptly, Conal must
have heard the click. But he gave no sign. 'What?' he
whispered.

'You heard me. The infant's a mongrel. Probably won't even live; you know how it is. Oh, Cù

Chaorach, it's a poor chance, getting live spawn from a full-mortal.' An irrepressible grin lit Cuthag's face; suddenly he was all joy and triumph and delicious hatred. 'The Lammyr have an expression for that rarity. Don't you, Skinshanks?'

It hissed, and smiled.

'Blood of a stone.'

Time slowed to a lurching crawl. I might as well have been a stone myself. I didn't want to look at Conal, but I had no choice; my own blood had turned black and slow in my veins, and if I didn't orient myself by him, I might lose contact with reality to the point of falling off the roan. But Conal's skin had turned ashen; his cheekbones beneath it jutted as if they'd break through; even his lips were dry and white.

It was Cuthag's turn to close his eyes, tasting the moment. He licked his lips.

'You promised Kate four centuries ago you would bring her the Stone,' he murmured. 'Do it. And you may still have your girl.'

He flicked the mare's reins and turned, presenting his unprotected back to us. I itched to bury a blade in his spine; but of course he knew I couldn't. None of us could, even as they rode away with all the contempt of easy victors. Skinshanks was the last to turn, giving me a final grin and a tip of its lank forelock.

My brother didn't move or speak till we'd watched the delegation dwindle in the distance, then vanish back into the gash between the hills. He didn't stir even after that; he might have been dead, for all the expression that crossed his face. All that moved was his hair, blustering in the rising breeze.

Somehow I hoped we could stay here, like this, forever. I wished we could be turned to stone, every last one of us.

But Conal moved at last. One fist clenched and flexed; something shuddered through his facial muscles. Then he swung down off the black horse and walked back to Jed. Avoiding our eyes, Eili followed him, her blade still naked.

Jed backed away. Conal didn't smile and he didn't speak. With two swift steps, he had the baby out of Jed's arms.

'Give him to me!' Jed cried. He'd have flung himself at Conal again, but I seized his arm and wrestled him back.

Flailing his free arm, Jed whacked me hard on the ear as he tore a fistful of my hair. I snarled in stupid superficial pain, then twisted his hand high and savagely behind him, doubling him over. I made sure it hurt so much, he couldn't speak. I had no wish to hear anything he had to say.

Not that I cared if he hated me. After all, I knew what was coming. I wanted him to hate me.

The baby gazed down in astonishment as Conal held it high and stared into its eyes. It laughed at this mad new joke and kicked in delight. Jed kicked too, lashing a foot savagely back at my shin, but I dodged with ease and twisted his arm farther till he gasped in pain.

Conal lowered the child gently to the ground. It

lunged forward to hug his knees, and Conal raked trembling fingers through the fine blond hair. 'He's hiding it.' Conal was dead-eyed and pale. 'Gods, Seth. Eighteen months old and he's hiding it.'

I swore too, much more profanely, then laughed, freeing Jed to stumble forward and snatch up his brother. 'So, Conal. The old witch's prophecy wasn't literal. Did your sainted mother consider that at all?'

'You know she didn't,' said Conal bitterly. 'I did; you did; but we were upstart boys and she was ancient and wise, wasn't she? Stones, spells, witchcraft, that was all she cared about. Oh, no full-mortal would have it in them to save *us*. Questioning her was heresy.' His gaze was tormented. 'She laughed in my face, Seth. And went back to her rocks.'

I looked away. I didn't want to witness his humiliation.

Sionnach gave a long, sad sigh, rubbing his healed arm. 'The child isn't full-mortal, though.' He glanced at Jed, eyebrows arched. 'Is he?'

'I don't know what you're on about. Leave him alone!'

'Too late,' I murmured, sick at heart. 'Too late for that.'

Eili's laughter was horrible, with all the warmth of an ice floe. 'Four centuries, Cù Chaorach! Four hundred years you've gone away from me to the other side, and you might as well have stayed by me, for your precious Stone wasn't even born for most of it.'

'Eili.' Conal's voice was as cold as hers. 'Shut up.'

'No, but just think,' she went on, her smile tight and intent. She had the look of someone ripping the scab off an awful wound. 'Your own child could have taught him swordplay.'

Conal didn't even look at her, but the glare he turned on Jed was terrible. 'Where did he come from? Who was his father?'

'I don't know!' yelled Jed. 'I doubt my bloody mother knew!'

There must have been someone!

Jed opened his mouth and shut it again. Self-preservation would stop him from contradicting Conal, if he had any brains and wanted to keep them.

But I sensed something else inside him: a stirring knowledge, like something horrible rising up from dark water. It rippled on the surface of his mind, buffeting mine. It was something he knew, something he'd forgotten for a long, long time.

Oh, hell.

'We're close to Kilchoran,' I blurted. 'It's protected, Cù Chaorach.'

'True,' said Torc, visibly grateful for a distraction. 'They can't come near us there. Keep what you have to say to one another till then.' He eyed Eili long and hard. 'And there's some things that should never be said at all.'

I could see what Torc could not: the gleam of tears tracking down her cheek. But her fingers smoothed them lightly away and drew a mask of angular hardness back across her face.

We rode on; we had no choice. We rode through birch and rowan and a deepening darkness, our horses so close, their flanks were almost touching. The miles melted into each other, and time blurred;

we were in shock, I suppose. Conal and I were ten yards ahead of the rest when we reached the bothy in the glade.

The stone walls of Kilchoran were just discernible among the rowans. Sionnach held the plank door open as Torc took the baby gently from Jed and carried him inside. I knew I couldn't join them; not yet. Conal walked on into the copse of ghostly trees that clung to the nearby rocks, and he expected me to follow. I knew that. Oh, what I would have given to defy him.

But it was out of my hands now. Everything was.

The moon was pale and cold, its light unforgiving. What a coincidence.

Conal was outlined in starlight, the silver pinpricks of his eyelight frightening in his shadowed face. I walked closer than I dared, and faced him. Oh, those bright, hard, pitiless eyes, heated by a spark of remembered love: the worn, hard-bitten love of centuries. Maybe it was the last dying spark.

He drew back his hand and struck me brutally on the side of the face.

My head snapped sideways with the blow. I staggered, but I didn't fall.

'Tell me,' he said quietly.

Shaking my head slightly, I lifted it to face Conal again, but I didn't retaliate. All I could do was let him in.

We stared at one another in silence for a very long moment. No point keeping anything back. A muscle twitched beneath his hollow eyes, but he said nothing of what he saw. Nothing. He didn't have to.

'And now,' he said expressionlessly, 'tell Jed.'

'Naturally.' Was that my voice? I didn't recognise it: so cold and hard and don't-give-a-damn. I stared my brother full in the face, searching his eyes till he was forced to avert them. He swore again, rubbed a hand down his face.

'Seth.' Hesitantly he extended a hand towards me. All I did was look at it.

Conal jerked his head upwards to throw a curse at the night sky. He turned and walked away from me, back towards the bothy. The black horse fell in at his back, its shark's eye swivelling towards me as it passed.

Then the horse and my brother and my past were gone, taking all that I ever was.

Jed

'Kate's known this for a long time. She'll be coming for your brother.'

Jed stared at Sionnach's kind, scarred face. 'She can't have him.'

Seth laughed bitterly. 'It won't be up to you, Cuilean. That's one thing you can be sure of.'

Jed knew he could have loved Kilchoran, in different circumstances. From outside it was nothing more than a down-at-heel barn; inside, it was one stone-walled space with soaring rafters and a worn timber floor. They all lay wakeful except for Rory, who snored gently in a nest of blankets. The only light came from the far end, where birch logs burned in a vast stone fireplace. In the flickering shadows, no-one's face was readable anymore.

'We have to cover good ground tomorrow,' said Conal. 'I barely trust this place for one night.'

'It's fine here,' soothed Torc. 'We'll start early, ride hard all day.'

'Don't waste energy worrying, Cù Chaorach,' said Sionnach. 'Kilchoran's safe. Get some sleep.'

Jed said nothing, only crouched, hugging his knees and gnawing his knuckles. All he could do was wait for his chance to run.

'Be ready to leave an hour before dawn,' said Conal, and the discussion, such as it was, was over. Rising, he buckled his sheathed sword onto his back, then reached down and took Eili's hand. She rose to her feet without a glance at him. Wordlessly Conal opened the barred wooden door and she preceded him into the night and the darkness.

Left behind, Liath whimpered, but all human conversation died. Sionnach and Torc turned over on their makeshift beds and settled to sleep. Branndair lay close to Seth, but it was Liath's skull the man caressed, and his gaze lingered on the door through which Conal and Eili had disappeared.

'You've this to look forward to, Cuilean,' he murmured. 'Ah, women. All the fun of falling out is in the making up. And I should think it'll take them a *very* long time to make this one up.'

Wincing slightly, Seth touched his left eyebrow, where a crust of blood had formed on the cut. The flesh around his eye was already swelling; everyone in the bothy had conspicuously avoided mentioning the state of his face. Jed shook his head slowly, and Seth grinned.

'You can't make us out at all, can you, Cuilean?' Casually Seth leaned across to Sionnach and found his left temple with his fingertips. He shut his eyes, looking momentarily unsteady, then shook his fingers as if shaking off static.

'I wouldn't want to,' said Jed. Scowling, he watched Seth stand up and step over Sionnach, then crouched to lay his hand on the back of Torc's head.

'That wasn't your mother's attitude.' Reeling very slightly, recovering his balance, Seth sat down close beside him.

'Shut up about my mum.' Jed glared at him and shuffled sideways. 'You don't know her. Didn't. Know her.' He blinked hard.

'Oh, but I knew her quite well. I was her lover for four years.'

Now Jed knew how Eili must have felt, when the Lammyr slammed its feet into her chest.

'No. You weren't.'

'Yes. I was.' Seth smiled.

'No.' But he was, he was *there*, on the edge of Jed's mind. The familiar ripples were stirring again, and this time Jed could do nothing to hold them back. The waves swelled, threatening to drown him, as a hideous shape hauled itself out of the dark water of his subconscious. He squeezed his eyes shut, then snapped them open again.

'I'd have known!'

'You did know.' Delicately, Seth touched his cut eyebrow again. 'You just didn't take much notice of me. Remember?'

'That's not possible!' Jed put a fist to his mouth.

Then, as if a withholding wall had been breached, the pressure collapsed over him like a wave. The swirling murkiness washed from his brain; the waves subsided and he could breathe and hear and see again. The memory was like crystal. He did remember.

'No. No, *no*.'

Seth was there whenever Jed came home: his eyes on Mila, and his hands on her too. Seth's hands on her waist, or touching her face, or trickling her long pale hair through his fingers. He'd be there into the late nights. He'd be there when Jed woke in the mornings.

Jed trembled violently. 'I remember you leaving. I remember I wasn't sorry to see you go.'

'No, you weren't.' Seth shrugged. Idly he fiddled with the rip in his T-shirt, examining his new scar. The blood was dry, a thin blackened ridge across his abdominals. 'You never liked me. But your mother and I understood each other. We were happy for a while.'

'I don't believe you!'

'That's your prerogative.' Seth shrugged. 'But that last day, as I left . . . you won't remember me taking hold of the back of your neck. You were mighty surprised at the time, but you won't remember.'

Jed shook his head, wordless.

'There was always a weird connection between us, you know. Our minds must be a good fit; I always knew my way around yours. I didn't much like that, but I got used to it.'

'If you've messed with my brain—'

'Call it that if you want. That day, the day I left your mother, I found the Veil in your head and I pulled it back for you. I shifted your perceptions. Rather a lot, actually. I hope you're grateful, because it wasn't easy.'

'Screw you! And screw your precious Veil.'

'I expect it already is, practically speaking. Anyway,

I had to obscure your memories to compensate. Rub myself out of them a bit more – even the parts of me you remembered. Fact is, it was way too easy to mess with your mind. I played with it so much, I think I've given you immunity. It's very hard to affect your brain now. We still have the link, but I can't do a lot with it anymore. Except know what's going through that hot head of yours.'

'How dare you. *How dare you*.'

'I told you, you ought to be grateful. And you will be.' The man's eyelight was like a frost-burn. 'But I did pull the Veil aside for you. It's why you've been there for our Finny. You could see her better than other people do.'

'You wouldn't do that.' Jed blinked at him in disbelief. 'Why would you do that for Finn?'

'I didn't do it for Finn.'

'What?'

'I did it for someone who needed looking after. Far more needy than Finn, believe it or not. You see, it was essential you paid him plenty of attention.' Seth smiled innocently. 'Even his own mother couldn't quite make him out.'

'Oh, God. Oh. God.' Jed's voice when he spoke was barely audible. 'So why didn't you do it for her?'

'Ah, too late. I got tired of walking in to find her looking for a vein. Tired of wiping blood off the wall before you got home, though I don't know why I bothered, since you're not stupid. I wasn't enough for her, but then you weren't either, were you? The drugs were more important than either of us.'

White rage and grief, creeping up Jed's spine to the

nape of his neck. Somehow, it was reflected in those frigid grey eyes that held his. Jed watched Seth like he'd watch a cobra with its hood up.

Seth shook himself, and smiled more easily. 'Mila was crumbling in front of my eyes, and you were a much better bet. Besides, I had my work cut out keeping her hidden.'

'You . . .'

Seth's smile mutated into a smug grin. 'Yes, I helped; course I did. Do you seriously think you'd have escaped the authorities' notice as long as you did if it hadn't been for me? It's a small town! That nosy bitch of a neighbour was quite a challenge, let me tell you. As for you and your endless thieving . . . oh, you made life difficult.' He watched Jed's eyes very intently. 'You were good, you really were, but you weren't quite as good as you thought you were. Say, "Thank you, Seth".'

Jed put his head in his hands.

'Okay, I'll do it.' Seth widened his eyes and mimicked a child. '"Thank you, Seth".'

Jed looked back up at him, hands over his mouth. He wanted to be sick, but he was too stone-cold.

'Jesus,' he choked at last.

'She was lovely, your mother. Could have been the saving of me. Ah, well. Good mother too, wasn't she?' A hint of bitterness entered Seth's voice. 'To you, if not to my son.'

'Yes,' whispered Jed. He stared at Seth, so beautiful and heartless. His mother had fallen for that; loved it, *followed it*. 'You're the reason we left the commune.'

'Yup. Mack threw her out when she got involved with me. She knew what I was, by the way. She was scared of our child even as it grew in her belly. Scared of that sickly thing! Afterwards, she almost forgot the boy existed. But she never forgot me. I wasn't enough,' Seth said again, viciously, 'but she *never* forgot.'

Jed said, 'You should have left her alone.'

'Of course I should.' Seth lifted one shoulder idly. 'But I liked your mother. I liked her a lot. Perhaps I loved her a little, if I'm capable of such a thing.'

'No,' said Jed.

Seth ignored that. 'I did try to put a stop to it.'

'Yes. You left her. And you know what she ended up with, don't you?' Jed was too empty to feel it; his soul was nothing but an echo chamber. 'After you dumped her? That *thing* came after her. Because of you.' Jed raised his eyes to Seth's. 'You know what you left her to and you did nothing. Skinsh . . .' His voice died. He couldn't finish the name.

Seth gazed into the fire. When he opened his mouth again, it was as if he hadn't heard.

'She got pregnant. Believe me, no-one was more surprised than I was.'

'You stupid bastard.'

'Hah! I suppose that does sound stupid to you, but it's not easy for a Sithe. I panicked. A half-breed child! I didn't think he'd survive long. They don't. How was I to know I'd fathered Leonora's precious Stone? And I didn't know, not till Cuthag came today.'

'You knew you were his father. You knew that and you left us—'

'I know. But you're a boy who spends his life running. Imagine how much faster you'd run if some benighted soothsayer had laid out your life five hundred years in advance.' Thoughtfully Seth examined the lifeline on his palm. 'I wonder if all her prophecies are going to be so blatantly self-fulfilling? I don't suppose I would have fathered the child if we hadn't been in the otherworld for so long. Wasn't the first time I'd got lonely.'

Jed didn't care. He remembered that day he'd met Finn and taken her home, the way Mila's eyes had widened. Tugging on his sleeve as he left, whispering in his ear as Finn went ahead of him down the stairwell.

Jed, that girl. I know who she is. If you're ever in trouble? Go to her uncle. He's a good man.

'Oh, God,' he whispered bleakly. 'She told me to go to you. I thought she meant Conal.'

Seth eyed him quizzically, then shrugged. 'Doesn't everyone?'

'What?'

'She *should* have meant Conal.' The man grinned. 'Strange, isn't it? Why not Conal? He'd be a much more suitable sire. And much as he loves Eili, he has not been faithful for four hundred years.'

'Conal.' Jed's heart contracted. 'Does he know?'

'Only just.' Irritably, Seth touched his eye again. 'How shall I put it? He wasn't happy. But it was time I owned up. He didn't know about me and your mother, you see. I can still keep secrets from my brother, and he has far too many scruples to probe against my will.'

'He's got too much respect for you,' spat Jed.

'Oh, way too much. He's so up front and honest! Well, he knows now, and so do you. He was adamant about that, by the way, so blame him if this is too much information. What does it make me, I wonder? Your uncle-in-law? Stepfather once removed?'

'It makes you a—'

'No.' Seth parried Jed's flying fist. 'No, you won't do that to me twice. You'll find no-one ever does anything to me twice, Jed. Now, let's not wake the neighbours, shall we?'

Jed staggered to his feet. Helplessly, he turned to Sionnach and Torc, but as far as he could tell, they weren't breathing. Liath sprawled on the timber floor, tongue lolling, her flanks barely rising and falling.

There was no help for him here. Grabbing his sweater, he twisted it, wishing it was Seth's neck between his fingers.

He wanted to say something, anything, but there was no way he could curse Seth foully enough. All he could do was turn on his heel, and run from the bothy.

Seth

The flames were dying and the fire was cold; I felt the bite of frost, a breath of the winter beyond the walls, but I knew it was imagination; I knew it was all in my heart and soul.

I put out a hand for Branndair to lick. He waited a long reproachful moment before he finally shuffled to me, nudging his head under my hand. The ends of my fingers were numb; I raked them into his thick neck-fur, trying to absorb his warmth so I could feel them again. But no mortal creature could give that kind of life.

He laid his black head on my lap, mourning the loss of me.

'Well, my only love,' I said. 'Will you come with me anyway?'

PART FOUR

Jed

Half-turning on his heel, Jed hesitated. Torc had said the bothy was protected. Even for Rory's sake, he didn't have to be in the same room as Seth.

He swallowed, hardly daring to examine the darkness. The wind was wild in the rowans, covering God knew what other sounds. And Lammyr could move fast, but Conal and Eili were out here somewhere. They'd head back to the bothy if there was any danger, and he'd see them.

Across the grass, twenty metres from the door, there was an outcrop of grey rock and a copse of rowan saplings. Tugging his jumper on, Jed squeezed into a cranny in the rock, keeping the door in view, his mind buzzing with obsessive hatreds. He was in no danger of falling asleep, so all he had to do was last out the chilling cold and discomfort till morning.

And then what? He didn't know, he *didn't know*. Somehow he had to get Rory away, but there was no-one to trust. Finn was gone. He loathed Seth so fiercely, he felt his heart might burn to a shrivelled cinder. Conal was a stranger in the grip of madness. The rest? They were fanatically loyal to Conal. If they were still alive.

Jed tucked his hands into his armpits to warm them. He could feel his pulse, strong, hard and hating: the beat was rhythmic, regular, the ticking of his own life. Lowering his head, he concentrated on it, on the repetitive thrum of his blood, low and ceaseless. Low and ceaseless . . .

Mila touched his jaw with her fingertips, smiling. His head jerked up, and in the sudden silent blackness, he knew he'd been dreaming. Jed shook himself.

Heart slamming, he stood up. The bothy door stood open, the blue roan motionless beside it. The shadow of a man rested something on its withers, then hoisted himself onto its back and took a blanket-wrapped bundle in his arms.

Jed squirmed out from his hiding place as the horse paced forward. Its rider glanced back, and so did the black wolf at his heels.

'Seth!' As Jed began to run, the horse's stride faltered, just long enough for him to run alongside. 'Seth, what are you—?'

Seth's white teeth flashed in the darkness, and Jed stared at the bundle he clutched against him. A small familiar snore was just audible, muffled by the depths of the woollen blanket. Jed clutched at the child, but Rory was out of his reach, snuggled into Seth's T-shirt. Seth had changed the torn one for a new one, Jed saw, staring at the clean black cotton and wishing, with all his heart, that the Lammyr's blade had gone six inches to the left.

There were hard lines at the corners of Seth's mouth. 'I wondered where you'd got to. Thought you'd be asleep by now. Assuming you weren't dead.'

Jed twisted back towards the bothy, thinking of Torc and especially of Sionnach and the way he slept like a cat, alert in an instant at the smallest disturbance. 'What have you done?'

Seth rolled his eyes and sighed. 'They're all fine. Only sleeping. I do hate confrontations. Besides, I don't want anyone to get hurt. I'm fond of them.'

'Conal . . .'

'Is too busy sorting out his personal life to worry about us.' Seth glanced into the woods. 'He's not looking, and he won't be back for a long time.' He smiled. 'Anyway, he trusts me.'

Jed's heart crashed painfully in his chest. 'I don't understand.'

'You never have.' Seth's face was almost kind as he urged the horse forward. 'Have you?'

Jed glanced back once at the bothy, despairing, then began to jog to keep up. 'What are you doing?' he panted. 'Where are you taking Rory?'

'Where he can do most good.' Seth's perfect calmness was what finally sparked Jed's panic. 'And where most good can come to him.'

'Why?' shouted Jed. He didn't care why. Anything to delay Seth till Conal came back.

'Why? Because he's the Bloodstone. Because I have a right to him. As much as you and, let's face it, probably more.'

Jed threw himself at the roan. Swinging its face towards him, it bared its teeth and was restrained only by Seth's hand.

'Give him to me! Give him back!' Jed grabbed the reins behind the bit and hung on for his life. Dodging the snapping jaws, he brought the roan to a snorting, slavering halt by the weight of his own body.

'Oh, of course. As if.' The sinews in Seth's forearms stood out as he fought to control the horse's rage. Snagged between his arms, nestled against his chest, Rory didn't even stir.

'You've no right! You didn't help him get born! You didn't even wait to see him!'

'I've warned you before, be wary of the horses. So this is for your own good.' Seth's foot lashed out, catching Jed a savage blow on his ear with a Timberland boot. As he staggered in pain, Seth seized him by the back of the neck, dragging him towards him. Jed was still hopelessly off balance when Seth struck him hard on the side of his head.

Flung a good distance, Jed landed against a heather tussock, the air knocked out of his lungs and his skull ringing. He heard the beat of hooves goaded to a canter, and he heard Seth's departing words as if from a great distance.

'Your own good. And your brother's.'

The world did not make sense for what felt like a very long time. There was too much chaos in his head, too much confusion, and – damn Seth to hell – there was too much pain. After a while he couldn't measure,

Jed rolled onto his side, put his head in his hands and let himself sob, softly and very briefly.

And that was enough of that.

He dug his fingers into mud and leaf mould, finding purchase and pushing himself groggily to his feet. He staggered; caught his balance. For a moment he stood in the wild wind, swaying a little. Above and around him, the noise of the trees was huge and hostile.

Conal. He could wait for Conal; except that Conal's rage and madness had set his brain on edge with fear. Jed had crept after the brothers earlier that night; had seen Conal strike Seth viciously, had seen him curse the sky.

Trust him, Seth had said; but what was Seth's word worth? He'd taken Rory. Conal wanted the boy too, and why should either of them give him back to Jed if they were insane enough to think he was important to them?

Hell no.

Flicking one last glance back at the bothy, letting one spasm of regret tighten his gut, Jed turned on his heel, and went after Seth.

Winter was days away. Jed felt it like a massing presence beyond the horizon, a building stormcloud. It was the light as much as the temperature, a chill of brightness that permeated the sky but barely lit the earth. Where sunlight did pierce the shadows it had a glowing honey intensity. Beyond the upsweep of streaked violet cloud the unearthly light of a concealed sun was intimidating: a warning to everything that crawled on the ground to scurry into holes and stay there till spring.

Jed wished he could do that himself. Lying flat on a slab of lichened rock, he searched the landscape, half-regretting his flight from the bothy. But that was only cold, and misery. He hadn't had a choice. Lifting his shaking fingers to the side of his face, he touched the swelling bruise that marked him from temple to jaw.

No. He'd had no choice.

Trouble was, he had no idea what to do, where to

go. Now that he knew what had happened to him, now that he'd been warned, he could keep his mind to himself, and he'd had enough of a start on Conal. The man had probably taken his small patrol back to his precious dun, for that matter. The fate of Jed wouldn't concern him.

But after the short day's journey, it was beginning to concern Jed very much.

In the ominous dusk that lay across the valley, the blue grey clouds were blotched with snow-light, the pale sky floodlit while the earth lay in shadow. The air smelt of frost and oncoming night.

Jed frowned. Only one chunk of the landscape drew the dying light, and that was a solitary hill, two or three miles distant. It looked lit from within, its summit glowing pink and translucent above thin blizzard-drifts of cloud. It was eerily like looking through rock to the bare flesh of the land.

He'd started to scramble to his feet when he felt his hackles bristle, and only then did he hear it: a clear hoof-fall. Jed froze. He wondered if Conal would only kick the shit out of him, or just kill him and be done with it.

'You're going the wrong way.'

It wasn't Conal's voice; it held a tinge of accent that Jed couldn't place. His spine crackled with fear. He knew he'd have to turn in the end, but it took every scrap of guts he had left to do it.

The horse was the colour of a fox, and it was no water horse. It was saddled, a Thoroughbred with a fine head, pricked ears, and a silver gleam in its otherwise ordinary horse-eyes.

A man leaned on the pommel. His face was Viking-handsome, his reddish-blond hair and beard cropped very short. He had a look of great curiosity on his face, and his eyes were simply the warmest brown eyes that had ever mesmerised Jed, the colour of melted sugar.

'And you are?'

Jed tensed, but not with fear. 'None of your business.'

'Well, None Of Your Business,' the man laughed, 'this is private land. So will you be moving on quickly, or will you be telling me what you are doing on it?'

'I'll *be telling* you that I'm looking for my little brother,' said Jed, managing to sound both mocking and aggressive. 'So if you won't *be telling* me where I can start to look, I'll be going right on. It's a free country. There's a right to roam. You can't throw me off this land.'

The rider was silent, half-smiling, as if he both could and would do just that.

'Nevertheless, you are going the wrong way. If you don't believe me, go on and get lost and die of exposure. See if that helps your precious brother.'

Jed grunted, bit his lip. Looked across the valley to the far hill. Came to a decision.

'I'm looking for Seth MacGregor.'

Indulgently, the rider rolled his warm brown eyes. 'Aren't they all. Well, I can take you right to him, if you ask nicely. *Cuilean.*'

Jed swallowed. It felt odd and wrong to have that nickname spoken by this unexpected man, but he beat down the rising fear and let himself hope. And for the first time in his life, he let himself beg.

'Please,' he said. 'Please.'

'Good!' The rider grinned and slapped the Thoroughbred's shoulder. 'You know when to swallow your pride. That makes you almost a man, not a whelp, and they're arrogant fools to call you one. Come, then.' Taking up the reins, he turned the chestnut's head and urged it forward. With his back confidently presented, Jed could see the bronze-hilted sword buckled to it, and the sleek modern crossbow that hung from the man's saddle.

He didn't feel like arguing anyway.

The light had gone from the far hill now, and its silhouette was fading into the wintry sky, but Jed kept up easily with the horse's pace. The warm gaze of its rider made his scalp itch.

The man gave a low laugh. 'Listen, mate, you stick with me. I'm no witch. Not like the freaks.'

'Aye, right,' said Jed. 'What are you doing here, then?'

The rider wasn't letting it go. 'I came with a woman, mate. Got me out of a tight spot.' He chuckled. There wasn't much humour in it. 'I'd stay in stranger places for a woman like her. But you watch these faeries. They're not like you and me. Can't trust them, mate. You watch that Seth.'

Jed gave him a cool look. 'Don't you worry about me, *mate*.'

At a distance, the hill had had a barren look, but as they climbed higher, the trees grew denser and the mist frayed. Underfoot Jed could feel heather and soft peat, alive with fungi, blaeberry and bearberry. Though the light faded fast and the night darkened, the forest was dappled with starlight, and the silver light stayed constant, so he wasn't quite aware when the sky vanished and a narrow twisted cavern opened into a hall flagged with grey stone and roofed with arches of ancient wood, high as a cathedral. Vines twisted up the pillars, moss and pale lichen frosted every edge and curve, and the air was white-scented with night flowers.

It could have been heartbreakingly beautiful, thought Jed. But only if your heart was the right shape.

He was aware of being watched, aware of murmurs of interest, of people loitering in the shadows to follow his progress, but he felt surprisingly unthreatened. When the echoing hoof-falls were silenced, the blond rider beckoned him forward and dismounted, keeping his hand on the bridle.

'Kate. Another guest.' A fragile green veil sighed as he drew it aside.

The woman who rose from the bed pulled crumpled linen sheets across her nakedness. She didn't seem so terrifying. She wasn't intimidatingly tall, but her beauty was breathtaking. Her hair was a bolt of copper silk that caught the light as she pushed it out of her heart-stopping eyes. They were golden, like the eyes of Conal's wolf's, but darker: the colour of honey. Her smile was wide, there were faint laughter creases at her eyes, and her expression was all warmth and kindness.

'Jed, darling one. Welcome home!'

Jed barely heard her. He was too busy staring at the man who rose from Kate's white-linen bed, who tugged on his jeans and came forward into the flickering silver light, buckling his belt. The bronze buckle was familiar; it had crossed Jed's mind to nick it. It might have been crass if it hadn't been so beautifully carved: the outstretched wings of a merlin.

Seth was all languid, loose-jointed, but there was a febrile glint in his eyes as he leaned on the wall unsmiling. His chest and arms and stomach were as hacked about with old scars as Conal's. Jed had thought of him as weaker than Conal, and he realised with a sickening jolt that he wasn't. He was smaller, and leaner, but his spare thinness was all strength, like one of those steel cables that if it snapped could take your head right off.

Seth's angular face was harder than ever, his left eye violently bruised and swollen and filled with a whole new intensity of pain and hate. It was impossible to go on looking into it, so Jed's gaze slewed to the tattoo on his shoulder muscle, intricate knotwork that came to a point at his biceps. It was identical to Conal's, to the one he'd seen when the man stripped to wash. Only yesterday, he thought. After Jed had slept on his shoulder. Something knotted Jed's stomach, and suddenly he felt like howling with regret, as if he'd made some terrible mistake but didn't yet know what it was.

'Where is he?'

'Safe,' said Seth.

'No. I said *where is he?*'

'Hush, lad.' Kate touched Jed's arm, but he tried to ignore her. 'Seth's telling you the truth,' she said. 'Rory is safe. And he's happy, happier than ever he'd be with bandits and rebels in the wilderness. I'll take you to him.'

She glanced back over her shoulder at Seth. She seemed to hold his gaze exactly as long as she wanted to, and when she broke it, Seth looked sick. This time he avoided Jed's eyes. He seized a white shirt from the tumble of sheets and pulled it on, covering the tattoo. The shirt looked thin and cool, but it clung to his damp muscles as if he was burning up with shame and desire.

All the same, he shot a look of contempt at the blond rider, who spat on the floor as he passed. Seth stopped. Loathing oozed out of him like sweat.

'You hurt the whelp, Laszlo, I'll have your balls on a spike.'

Jed swallowed hard and stared at the blond, whose lip was curled in something not unlike amusement. Though not much like it, either.

'Boys,' murmured Kate. 'Laszlo won't touch the young man, Murlainn. Jed is my guest. Although if you're keen on him yourself . . .' She left it hanging, her mouth quirking with the joke.

Seth turned and searched Kate's golden eyes. 'Oh, I believe he's taken.'

Kate's facial muscles tightened ever so slightly, but her smile remained fixed. 'Murlainn?'

'Isn't he? Spoken for? I thought that was Laszlo's whole problem.'

'Naughty.' With an air of barely contained patience, Kate flicked out her hand towards Seth, presenting the back of it.

He stared at it for long seconds, then sullenly took

a step back towards her. Lifting her hand, he kissed it and pressed it to his forehead.

'Better.' Kate's lively air was restored. 'Now, Nils. You and I will take Jed to his brother.'

Seth strode out of the hall in silence, the dark shape of Branndair loping to his side as he disappeared through an archway.

'Such a sulker.' Kate tied a leather belt round her dress and ushered Jed and Laszlo from the hall. 'Now, you're my guest, Jed! Go where you like. Treat my home as your own. Because that's what it *is*.'

She made his flesh crawl. Having her strolling languidly at his back gave Jed a horrible sense of being stalked by a spider. For all her warmth and delight and her beauty, he didn't like this place and he didn't like her. The beauty left him cold, especially the wind-chill from her fluttering eyelashes.

The passageway seemed interminable, but ahead of him Laszlo stopped quite suddenly and smiled. Jed became aware of a fast, itching beat of music; with a flourish, Laszlo ushered him into a room where maybe a dozen women clustered round something on the floor. In the centre sat Rory, focus of all their attention, his barleycorn hair catching the light as he slapped at a hide bodhran. Losing the rhythm entirely, he giggled and fell over, ending the music and sending the women into gales of laughter.

The laughter hesitated and died as Jed shoved forward to Rory and hoisted him into his arms. Some of the women glared, but Kate was behind him, smiling and stepping forward. As if catching their cue from her, the women relaxed and sighed indulgently. Jed shut his eyes, hugging Rory, afraid to let him go again.

A woman leaned over Jed's shoulder to tickle Rory's chin. 'He's a darling,' she cooed.

'But not your darling.' Jed jerked him away from her hand, but his frown slackened in puzzlement. 'I've seen you before.'

'I don't think so.' Her smile was coy but wary.

'Black jumper.' He looked her up and down. 'Cheap red blazer.'

Kate stepped between them, dismissing the woman with a warning glance. 'Come, Jed. I'm sorry it had to be this way, but you'd never have brought him to me otherwise. Your brother is where he belongs now, and so are you.'

'Don't use my name. You don't know me.'

'Ah! Too long with bandits.' Kate laughed softly. 'Oh, Cuilean, not all the Sithe are psychotic. If Conal wants to ride around the wilds with his gang, looting my farms and taking his sword to my men, let him. Let him see where it gets him. Cù Chaorach is a sorrow to me, but I wish him no harm, despite all he's done.'

'That's not what—'

'Ah, you've heard a different story? My dear, Conal may seem old to you, but believe me, he has some growing up to do.' Closing her eyes, Kate sighed. 'I'd so like to see him get the chance.'

'Is that a *threat*?'

'Oh, come, don't be like that. I love that man with all my heart, but Cù Chaorach is a bomb with a very short fuse. Even Finn agrees.'

'I doubt that,' muttered Jed.

'Then she can tell you herself. Can't you, my dear?'

In the silence and stillness, there was movement. Out of the shadows farther back, one of the women slowly stood up: the youngest of all of them. Only by blinking and squinting into the dimness did Jed recognise her, and his gut turned over.

'*Finn?*'

She reddened as she came forward, but she didn't avert her gaze. 'Hello, Jed.'

'There.' Kate clapped her hands. 'I think we'll let you two catch up. Hmm? You must have *such* a lot to talk about.'

'Don't take this the wrong way,' he told her, searching Rory fruitlessly for signs of mistreatment: bruises, nits, unscrubbed fingernails, anything. 'But I kind of expected to find you in a dungeon.'

Finn twisted a strand of hair manically between her fingers. 'Well. That's what I'd have thought too. Before. You know. Now.'

'Conal's so worried about you.'

She laughed. 'I was worried about me too. But only till they brought me here. Jed, she hasn't hurt me, she hasn't threatened me; she hasn't even tried to scare me.'

'Yeah, she's lovely. The lights are on full-blast. But nobody's home.'

'Are you seriously calling her *stupid*?'

'I'm not talking about her brain. Have you not seen? There's nothing behind her eyes.'

Finn opened her mouth. Shut it again, and frowned. 'Watch yourself. Remember she can see in your head.'

'It's all friendly little threats in this place, isn't it? If I can keep Seth out of my head – and I can, now – I can keep her out.'

Finn blinked at him then as if seeing him for the first time. 'Jed.' She leaned close and stroked his jaw with a trembling fingertip. 'What happened to your face?'

He'd forgotten all about it. Absently he touched it, felt the throb of pain in his flesh. It was like the ache of a very old, scabbed-over cut.

'Seth,' he said shortly.

'Yes, I thought so.' Slowly Finn nodded. 'He didn't understand.'

He raised an eyebrow. 'Didn't?'

'You can imagine . . . when he brought Rory. When he found me here. He didn't understand that I . . . wanted to stay.'

'Jesus. I bet he didn't.'

Silently Finn picked at her nails. 'There was a time . . . listen. Him and Conal, they both used to be her men. They believed in her. I don't know what's gone wrong, but it's politics, that's all it is. Stupid politics.'

He rubbed his eyes, exhausted. 'Finn . . .'

'Seth's come back to her. It doesn't matter what I think of him or—' Gently she cupped his bruised face. '—or even what you think. He'd never do anything to hurt Conal.'

He studied her face sadly. 'And neither would you.'

'Of course neither would I! I don't want anyone

to get hurt. Be better if they talked to one another, wouldn't it?'

Jed sighed and went back to hunting Rory's scalp for nonexistent lice, but then something struck him, and he narrowed his gaze at her throat. 'What happened to your other necklace?'

Absently she touched the pendant and glanced down. The crude raven's-talon was sharp and hollow, the chunk of emerald gone. Perhaps to stop the claw pricking her skin, it lay against a slender toothed leaf, delicately carved out of polished wood and strung on a woven thong.

'Oh, the stone. It fell out. The setting was loose, remember?' She grinned. 'Rush job.'

'Yes . . .'

'Kate's got the emerald. She's going to get Gealach to set it properly.'

'Nothing could be easier,' said Kate's laughing voice. 'I can fix a lot of things now.' She sat down and put an arm round Finn's shoulders.

Jed's disbelief must have shown on his face, because Kate wagged a finger at him. Behind her, in the shadows, stood Laszlo, his arms folded.

'I adore Cù Chaorach,' said the queen, 'but he is *such* a one for giving one side of a story.'

'I suppose most people are *such* ones for that.'

Kate's lips thinned disapprovingly as her arm tightened on Finn's shoulders. 'Conal loved Finn's father; her father loved him. But Conal led Aonghas to his death for his own obsessions. Cù Chaorach is a noble man, and a bonny fighter, and he means well. But he can be the most selfish of brutes.'

Finn started at that. 'He's not selfish—'

'No, dear one.' Kate tutted mischievously. 'And he isn't the violent type.'

Finn blushed and gave her an embarrassed grin. 'I know, I know.'

Jed's lip twisted in disbelief. 'Finn?'

'Oh, honestly, young man. Finn isn't stupid. I don't know what Cù Chaorach's told you, but I'm not on some mass suicide mission.'

Jed pressed his cheek to Rory's hair, unwilling to meet her alarmingly brilliant eyes.

'Jed, my people love me. You think that's because I ask it of them? Oh, please. My people love me because I indulge their whims. Why shouldn't I?' Kate tossed her hair back from her shoulder. 'I gave them their desires in the first place. Give your people what they want, Jed, and they'll always want what you give them. And I can do the same for your people. I've wanted to help them for so long, but how can I do that when they're barely aware of me? The full-mortals, listen to me? They can't even *see me*.'

If he could have stuck his fingers in his ears, he would have, but he had a feeling that would be a tactical error. 'So why'd you come after my brother?' he muttered.

'*Come after* him! Heavens, you have such a pejorative way of speaking.' Kate sniffed disdainfully. 'Would you have let me persuade you? Your bandit friends would have had my throat cut before I could get a word out.'

'So you just stole him.'

'Oh, hardly. His father gave him to me. Which, as it happens, was precisely what was predicted. His parents were supposed to give him up voluntarily. And they both did!'

'My mother didn't—'

'Yes, dear, of course she did. She gave him up for a fix. What did she think would happen to him if anything became of her? For heaven's sake! Thank goodness you were there, Jed. Although Skinshanks would have looked after him well enough, if you hadn't arrived.'

'Hang on.' Jed rubbed his temples. 'You weren't looking for him, or you'd just have taken him. You were looking for a *stone*.'

Kate fluttered an elegant hand. 'Yes, yes, but I always had my suspicions. Which were confirmed by an oracle, ooh . . . two centuries ago? I had to wait for the blessed creature, of course, and it took me a little time to trace the right child. But heavens, you could have knocked me down with a chicken feather when I found out who'd fathered it.'

Jed couldn't speak. His head was too full of Skinshanks, and the smile on its face when Jed had turned up at the last minute and rescued Rory. No wonder the Lammyr hadn't looked very bothered. They'd had a contingency plan, and Jed was it.

Kate draped her free arm around him; now she enclosed them both in her scented warmth. 'I was fond of Finn's grandmother, and I miss the old dear, but I always had more imagination than she did. She couldn't see past magic rocks, that was Leonora's trouble.'

Jed peered past her at Finn, waiting for her to leap to her grandmother's defence, but all she did was smile a little sadly. *For God's sake . . .*

'Well. Now that Rory's in my keeping, he can help me dissolve that choking shroud of a Veil. We'll work at it together, as he grows. Then the full-mortals will see me as my own people do; all of them, easily. Not one at a time, with an effort.' She blew a flirtatious kiss at Laszlo, and he grinned. 'I can make them as happy and secure as I've made my Sithe. Your people live in a prison of fear and doubt, Jed, but I can free them. See?' Her warmth made the hair on Jed's skin lift as she leaned over him. 'I'll protect you full-mortals from all your enemies. I'll let you see who your real enemies *are*.'

The gist of it seemed reasonable, logical even. He couldn't imagine why it was wrong; so wrong, it was as if every word she spoke was misshapen, spelt and spoken backwards. Shaking his head violently, he remembered something beyond Kate's words, something of her that seemed more real: cruelty, and bright malice.

'Finn,' he said, craning past Kate once more. 'Do you remember Cuthag?'

She frowned. 'Who?'

Oh shit.

'If the Veil goes,' he said, turning sharply back to Kate, 'we'll see people like Finn properly. That what you mean by showing us who our enemies are?'

Kate's breath caught in her throat, as if she was mildly exasperated. Then she relaxed and turned her focus only on Finn.

'Finn knows the Veil has kept her hidden. It's made her a nobody. Well, Finn, you're *not* a nobody. You're a *Sithe*! Think about it, Finn! Those dull-wits who think they're better than you, those girls who make your life a misery! Wouldn't you like to get your own back?' Kate trailed a finger along her jawline. 'You're a lovely girl. Why should you stay unseen while those cattle preen themselves? You can be top dog for a change. You can be queen of *your* circle.'

Jed shrank back in disbelief. *Finn*, he thought. *Finn. You know fine you aren't lovely. I've heard you bitch about it. You laughed about it.*

'The Veil is a moth-eaten rag. We've crossed over everywhere, we cross-breed more and more, and now their kind have begun to come to us.' Kate glanced at Laszlo, back in the shadows. 'The Veil's going to die, but we'll turn that to our advantage, won't we, Finn? We won't go down with it. We'll join with the full-mortals on our own terms.'

Kate tipped Finn's chin so she could look directly into her eyes, and Jed knew how it was. Those slender fingers, cool and dry against the skin, the touch of them travelling through the jaw and into the skull.

'It's dead skin,' Kate murmured. 'It's already rotting. Even if Conal were right, the Veil's death is inevitable. It's only madness that fights the inevitable. *Madness.*'

And Jed remembered what that looked like: Conal's wild face as he seized Rory, Conal striking Seth almost hard enough to snap his neck, Conal cursing the night sky like a lunatic. There was the bitter rage of Eili too: the pointless waste of four hundred years could make you mad. For a crystalline moment, Jed believed that absolutely.

It lasted fractions of a second, no more. But in the same instant, he saw how it was for Finn.

People lied to Finn. They'd done it all her life. How would she recognise a lie? She didn't know what one looked like.

Oh, Finn. His stomach turned over.

Kate nodded. 'Finn sees it perfectly clearly. Our two worlds are like parallel rivers. Rivers always join, forge a channel together. One day the worlds will collide, and this side will be swallowed up, but so what? There's a watersmeet at Tornashee, but does the smaller river vanish? No! It's absorbed in the larger one. There's turbulence, and dangerous water, and then?' She stroked Finn's cheek as she smiled. 'Clear brown water, and the sound of the trees, and birdsong, and cool shade. It's beautiful.' She gave a small, sad sigh. 'Conal taught you to swim there, didn't he?'

Finn nodded, unspeaking.

'You love him. That's understandable. He's been your father since he lost you your own.' Kate's voice held infinite melancholy. 'Ah, Finn, Conal can be saved.'

The battle was lost, but Jed flailed one more time. 'Finn . . .'

Kate spun and faced him, righteous anger lighting her eyes with gold.

'You see, Jed? That's why Finn will stay with me. She'll stay. Because together we'll save Cù Chaorach.'

'Ed! Down!' Rory hammered Jed's shoulder with furious fists.

When Jed had first picked up his brother, he'd had no intention of ever putting him down. But over the long hours since they'd come here, he'd had to. Hours? It could be days. He had only his own body clock to go by, since his cheap watch had never recovered from its soaking and there were no windows in this warren. He and Rory had slept and eaten when they felt like it. No-one had tried to snatch Rory away, and gradually Jed's confidence was returning. He could let Rory go more than a metre from him, for – oh, whole minutes at a time. Now, reluctantly, he set the squalling child on the ground and was rewarded with instant silence.

Jed stuck close behind him as the toddler trudged down a new corridor. There didn't seem to be much chance of getting lost, anyway. Either they'd lose their bearings in these tortuous caverns – in which case,

Kate would be bound to send Laszlo after them – or they'd find a route to the outside world, which was frankly too much to hope for.

The passage opened into a bare rock-walled space where water fell in a spray into a clear greenish pool. At the pool's edge lay a black wolf, its yellow eyes fixed on them. Jed stood still, shocked, but Rory marched heedlessly forward. Only when he was about to plunge feetfirst into the pool did Jed run forward to grab him. Branndair lifted his head but made no sound.

Seth stood barefoot but fully clothed beneath the fall of water, eyes closed, his jeans and white shirt soaked, singing quietly to himself: a lilting tune Jed's mother used to sing. "My Lagan Love." Had Seth taught it to her, or had she taught him? Suddenly Jed couldn't stand the sound of it. Hatred constricted his heart. Seth would leave him nothing of her, in the end, not even some old song. *Nothing*.

Falling silent, Seth shut his eyes tighter, turned his face up to the hard lash of the water, and let it wash out his mouth in a fountaining spray. Jed began to back away, then hesitated, heart thudding. He wanted to know how Seth could do it. Stab Conal in the back. Seduce Mila. Steal her baby, the baby he'd abandoned, and give him to that slapper of a witch for the sake of *politics*.

Seth spat out a mouthful of water, shoved his hands through his hair and without opening his eyes said, 'Have you a weapon with you?'

If only. Remembering the pistol in his belt, Jed gritted his teeth. 'Not one that works.'

'Ah.' Seth tipped his head forward, opening eyes that were starred with silver light. The right one opened properly. The left one was still swollen, bruised horribly by Conal's blow. Stepping out of the pool, Seth glanced down at the child squirming in Jed's arms. 'At the risk of my own throat, I suggest you find one. And don't turn your back on Laszlo. Not ever.'

Jed frowned, curiosity overcoming his contempt. 'Laszlo's not going to bother with me.'

'He will. Kate knows it, but she leaves me to do her dirty protection work.' Seth spat again into the pool. 'Laszlo's afraid of you. And fear makes men do terrible things.'

'I've got nothing against Laszlo,' said Jed. 'You're a different matter.'

'Right. Well, allegedly,' said Seth with a sarcastic grin, 'no Sithe can ever kill Laszlo. He'll only be killed by a full-mortal. Someone like himself.'

'I see.' Jed paused, thinking about that. 'There's a lot of us about.'

'Yes, though not many over here. And he's done enough killing in his time to make plenty of enemies.' Seth shrugged. 'Of course it's all bollocks. Witchcraft, superstition, whatever. Don't talk to me about prophecies.' His lip curled in loathing. 'I've had enough of those to last me three Sithe lifetimes. The point is, Laszlo believes it.'

That made Jed shiver. 'He had every chance to kill me on the way here, and he didn't.'

'Wouldn't dare. Yet. Skinshanks wants you.'

Jed froze. 'What?'

'It's bored with Laszlo. Taken him as far as it can. Wants a new protégé, and you're it; it's had its eye on you for a long time. It's already worked on you, from a distance.' Seth shrugged. 'Well, what Skinshanks wants, Kate'll give. Good luck with that.'

Jed found himself holding Rory closer. 'But that means Laszlo won't—'

'Oh yeah, he will if he gets a chance. He'll slide a kitchen knife between your shoulder blades and apologise for being clumsy.'

Jed swallowed, his throat dry. 'Why would you care?'

Seth's eyes strayed to Rory. 'I thought I'd made that perfectly clear.'

Rory squealed, delighted to have some more adult attention, and kicked free of Jed's grip. Cursing, Jed snatched at him, but he was a fast mover for a toddler. He collided with Seth's legs and was thrilled to be swept up in his strong hands.

Jed clenched his jaw. If the man so much as looked at Rory the wrong way, he'd take his eyes out with his bare fingers. But Seth only held the baby at arm's length, gazing at him as if looking for a little bit of himself. Rory's eyes were wide and fascinated as he returned the stare. Stretching out a stubby hand, he touched Seth's bruised eye, and the man flinched in surprise.

'Ouchy,' said Rory, and grabbed Seth's neck, hauling him in for a proper hug.

A look of utter shock dawned on Seth's face, and he would have dropped Rory to the stone floor had the child not locked himself so securely round his neck. Seth pressed his face to Rory's, so close that his black eyelashes brushed the small cheekbone, and his arms closed in on the little body to hold him far more tightly than Jed thought was necessary.

Seth crouched to set the child down, pushing him gently back in Jed's direction. Jed lifted him. Rory's clothes were soaked now, and Jed was on the point of saying something vicious about Seth's carelessness, but one look at the man's unguarded face stopped him. Instead he said softly: 'Why did you do it?'

Seth stood up, his gaze chilling. 'Partly because of you, you'll be sorry to hear. Kate's been trying to entice me back.' He grinned ironically. 'That bitch-queen plays a long game. She was very subtle. But I wouldn't have done it, you know.'

'Wouldn't?' Jed's mouth was dry.

'No. But then you came out with that ghetto remark of yours. I thought a lot about that. Why should we live in a ghetto, after all? It's your kind need to be controlled and corralled, not ours.'

'But I thought . . . you'll all be destroyed.'

'It's one theory. Me, I think we're strong enough, clever enough to survive the worst. But only if we do it on our own terms.'

Those words echoed. Jed remembered Kate saying them.

'You know, I saw Belsen, Cuilean. I saw it liberated. It made quite an impression. I've been all over; I'm quite the world traveller. Rwanda, Kosovo, Sierra Leone. Have you heard of those? Did they register with you?'

'Kind of . . .'

'Quite. Kind of. Anyway, when I got tired of being a soldier, I joined the police, and I ended up pulling the corpse of a six-year-old child out of a ditch.' He smiled coldly. 'You never stop, do you? If the Veil rots away, what in the name of the gods will we do? The thought of it turns my guts to ice. We'll need someone strong, someone who'll protect us. Someone as ruthless as you people are. Because, gods, you are. Do you have any idea how much I've seen of you? You kill your own children. Your *children* kill children.'

'Not all of us.' Jed decided Seth was a little more insane than Conal.

'More than enough.' Seth shrugged. 'You're beyond belief, or you would be if I hadn't seen the evidence. Well, with Kate in charge, we might just be all right. Kate's nothing if not ruthless. She's wicked, but she's one of us.'

'I'm amazed you can even touch her. After my mum.'

'Don't push it, Cuilean.' There was a snarl in Seth's throat, fading to silence. 'Though it sometimes amazes me too.'

'Kate doesn't care about you!'

'It never once occurred to me that she did.'

'I don't mean just you. She doesn't care about any of you. Nobody but herself!'

'True, and of course, I know now why she targeted me and not Conal.' Seth eyed his baby son with a tight smile. 'It was never going to be my superior charms, was it? But Kate's got the right idea, you see. Caring's so overrated. I've been alive a long time,

Cuilean.' The pitch of his voice rose. 'Have you *any* idea how much love you can give and take in a life that long?'

Jed tensed, but the man only shrugged, his voice cooling again.

'Caring. Loving. What do they get you but grief and horror and death? Conal cares, and what has it got him? Exile, and a rage he can't control anymore.' Seth's teeth bared, but it wasn't what Jed would call a smile. 'It used to be so easy, Cuilean. I used to draw in the Veil as if I was pulling a hat down over my eyes. Now I try to seize it, and it disintegrates where I touch it, or vanishes like a mist-phantom. I wore out the last of my kindness keeping you and your family protected. Now I've had enough. This way, it's our own choice. I'd rather take my chances with Kate than wait around for the Veil to dissolve and for everything I've ever loved to vanish.'

'Thought you didn't love anything.'

Seth's eyes were brilliant and intense. 'Slip of the tongue. But if you insist, there's one person I do still love. And in the end, he was my only reason.'

Jed's temper flared. 'You don't love Rory!'

'Rory? Certainly not. I'm talking about the noble fool who loves a girl who'd drop him like hot silver for the chance to be in her own gang. He loves Finn more than his own life, and he'd have given that up for her like a shot.'

'Aye. That's what worried me.'

Seth shut his eyes, sighing. 'Listen to me, Cuilean: Conal would never have given up your brother. I told you to trust him and you didn't. You blew it. If you'd stayed with him, put your trust in him . . . well.' He shrugged. 'You didn't.'

The blood in Jed's veins was icy. '*You* took Rory.'

'But Conal never would have. Give up an innocent child? It would kill his soul. Cold iron, Cuilean: I don't expect you to understand. The thing is, Finn's death would have done the same. You see? I didn't have any kind of a choice. My brother will never forgive me for this, but he'll remain himself. I've saved him, Cuilean, at the expense of my own son. Oh, and possibly my own soul, but that was a goner anyway.'

Jed stared at him. His voice would barely come out, and when it did, it was scratchy. 'And Finn . . .'

Seth tilted his head back into the water, took a mouthful, then spat it out.

'Ah yes. Imagine how I felt when I got here. When I saw her. When she told me.'

An unexpected pity wrung Jed's guts, but Seth's expression didn't change.

'It's almost irrelevant, though. The child's bewitched. Literally bewitched, I mean. Spellbound tighter than a witch's arse.' He shrugged. 'But at least she has her life, and Conal has his soul. It's as much as I expected. And it's as I say: Kate's probably our only hope. I'll get used to being her henchman. I've been that before.'

'You're not even convincing yourself,' said Jed, nuzzling Rory's head. 'She'll destroy everything you love.'

Seth half smiled. 'There are few people who know of those things, Cuilean, and you ain't one of them. I'm out of respectable choices: Kate's my hope now.'

Jed wanted to shake him. 'You only have to *look at her*. I used to think your pal Gocaman was a psycho. Now I've met Kate, I know what a real one looks like.'

'You're a talented whelp, you really are. You've got instincts, I respect that, but you don't know what you're talking about. There's more to it than Kate's personality.'

'Yeah, right. Sure there is.' Jed picked up Rory, but hesitated. 'Tell me one thing. Why didn't she just take him? She could have taken him anytime.'

'Ah, no. No, she couldn't, not if she wanted her blessed prophecy fulfilled. She wanted it done right, and his parents had to abandon him, of their own free will.' Seth smiled sourly. 'Well, I did. And his mother would have done, long ago, if not for you. You were quite an obstacle for them, Cuilean. Take a little comfort from that if you like.' Under his breath, he added, 'I do.'

Jed shook his head and turned away. 'Bye, Seth.'

From the corner of his eye, he saw the man's hand move towards them, but at the last instant Seth clenched his fist and drew his hand back to his side. Jed didn't look back, but he could feel Seth's stare between his shoulder blades, and he felt it long after they were out of his sight.

Finn

If there was uneasiness in Finn's soul, it was balanced by her livening instincts. She'd known as soon as she was tugged through the watergate that she belonged in this world, and she'd known by some ancestral memory how to free herself from a hungry kelpie. Her mother had become more real to her here than she was at Tornashee, albeit a mother in dreams. And the knife Eili had given her that first night should have felt awkward and strange; instead it had felt like an extension of her hand, and one that she could have used—

Though against whom, she couldn't remember.

Now it was Kate's stronghold that was rapidly growing familiar. The labyrinth might be contorted, but it felt warm and secure and like home, as if the tunnels had been dug a long time ago through ancient ground where she'd first taken root. Kate had taken her in with no questions asked, she had welcomed her into her inner circle, she listened to her and talked to her and—

Answered questions.

Finn rubbed her temple and paused to steady herself on the stone archway. The morning fuzziness – if it was morning; she wasn't sure – had verged on a headache for about an hour, and she was inclined to blame it on what she'd remembered. She was used to the truth now, that was the thing. An unanswered question would fester, now that she recalled it.

'Kate?'

The woman looked round, smiling, dismissing a disgruntled captain with an idle wave. 'Fionnuala. Come in; we're finished for now. Is something wrong?'

The candle flames in this chamber didn't glow that unearthly silver they did in the great hall, but a subdued gold that sparked off precious stones and made silk and velvet glow with inner light. God, Kate's home was beautiful.

'Wrong? Hardly,' said Finn dryly. 'No, I had a – I remembered I wanted to ask you something.'

'You can ask me anything I know the answer to. Let's get those nagging questions out of the way.' Kate tutted, and murmured, 'I don't know what your mother's been thinking.'

'So.' Finn lowered her voice. 'Kate, what's a fetch?'

'A fetch?' Kate frowned. 'It's a doppelgänger. Do you know what that is?'

'Someone's double. Yes?'

'Yes. But a phantom double. Why do you ask?'

Finn hesitated, but the thick heaviness was back in

her head and she wanted rid of it. 'I saw one. In the forest. It looked like Conal.'

Kate took a step back. 'You saw Cù Chaorach's *fetch*?'

'That's what he said it was.'

'You told him?' There was a hint of a screech in the queen's voice. 'You *told him* you'd seen his fetch?'

'Yes. I didn't know what it was.' Finn was sorry she'd asked, now. 'He seemed upset.'

'I'm not surprised!' A muscle jerked in Kate's face, and tears started to her eyes.

'Kate, are you—?'

'Oh, the silly man, he loves to fight.' Recovering, Kate reached for Finn's hands and smiled gently. 'You don't have to worry anymore.'

'Meaning what? Is it bad?'

'Oh, my dear young woman.' The queen cupped Finn's face. 'It's the best news I've had in weeks. A fetch is the best of all possible omens. It means Conal is coming to a crossroads in his life, and I suspect that bodes well for peace talks.'

'Peace talks.'

'Yes. Because you're right, of course, and we can't go on like this. We're Sithe and we shouldn't fight one another; there aren't enough of us as it is. You've made my morning.'

'Well. Good.'

Kate's ivory-pale arm rested gently on her shoulders again. The coolness of her touch at least made Finn's head feel lighter, and she found herself leaning into the queen, and hoping vaguely that she wouldn't be offended.

'Oh, Finn, thank you for this. Now, there are things I have to do, but we shall talk later. We have so much to talk about, you and I.'

Jed

Jed hesitated where the passageway opened out to the green pillared space. It was vast, beautiful, ringing with laughter and music. Still, Jed found himself nostalgic for the bare silent austerity of Kilchoran.

Kate was draped elegantly across a chaise, laughing at something Laszlo had said. His head was bent close to hers, his fingers resting confidently on her thigh. Finn sat cross-legged on a cushion, concentrating on a chessboard set out between two women. One of the players, small and almost scarlet-haired, caught Finn's eye, and a look of conspiracy passed between them before she moved her knight.

'Hey, Gealach, cut it out!' laughed her opponent. 'I can't play two of you.'

Two men strode into the hall, both in combat trousers, khaki shirts and mud-spattered jerseys, swords on their backs and bows in their hands. The scarlet-haired woman, forgetting her chess match, leaped to her feet and flung herself at one of them with a shriek of delight. As she clung onto him, legs and arms wrapped round his torso, he dropped his bow to grab her, laughing.

The other swordsman, heavier-built, head close-shaved, and wearing a plain gold torque round his neck, did not smile. When Kate held out her hand to him, he took it and pressed it respectfully to his forehead. Drawing back, he exchanged a look with her and with Laszlo.

'Uncouple yourself, Iolaire, and give us a report.'

Laszlo was all tolerant amusement as Iolaire detached his girlfriend and set her down, kissing her. Watching from his alcove, Jed shivered for Iolaire. Laszlo's easy geniality was nothing but a mask, and for all the snide remarks about faeries, it was Iolaire who looked like a real human being.

Kate wasn't looking at Iolaire anymore, or the other fighters. Her golden eyes had sparked with pleasure. 'Jed. There you are! Come out from there, dear one.'

Beside the chessboard, Finn stood up, smiling a rather awkward greeting. The small group around the chaise turned to look at him in surprise, and the hall fell silent.

Reluctantly Jed eased out from his archway.

'Oh, don't look so cowed. I've been waiting for you. It's time for you to go home.'

Jed swallowed, frowned, forced himself to walk forward. 'Me and Rory, you mean?'

'Oh please, don't tell me what I mean. I can't bear that.' Kate lifted her copper hair with one hand and tossed it back over her shoulder. 'Heaven's sake, boy.

That was a joke!' She stood and walked down to him as the three fighters behind her exchanged glances.

'Yeah, but—'

'You must be longing to get home.' Lightly Kate traced the contour of his cheekbone, smiling. 'But Rory? By no means.'

He jerked away from her touch, clutching his brother. 'Hang on, you—'

'Now, Jed.' She took Rory carefully from arms that were suddenly too weak to keep their hold, passing the boy to Iolaire. 'You'd give this child back to barbarians. Killers. Would that be in his best interests?'

'I wouldn't go near them!' Panic rose in his throat.

'Yes, you would. Don't be disingenuous, dear.'

'I don't trust them. I don't trust any of you. I'd take him *home*.'

'Don't be silly. He *is* home.'

Jed stared up into the face of the swordsman Iolaire, who had looked so human. He had sea blue eyes, and curling dark brown hair, and a gold ring soldered into his earlobe. He had small scars on his left cheekbone and temple, a mouth with creases where he smiled a lot, a tiny thistle tattoo on his collarbone. He did look human. He looked unhappy too, and sympathetic, but he held the child firmly out of Jed's reach.

'You can't do this!' yelled Jed.

'No, Cuilean. It's you that can't do as you please.' The second swordsman stepped forward, blocking his view of Iolaire, and seized Jed's arm. Staring down at him, the man rubbed the palm of his hand distractedly across his shaved head. 'Would you give your brother to them? What kind of people do you think they are? Cù Chaorach's woman killed mine, *boy*.'

Jed fought back panic as he wrestled his arm out of the man's grip. 'In a fair fight, I bet.'

'A fair fight, yes, and one that had no reason to happen in the first place. Bandits.' The swordsman spat. 'Killers.'

'All right, Cluaran. Hush, now. There's no argument.' Kate touched the man's arm.

'I only want to take him home!' Jed screamed.

'That's enough, Jed. Leave now, and one day you'll see Rory again.' Kate nodded to Cluaran, who grasped Jed's arm. 'Give him a horse, Cluaran. A good horse, one that'll take him where he wants to go.' Her lips curled in a smile. 'He mustn't walk all that way.'

'Kate, please let him stay.' Finn pushed forward, almost knocking Cluaran over.

'No, Finn,' said Kate. 'Jed's unhappy here. He can't stay if he isn't happy.'

Jed breathed hard through his teeth. 'I'm going. Don't worry.' He looked again at Rory, sleepy and puzzled in Iolaire's arms. His heart was in shards, but he had no choice.

Finn grabbed his elbow. 'Jed—'

'Forget it, Finn.' He flung her off. 'I'll be back.'

Kate shook her head, smiling at him slightly. ~ *Oh no, Cuilean. No, you won't.*

He shot her a look of pure loathing before jerking his arm out of Cluaran's grasp and marching ahead of him to the great archway at the entrance to the hall. Finn was at his heels, running to keep up. 'Jed,' she begged in a low voice. 'Please. She'll let you stay if you ask to stay. Please.'

He couldn't believe he was walking out of here without Rory, after all that had happened. He couldn't believe Finn was on Kate's side. And he could barely believe it, but he didn't actually care what Finn thought anymore.

'Look, Seth's one of us and he doesn't think she's all bad. He's in love with her!'

'Why can't you see things right?' Jed shook his head, staring at her. 'Seth *hates* her.'

Finn turned away, absolute confusion in her eyes. Jed had the feeling she was hunting around for Seth, but he was nowhere in sight. Trust him, thought Jed bitterly: well out of the way of a confrontation. Maybe his conscience couldn't take it. If he had one.

Grabbing Jed's arm again, Finn nodded towards Cluaran. 'You think they can all be wrong? You think he's wrong?' she pleaded. 'Eili killed his lover. They didn't start this war, Jed. Conal did. I love Conal, but maybe he's just wrong, okay?'

'You forget fast.'

'And you're so pigheaded,' she retorted. 'He got my dad killed, didn't he? Why do people have to die for Conal's beliefs?'

'Yeah. Nothing's worth dying for. That what you think?'

'There's nothing worth killing for.' She seized his arm.

'Anything worth living for, Finn?'

Sharply she let him go. Her fists clenched and the silver light in her eyes gleamed hard. 'Think about Rory, Jed.'

He paled. 'Don't ever try that line on me again.' Turning on his heel, he hesitated, his voice trembling. 'Look after him, all right?'

'We'll all do that,' said Cluaran.

Jed gave him a hateful glare, then went on before him towards the daylight. He didn't look at Finn again.

The sun was blinding as he stepped from the passageway, and only then did he realise how cold and encircling was the darkness in Kate's stronghold. No windows. Just like Kate, he thought suddenly. No windows, nothing but darkness, nothing to see. *The lights are on but . . .*

A chill shivered through him. Nothing behind her eyes, nothing between her eyes and her brain. *No soul.*

A movement to his left caught his eye. Thin, half-translucent, and stripped to the waist, the Lammyr basked on a huge mossy boulder, absorbing sunlight like a pale lizard. Despite the brilliance of the overhead sun, it cast no shadow, its flesh too pale and insubstantial even to make a mark on daylight.

Cluaran recoiled, his face twisting with disgust, but it ignored the man, curling upright at the sight of Jed like a slug eyeing a glassful of salt. Its pallid fingers clutched the stem of a wineglass and as Jed stared, repulsed, it took a drink, eyes fixed on him. Jed could see the shadow of the dark red wine slipping down its throat, the stretched muscles working beneath the skin. It set down the glass and grinned, and then it spoke.

It was the voice of authority, the firm and steady voice of a police officer. It was gruff, reassuring, and completely alien coming from those thin yellow lips. Jed felt for a terrible few seconds that he was back at the Fairy Loch, the water freezing, weed-clammy, ready to swallow him.

'*Come on, laddie, it's not worth it.*' The Lammyr grinned. '*Calm down now. Come and get a cuppa at the station. We want to help you and the baby.*'

Jed swallowed hard, wanting to be sick. 'You killed my mother,' he whispered.

'Ingrate.' The voice had changed altogether. It was like the rattle of bones but it was recognisably human, and he'd heard it before. It was the voice of his mother's dealer. 'The killing of her was the making of you. And it wasn't as easy as it looked.'

'Good.' Jed's mouth twisted. Despite the bile in his throat and the horror in his heart, he took an impulsive step towards Skinshanks.

Cluaran's hand fell on his shoulder and held him back. 'Don't. That's what it wants.'

'Ach, Cluaran. Don't be such an old woman.' Skinshanks drank again, Jed watching the wine go down with fascination. 'I like the boy. I like him a lot. I wish I'd had more time with you, Cuilean. See you again, hm?'

Cluaran growled threateningly and pulled Jed on, more gently this time. In the copse beyond the arch-way, horses stood tethered, and Cluaran brought forward a bay mare with soft silver-pricked eyes. 'She's a good girl, this one. She'll take you where you choose to go. But listen, if I meet you again, it'll be as if I've never met you. Do you understand?'

Jed nodded silently, taking the bay's reins, unable to speak.

'Don't be afraid of her, Cuilean. She's a horse, not a water demon.' He gave Jed a swift boost onto the mare's back. 'All you have to do is hold on. Now, go. And remember what I said.'

Cluaran slapped the mare's rump and she shook her head and moved off in an easy trot. She wasn't a difficult ride. She guided herself through the forest while Jed held the reins like someone in a trance, not seeing the green and golden light, not hearing the birdsong or smelling the resin of the pines, not even looking back until the mare paused, snorting, at the foot of the hill, where the trees gave way to the moor where he'd run into Laszlo. That seemed like a century ago.

The low winter sun was lovely on the wind-cropped heather, and the mare's nostrils flared with delight at the long uncluttered stretch of land.

Coming to himself, Jed looked briefly to the east and then towards the northwest, silently trying to get his bearings after the timeless, directionless darkness of the caverns. Briefly he flailed with his mind, searching, but the effort felt clumsy and amateurish, and besides, he felt as if he'd never connect with another human being as long as he lived.

The mare turned her head to look back at him, silver light sparking in her gentle dark eyes.

'You're not a dumb animal,' Jed told the mare, past the choking misery in his throat. 'You know where I want to go.'

Her ears flickered back and she watched him, blowing softly. Then she trotted forward again and broke into an easy, rhythmic canter before Jed had time to be scared.

Finn

'Oh, he can have *that* one back.' Kate smiled at Laszlo. 'I think you'll find it's worth it.'

The horses in the stabling cave moved restlessly, anticipating fresh air and action, silver sparks in their eyes. The twelve fastest were saddled and bridled, four of the riders already mounted. Laszlo's hand was on his chestnut's neck, caressing its twitching muscles, but the other hand laced into Kate's hair, turning her face to him for a long kiss.

Wish Seth could see that, thought Finn viciously.

She crouched in the corner of the feed store, nibbling her cuticles, waiting for them to go. Till an hour ago, she'd planned to ask permission to go hunting; she was starting to miss the sky. Since Jed's enforced departure, she'd lost the urge.

Not in the mood for company, she'd cloaked her mind in the blackest block she could conjure. Not that she couldn't see Kate's point; it made complete sense that Jed had to leave. It was only that questions had started to fog her mind again and she hated it, hated it. *Damn Jed*. He'd whacked her new certainties with a dirty great mental bludgeon. She needed space and thought and time to get her balance back, and she needed to be alone.

And Kate's mood was so star-bright and bouncy, Finn didn't think she could bear it.

Please go away. . . .

They didn't. Too busy flirting.

'I don't see the point,' grumbled Laszlo. 'I thought the whole idea was to break him.'

Huh, thought Finn, glad that Kate was there to restrain the big thug. *Good luck breaking Jed the Ned, pal.*

'We will. Him, and Finn's traitor mother.' Kate slipped her arms round Laszlo's waist. 'Hardly need Jed to do that.'

Finn frowned. Wiggled a finger in her ear to clear it.

'Would've been better to kill the boy, though.'

'You're so crude,' complained Kate.

'Hasn't bothered you before now.' A big grin in his voice.

The queen slapped his stomach playfully. 'You don't kill a man's soul with a blade or a bullet, you hopeless full-mortal. You do it with love.'

'That's why the girl's still breathing, then?'

Not now, she wasn't. Finn was very still in the darkness and shadow.

'She will be as long as he is, dear. She won't stop breathing till Cù Chaorach does.'

· · ·

'A dozen men and Skinshanks. That ought to do it.' Kate and Laszlo had moved on into the main stabling cave so that Laszlo could mount. Finn shut her eyes, but the stupidity of that was too much. She opened them, focused on the slit of silver candlelight beyond the door of the feed store, and the dark block in her mind. *Keep it there. Keep it there. Keep it there or die.*

'What shall I bring you?' Laszlo had laughter in his voice.

'Hmm. Let me see.' Kate tutted softly, as if she were thinking hard. 'A deer and a fox and a boar. As for the dogs: if you find them, feed the birds.'

'That'll be my pleasure.' He kissed her again. 'More my pleasure than you can imagine.'

'Don't be sure of that, my love. Happy hunting.'

In a dull clatter of hooves, the hunting party moved towards the tunnel that would take them out to the hillside. As the hoofbeats picked up speed, they echoed and faded, till only silence and a breath of wind filtered in from the outside world.

If Finn could have pushed herself back through the stone wall behind her, she would. As it was, she crouched, very still, letting air barely stir in and out of her lungs. Kate had paused to murmur to her favourite mare, but at last the silk of her dress whispered as she turned, and Finn smelt her hazelnut scent. Her shoes clicked lightly on stone, and faded past her hiding place, and then Finn did close her eyes, because the wave of happiness threatened to drown her.

It seeped from Kate, but it was overwhelming Finn.

For a timeless instant the queen's contentment and delight were hers, familiar and powerful. Finn ground her teeth, bit hard on the inside of her lip. Useless.

Clutching at her throat, she seized the empty raven's claw. *Faramach*, she thought, *why did he leave me?*

Because I left everyone else . . .

She jerked the slender chain hard to snap it, and the claw fell into her hand. Finn tightened her fist, piercing her flesh with the jagged points of silver.

It hurt beautifully, so she pressed her other hand to it and forced it deeper. She couldn't help gasping as the talons plunged deeper into her palm. Briefly she thought the pain might make her faint; then her vision focused, and her misty befuddled mind was as clear and sharp as the silver points of pain.

She stumbled out of the feed store, and ran.

She found Seth far sooner than she'd expected; halfway down a narrow passageway, an arm shot out and grabbed hers.

'Ow!' she yelled.

'Shut up.' Seth flung her into an empty room. 'Block.'

As if he had to tell her. She jerked her arm out of his grip, and he saw her bloody palm. He blinked, made a grab for it, but she snatched it away, digging the talons back into their holes.

'What have you done to yourself this time? No, never mind. What's Kate up to?'

'She's sending out hunters.'

'*Now?*'

'Twelve. And the Lammyr.' She gulped down nausea. 'It's just a hunt. But—'

He shook his head impatiently. 'Never mind hunting. What's she so unnervingly happy about?'

'I think—' Tears of uncertainty burned her eyes; then she bit her lip hard. '—Conal's fetch.'

Seth went white, his pupils dilating in the shadows.

'What?'

'I saw a fetch. Conal's. That first night here, while you were hunting. I told Conal, but he wouldn't tell me what it was. I told Kate, and she's been like a pig in shit ever since.'

'Jesus. Gods.' Oddly enough for Seth, it didn't sound like blasphemy. He sounded as if he was calling for help. Hands splayed on his mouth, he stared at her. 'Oh, gods, what have we done with you? Why wasn't I told?'

'You weren't there.' She trembled. 'And Conal told me not to tell you.'

'I'll bet he did.' Seth snatched up the sheathed sword that lay on a bench behind him. 'Where's Jed?'

Finn paled, realising he didn't know. 'Jed's gone.'

'*What?* When?'

'Two hours ago. Kate made him leave.'

She didn't think Seth could go any whiter, but he did. As his hand shot out to her throat, she flinched, but he only seized the empty raven's claw. 'Where's your stone?'

'Fell out. Kate's got it.' She felt sick.

'That explains a lot.' He finished buckling on his

sword and tucked his shirt into his jeans. 'Otherwise, you might have the brains to know it.'

Her whole body felt bloodless. 'Know what?'

'That there's only ever one reason to send out a Lammyr.' He strode from the room without looking at her again.

The pain in her hand was gut-sickening now, and she thought she was going to pass out. Gritting her teeth, she clenched her fist on the claw again, and the distant sounds of the hall finally encroached on her brain.

She heard the click of Gealach's chess pieces, the whicker of horses in the stabling cave, the slow thrum of a distant mandolin, a ripple of laughter among men and women just back from a patrol. After a little, it occurred to her that she hadn't breathed for a while, so she filled her lungs; and that allowed her limbs to move.

She ran.

The stronghold was a maze of tunnels, but some compartment of her mind recognised Seth's path as clearly as if he'd left prints in snow. She didn't pause to question the knowledge; but pelting round a corner at full tilt, she skidded and stumbled, banging her shoulder on the wall.

Five women were ahead of her, walking abreast and talking in low laughing voices, effectively blocking her way. Finn blinked. She could be back in the corridor at school, with Shania's gang approaching and no way of avoiding them. Her heartbeat tripped and thudded; then as her vision cleared, a voice called out her name, including her in their gossip and their company.

And she'd fallen for it.

She'd argued with Conal barely a month ago, screaming with rage, taking it out on him instead of Shania's gang. *One day I'll be One Of Them!*

Oh, no, you won't. You're better than that, Finn.

She hadn't been better than that. She'd pawned her soul to be in a gang. What was it going to take to get it back?

The women had fallen silent, bewildered, glancing uneasily at one another. Finn made herself smile, though she was picturing Jed as he walked out of Kate's caverns and it made her feel as sick as if a Lammyr had run pale fingers through her hair.

Tears sheened her eyes, and the women blurred. Gealach walked tentatively forward, but Finn desperately did not want the woman to touch her. Her self-respect was balanced on a wire, and if Gealach touched her, it would spin down irretrievably into the gaping hole where her pride used to be.

'Finn?'

She barged through them as if they were thistledown and sprinted on in Seth's path. They could never catch her. Every feeling she had was concentrated in the palm of her hand, and the rest of her body felt as if it were flying. She could run this fast forever.

'Finn!' The cry went up behind her, anxious and desolate. Her heart ached. She did like them; she liked them a lot. They were like her: They believed Kate, trusted Kate. . . . She beat away the regret and kept running. They'd be all right. She'd be all right too, if she could—

The passageway ended abruptly in a forest clearing. Finn glanced over her shoulder, expecting the entrance to have vanished like a magic trick. But there it was, a stone arch rather smaller than the main one. Around her, the sun filtered through winter-bare branches and yellowed larch, and the forest litter beneath her feet was crisp with a delicate rime of frost.

A sound made her spin on her heel. Seth stood watching her, a shadow among tree-shadows, his sword in his hand, the blade glinting dull grey as his eyes. His stillness was eerie.

He hefted his sword, flipped and flung it hard and straight at her.

Reflexively she shut her eyes. It was all she had time to do. She felt the blade's whisper along her flesh, the sudden bite of cold where it sliced the fabric of her shirt. And then a rattling dry-bone sigh echoed in her ear, and a clammy weight sagged against her shoulder.

She gave a shuddering sob of revulsion. Panicking blindly, she scrabbled at the thing that lay dead against her, but her hand was slippery and clumsy with her own blood, and she was dizzy with nausea. She couldn't get rid of it. Seth had to grab it by the skinfolds of its neck and fling it aside.

Ignoring her, he snatched up his blade and thrust it into an ice-fringed burn on the edge of the clearing. When he drew it out, it was clean of the pale ooze of Lammyr blood.

'Wild running water,' he remarked to the air rather than to Finn. 'There's a stroke of luck.' Reaching deep into a jagged gap between two stones, he drew out a bridle and flicked dead leaves off it. The blue roan moved in the shadows beyond the clearing, and he slipped the bridle over its head.

'Block, you wee fool, or you'll be the death of me.'

'I am blocking,' she stammered. 'You saved my life.'

His voice dripped contempt. 'Don't take it personally.'

She shivered. 'Thanks anyway.'

'Wish I could stay and chat, but I've an urgent meeting.' He scrambled onto the horse's back and took up the reins. 'Bye, Finny.'

'Seth!' she screamed as Branndair loped past.

He spun the horse and looked at her hatefully. 'Stay with your coven, Dorsal. You're happy here, aren't you? Finally, somewhere you belong.'

She tore after him, stumbling on fallen branches, just snagging the horse's reins in her fingertips as it whirled on its hind legs and bared its teeth, the toss of its massive head pulling her off her feet. Seth raised a hand to strike her away.

'You too,' she gritted fiercely. 'Did you belong here too?'

'I haven't got time for this.' He glanced back at the stone archway.

'Give me some time, you selfish bastard!'

'Ooh, that's a common mistake.' He grinned, hauling hard on the horse's mouth so that its teeth couldn't close on her arm. 'You're mixing me up with someone who gives a *spider's fart what you think of me.*'

She moaned with the effort of holding on as the

roan swung its muscled neck violently. Her arms felt
as if they were popping out of their sockets, but she
wouldn't cry. If she cried she'd be left behind and if
she was left behind she would die. 'You cared what
Kate thought!'

'Big misjudgement, much like hers. Oh, you fell
for Kate, didn't you? What did she do, come into
your dreams? That's how she got me.'

'I didn't know her. I thought it was Mum, I thought
she – Stella. The right part of her . . .'

'Your real mother,' he sneered. 'You thought she
was your real mother. Better than the one you had.'

Finn gave another desperate sob.

'Ah, she'd have to use dreams till she got that shield
stone off you. It could protect your conscious mind,
but it couldn't keep her out of your dreams, not our
Kate. Isn't she lovely? All that charm! All that os-
tentatious compassion! Ah, Finny, it rubs off like a
cheap child's tattoo, and then you get to see the
malice, and that gets wearing, let me tell you. But I
never gave a toss for her, never. I hadn't a choice. I
had *no choice*.'

'So why are you leaving?' She shut her eyes tight
and gritted her teeth. Soon she would let go and fall,
and if the horse didn't kill her, Kate would. *Only to
spite Conal. Only to spite him* . . . A fire was burning
in her palm where her blood soaked the reins.

Seth sighed. 'Don't get me wrong, now. I'm not responsible for your little boyfriend and I never will
be. But I'm not going to let Laszlo murder my son's
brother.'

'Seth.' Finn's grip was failing, her ears roaring. 'Going to let him murder me?'

He looked down at her, unblinking. Through the sweat that stung her eyes, he did look like a falcon, she thought irrelevantly, and a rabbit's last sight of a striking talon probably looked much the way his hand looked, raised above her head.

His fingers clenched and unclenched and then, instead of striking her, he reached down and seized her arm, effortlessly swinging her behind him onto the roan's back. He gave her no time to catch a breath before he kicked the horse into a furious gallop.

Gripping him for dear life, Finn felt his shirt wet beneath her hand and knew that it was her blood soaking it. She pressed her cheek to his back and locked her arms harder around his waist, knowing with only seconds to spare that she was going to lose consciousness. An instant later, she did.

When she opened her eyes, surfacing through a haze of pain, something was wrong with the view. It took a moment to register that she was staring at the horse's neck, not at Seth's back, and he was steadying her with an arm round her waist. Groggily she craned to glance over her shoulder. Despite the winter bite of the wind, Seth was stripped to the waist, the blood-stained shirt twisted and knotted round his own waist and hers, tying her to him. Part of a sleeve had been roughly hacked off and wrapped round her hand. Despite the throb and sting, she grinned and shook her foggy head.

'You big soft git.'

A grunt was his only reply as he goaded the roan back to a gallop, the burst of speed whipping any more smart remarks back into her throat. Then, horribly, she remembered.

'Rory!' she shouted, half-turning. 'I promised Jed I'd take care of him.'

'You?' he barked. 'You can't even stay awake to save yourself. You nearly fell off!'

Somehow Finn knew from the way he said it that he'd almost let her go, let her fall. She wondered what had stopped him.

Seth reined the roan back to a canter and sighed, his voice softening a little. 'The best thing you can do for Rory is stop Laszlo killing his brother. Kate's people will look after him, better than you ever could. You think I liked leaving him? But Kate won't harm him. We have friends in a lot more danger than that baby.'

She let her thoughts roam horribly, as the wind speed stung her skin. *Friends. Danger. Oh, God.*

'Does this thing go any faster?'

'Are you going to faint again?' he asked with mild contempt.

'No.'

'Then sit behind. And hold on. And shut up.'

Jed

The bay mare blew gently, ears flicking, and Jed laid his fingers against her neck to feel the soft prickle of horsehair, damp sweat, the warmth of blood in her veins. She felt placid and solid and normal, and it seemed to Jed she was the only thing locking him down to reality. All the same, he wouldn't mind terribly if she stumbled, if he fell and was killed beneath her.

Someone was riding fast towards him across the rock-strewn plateau, but Jed's eyes were hot and blurred, and anyway, he didn't care enough to look. He didn't know if the rider was friend, foe or indifferent stranger, and he'd stopped caring somewhere in the middle of the valley. His mother was dead. He was trapped in a place where he didn't belong, and the only alternative was a place where he didn't exist. He knew he had no chance of getting back to the caverns, that he would never see Rory again, that there was no longer a life much worth living for him.

When the other horse drew alongside, Jed didn't

look at it. He didn't care when the mare's reins were seized from him. He didn't struggle when arms went round him and dragged him off her back, straight onto the other horse and into the fiercest hug he'd ever known. He smelled the sleeve of a familiar woollen jumper as it wiped the tears from his filthy face, and then his head was tucked into a warm shoulder, and a strong arm held him tightly.

Conal did not gallop back. He led the mare at an unhurried walk, Jed in his arms, and he talked quietly all the way. Some of it Jed barely heard, and the rest he would never tell another living soul, but after a little while, feeling crept back into his heart. He began to feel he might survive this, might even want to. He even felt a spark of awkward stirring happiness. It was belonging, and being wanted, and missed, and loved. It was, for once, being looked after.

Conal drew rein, and looked back over his shoulder, and Jed felt him sigh deeply. Then he turned again to his waiting friends. Even then Conal didn't hurry, but let the black horse lead the bay mare at an easy amble into a belt of trees.

'We still have time, Conal,' said Eili. 'We can ride away.'

'Ach, Eili, my brother is back there.' Conal jerked his mouth into a smile. 'I'd like a sharp word with him before I go anywhere.'

'Conal.' Sionnach's voice was gentle. 'Your brother is lost to us.'

'No,' said Conal harshly. 'Not to me.'

Sionnach opened his mouth again, but Torc glared him into silence.

'Conal.' Eili's mask slipped, and in that second she was no longer his lieutenant, only his lover. 'Please,' she whispered. 'We can ride away.'

Jed rubbed his scalp, confused. Conal's arm was still tight around him. It was reassurance and comfort, but Jed could sense it was something else too: Conal did not want him to turn round. Jed twisted anyway and peered past Conal. There was a smudge of motion across the valley. He screwed up his eyes, focusing. Then he made out what it was, and his heart cracked.

'Conal,' began Sionnach.

'It is *too late*,' said Conal through his teeth. Releasing Jed, he let him scramble clumsily across onto the mare. 'She's taken my brother and Jed's too. She's taken Finn. I *will not* leave without them. But I don't ask any of you to stay.'

None of them even bothered to answer him. They fell in behind as he rode the black horse to a high stretch of ground. Its eyes were green-pricked, its nostrils scarlet, and Conal held its reins lightly in one hand, watching the thirteen riders now lining up on the opposite slope. Liath leaped up onto a rock outcrop and snarled into the oppressive air.

They waited. No-one seemed in any hurry. Conal's horse paced eagerly back and forth, hooves thudding hard into the peaty ground, tossing its massive neck. Above them the sky was blue, streaked with high cirrus, but cloud lay low over the far hills, swollen and discoloured with imminent snow. Beneath Jed's breastbone was a wrenching pain, like a wet rag being wrung out in his chest cavity.

'Cù Chaorach! Your godchild's gone over to Kate. She's left you!' Laszlo rode forward, his voice floating mockingly on the clear air. 'Sweet, but once you're dead, Kate'll hang her. She wants you to know that.'

Conal said nothing, but he didn't take his eyes off Laszlo.

'Oh, your brother's betrayed you too, of course! Even the wolf-whelp's led us straight to you. Tell me, how does it feel?'

The horsemen at Laszlo's back stirred restlessly and one of the horses whinnied. Jed's mare whickered quietly in reply, but Conal's black horse stopped still, ears flattening, gills rippling, its snorting breath deepening to a growl. On the far hilltop, the horses spun and backed while the riders fought to control their heads.

'I'm sorry, Eili,' said Jed, barely audibly. 'I'm really sorry.'

She turned her dappled horse and rode a circle to end up at his side. 'Don't say that. You had to come looking for us, you had no choice. Conal found you through your horse and he guided it in.'

'But Kate couldn't—'

'She tracked your head all the way from her caverns.' Eili's voice was curt. 'Now, take this. Conal's orders, before you ask.' Smiling slightly, she handed Jed a sheathed dagger. 'More use than that ridiculous gun of yours.'

Jed fumbled with the buckle of the belt. 'I thought she couldn't get in my head.' He was so ashamed of his arrogance, he wanted to be sick. 'I was so sure, I—'

'Cuilean,' Eili said gently, 'she can get in anyone's head.'

It didn't help. He should have realised. 'Can't Conal call for help? From his dun?'

'You don't understand. They tracked you, it's true; but all that changed was the timescale. Conal never had any intention of returning to the dun, not once she took Finn and Rory.' Eili shrugged lightly. 'Besides, we can't contact the dun; we're too far away and she's blocking us somehow. Torc can't even reach his own son. Her witchcraft's that strong. So don't be ashamed. You're strong too, but you're no match for her.'

'We shouldn't have stayed,' said Sionnach, at his twin's side. 'But Conal was too angry. Not with you. With himself and Kate. He wouldn't leave you or Finn. And he wouldn't leave—' Sionnach's voice caught in his throat, and Jed realised he had choked on Seth's name. '—and we would never leave Conal.'

Sionnach was trying to make him feel better, but it was too many words for the man, and a clumsy effort. It only made Jed want to slink away, and curl into a ball, and hide till the end of time. 'Eili. I know I shouldn't have – it's just that – Rory—'

'Gods, how much do I have to explain? Conal considers the taking of Finn and Rory a defeat. That means he has a – a final right to even things.'

Jed wanted to say, *A last right?* But before he could say it out loud, he heard how it sounded in his head. No. He wouldn't say the double-bladed words.

'So it's not your fault.' There was naked ferocity on Eili's face. 'We're on our own.'

'Son of the hound Griogair!' shouted Laszlo. 'Come and get flesh!'

Conal's lip curled back from his teeth. 'You heard my claim, then? You're getting better.'

'Kate let me know.' Laszlo laughed. 'I'm more than happy with the challenge.'

'I doubt that. But nothing else would get you to stick your pretty head out of your hole.'

Eili and Sionnach urged their horses forward to his left and right side. Eili muttered, 'This is a trap, Conal.'

'I know it is.' Beneath him the black horse shuddered with aggression, flanks streaked with sweat, and Conal laid a soothing hand on its withers. 'But some traps have to be sprung.'

He turned to Jed, smiling, and rode back to him. 'Listen. Stay here. That dagger's for self-defence, nothing else. Don't get involved, whatever happens. That is an order. Okay?'

'But—'

'Jed. You barely know how to hold it.' Conal laughed but his eyes were kind. 'Don't even touch it unless you have to. You'll cut yourself.'

Jed tried to laugh too, but he couldn't.

'We'll be back in a minute, right? No big deal.' Conal leaned closer to him, reaching out a hand to cup the back of his head. 'Jed,' he murmured. 'If it all goes pear-shaped, just ride. Ride northwest like stink.' He grinned, swivelled Jed's skull and pointed. 'That's that way, all right? Don't look back. Keep riding, and one of our clann will lock on to you and find you. Tell them I sent you.'

Clenching his teeth, Jed glared at him. It was all he could do to stop himself crying.

'And for gods' sake, let them look in your head, you stubborn pup, or they'll cut it off. But we'll be back, 'kay?' He turned his horse to stare back at Laszlo and his men. 'We're just going to sort something out here.'

He flexed his fingers, stroking the black shoulder beneath him, and spoke to the horse in a soft voice. Its ears flicking forward, it snorted and plunged onto the slope and down, leaping from rock to tussock onto the boulder-strewn plateau. The twins were right behind him, but Torc hung back, keeping Jed company.

Laszlo rode forward to meet them, his smile reaching his warm brown eyes. He and Conal circled each other at a respectful distance as each slowly drew his blade.

Conal grinned. 'It's about time.'

'Past time. You won't be running back to the shadows this time, Cù Chaorach. Kate has taught me to block you. You won't get into my head, if that's what you're hoping.'

Conal gave him a thin smile. 'I wouldn't want to go there.'

'You have no idea how true that is, warlock.'

'You have to throw names?' Conal shrugged. 'Listen. Leave the boy alone.'

Laszlo's mouth twitched. 'The others will. That I guarantee. The rest is up to you.'

'No more deals, then.' Conal lifted his sword to

his face in salute, laughing when Laszlo mirrored the gesture with his middle finger raised.

The black horse leaped forward and thundered towards Laszlo's. Jed's heart bounded raggedly, and his teeth clenched hard. The impetus was so fierce, it looked as if the horses would collide and explode into fragments, but as they came abreast, the black veered and snaked its head sideways, sinking its teeth into the neck of Laszlo's chestnut. Conal leaped from its back, crashing into Laszlo and flinging him to the ground.

They rolled together, blades glittering wildly so that Jed couldn't bear to look. Then they were on their feet, breathing hard and edging round each other. Laszlo lunged, Conal parried, and then they were at it in earnest, slashing, dodging, leaping, the air split by the furious ring of steel.

Jed's heart might have been slamming right against his breastbone; it was that hard to breathe. 'He's faster than Laszlo,' he said desperately. 'Isn't he?'

'Laszlo isn't so slow himself,' said Torc. 'And he's good with a blade. Very.' He paused; then his face lit up. 'Ah-hah! You dogshits!'

His laugh was aimed at the twelve horsemen, who were riding down the opposite hill in a thundering pack. 'I knew the bastards wouldn't leave it to the Captains! Brilliant!' He kicked his heels into the iron grey and it sprang forward with astonishing lightness. Swaying perilously, Torc turned to give Jed a cheery wave. 'See ya, Cuilean!'

Eili was first to turn on the enemy detachment, yelling in infernal excitement, and before her two swords had completed their first arc, one of the riders was rolling half-decapitated to the earth. The woman was a psycho, thought Jed, just as his terrible shock was overwhelmed by a cold and eerie calm.

Eili sprang from her own horse to the fallen rider's, then down to the ground, beckoning on the next man. Torc's huge iron grey was lashing out with its feathered hooves as Torc swung his sword one-handed from its back, and Sionnach rode like a fiend between them all, reins knotted as he wielded his own slender swords with an economical grace.

'Only twelve?' Eili laughed wildly as she yanked a blade from the breast of the man who sagged against her. Another was behind, flying at her, but the white wolf met him before he could connect. Liath bowled him aside in midair, sinking her teeth in his jaw. Blood spurted across her muzzle.

The bay mare was peaceful beneath Jed. She at least wasn't itching to join in. And nor should Jed be, but he was. Sitting here on the mare's back felt like disgrace, like a punishment. Oh, now he felt like a puppy; an infant left at the side of the field while the grown-ups got on with business. The shame was thick in his throat, worse than the fear. He wasn't to fight at all, not even to save himself: he was only to run with his tail between his legs. That was the worst scenario. The best was that Eili, Sionnach and Torc would make mince of Laszlo's little army and he'd have contributed nothing.

And yet he was afraid, really afraid, and he didn't want to go down there, and he was glad of Conal's orders. Jed spat on the ground in disgust at himself.

At that moment, a great instinctive shudder went from the nape of his neck to the base of his spine. Something was moving through the melee, an emaciated figure with a long trench coat flapping loose behind it. Its path through the fighting was effortless, because Laszlo's men were flinching out of the Lammyr's path, clearing its way to Torc. It strolled on quite nonchalantly, not even bothering to hurry.

Skinshanks. Jed closed his trembling fingers tight round the dagger's hilt. He would not, would absolutely *not* cut himself.

Torc was off his horse now, fighting hand to hand with one of Laszlo's men. He didn't see the Lammyr approaching. *Not Torc*, thought Jed in despair. Torc couldn't run from a Lammyr; Torc wasn't quick enough. And Torc couldn't see it coming.

A thin thread of anger coiled round Jed's heart, loosening the grip of terror. It was only a sliver of courage, but if he just sat here and let the Lammyr walk unseen up to Torc, he wouldn't be able to live with himself. Jed kicked his legs clumsily into the bay mare's flanks, and she nickered tolerantly, but she didn't move.

He kicked her again. She lowered her head and stood foursquare.

Jed looked up sharply at Conal, parrying Laszlo's sword with a clash of steel and turning it as it slashed at his shoulder. The tosser. The Boy Scout. The big *idiot*. All his attention ought to be on his opponent, but it wasn't. Conal was cheating. He had a hold on Jed's horse.

Two could cheat at that game. Angrily Jed slid

from the mare's back and ran, as fast and as hard as he ever had. If he tripped and cut himself, it'd be Conal's fault; but he didn't. Jed hurtled down the slope and across the plateau, leaping the boulders, desperation making him sure-footed. Before he had time to change his mind, he was in the thick of it.

Laszlo's men were true to their leader's word, dodging Jed with lightning ease and staying out of his way. Jed was behind the Lammyr very suddenly, and he skidded in the churned earth, yelling. It turned, unconcerned, as if all he'd done was tap it politely on the shoulder.

Maybe this wasn't such a good idea. As the Lammyr took a step towards him, Jed lashed out clumsily with the dagger.

'Tsk. Don't get involved.' Skinshanks's bony-knuckled hand caught Jed's blade as it slashed wildly, pulling him in so close, he could smell its dry sweet breath. 'Do as your Captain tells you, you disobedient pup.'

Pale blood trickled from its palm, over Jed's hilt and onto his hand. Jed clenched his teeth, waiting for the swamping sickness, but it never came. Instead he felt Mila's touch on his cheek, a breeze like her soft murmur in his ear, and he clasped the hilt of the trapped dagger in both hands. Then he hacked it as hard and deep as he could.

Skinshanks stumbled backwards, gripping its split wrist and the loose-hanging thumb, trying to clamp the two halves of its hand together. Opening its mouth in a wide smile of delight, it turned with a swirl of its coat and walked away, colourless fluid dribbling from its sleeve. The heather withered where it fell. Shuddering, Jed lifted his dagger. Before his eyes, the blade cracked into glistening shards and tinkled to the rock at his feet.

'Torc!' screamed Sionnach, whose snarling dapple-grey, blood leaking from a gash in its rump, was lashing obsessively at its attacker. Sionnach jumped down and sprinted for Torc, but two of Laszlo's men intercepted him, one for each blade.

The Lammyr was making its unhurried way towards Torc, reaching into its coat with its good hand and drawing out half-seen curved things that glinted evilly in the winter brightness. Torc raised his sword, a snarl on his face, but the Lammyr's first spinning blade wasn't aimed at him: it thunked into his rearing horse's neck just below the throatlash of its bridle. The horse screamed hideously and stumbled forward, crashing to the ground, and a wide fan of aortal blood sprayed Torc from head to thigh.

Howling with rage, Torc took the sword in both hands, deflecting two blades in quick succession. The second spun wildly, ricocheting into the neck of one of Laszlo's men, making Skinshanks shake its head with ironic laughter. Still chuckling to itself, it drew the third blade, feinted in a blur to the left and flung it deep into Torc's chest.

'No, no, no!' Eili's scream cut across the uproar, drowning out Jed's, as Torc fell forward onto his knees. The big man looked up at the Lammyr with defiant loathing as Skinshanks drew a dagger, grasped his jaw to tug it back, and slit his throat.

It closed its eyes blissfully as a fountain of blood

jetted across it, but it didn't wait to see Torc topple
forward like a felled tree. It turned lightly away, an
ecstatic smile lighting its face. Liath stalked forward
with head lowered and hackles high, but Skinshanks
only flicked its wounded hand at her, sending a spurt
of colourless blood across her savage jaws. The wolf
howled in pain, pawing at her muzzle, and fled with
her tail between her legs.

Jed looked helplessly across the field to where
Conal and Laszlo stood apart, panting, eyeing each
other in a hideous stalemate. Blood matted Conal's
hair and ran in streaks down the left side of his face
and neck; Laszlo's arm and hand glistened scarlet
with it, a vicious slash gaping on his upper arm. Both
of them turned to watch the Lammyr's carnage,
swords still held defensively high. Then they glanced
at each other, coldly half-smiling, and hurtled back
into combat.

Eili slid to her knees beside Torc, pushing him onto
his side with one hand, the other poised to mend the
wounds. His hand still twitched on his sword hilt, but
the blood no longer spurted from his gaping throat;
the thrown blade had stopped his heart. There was
nothing for Eili to do but close his lightless eyes.

Jed caught a slick movement at the edge of his vision, but the warning he shouted was far too late. He
ran towards Eili, but one of Laszlo's men sprang into
the air and kicked out, catching him below his rib
cage and sending him sprawling.

The Lammyr flew for Eili's back, clutching her lovingly as it sank its teeth into her shoulder. Roaring,
she rose from Torc's body, lifted both swords and

jerked them in an arc over her head. The Lammyr dodged, snaking its head and torso sideways.

'For goodness' sake!' it hissed. *'Cooperate!'*

Its bloodied mouth bit into her again, closer to her neck, lips curving around her flesh in a wide smile as its teeth went harder and deeper. Clenching its wounded fist, it squeezed its own colourless blood into the bite. It must have found better nerves on its second attempt, because Eili dropped her swords, scrabbling at the thing that clung to her, and her tormented scream merged with Sionnach's yell of terrified fury.

Skinshanks dropped off her, licking its lips as it admired the blood flow. Jed, staggering to his feet, saw her lunge for her swords, but two of Laszlo's men had seized her almost before she moved. One jerked her head back to hold his dagger to her throat.

'Back off, Sionnach. I don't want to hurt her.'

'Speak for yourself, Lus-nan-Leac,' said the other dryly.

Sionnach, watching his twin, lowered his swords slowly.

'Sionnach, no.' Eili's voice was thick and hoarse, her eyes dazed and filmy. 'Bradan, my brother'll kill you if I don't.' Digging her trembling fingers into the Lammyr's bite, she clenched her teeth.

Bradan snorted. Eyeing Torc's dead horse, he gave its head a savage sidelong kick, and Jed noticed he had only two fingers on his left hand.

A shout of contempt pulled all their attention. Conal crouched before Laszlo, clutching his sword hand, blood running freely between his fingers. The sword itself lay ten feet from him, where Laszlo had struck it from his grip as Conal turned towards Eili's appalling scream. Now Laszlo's sword was at Conal's throat, already pricking blood from the hollow of it.

'Filthy mortal,' snarled Eili into the sudden silence, her bloody hand clamped inside her shoulder. 'Sionnach, please!'

'Sionnach, if you even move in Cù Chaorach's direction, I'll cut her throat myself,' said Bradan calmly. 'You know Lus-nan-Leac was fond of Eili, but for me it'd be a pleasure, so don't tempt me. Drop your swords.'

'Sionnach, *no*!' she screamed. 'Go to Conal!'

Watching his dark eyes, Jed saw the exact moment Sionnach's heart broke. Meeting his twin's gaze, he shook his head very slightly. The slender curved swords rang discordantly as they clattered to the stones.

In the silence, something sounded like rock scree tumbling, but it was only a dry mocking sob from the Lammyr, perched on a granite outcrop above them all.

'This is so touching,' it hiccupped, wiping a fingertip delicately under a dry eye. It used its hurt hand, lifting the dead finger with its good hand by way of a macabre joke.

Lus-nan-Leac shuddered, his blade scraping Eili's skin. 'Sorry,' he muttered.

'Tsk! Where's your honour, Nils?' Skinshanks sprang down, darting to Conal's sword.

Conal's gaze never left it as it picked up his sword. There was absolutely no hope in his expression, only a dead-eyed loathing.

The Lammyr raised the sword high, smiled, and drew the blade down through the ugly split of its hand, cutting even farther into the gaping wrist. It tossed the weapon to Conal, who caught it reflexively by the hilt and studied the ooze that coated it, flicking the blade with a finger.

Laughing, Laszlo rose and withdrew the tip of his sword from Conal's throat to give a mocking salute. 'Come on, then, Cù Chaorach. Let's do this the chivalrous way.'

'Let's do it my way,' said Conal, and tossed his sword high into the air.

They all watched it spin, glittering in the snow-light. Even Laszlo gaped at it, hypnotised. It had yet to touch down when Conal took a running leap and fell on Laszlo.

Dodging the man's flailing blade he slipped round his enemy like a python, grabbed his head and locked a forearm round his neck, struggling for the leverage to snap it. In the awful stillness, Laszlo snatched grunting at Conal's arm, jaw clenched, straining with the effort not to die.

Then Conal's sword finally came to earth, plummeting into the peat point-first. Where it should have stood quivering, it shattered into razor shards, showering both men.

Starred with pinpricks of blood, Laszlo seemed to recover his focus. His sword arm swung back hard, the blade biting into Conal's side deep enough to loosen his hold. Laszlo flung him off.

Conal looked once towards the group at the foot

of the hill. Seeing Eili still alive, he turned away, smiling. His eye caught Jed's.

Jed's pride was all gone now. Conal was the closest thing he had to a father, the only father he'd ever known, and he was standing down there alone without a sword. Jed let Conal into his head, pleading. *Please win. Please win. Please live.*

All Conal could give him was a wry smile. Then all his attention was back on Laszlo, who was striding confidently forward, sword held back for a vicious sidelong slash.

Conal sprinted forward almost into the teeth of the blade and just as it swung to disembowel him jumped high, twisting in the air like a cat. Laszlo stumbled with his own impetus, rolling as he fell, and gaped up in disbelief. Conal was falling towards him with hands outstretched for his throat. Yelling, Laszlo grasped his sword two-handed.

There was a fraction of time, and he snatched it. He wrenched up his weapon, thrust it savagely into Conal's belly. As the weight of Conal's own body bore him down, Laszlo twisted the blade sideways and upwards till it ground into his breastbone.

Laszlo grunted in pain as Conal thudded onto him, then heaved hard and shoved him off. Staggering to his feet, he grinned down into Conal's face, seized the sword-hilt and yanked out the blade in a spray of blood. Conal's body arched upwards, sank down, and he sighed almost dreamily.

'God, but you've been a troublesome vermin,' said Laszlo, trailing the tip of his sword down Conal's rib cage and back up to the hollow of his throat, where the pinprick wound of his first attempt was beaded with blood.

'Shall I finish what I started, Cù Chaorach? Or shall I obey my queen, and let the buzzards do it?'

Jed barely knew he'd run until he was stumbling forward across Conal, knocking Laszlo's blade away and splaying his cut arms across the body. 'Get off him! Get off!'

Laszlo rolled his eyes. 'Oh, not you again. Well, well, I suppose it saves the effort of coming to you. Two birds with one stone. Is that the expression, *mate*?'

Jed scrabbled at his belt, hauling out the pistol and pointing it at Laszlo's chest. For an instant the man's eyes dilated in fear, and then he laughed.

'So. I guessed you had that. Ten out of ten for effort, but you know it's wasted.'

'That's what you think.'

'The safety isn't even off!' Laszlo bellowed.

Jed thumbed it quickly. 'It is now.'

Laszlo eyed him, lips twitching. 'It doesn't work, you stupid brat.'

Jed's pulse beat so hard in his throat, it was choking him. *He's right. You tit. And now you're dead. You tit.*

'Look, can I get on with my work? We'll talk after that.' Smiling, Laszlo lifted his blade and winked.

Superstitious. Seth said Laszlo was superstitious. He believed in idiotic prophecies. 'It'll work on you. Kate told me. You killed somebody with it, so it can kill you. See? It'll kill the one who's murdered with it, she said.' Jed hoped that sounded vaguely like Kate. 'Part of its – um. Its charm.'

'That's a good one. You're a liar as well as a thief. Skinshanks!' roared Laszlo. 'Deal with this whelp!'

'No, no. He's quite right, you know.'

Laszlo twisted his head to stare at the Lammyr. Reclining on a rock, it laughed and wiggled its mutilated fingers at him.

'What?' Laszlo's eyes, for the first time, held sparks of fear. 'Skinshanks, don't piss around. This is serious.'

'So am I, Nils. You're on your own. I'm interested to see how this turns out. Besides, I've told you already: I like the boy.'

Disbelief and betrayal darkened Laszlo's face. 'So you have a new pet. It doesn't mean you need to kill *me.*'

'Would I? Nils, you wound me.' Pouting, Skinshanks nodded at Jed. 'But it'll be terribly funny if *he* does.'

'The bloody gun doesn't *work.*'

'Oh, it's like a movie!' Skinshanks clapped its hands. 'Will it go off in your face? Won't it go off in your face?' It folded its arms, looked brightly from one to the other.

Jed stood up, levelling the gun at the bridge of Laszlo's nose. 'Get away from him.'

'I think I'll take my chances.' The man took a step forward.

Jed made himself smile. *Like a Lammyr,* he thought. *Smile like a Lammyr*. And he saw Laszlo pale.

'I'm going to kill you. I'm the one. But if you back off now, I won't do it today.'

'Oh, so what?' Laszlo eyed the gun once more, then stepped back, trembling, and spat in Conal's face. 'You'll be a long time dying, Cù Chaorach. But you will die.'

Not a muscle moved in Conal's face as Laszlo backed away, then turned and loped to one of the dead men's horses, treading on the corpse of his own. 'Bring the twins back to Kate!' he shouted over his shoulder as he mounted. 'The boy to me; you hear me, Skinshanks? Leave Cù Chaorach to the crows.' He kicked the horse into a gallop, his yell sharpened by humiliation.

Leaderless, Laszlo's men exchanged glances, their eyes quicksilver-bright. One, in an indigo shirt, took a step towards Jed, but Lus-nan-Leac, his blade still at Eili's throat, shook his head. Indigo Shirt stopped in his tracks, gave Jed a single pitying glance, then averted his eyes.

Conal was staring at the sky, motionless, but when Jed fell to his knees beside him, his left hand moved very fast, gripping Jed's jaw and forcing his face round to look at his own. The other hand, his right hand, was clutched across his torn belly, holding in his innards.

'Don't look down,' he whispered.

'Okay.' Sniffing, Jed rubbed the spittle from Conal's

face with his bare hand, his tears blotching the skin, and smoothed back the sweat-stiffened hair from his forehead.

'Look up, Jed. Look at the sky. It's lovely.' Conal's eyes blurred; then his lips moved again, inaudibly. *Praying?* Jed thought, and then the wild hope hit him: Conal was muttering some magical Sithe incantation that would mend the hole Laszlo had put in him. A heartbeat later, as a single clear word formed, Jed knew that he was only swearing through gritted teeth at the pain of it.

When Conal caught sight of Jed's face, he stopped. 'Disobedient pup.' He half smiled. 'Brave lad. Thank you.'

'Conal. Oh, God. Conal.' Jed began to cry in earnest.

'Gun didn't scare him, Jed. You did.'

'You can still talk,' said Jed desperately. 'You'll be okay.'

'Be talking for a while. Y'll be begging me to shut up.' Conal grinned, the corners of his mouth flecked with bloody spittle. 'But'm not going to be okay.'

Jed opened his mouth to argue, but Conal silenced him with a beautiful smile of genuine happiness. 'He's coming,' he whispered. 'I knew he'd come.'

The scream of a horse split the air, and hooves thundered on peat and rock.

'Oh, what now?' said Skinshanks testily. It raised itself on one arm, then got to its feet just like an interrupted moviegoer. Turning, it was in time to see the blue roan gather itself mid-gallop, and spring.

'Tiresome!' was all it had time to say before Seth's

sword split the air and its head flew from its shoulders. The figure clinging to Seth's waist gave a short scream and pressed her face between his shoulder blades.

Jed was surprised to feel a little sorry for Laszlo's six surviving men, who swore and spun and panicked as Seth cut through them like some insane reaping machine. The Lammyr dealt with, sheer surprise allowed him to kill Indigo Shirt with barely an argument. By the time the rest had realised he was not here on some incomprehensible errand of Kate's, his own impetus was carrying him forward in such a red rage that the others stood no chance.

Only one of them survived. Eili, finally free to move as her guards leaped to defend themselves, slammed her forearm back into Lus-nan-Leac's face. He reeled back, stunned, and slumped to the ground. Eili did not even look at Bradan. Tugging her hand from her ragged half-healed wound, she walked away from him without a backward glance.

Casually, Sionnach lifted his swords and flung them as one. Bradan slammed against the rock wall, impaled, as the light died in his shocked eyes.

Then Eili was running, sprinting past Seth as he hacked the last man down, heedless of the blood soaking down her jersey, running like a hunted deer. She didn't spare Jed a glance as she fell to her knees and stroked Conal's hair, smoothing down the spikes of sweat and gore.

'You're alive. You're alive.' It was the first sound she had made since she saw Conal fall to earth, but her throat oozed a red line where she'd strained against the blade. Hesitantly her hand hovered over his gap-ing wound, and he gave a single sobbing cry as she lowered it.

Blinking hard, he clamped his mouth shut, a trickle of blood leaking from the corner. Something like a laugh wheezed in his chest. 'You 'kay, my lover? You can run.'

'I'm fine,' Eili said distractedly. 'I'm sorry, I'm sorry I screamed like that.'

'Don't. Couldn't help it. Told me it was a trap.' He was the colour of ash, but he grinned as a shadow fell across his face. 'Hey, Prodigal. Knew you'd be back.'

Seth fell to his knees, letting his sword clatter to the ground and laying a hand against his brother's cheek. Leaning forward, he pressed his forehead to Conal's, then kissed his pale skin. Jed thought he saw a tear fall from his eye onto Conal's cheek, a single spasm of grief tightening his face.

Conal's eyes widened. 'Seth, no. Please.'

Jed's head jolted up. He would have flung himself at Seth and dragged him away, but Finn grabbed his arm, holding him back. One angry glance told him she was Finn again.

'Get out,' whispered Conal, and his brother jerked back as if he'd been flung away. Seth clutched his belly in agony and sucked in a silent cry.

Conal's voice grated against his throat. 'Don't risk it. This one's mine, Seth.'

'Conal, I'm sorry.' Finn shut her eyes, against tears and the sight of him.

'Not your fault, love, 's my own.' Conal let go his grip on Jed to reach for her, but all he could manage was to stroke her cheek once with a finger. 'Saw my fetch, toots.'

'I didn't mean to see it. I didn't want—'

'Course not.' He bit his lip hard as a shudder went through him, and his voice dropped to a rattling whisper. 'Listen. The things you thought? Kate had you spellbound. Poor Finn. Where's your stone?'

'I lost it.' She bit blood from her lip. 'It wasn't Kate. I was One Of Them, it was me, I—'

'It was Kate.' Conal's eyes were hot silver. 'Believe that.'

Eili gave a strangled shriek of frustration then. Pulling her bloodied fingers from Conal's innards, she eased back the edge of the wound and slid both her trembling hands inside.

Conal's grip closed on her arm, and her tears fell onto his hand unhindered.

'Eili.' It was barely audible. 'Too much. Please stop.'

'You said you'd stay,' she howled. 'You said this time you'd stay! *You promised!*'

'I'm sorry, I'm sorry. Eili. Please stop. Please.'

Slowly she took her hands from the gaping mess of the wound. For the second time that day, Jed disobeyed Conal, and looked. His gorge rose.

'Forgive me, Eili,' gasped Conal through gritted teeth. 'Stop.'

'I don't want you to die!'

'Don't want to die.' His smile was stretched thin. 'Ach, Eili. Don't want to die badly.'

'You couldn't,' she said fiercely.

'Not if you help.'

Wind stirred like a whisper on the moor. Close by

the black horse stood, head lowered, its snorts deep
and guttural. A white shadow moved, whining as she
limped to Conal and lay down with her muzzle on
his sprawled foot.

'No. I can't.' Eili shut her eyes.

The sound of a drawn dagger ripped the stillness.
Eili's eyes snapped open. 'No. Don't you *dare* touch
him again.'

Seth put his hand to Conal's face, his eyes lightless. 'I'm his brother.'

'You're a traitor!' she shouted. 'It's my work, not
yours!'

'I'm cold, Seth. Gods, 'm so cold.' Conal's teeth
were clenched hard.

Both Seth and Eili fell silent, and Conal's head lolled
towards Eili, a gout running from the corner of his
mouth to join the rest of the blood that soaked his
hair. He spat more of it, shivering. 'He's my brother,
Eili. Deny him this, he's paid. Understand?'

'Yes.' Her voice was level, but her hands trembled
violently.

'Eili.' The pitch of Conal's voice had risen. 'I need.
You. To *do this right*.'

She closed her eyes, and her hands stilled. Stroking
his face, she rested his head on the palm of her left
hand, then bent down and kissed him till he stopped
shivering. Her right hand moved to the sheath on
her belt. Conal smiled into her eyes.

Jed grabbed Finn and tugged her face against his
neck, but the motion of Eili's hand was barely visible
anyway. She never let her gaze drop from Conal's as

the blade in her steady grip flashed bright across his throat.

Blood spurted across Jed's cheek; he heard the suck of air in an open windpipe, the squirt and gurgle of blood. There was awareness in Conal's eyes for interminable seconds, and he spent it looking into Eili's.

Then the silver light faded, and went out.

PART FIVE

Seth

'Oh,' said Finn. 'Oh.' She pushed Jed away and stumbled back, and looked to me for help.

I said nothing. I did nothing. I watched my brother's empty face.

Eili was still on her knees, eyes locked on Conal's as Sionnach stepped from behind her and knelt to draw down his eyelids. She gave one strangled howl before she fell silent again and rose to her feet. The bloodied knife was still in her hand, and she moved it, trancelike, till the tip of it was pressed below my ear.

Sionnach pressed it gently away from my jugular. 'Like it or not,' he said quietly, 'Seth's our Captain now.'

Eili's voice was all contempt. 'I'll go with him and I'll ride at his back and I'll fight at his word, but he'll never be my Captain. And if I'm called upon to kill him, it'll be my duty and my joy.'

'You may be,' said Sionnach. 'And soon. Let the clann deal with him.'

Did they think this was over? Perhaps, for them, it was. And that was probably best. I turned to Jed.

He'd walked away, back to the bay mare, pausing with tight-shut eyes and shaking fingers to prise a sword from a dead man's hand. The mare whickered and walked to meet him, her dark muzzle blowing affectionately into his ear. Jed put his arms around her neck and pressed his face to her warm skin. He stood there for a long time, as if he no longer had the will to move.

Getting to my feet, I took up my un-blooded dagger, then grasped a handful of my hair and slashed through it, close to the scalp. Jed watched me for a few seconds, then turned away.

When I went to him, what felt like an age later, he flinched back and blinked. He didn't recognise me, I realised.

Fair enough. 'I'm sorry I hit you,' I said.

'Oh.' Jed frowned, touching his face. 'I forgot. Okay.'

'I wanted to hit my brother, but he wasn't there.'

'Bet you wish he had been.' Jed looked right into my eyes. 'Now.'

'Yes,' I said. 'Things might have . . . well.'

'Funny,' said Jed. 'You calling me a Lost Boy.'

I clenched my teeth. 'I loved your mother, okay?' Gods, the words tasted bitter, but I had to get them out before I thought better of it. I might not get another chance. 'I know fine it wasn't enough, but I wasn't capable of more. If I'd stayed around, I might have protected her from the Lammyr, but I didn't. I betrayed her like I betrayed my brother and if there was an afterlife I'd be down on my knees to their ghosts, but there isn't, so that's that.'

Jed listened to me in pitying silence. I stood there and took it.

Resentment warred with grief inside me. 'But nothing I say or feel is any use to you. So I won't apologise.'

'Thanks,' said Jed curtly, and I knew he meant it.

I gazed at him for a long moment. 'You look different.'

Eyeing my scalp, Jed gave a short laugh.

'Yeah. Don't say it.' I handed him the belt and scabbard that matched his sword. 'Here. Hard to ride with a naked blade.'

'Thanks.' Awkwardly Jed worked his looted sword into its sheath, then buckled on the belt.

'Not like that.' I rolled my eyes. 'Here. This strap. It's not fecking rocket science.'

He submitted to my assistance. 'Nice shirt.'

Dispassionately I touched the sticky stain over my heart and fingered the ragged rip in the indigo cotton. 'Feorag won't be needing it, any more than he needs his sword belt. And I'm tired. I was starting to get cold.'

'Uh-huh,' said Jed. 'I guess Feorag wasn't.'

'Not that he'll ever feel.' I raised my eyes to the sky. 'Y'know, Cuilean, when I was nine and Feorag was eight, we were never apart. What a war it is, Jed. What a war.' I shut my eyes, letting myself wallow in half an instant's useless nostalgia, then blinked them open. 'So. I know where you're going.'

Carefully Jed tucked the gun out of the way into his jeans. 'I left Rory there. I have to go back for him.'

'I left my favourite T-shirt. Doesn't mean I'm getting it back.'

Jed looked me up and down. 'You don't change.'

'What, and let her win? Good luck to you, Cuilean.' I cupped my hand for the boy's foot, boosting him into the saddle and slapping the mare's flank.

Jed didn't look back, didn't even look sideways. He was fixing his focus on what was in front of him, not letting the chill of fear back inside his belly. I recognised it all.

Well, at least he'd get to the caverns, even if he never got out again.

Jed rode past Finn without acknowledging her, gaze still fixed between the mare's ears, but he raised a hand quickly and belatedly from the reins to wave good-bye. Dazed, she watched him go, rooted to the spot as the mare carried him out of sight over the ridge.

She could see nothing else for those long moments, so I took my chance. Drawing my hunting knife, I approached her back in silence. Taking swift hold of the leaf necklace, I slit the leather thong before she could even flinch.

With a small gasp, she turned and stared at the carved wooden leaf in my palm.

I closed my fist over it. 'Rowan. Gods, girl, but you're too strong.'

'What—?'

'She's been using you since you got here,' I said.

Studying the thing, I stroked its delicate toothed leaves with a forefinger. 'This is enchanted, of course, but it only helped; made her connection with you stronger. Your mind's a fierce thing, Finny; you might as well have been carrying a loaded gun. All that power, there for her to take, and you never even knew it. It was you making the air thick. All that interference, all that white noise. Your block. Your mind.'

Her voice was hoarse with horror. 'I was stopping you? I was stopping you communicating?'

'Nope. She was.' I balanced the leaf on a boulder, drew my sword, and slammed the hilt into it twice, three times, then used the blade to sweep the charmed splinters into the grass. 'That was an amplifier; you were the weapon. That's why the shield stone was no help; there was nothing to protect *you* from. But she never had to use her own mind; she had yours to play with. All the more when you were wearing that. I tell you, you're too strong.'

Her throat jerked as she swallowed hard. 'Meaning what?'

I shrugged. 'How would I know? Forget it for now. She can't do it again. The talisman's broken and you're aware of her. Let's talk about Jed.' I watched her eyes soften at his name. 'So, would you die for him? For old times' sake?'

She went as grey as the stones.

'Finn,' I said softly. 'You don't have to be a coward with a mind like yours.'

'I know I'm a coward.' Averting her gaze, she

tugged at the rough linen bandage on her hand, twisting it savagely, as if she wanted to make it bleed again.

I grasped the bandaged hand, stopping her. 'Listen.' I leaned closer. 'Laszlo can kill you. The Lammyr can kill you. Kate can't.'

She narrowed her eyes. 'Is that the truth?'

'Think what you like of me, I don't lie. It's the bargain Kate made for her . . . magic tricks. Others have to do her dirty work. That's how she kills with such a happy heart; those laughter lines of hers are genuine, believe me. That's how she can talk so glibly about not hurting people. Just like she promised me she wouldn't hurt Conal.'

The blood drained from her face. 'She told me she wouldn't hurt Jed.'

'She won't.'

'She *did* kill Conal. She just used Laszlo.'

'Ah, no. Kate's too clever for that. Strictly speaking, Laszlo killed him. And Conal delivered himself to Laszlo because Kate knew how to play on his recklessness. Sh! All right, his courage, if you want to be sentimental about it. And she knew how to play on his obsessions too, and his temper, all the things that put the fear of the gods into Jed and drove him away.' I laid my fingers against her lips before she could get the retort out. 'Don't bother saying it, Finn. I caused my brother's death and I'll pay for it. I already am.'

'Are you?' Her lip twisted.

'Never enough for Eili, that's for sure.' A shiver ran through me.

'Don't go feeling sorry for yourself, will you? We've brought it on ourselves, whatever Eili does.'

'She'll do nothing to you, Dorsal. You were beloved of Conal.'

Her tear ducts filled. 'He was worth ten of you. A hundred.'

'Didn't I tell you not to say it? I can read your mind. Think I don't know it myself?'

'No.' She shook her head. 'No, I don't think you do. Conal's temper, Conal's obsessions, that's all you can talk about. Want to blame him for anything else?'

'Okay, I'll oblige you.' I grinned viciously. 'Kate even knew how to play on his love. He loved you, he loved Jed, and fool that he was, he loved me. And I killed him. *We* killed him. Is that what you wanted to hear? He loved us all and it killed him, *Finny.*'

Her eyes were dry and disbelieving.

I met her stare, then ground the heels of my hands into my eye sockets. 'Would you listen to me? I'm sorry. I'm so sorry. Damn it, Kate's good at what she does.'

She made a slight move forward, and for an instant I thought she was going to put her arms around me. I dropped my hands from my bloodshot eyes, frozen cool once more, and she backed off.

'Finn. Kate'll try to suck your self out of you till you don't even exist anymore. But you have to consent to your own destruction. Keep her poisons out of your mind and you'll be okay.'

'Like you did?'

I laughed. 'Be my guest. She always enchanted me, that woman, and if she was standing here, I'd want her even now. I'm not saying it's easy. But you've already managed it once.' Gripping her mutilated hand, I wrenched it up to her face. 'You didn't need any stone, did you? You can rely on those damn things too much, that's what Leonora didn't tell you. You can stop listening to your own instincts. But you did without it in the end: clever girl.' I put the palm of my hand against the bloody bandage and interlinked my fingers with hers. 'Use your instincts and you'll be fine.'

She stared at my hand, swallowing, and I remembered that was exactly how Conal used to hold her hand after a bad day at school. Something that might have been a heartstring twanged in my chest, and I let her go.

'Then Jed will be fine too,' she said. 'He can fend her off.'

'Yes, funny, isn't it? He has talents, your full-mortal.' I smiled. 'But he still has a soft belly for cold steel.'

Her skin paled as she put her wounded hand to her throat. 'I'm going back.'

'I imagined you would.'

'You're not going to try and stop me?'

Did I look like a responsible older relative or something? 'Want me to save you from yourself, Dorsal? No point. Jed can't do it on his own. If you don't go back, we've all had it.' I lifted a shoulder. 'If you do, we've probably had it anyway, but it's worth a shot. I never really believed in that mythical Stone, but I believe in Rory. A bit.'

A determined expression settled on her face. 'You'll have to give me your horse.'

'Finn,' I sighed, 'I can no more give you my horse than give you my arm. In fact, the arm would be easier. So you'd better have both.'

'Arms?'

I rolled my eyes. 'Me and the horse, you great thickbrain.' I whistled a low note between my teeth and the blue roan lifted its head from its blood-soaked grazing and trotted to me. 'I suppose I'm going back with you. Seeing as you've lost Conal, the notion of me breathing my earthly last won't bother you. Up.' I boosted her onto the roan and it snorted, its dark muzzle stained as red as its nostrils. Its whicker was like an excited laugh.

One hand on its wither, I paused. There was a patch of dead twisted heather beneath a granite outcrop, and I remembered suddenly why.

I crouched to lift the Lammyr's head by a handful of lank hair. The severed neck had clotted already with mucal blood. I brought it back to the unimpressed roan, weaving and knotting its sparse strands of hair into its black mane so that the grinning head dangled against its neck. Rigid with disgust, Finn stared into the Lammyr's eyes as I scrambled up behind her.

'Sionnach!' I shouted.

Sionnach's head lifted, his look cold.

'Get out of here. Take them to Brokentor. We'll be with you by dawn, if we're coming at all.' I kicked my heels into the roan's flanks, and it leaped forward, hooves flying over the rough ground, Branndair falling in at its side.

The severed head bounced against my knee, still smirking. I couldn't help giving it a glance, and that's when a blur of white caught my eye.

Alongside Branndair a pale wolf ran, a scar like an acid burn across her muzzle and a glint of hatred in her amber eyes.

Finn

In the moonlight in the trees, Jed held Liath's face between his hands, stroking the livid hairless scar with his thumbs. 'I don't get it. Its blood splashed on me. I didn't like it, but it didn't do this.'

'It's animals it affects like that. Animals, and things that grow in the earth.' Seth was focused on the granite maw of Kate's caverns, a darker blackness on the other side of the clearing. 'Humans? We grow skins fast, we're adaptable. It's not so long ago, Skinshanks could freeze you in your tracks in broad daylight, just by being in the vicinity. Remember? You'd throw up at the sound of its name. Now you could reach out and touch its head in the dark if you felt like it.'

Jed glanced at it and then at Seth. 'I don't feel like it.'

'No? You'll do it for a dare when your mood is different. Your heart grows a little harder. Tomorrow it'll be harder still, if you live to see it. Another skin layer. We get used to anything.'

'It isn't bothering your horse,' said Jed.

Seth's white teeth flashed in the darkness. 'Well. That isn't really a horse. Now, leave the sword here. You won't need it.'

Finn waited, her hand on the nose of the nervous bay mare, who very clearly did not consider the blue roan a horse. She called Seth's name softly.

He turned with a look of mild surprise, then grinned, and only then did she realise she hadn't spoken out loud. Backing away from Jed, he half turned to her.

'You're getting the hang of it,' he murmured.

'Seth. Are you sure she doesn't know?' It seemed so fantastically unlikely. Even in the arrogance of her victory, wouldn't Kate keep her guard up? On the other hand, she was so sure of herself, and so certain of her hold on Seth . . . A tremor went down Finn's spine and she frowned. 'Seth? Are you sure?'

'No.' He shrugged, looking away. 'But I'm blocking her the best I can, and as far as I know, she still trusts me. Got a better idea?'

She shook her head.

'Finn.' He sounded gentler than she'd ever heard him. 'I didn't mean that, about you being a coward. I was hurt and I wanted to hurt you. Again.' He reached out briefly, not quite touching her arm before he snatched his hand back. 'You can still go back. Sionnach will take you to a watergate. Rory's not your responsibility.'

'Jed is.'

'Huh! You care about the whelp, don't you? Should I be playing the chaperone?'

Well, since he'd brought it up . . . 'Seth?' She rubbed the bay mare's muzzle.

'Uh-huh.'

'You're not my uncle, and it always seems like you're closer to my age and you're—'

'The bane of your life.' He put his forefinger to his temple and shut one eye. 'What else? The demon relative. The stroppy adolescent. The family werewolf, for crying out loud.'

'Oh.' She flushed. 'You knew I said all that. Only, Seth? Conal said we were going to need each other, but we've never got on. Have we? I—'

'That's right.' He made an exasperated sound through his teeth. 'So, no. Don't look to me as a substitute.'

'Okay.' With one finger she scratched the star of hair between the mare's eyes, embarrassed and furious that she'd even tried to like him, tried to connect. 'I wasn't going to.'

'A godfather's a godfather.'

'Too right.' As if she'd want any paternal concern from him. Friends, she'd thought, maybe, but hell's teeth, not if it was any kind of an *effort*.

It hurt, though. Even though she was angry as hell at him, it did hurt.

Awkwardly he rubbed his neck. 'I'm not good at it, okay? That kind of—'

'Yeah. You can shut up now if you like.' Glaring into the mare's brown eye, she saw Seth's reflection distort and grow larger as he sighed and stepped close.

Gathering her hair in one hand, he pulled her head clumsily under his chin and hugged her hard. 'It isn't the time,' he growled as her chest heaved against him, his thumb wiping tears ruthlessly from her eyes. 'Not now. Grieve at his wake, if you live to enjoy the luxury.'

'Sorry.' She pulled away, digging her fingernails into her wounded palm.

'And stop apologising. Let's go.' He paused and shut his eyes. 'Finn. I'll do my best. I will, I truly will. But don't believe in anything from now on, okay? Or anyone.'

She nodded, bewildered, as he drew his sword. Then he grabbed her by the shoulder and thrust her, stumbling forward, across the clearing. His hand went to the back of Jed's neck and forced him on too, into the darkness of the granite mouth and the first silver glow of candlelight.

'Murlainn,' said Kate silkily. 'You have some explaining to do.'

She stood up as the laughter and celebration in the hall faded into silence. Seth shoved Finn forward, and flung Jed at Kate's feet.

'Hi, babes,' he greeted her cheerfully. 'Do you want the puppy dog or not? He went straight back to my brother and his bandits.'

Finn's neck throbbed. She didn't dare look at Seth for fear of what she'd see.

'I know that well,' Kate said, frowning. 'Where are the six men I had left?'

He made a disparaging sound. 'I killed them all but one, and he's walking home. Lus-nan-Leac, it was.'

A sigh like a whisper went round the hall, and one woman let out a gasping scream, one a stricken cry. A man stepped forward, staring at Seth's indigo shirt with its patch of darker darkness over the heart. 'Feorag,' he said, his voice raw. 'Feorag.'

Kate raised her hand. Silence fell, broken by a single helpless sob. 'You may pay for that, Murlainn.'

'It's already paid for.' His voice darkened with bitterness, and Finn felt a little reassured, because she hadn't liked that easy lightness in his tone. Not one bit. 'Five seems a fair price for my brother, Kate. Butchered by Laszlo despite your assurances.'

'Murlainn. I'm sorry.' She turned to Laszlo where he stood in shadow behind her, and shook her head sadly. 'Did I ask you to kill his brother, Nils?'

Laszlo's mouth tightened, but his satisfied smile stayed in place.

Kate gave Finn a sly glance. 'I seem to have misinformed you, Fionnuala. Not so much a crossroads for poor Cù Chaorach: more of a dead end. But I liked your uncle,' she murmured a little hungrily. 'He was such a challenge.'

If Kate was chocolate, Finn thought, she'd actually melt before she could eat herself. Maybe her vanity really was her big weakness. Maybe they even had a chance, or a ghost of one.

Seth spat on the rug at Kate's feet. 'A challenge you never met. Never will now.'

'Ah.' She sighed almost apologetically. 'That's a matter of perspective, isn't it? Honestly, Nils, that was clumsy of you. I had high hopes for Murlainn and Cù Chaorach both. Well, I hear the brainless boar

Torc got what was coming to him. What about the twins?'

'Your men killed them as I arrived.' Seth laughed contemptuously, and Finn realised with unease that, in fact, Seth could lie very well indeed. 'What a panic. Was it you that taught Laszlo to abandon the field before his men?'

'I thought it was all over.' Laszlo took an aggressive step forward.

Seth arched an ironic eyebrow. 'It is now.'

'You're blocking me, Murlainn.' Kate put her fingers to her temple. 'Why?'

'What, when Conal . . . when he's still . . .' His voice was shaking and he stopped. 'You've no business in my head,' he said at last. He went to Kate, putting a hand on the back of her neck as she smiled provocatively. 'Not right now. Not in my head.' He gripped her hair and kissed her with a passion that was close to violence.

There was something disturbing about Seth's kiss, Finn thought. It was just too good to be an act, his pulse leaping in his throat, his fingers white-knuckled where they gripped Kate's shining hair, his eyes open and tormented with lust. Beyond them, Laszlo's face had warped into a mask of hatred, and the warmth was gone from his burnt-sugar stare.

'Of course. You're upset. I understand that.' Drawing away, Kate caressed Seth's cropped skull. 'I like the new look.'

Even in his obvious pain, he looked bemused. 'You know fine there's a reason for it.'

'I've told you I'm sorry. I would never want to hurt you, Murlainn.' Gazing at him with open adoration, she drew her fingertips idly down his stomach.

Stroking her neck, he met her eyes. There was such fanatic desire in his face, Finn wondered if he could even remember all the others she'd promised not to hurt. Kate's attention, though, was not all on Seth. Finn could sense the woman's mind reaching past him, past them all, far beyond the caverns. Kate looked at Seth as if looking through glass.

'Seth!' gasped Finn, but Kate had already taken a sudden step back from him, her eyes narrowing to slits of gold.

'The twins are not dead,' she whispered.

Seth's fingers slid into the silver chain that hung round her neck, and tightened it. Pulling her hard against him, he flicked his hunting knife against her throat. Jed scrambled to his feet, tugging Finn after him.

'How dare you, Seth,' Kate hissed, her tongue flickering like a snake's. 'How *dare you*.'

Seth pressed his face to hers. 'I know the position of everyone in this hall.' His voice rang quiet but clear. 'If anyone tries to help her, they'll be killing her.'

'The nerve – the insolence – the heresy of you!' Kate was spitting and choking on her rage, her eyes glowing. 'You'll die for this. Choose how. Choose by what you do next.'

'Shall I take you with me, though?' There was a bead of sweat on his temple.

'Get your hands off me, you *cur*.'

'That's a new one, babes, coming from you.' Seth brushed her cheekbone with his lips, as if he couldn't help himself. 'I will kill you. You know it. Tell them.'

'He wouldn't dare!' shouted a voice. Gealach. 'We'd rip him in quarters.'

'And still be too late.' Seth smiled thinly, his gaze locked on Kate. 'My brother was gralloched by her man today and left alive to the birds. Torc was slaughtered by her pet Lammyr just to trap the healer and her twin. You all think we deserved it. But you know I'd dare. I saw the state of my brother and I was in his head and I *guarantee I would*.' Air rasped hard in his throat. 'How much do you love your witch queen? Bring me the infant.' When no-one moved, he pressed his blade into Kate's flesh, drawing a thin trickle of blood.

'Bring me my son!' he yelled.

There was movement at the entrance to one of the passageways, the press of bodies divided, and Rory tottered forward.

Jed swore in relief, and would have run straight for him had Seth not jabbed his blade tighter against Kate's throat, provoking a shriek of thwarted rage.

'Get rid of that,' he said viciously. 'What is it, a cat? A piglet?'

'Ah.' Kate's sigh was almost fond. 'You're strong, Murlainn.'

'Me and Cù Chaorach. He is in my heart and my head and you have us both to deal with. Now, bring me my son. Another changeling and you'll lose an ear.'

Where Rory had been, there was nothing now, but

distantly, from one of the passageways, echoed the rowling shriek of an offended cat.

'Bring the brat,' Kate told Laszlo acidly. 'We can always get him back.'

'Over my dead body,' snarled Jed.

'Quite,' said Laszlo, and he strode to a group of the women, lifting a child from reluctant arms. Grey eyes sparked in the infant's tear-blotched face, and he stretched his arms to Jed.

'Ed!' he sobbed, as if he'd been abandoned for a month.

Jed swept him up and nodded at Finn. She swallowed, her throat dry as dust. Now would come the tricky part. She had no idea how they were going to get out of here, and she hoped against hope that Seth did.

'Seth,' she said. 'It's him. It's Rory.'

'Good,' said Seth. 'Now, go.'

Jed and Finn looked at each other, then back at Seth. In unison they said: 'What?'

'Go!' he roared. 'Or do you think they'll let us live just for chess partners?'

They didn't need a third telling. Finn looked back at Seth once, standing at bay with his arm round Kate's neck and his knife still pressed almost lovingly to her jugular. His glance was so swift, she only just managed to catch it; then his focus was all on his faery lover once again.

The crowd parted reluctantly as they edged out with Rory. In the tunnel beyond the hall, they took to their heels, and reached the bay mare running. She whickered fondly to Jed and struck the ground with a hoof.

'Do we just leave him?' said Finn desperately as she hauled herself into the saddle.

Jed handed Rory up, but he didn't meet her eyes. 'We have to.'

As she pulled Jed awkwardly up behind her, they saw the two wolves stalk forward towards the archway. Then the bay mare was off at the gallop, and they saw no more.

Seth

He backed slowly towards the cavern mouth, feeling the inches with his mind. It was harder now. She was inside it and it hurt, and she wasn't alone, an insidious pressure building from the combined malevolence of everyone in the hall, not least the ones whose lovers were newly dead.

'Ah, Seth,' Kate murmured hoarsely against the chain that bit hard into her neck. 'Never to see your son again, after all your efforts!'

He shut his eyes, the better to focus on them all, but he was losing them; they were drifting out of the map in his mind, and in a few moments it would be impossible to protect his flanks. When that happened, he would be as good as dead, or perhaps not as good as dead. It wouldn't be so quick as death. For all his stupid bravado, he didn't want to be ripped in quarters, and Gealach was not bluffing.

Then he felt the warm presence of the wolves at his side, heard Branndair's low growl. It made him oddly happy, and a little courage trickled back to him. Despite everything, they were with him still. Even if their protection couldn't buy him enough time, then to die with friends, however slowly, however badly, would be better than dying alone.

He wanted to link his mind to Branndair's. He needed the comfort it always gave him, that wild half-wolf feeling, but he couldn't spare the concentration. Maybe later, when they had him, maybe he'd get the chance then, if Branndair lived long enough. Maybe it would help a bit. He couldn't imagine it would help much.

'Well,' Kate went on. She knew his fear, and despite the bite of her own necklace on her throat, her mouth twitched with merriment. 'At least you'll be seeing your brother soon enough.'

'Is that how it happens?' Sweat trickled into his eye. 'Tell me.'

'How would I know better than you?' she crooned. 'It's a comforting thought, isn't it? But in line with current scientific thinking? On balance, perhaps not.'

He let out a gasp that was almost a laugh. 'You're funny.'

'I always thought you were too. What a shame it is, what a shame. You could lie down with me this very moment, couldn't you? Ah, Seth. What a waste.' She sighed dreamily. 'You see, when I said you'd be seeing Conal soon, I didn't mean very soon. It won't be nearly soon enough for you. You'll be begging me to make it sooner.' She licked her lips. 'I'll like that.'

'I know you will. Don't go thinking I had any illusions.' He breathed hard through his nose, trying to loosen the numbing knot of terror in his guts.

She laughed.

That did it. In his head, he could feel the last traces of Conal, dissipating slowly but inexorably. He couldn't hold on to him, couldn't keep him. Reckless hate raced through his veins, chasing out the fear. 'See, when you've got me begging for mercy?' he hissed in her ear. 'You remember this, witch: However much I beg, whatever I tell you, I *don't mean it.*'

From her throat came a sound of frustrated fury. He'd spoilt her fun. A tiny fraction of it maybe, but it was enough to madden her, however he paid for it in the coming hours and days. It was Seth's turn to laugh. A small, hollow sound, but he'd laughed in her face, at least.

Behind his back was the passageway to night and blackness. On the nape of his neck he felt a breath of wind from the north, the tang of winter on it, but it was gone in less than an instant and he could smell nothing but the scent of her flesh. Grinding his teeth, he heard as if from a long way off the growling snort of the roan, the sparking ring of a hoof on granite.

He took the blade tip from her neck and kissed the welling blood on her skin. Kate sighed, arching her neck blissfully. Twisting the knifepoint into the jump ring of the necklace, he snapped it, and caught the emerald pendant in his palm as it fell. 'This isn't yours.'

She stumbled and he shoved her forward with his foot, seeing Laszlo reach for a crossbow even as he turned to the passageway and ran.

'Kill him.' Kate's calm words echoed in the hall behind him. 'Slowly, now.'

The weight of their hate slammed into his head, almost making him lose his footing, but he recovered and ran stumbling on, the wolves at his back, a flimsy block barely protecting his mind. Sheathing his knife, he drew his sword. The horse was a pale impatient shape at the mouth of the cavern, and he reached for its withers and flung himself onto its back even as they swarmed from the archway. *I'll grow up now, Conal, I promise. I promise I will. Please let me.*

'Shoot the kelpie!' yelled Kate, and the beast beneath him screamed and staggered sideways with a cross-bow bolt in its flank. Snatching at it, Seth hauled the thing out with an effort. Green-eyed, the roan turned on Kate's fighters, pawing the earth, while he fought it, swearing obscenely. Its fury was too demonic now to carry him away.

Kate smiled, wide and lovely. 'Skinshanks! Where's Skinshanks? Fetch the Lammyr!'

Seth gasped as a thrown dagger sliced into his arm, making him drop his sword. He thanked the gods for that order to kill him slowly; Alainn's aim wasn't truly as bad as that.

Drawing his hunting knife once more, he grinned at Kate. 'You want Skinshanks? All yours.'

He reached down for the Lammyr's head, slicing through its hair to free it from the roan's mane, brandishing it in his fist.

All sound died. Watching their shock turn to predatory scorn, he could feel their collective dare in his mind. They knew he wouldn't do it; he didn't have the guts. He wasn't the man his brother was.

Well, he wasn't. And he wasn't sure he did dare. Seth thought of what it might bring. And then he stopped thinking of that, because what was the point?

He closed his eyes, half-smiling, then snapped them back open.

'I curse the ground you cross!' he screamed. 'On my life and my soul and my heart, I curse it for your children and your children's children.' Viciously he flung down the head between himself and the horde.

It seemed to grin, one final time. Then it exploded into vile fragments, showering the ground between Seth and the Sithe, burning all that it touched in sparks of congealed blood like pale flame.

He heard Kate's shriek of unearthly fury, felt the turmoil of incredulous minds, but he didn't wait to enjoy their horror, finally dragging the roan's head round as it recoiled from the Lammyr's spattered remains. It fought him for a second more before springing forward into a gallop, and that was long enough for him to feel two hard blows in his back that knocked him forward against the roan's neck, the air stunned out of his lungs. Then they were both running with the wind into the northern winter.

Finn

She reined in the bay mare, who stopped gratefully, head down, limbs trembling with exhaustion. Leaning forward, hugging her neck, Finn slid off.

'What are you doing?' Jed glanced back into the darkness. 'We have to keep going.'

'Do that. Go on, take Rory. I'll catch up. I can track you. I can *track*.' She hoped that was true. But whether it was or not, she couldn't go any farther. Not without him. Scum, traitor, turncoat: whatever he was, she was. Besides, he'd saved them, and she wasn't going to abandon him.

'But you haven't got a horse!'

She shook her head violently, needing to convince herself as much as Jed. 'Yours can't carry us all anymore.'

'That's not what this is about!' Jed's voice cracked. 'Is it?'

'I can't just leave him. I have to wait and see, at least. Find out what happened to him.'

Clutching Rory, Jed wriggled forward and gathered up the reins. 'Look, if this is some kind of thing you think you've got to do for Conal—' He hesitated. '—it's pointless, you know? Is that what it's about?'

'No, no. Really, that isn't it. Please go on, Jed. Please.' *Before I start crying and begging to come with you after all.*

'Well, you'd better come soon.' There was an obstruction in his throat. 'I don't want to have to come all the way back to get you.'

She couldn't bear to watch him ride away, so she climbed to a jutting spar of rock that glittered with mica in the starlight. Cold, it was so cold. Finn lay on her stomach, feeling the deep chill radiate through her blood and into her bones. She let her focus dissipate, let her instincts kick in, and suddenly she knew how it was done. There in her brain she found the place, tweaked it like a proud apprentice mechanic, and felt warmth churn in her bones. So that was Seth's secret. She smiled.

Seth. Remembering, she lifted her cheek from the stone and peered out across the moor. It wasn't her amateur efforts alone that had chased away the cold. In the short time she'd lain there, mildness had blunted the weather, and now the stars had vanished. For a moment she thought they were drifting to earth, then saw it was only the first flakes of snow.

He isn't coming, she thought, and the stab of grief surprised her.

She stood up, limbs stiff, a dull ache in her heart. Both of them: she'd only gone and lost both of them. She might as well set out on the long trudge after Jed, though it barely seemed worth the effort. It seemed so terribly pointless, that was all. And now it was snowing.

In the distance, between earth and sky, movement caught her eye, then running shapes. Shinning down from her perch, she ran awkwardly down the stony slope, squinting into the gathering whorls of snow. Through it the blue roan cantered, the wolves at its heels, a figure slumped across its neck.

'Seth!' she yelled, the snowflakes drawing in her voice and absorbing it. *'Seth!'*

He drew himself up. Briefly he seemed to have trouble focusing; then he was nudging the roan with his heels, steering it straight for her. It didn't break pace as he leaned down and with a grunt of pain swung her up by one arm. For a horrible instant, she hung between the horse and the earth, then dragged herself up behind him.

Unexpectedly she knocked against some obstruction, and Seth screamed. Then she did too, and clapped her hand over her mouth. He hung forward once more against the horse's neck, gratefully clinging to it as Finn gripped his belt and stared at the two shining shafts that stood out from his back.

They overtook Jed just before dawn, the bay mare breaking into a canter to keep up. Brokentor was not hard to spot, a volcanic remnant that jutted from the moor maybe three hundred feet, its eroded plug split and tumbled by the aeons. Sionnach and Eili rose as they approached. Eili's jumper was crusted with dried blood in a swathe from her neck to her side, and her ragged hair was gone, hacked down to dark red stubble.

The bay trotted to an exhausted halt a respectful distance from the roan, and Jed lowered Rory to Sionnach's arms. 'Potty!' the child wailed.

'I'm sorry, angel.' Jed slid off the mare and tugged at the sodden baby jeans with some difficulty. 'It really wasn't the moment.'

Finn clung to Seth's immobile form, afraid to move in case she disturbed the crossbow bolts again. 'Eili!'

Eili walked calmly to the horse, speaking soothing words in her own language as she stroked its flank. As she put her hand over its wound, a shiver rippled through its muscles.

'Eili, please!'

Branndair whined as desperately as Finn did, and nudged Seth's unresponsive leg with his muzzle.

Eili pressed her mouth to the hole in the horse's flank, tasting it. 'That's a good wound,' she told it. 'A clean wound. It'll heal fast.' The roan whickered to her as she turned to peer with clinical interest at Seth's back. 'That isn't.'

'Please!'

Eili glanced up. 'Begging me now, are you? For this scum?'

Finn bit her tongue, very hard, tasting blood and not caring. If she cried now, Seth was lost. She knew it by instinct; she knew it by looking into Eili's emotionless eyes.

'Yes, I am. I'm begging.'

Branndair was pacing frantically, pausing only to

lick Seth's foot and stare beseechingly at Finn, but she wouldn't look at the black wolf. He too might make her cry.

'I'm begging you. Please. For Conal.'

'No,' Eili said at last, coldly. 'Not for Conal. For me.' She turned. 'Sionnach!'

He pulled Seth off the horse without gentleness, ignoring Branndair's frightened snarl, and carried Seth to the bowl-shaped hollow in the side of the hill where they'd made camp. Sionnach dumped him facedown in the thin snow beside Conal's corpse.

'Let that be the first thing you see when you wake up,' he said as he ripped the indigo shirt from Seth's back.

It was. Finn was too afraid to interfere, too afraid of Eili changing her mind. It was hours later when Seth's eyes blinked twice and then opened. He didn't flinch, gave no sign at all, only gazed at Conal's cold peaceful face a metre from his own.

A shadow fell across the dead face and the living one, but Seth didn't look up. 'Thank you, Eili.'

'Don't mention it.' Her eyes were concealed behind the sunglasses Conal had brought her, a fierce winter sun glinting on the lenses. 'You're mine to kill, not hers.'

A smile twitched his mouth. 'Understood.'

She nodded and walked away. Seth's eyes met Finn's across the two corpses.

She'd never been so glad to look at him. Hour after hour she'd tried not to see Conal's wounds; instead she'd stared at his blue bitten nails and wept in silence. Branndair had stretched himself against Seth, and Liath lay at Conal's feet, her amber eyes bereft, but Jed had withdrawn hours ago to the far side of the hollow, hugging Rory and staring out empty-eyed across the valley. Finn understood he couldn't sit by Conal and Torc, not with the baby, but nor could she leave Conal. Somebody had to sit with him, besides a wolf. Somebody had to sit with Seth too. For when he woke up. For when he opened his eyes.

Seth stretched out a hand, wincing. 'Here.'

She scrambled across the slope to him, taking the emerald splinter from his hand.

'Do me a favour,' he said. 'Get rid of it. Give it to somebody who needs it.'

Grabbing a snowy boulder, he dragged himself into a sitting position. Branndair rose, stretched and slumped close against him once more, and Seth put his arms fiercely around the wolf's neck. The skin of his naked torso was almost as blue as his brother's. If it hadn't been for Branndair's warmth, he would have frozen to death, and Eili and Sionnach would have done nothing to stop it. Finn remembered what Leonie had told her: The Sithe were cruel, vicious, cold. *Watch it, Finn. Don't let iron into your soul. Stay human.*

Right now, winter seemed to be sinking into her bone marrow. Well, it didn't have to. She was going to stay human if it killed her. She smiled at Seth. 'I'm glad you're okay.'

'You're in a minority.' He gave her a rueful grin as he fought the chattering of his teeth. 'But I'm with you.'

Eili be damned. Finn opened Conal's pack, pulled out his spare jumper and thrust it at Seth. He took it,

gripping it against his chest till his shivers began to
subside.

'I don't want you to think, Finn . . . ,' he said, and
hesitated. 'Don't start thinking well of me, or anything. There was a moment back there . . . I didn't
know which way I was going to go.'

'I know that.' She looked into his eyes. 'I do know
that.'

'You do?' He clutched the jumper as if reluctant to
take it away from his skin. 'Okay.'

'How did you get away?'

'Oh.' He laughed. 'A load of mumbo-jumbo and
Lammyr blood. They won't be following. It takes a lot
of time and effort to clean a curse that's sealed with
a Lammyr head. That's what I love about superstitious faeries.'

'Don't you think you're a bit cynical?' Finn said.
'With your lifestyle and everything?'

'Ah, if I wasn't, I wouldn't be me, would I?' He
winked. 'And that would be a shame. Besides, you
should have seen their faces. They couldn't believe I'd
done it, couldn't believe I'd bring such anathema on
myself. What's the use of that? To be frozen useless
by a few words and a piece of dead flesh?' He lifted
Conal's jumper and stared at it.

She didn't know what *anathema* was, but already
she didn't like the sound of it. 'Are you sure they're
not right?'

Seth pretended not to hear her. 'Now.' Grunting
with the effort, he stood and pulled the jumper awkwardly on. She was never to know if the pain on his

hard face was due to the holes in his back or to the smell of Conal that still clung to the dark wool and that had almost made her cry herself.

'Sionnach,' he said. 'Give me my brother.'

Sionnach glanced their way, and after looking to Eili, he came across the hollow to lift Conal with incredible gentleness. As he passed him into Seth's waiting arms, Finn could see he was tempted to thrust the body hard, just for the jolt to Seth's wounded back. But he resisted, maybe for the sake of Conal's dignity.

She had no idea how Seth struggled up the hill with the dead weight of his taller brother, but he did, right up to the cracked and worn rocks at its summit, the wolves flanking him and Sionnach and Eili behind, carrying Torc. They laid the two corpses together on the rocks.

Clutching Rory, Jed looked from one to the other as they turned and started down the hill. 'Aren't you going to—' His voice shook. '—burn them?'

Sionnach bristled as if he'd suggested something obscene. 'Not when there's time to do it properly. At least Murlainn bought us *that*,' he added contemptuously.

'You're going to leave them there?' Jed stared at the Sithe.

Avoiding his eyes, Finn moved closer to Seth, her gaze fixed on the bodies. *Family. Seth's my only family in this place. And he isn't even family.*

God damn it. I'm an orphan.

'We don't like the smell of burning flesh, Jed.' Seth

turned to limp down the hill, and Finn fell in at his side. 'The ground's frozen, even if I wanted to feed them to the worms. They'll go to the foxes and the wild-cats and the ravens and the buzzards. And I'll stay with them till they're stripped bare, and when I re-trieve their scattered bones, I'll make a barrow for them. That's my job, and this one I *will* do.' He stared at Eili.

'And I will guard their backs,' she said stiffly.

Seth lifted his sword belt and buckled it across his back, his lips white as he fought not to flinch from the weight of his own weapon. 'You will take Jed and Finn to the dun,' he said. 'You'll do it because I tell you to.'

'If you follow us,' said Sionnach, 'the clann have the right to kill you, Murlainn.'

'They may do, but at least they'll do it quickly,' Seth said sourly. 'For now, I will stay with Conal and Torc, I will guard their front and back, and nothing but the wild things will come near them. When their bones are buried I will come to you, and when their wake is over we'll all be done mourning.'

'I will never be done!' shouted Eili.

'You will, to the world outside your head, just as I will.' He stared into her angry eyes, and this time it was Eili who looked away. 'Your head is your own. Like mine.'

Snow came, burying the land, muffling every sound but the keen of the wind and driving across the moor like a vengeful white ghost. It had gone again, lying only in hollowed patches, before Seth returned to the dun, gaunt and hard with hunger and cold and grief. Finn never did ask him about the weeks he stayed at Brokentor, and he never offered to tell her.

Seth

He eyed them all, the men and women of his clann.
If he kept his arms folded, they wouldn't see his
hands tremble. He'd fought with them, ridden with
them, squabbled with them; he'd danced and sung
and got drunk with them in this hall. Some of them
he'd loved. Now they might have to kill him.

No-one spoke. He felt unafraid, just listless and
very, very tired. Maybe nothing could be worse than
the long weeks at Brokentor. At least that was over.
One day this would be too.

There was no point protesting. It wasn't up to him
anymore, and he wouldn't even if he could. Eili stood
to the side. Her eyes hadn't left him since he rode
through the gate of the dun and they disarmed him.

Grian, who seemed to be their spokesman now,
rubbed his forehead. 'It's Eili's choice. Do you understand, Murlainn?'

'Yes,' he said.

They all looked at her. It was her milking of the

moment that told him he was not going to die. Death, she'd have pronounced on him quickly. Eili wanted to keep him in suspense, and paradoxically, that told him what he needed to know. He closed his eyes.

'If it was for me alone,' she said at last, all dignity and coolness, 'I'd choose death. But it isn't. He is the father of the . . . child. He is the Captain of this dun.' She smiled unpleasantly. 'If he can take it back.'

He heard a hundred and more sighs, but his own wasn't one of them. Trying not to let his fingers tremble, he reached for Conal's now threadbare jumper and pulled it off over his head. He was determined to do that, at least, before they told him to. The constant acute ache in his crossbow scars was gone, and he allowed himself a wry inner smile. Obviously Eili did not want anything to distract him from what lay ahead.

'Murlainn,' said Grian.

'Grian,' said Seth, tossing the jumper to him. 'Get those two – newcomers – out of here.'

Grian blinked, a little shocked, as if he'd forgotten their existence. 'Of course. Yes.'

Jed resisted, half-turning back, but it was Finn who cried out, 'Seth?'

'Go on, Finn,' he said as two men came forward to flank him. 'We're just sorting something out. I'll be along in a bit.'

Jed made an angry terrified sound, as if Seth's words had reminded him of something else, but the two of them were half-led, half-pulled from the hall, and Seth shut his eyes, relieved, when the door slammed on them. He turned away, put them deliberately out of his mind, and raised a block against the rest. That would not come down till it was over. Whatever else they did, they weren't going to beat their way into his mind.

He could feel Orach trying to get into his head, desperate to take some of what was coming to him, but he shoved her away. Not even her.

Besides, he wouldn't do it to her.

At the top end of the hall, they were already swinging the straight pine trunk into place, suspended horizontally at shoulder height on the iron brackets. It hung precisely in the gap between the walls of a huge arch that led to the anteroom beyond the hall, at the top of a shallow flight of three steps. A prominent, clear position; a good place for setting examples.

Thanks for that, Father, he thought bleakly. *Finally gave me my moment in the spotlight, you fecker.*

There was something about the simplicity of the thing that sent a shudder through him, and he looked only once, swiftly, at the dappling of brown spots concentrated in the central section of it. At least the clann weren't making a meal of it. None of them were enjoying this.

Well, except for one. Eili's eyes were bright and hating.

Nothing for it. He walked to the pine trunk, hell-bent on keeping his limbs steady as he reached the last step. His throat was as dry as a dead leaf, but they didn't have to know that. The men on either side of him took his wrists and caught the lengths of cord thrown to them.

'You don't have to do that,' he told Carraig bitterly.

The fighter swallowed and cast his eyes down. 'I know, Murlainn.'

'Then don't tie me, Carraig,' he muttered. 'I won't fight. You know I won't try to run.'

'Murlainn. Please do this. You don't have to but—'

'It stops you falling, Murlainn,' interrupted Fearna in a soft voice. 'Because otherwise you will. Whatever you think, however strong you are, you will fall. Carraig's right. Please.'

Seth hesitated, then nodded, and they looped the thin ropes round each wrist. Closing his eyes, he let Carraig and Fearna stretch his arms against the timber. He'd ridden and fought and drunk and laughed with both of them, and now, though each of them pulled the cords tight, they also clasped his fingers with their own. He was more grateful than he could say, but he said nothing, suddenly afraid of weeping. He was not afraid of the pain, not yet, but he was terribly afraid he might weep with the bloody awful sadness of it all.

They were making it quick, he knew it, but it still felt like forever before silence fell with that particular dreadful quality. He glanced briefly at Carraig.

'All right, Murlainn?' he whispered.

He was letting him know it was coming. Seth gave him a very fleeting smile and closed his eyes.

He felt the evil breath of the lash before it even hit him.

Finn

'The hell with this,' said Finn. She took her hands from her face and ran round the passageway to the anteroom at the top end of the hall, Jed at her heels.

'Will we get in there?'

'Nobody's going to stop us.' She glanced back at him. 'Because they're all in there. All of them watching. The bastards.'

She was right: the anteroom was empty. The hall was full, but no-one was taking any notice of two figures easing in through the gap in the darkness around the anteroom door.

The crowd of watchers stood in absolute silence, and there was no screaming. There was only one sound: the light song and snap of a whip as it cracked into flesh. Finn froze, briefly incapable of moving.

Facing them was Seth, bound to a stripped pine log, but his eyes were shut tight. With each lash, his body jerked involuntarily against the log, but it was his only reaction, so for seconds Finn didn't understand. Then she made out the fine spray of red, the droplets spattering the wood, and she clapped her hand over her mouth. Seth's jaw was rigid, his skin white and stretched, and blood trickled from the corner of his lips.

Like a ghost behind the hideous image there was another one in Finn's head: Seth stripping off his jumper, throwing it to Grian. He was taking this of his free will. She clenched her fists till her nails drew blood in her palms, reopening the gash she'd made with her pendant. She still hated them all. Her body seethed with terror and pity and a murderous hatred. There was no pleasure in any of their faces, even in the face of the man who wielded the brutal whip. He was not enjoying his work, but neither was he holding back. The flogging was thorough, professional, brutal. The clann were only enduring it, but she felt no shred of pity for them. Even Sionnach was looking on stony-faced and miserable. But his sister's eyes came alight with glee as she found Finn in the shadows, and there was fervid hope in her expression.

No, Finn thought. *You can wait forever, you vengeful bitch. I won't scream.*

Seth opened his jaws and sank his teeth into the pine trunk, blood from his bitten tongue spilling down the timber. Her own back jolted with every lash of the whip. *Oh, please,* she thought each time: *Make it stop. Not again. That's enough. You'll kill him. Stop now. Please.* But every time, the whip was drawn back, every time she heard the crack of it, duller and wetter now.

The guards seemed to be holding Seth tighter, and

the one she could see had tears in his eyes. As Jed closed his arms tightly around her chest, she felt something trickle hot into her hair, and knew he too was crying. They couldn't leave. She had not abandoned Seth at Brokentor, and she wouldn't abandon him now. But if the lash did not stop that relentless, endless cracking, she thought she might throw up or pass out, and she didn't want to do either.

And then, when she thought she could stand it no longer, it was over.

Seth

He lay facedown on his own mattress, staring at the wall. So he'd got here by himself. He remembered that.

He had not fallen when they took the ropes off his wrists. He'd walked out of the hall by himself, in front of them all, the pain a stabbing demon with its flaming claws deep in his back and its tentacles around his throat, threatening to cut off his air supply. Some of the clann were weeping. But he wasn't. *Never. Would.*

He'd climbed the stairs to his rooms alone, their watching eyes keeping him upright as far as the landing. But he didn't know how he'd made it up the second flight. He didn't know. He didn't even remember the climb, though he vaguely remembered throwing up at the top of the stairs, the pain flaying him in a vicious circle and making him vomit again.

Damn them all to the seventh hell and beyond. He let himself feel the hatred, because after tonight he must not feel it again. When the pain subsided, in a couple of centuries, he wouldn't. They were his clann.

He hadn't made a sound. He had not passed out. He'd got his dun back, got his clann back. He was the son of Griogair Dubh and he was their unchallenged Captain. He'd atoned for the death of their leader, at least in the eyes of the clann if not in the merciless eyes of Eili. Or, indeed, his own.

None of it helped at that moment. It had got him through the punishment, but it couldn't dull the pain. Blood still trickled down his sides, wetting the sheets, and his jeans were soaked with it, but he hadn't been capable of taking the damn things off. He'd only barely been capable of crawling to his own bed and hauling himself onto it. Silently he wept the tears he couldn't weep in the hall. *Sod it. So much for that resolution.* Silently he reminded himself that nothing they could do to him could compare with the pain he'd brought on his own heart.

But it didn't help. Not this instant. Because oh, gods, it hurt. A tiny whimper of agony choked in his throat, but he still couldn't sob or scream, because they still might hear in the unnaturally quiet dun.

Branndair was slumped against the bed, his tongue occasionally licking Seth's fingers and his raw left wrist. They'd locked the wolf up, of course, in this room, and there were deep gouges in the door and the floorboards where Branndair had tried to get to him. He wouldn't fix them, Seth decided savagely. They'd remind him.

Branndair stayed close now, but the wolf knew not to touch him – he'd felt Seth's terror that he might – and Seth hated them most of all for that. But even the light fleeting glance of that wolf-mind was comforting, because Seth had never felt so alone in his life. If it wasn't for Branndair, his heart might have broken.

The wolf sat up and snarled, and Seth gazed in a stupor at the door. He didn't have a thing left. If it was anyone come to gloat, let them try. Branndair must be hungry by now. Seth let himself smile a little. Gods, even that hurt.

Then Branndair was on his feet, hackles high, teeth bared. The door opened hesitantly, but the wolf made no move to attack. Reaching out with his exhausted mind, Seth saw who it was.

'Branndair,' he murmured. 'No.'

The wolf lay down, sulking, as they came in. They shouldn't be here; but Seth didn't have the energy or the will to send them away. He made another abortive attempt at a smile.

'Hey, Finn. Jed.'

His voice seemed croakier than it should have been. Ignoring Branndair's warning rumble, Finn reached out a hand to Seth's face, clenching it at the last moment. After a little hesitation, she bit her lip and touched his hair.

'Yeah, that's okay,' he mumbled. 'That bit of me doesn't hurt.'

Her face was wet with tears, he realised with an odd rush of affection. And Jed didn't look much happier, funnily enough. Finn held a bottle to his lips and he felt water against his burning throat.

'Thanks,' he said, wishing she'd give him more.

'They're bastards,' said Jed, wiping his nose with his sleeve. 'Bastards.'

'I hate them,' added Finn quietly.

'Thanks for that. I love you both.' Seth laughed very quietly, wincing at the pain that surged through his back and threatened to make him vomit again. 'But please don't. They had to.'

'They're all walking round like zombies, if it helps.' Finn's eyes were brilliant with rage. 'Half of them in tears, the hypocrites. Sionnach too.'

'Oh, Finn.' He was too tired to argue. 'This or kill me.'

'They pretend it's for Conal,' she said softly. 'Liars.' She stroked his hair and he closed his eyes briefly.

There was a point when he'd thought he felt Conal with him, down there in the hall: the touch of his mind, his fathomless pity and grief. He'd thought he could feel Conal's touch, Conal's hand against his face. He'd thought he heard him whisper, telling him *Stay on your feet, little brother, stay quiet, it'll be over soon;* but hey, that was pain and humiliation for you. Made a man hallucinate. Seth certainly couldn't feel him now.

Jed ducked back out through the door and returned with a bowl of faintly steaming water and a pile of white cloths. This time Branndair did growl.

'Branndair,' Seth growled back, and the wolf lay down again, fangs still bared.

'Grian gave us these. He wanted to come himself, but Jed and I wouldn't let him.'

'Good.' Seth's lips twitched. 'Good for you. Listen. I can't face a healer at all, but the one you mustn't let near me is Eili. All right?'

Jed frowned. 'She wouldn't even try, would she?'

'You'd be amazed. I'll explain. Later.' He made a pathetic shot at a laugh.

'Can you bear it?' Finn nipped her lip hard. 'I think I have to clean it. Even though . . .'

'Even though.' His voice shook, and he was annoyed at himself. 'Yeah, there'll be muck. Won't do me any good. Go ahead.'

It stung like nothing had ever stung him before: like a byke of angry wasps loose on his back, even after Jed found his hip flask and emptied the whisky carefully down his throat, but he managed not to scream. He just buried his face in the pillow, ripping the linen with his fingernails, wanting to die, while Finn peeled off the blood-crusted jeans. At least then Jed could get at his belt, and slide it between his teeth.

Finn cried the whole time, but silently, trying not to get salt tears on his flayed flesh. She was so businesslike, so brisk, and underneath it all was a terrifying cold anger.

'I'm sorry,' mumbled Seth.

'Don't you dare. Don't you *dare* apologise again.'

'I mean for this. You shouldn't see. You're angry.'

'If it's all right for them to do it, it's all right for me to see it.'

Fine. Seth had no energy left. Everything he had was fighting pain. ~ *You're too young* was all he managed.

He thought she'd throw a temper. Instead she was silent for a long time. She touched the very top of his shoulder, somewhere there wasn't an open wound. Her touch was very gentle – so light, it could have been the touch of her mind – and suddenly she seemed far less certain.

~ *Not forever* was all she said.

'You okay?' Finn chewed her lip.

'I'm okay, Finn.' At least, weeks later, he was no longer afraid to move or breathe. Seth stood watching Rory play on the rug with the wolves. Liath crouched submissively in front of Branndair, playfully nibbling his throat fur. 'I need to go down to my clann now.'

Finn flushed with anger. 'No, you don't. Not if you don't want to. They can wait.'

'She's told them so,' said Jed. 'And she's just slapped Grian.'

'Dorsal, you did what?' He did his best not to laugh, and nearly succeeded.

'He's got nail marks on his cheeks, wait'll you see. She's drawn blood. And when he told her you were lucky not to be dead, she told him *he* was bloody lucky you weren't.'

Oh, gods, he mustn't go on finding this funny. It had to stop. 'Finn, you're not helping. What did I tell you, you disobedient—'

'Bag of wolfmeat?' Her bitter smile flashed. 'I will never obey you on this. You've got your traditions; well, so have I. Civilised ones. If I live to be a thousand years old, I won't forgive them.'

In the awkward silence, Jed coughed. 'There's good news,' he told Seth brightly. 'A lot of the women are feeling awful sorry for you.'

Seth grinned wickedly, but Finn's face darkened. 'It's not funny.'

'It kind of is. Anyway, Finn. I couldn't stay in exile, I'd have died of misery. It was this or kill me. They're my clann and I love them.'

'Well, I don't, and you can't make me.'

'I thought your grandmother had this conversation with you. Stay human, don't hate. They had to do it. Eili demanded it, and I deserved it.'

'You did *not* deserve it. Conal would have killed them.'

'She told them that too,' added Jed, wiggling his eyebrows.

'Wow. Did she really?' Seth wished he could have seen their faces.

Well. He'd be seeing them soon enough. Gritting his teeth, Seth crouched and lifted Rory. The boy was such a fragile thing still. It didn't hurt too much.

'You worried?' Finn asked him softly. 'About going down to those pious bastards?'

What worried him most was Finn, so willing to hate on his behalf, but he decided to keep his mouth shut for now.

'Worried? Nah. Terrified.' He smiled at her. 'Let's go.'

The silence that fell in the great hall was nearly as
oppressive as the silence that had met him when he
rode back into the dun. Seth wondered fancifully if
the whole clann was dead and stuffed, and whether
he'd mind very much.

He watched their eyes, every one of them, Branndair
snarling softly at his heels. There was an arrogant
swagger in his step, in case he needed to walk through
scorn and derision, but he could make out nothing
but respect; and in that instant, it was worth it. He
wanted to howl with relief. In only one face was the
hatred undying.

Eili sat watching him through narrowed lids, her
hands clasped tightly. Beside her, Sionnach got to his
feet, his eyes on Seth, his fingers splayed on the table.

'Murlainn,' he said.

Eili remained in her seat, but around the hall, the
rest were all getting to their feet, clumsily, as if their
tardiness embarrassed them.

'Seth.'

'Murlainn.'

'Captain.'

Finn opened her mouth at him, mock-awestruck.
~ *Get you.*

~ *Finny, give it a rest. I'm dying of embarrassment
here.*

Every clann member but one was on their feet as
Seth reached the top table, and Grian and his advisers
backed off. He didn't look at the archway beyond
the table: couldn't bear to, didn't have to. He went

straight to the central chair, the one with a scabbard
and sword belt laid across its arms like a barrier.

Seth set Rory down on the table, tweaked his nose,
then laid the scabbard and belt on the table beside
him. He only had to snap his fingers to make Finn
and Jed drop obediently into the places to his right
and left.

He made himself not grin. He could only hope *that*
attitude was going to last.

Lifting Rory again, he sat down casually in the forbidden chair, Rory curled in his lap. The exhalation
from hundreds of lungs went around the hall like a
single sigh.

Seth looked up at them all. His clann.

'Tomorrow night,' he said. 'The wake for Cù Chaorach and Torc. You've left it long enough.'

He rested his left ankle on his right thigh, and
bounced Rory on his lap, smiling into the infant's eyes.
He hadn't leaned right against the chair back, but he
was fairly sure nobody noticed.

'The captains will come to my rooms at noon for
their orders.' He studied the ranks of stunned faces,
and widened his eyes, shrugging. 'That's all.'

'Murlainn.' The whispered word echoed eerily
around the hall.

The clann began to talk again, uncertainly, as
muted as they had been on that night he hated to
remember. He got a wicked pleasure from seeing that,
once again, more than a few were in tears. Branndair
lay at his feet, restless, his hungry yellow eyes on the
clann.

One by one they stood up and came to Seth, clasped

his hand and pressed it to their foreheads. All of them, one by one, returned quiet to their seats. Not for a single one did he put Rory down: not even for Grian, not even for Orach. When he'd counted them all – all but one – he got to his feet, handed Rory to Jed and slung an arm round him and Finn.

'You,' he murmured, 'have given me back my clann and my dun and my life. Now let's get out of here. And oh, *gods,* do I need a drink.'

EPILOGUE

Finn

'Finn,' said Sionnach. Leaning on the stone archway, he gave me a sympathetic smile. 'Your mother is here.'

'Okay.' I hugged my knees and stared out beyond the parapet. 'Thanks, Sionnach.'

Jed and I sat close together on the broad battlement of the dun, backs against the low wall, staring out to sea across the early spring machair with its smattering of wild flowers. Sionnach's footsteps faded down the stairway, back towards the courtyard. Hooves clattered on stone and were muffled by grass as a patrol rode out. A horse whinnied in the stables, a hammer rang on metal; there was laughter, and the start of a quarrel. The yells from an anarchic twenty-a-side football match were drowned by the closer racket of four off-duty guards playing Jenga. Behind it all was the lazy growl of wind turbines, the blade shadows sweeping hypnotically across the battlement.

The only silence in the place was the one between us. Jed looked sideways at me, chewing his knuckle.

'Kind of ironic, this, isn't it? You going. Me staying. I'm really sorry.'

'That's okay.' Though it wasn't.

Music burbled quietly out of the courtyard amplifiers: nobody had bothered to change it since last night's full-moon party. I wanted to be back there, before the dawn I'd been dreading, curled sleepily against Jed with his arm around me. Watching Orach drag Seth up for a dance; trying not to read Eili's lethal gaze as Seth's face registered a kind of happiness. Trying not to fall asleep in Jed's arms; an awful premonition twisting my heart. I hadn't wanted the sky to pale: I didn't want to wake and find the night gone. I wanted to stay more than I'd wanted anything in my life.

Jed picked awkwardly at a nail. 'They honestly think Rory's their great hope. Seth says it's superstitious shite, but Rory will have a good life here. Much better than over there.'

'I know. It's fine.' I stared across the machair. 'You'll have a good life too.'

He said quietly: 'It's the only place I've ever existed.'

A familiar gurgling giggle drifted up from the courtyard, so we both peered over our shoulders. The Jenga game had been interrupted but nobody seemed to mind. Rory was settled happily between the four guards, two men and two women, who lay on their stomachs, helping him build and destroy a Jenga-brick tower.

Jed chewed his knuckle. 'I'm not staying just so Rory can be some sodding figurehead. He's too little to get lumbered with that. But . . .'

'But Seth doesn't care that he's the Bloodstone, does he?'

'Nah. Couldn't care less. He's just besotted.' Jed gave me a twisted grin. 'Bit late in the day, but I couldn't separate them now, could I? Seth came barging into my room at four o'clock this morning.' He rolled his eyes. 'Panicking his hungover head off 'cause Rory had a tummy bug.'

'Aw, Jed. He isn't used to it, pure Sithe don't get bugs. Cut him some slack.'

'Aye. He's a troubled man.' We started to laugh, till our eyes met.

Jed looked away sharply, out towards the grey sea. 'You'd better go and see your mother.'

'Don't get into any scraps, right?' I cleared my throat. 'And don't cut yourself. And don't ride water horses. And don't let Seth boss you around, 'kay?'

'Look who's talking.' He managed to smile. 'Want me to come? Moral support?'

I shook my head as I got to my feet. This was one I'd have to face on my own.

At the foot of the stone steps, someone barred my way, and as I met Eili's brittle gaze, my heart sank. I knew the woman was going out on a reconnaissance patrol and wouldn't be back for three days. I'd hoped I wouldn't have to see her again.

'So, Finn. You're going with your mother?' Eili was almost smiling. 'I know you're angry, but weren't you going to say good-bye?'

'Eili,' I said. 'Conal didn't want you to do what you did to Seth.'

Eili's face was perfectly still; she didn't lose her

temper. 'Conal lives in my heart,' she said, 'but he doesn't have to live in my skin. Seth is my Captain: I have to protect his life, and I have to rely on him to protect mine. I had to do it, Finn, and Seth understands that, even if you don't.' She paused. 'You watched. You disobeyed him, I saw you. I hoped you'd scream or weep, shame him, but you didn't. Well, good for you. But you shouldn't have watched at all if you couldn't take it.'

'It's because of what you did that he's making me go back.' Resentment choked me.

'No, it's because of how you reacted to it. Anyway, there's your mother to think of.' Eili set her jaw. 'Con . . . al would agree with him. Conal would want you to go with Stella.'

I could hear how much it hurt to say his name, and my heart stopped thudding so angrily against my rib cage. She could have insisted on Seth's execution, after all, but she hadn't.

'Eili? Is it over, with Seth? Will you leave it at that?'

'I don't know. I wanted him to die, Finn, and I still wish he had.' Eili stared at me for a long silent moment. 'I don't know. But I'll try.'

I nodded unhappily. 'Bye, then.'

'Finn,' Eili called after me. 'There's something else Conal would want.' As I turned, she smiled. 'He'd want you to come back.'

'Yeah.' I smiled too, properly. 'I will.'

Upstairs, outside Seth's rooms, I hesitated, aching with nerves. I could hear raised voices even through the solid oak door: Seth and my mother, at each other's throats again, only it didn't make me so happy as it once did.

Stella's voice was harsh. 'How typical of you, Seth, to make me come to you.'

'Nobody made you come here.' He was angry too, but his voice was low. 'It's your own stupid oath you've broken, Reultan.'

'Don't call me by that name. *Not ever.*'

I'd lost my taste for eavesdropping. As I shoved open the door, they both fell guiltily silent.

Stella recovered first. 'Finn,' she said, a funny catch in her voice. 'Finn.' She strode across the room and wrapped her arms round me ferociously.

I was briefly shocked rigid; then I hugged her back, burying my face in her shoulder so that neither she nor Seth would see I was crying. Seth kept awkwardly quiet, taking a new and intense interest in the stone walls. As Stella let me go and cleared her throat, recovering her composure and her ice, I felt the hesitant glance of a mind against mine, wilder and more wolfish than Conal's but suddenly just as protective. I knew what Seth was telling me.

~ *Steel yourself, Dorsal. 'Cos your mother is.*

'Finn, you're coming back with me tonight.' Stella tried to smile. 'I've only left it this long because of Conal. I'm sorry.'

'Stella, be careful for her,' said Seth. He whetted his sword as Stella looked on with distaste. 'Finn's a talented girl.'

'She'll learn to keep that quiet, like I do,' said Stella. 'She'll learn to live with the natural laws God intended.'

'Zealot.'

'Leonora had her way,' she said. 'She's dead. And now so is my brother.'

'He was my brother too,' said Seth quietly, stropping the blade.

'I was in a black taxi when I felt him die,' said Stella, quite dispassionately. 'The driver thought I was mad, or drunk. Ah, what does it matter? What do you think you can do without him? One day this world will die, and I don't want Finn's heart to break when it happens. And I don't want her to come to the same end as Conal, or her father. She doesn't belong here.'

Seth looked at me. 'Yes, she does.'

'She is my daughter!'

'That's why she's going back with you.' Seth held up his blade and turned it in the light, then looked along it into Stella's blazing eyes. Turning on her heel, she stalked out.

'I don't want to go back,' I told Seth tearfully.

'It isn't up to you. Or me.' Seth went on obsessively honing his new sword blade. He'd wear it away altogether before the day was out. He was driving me mad.

'You're the Captain of this dun!'

'That doesn't give me authority to come between a mother and her daughter.'

'You could if you wanted to.'

'It's not about what I want.' He rubbed his arm across his eyes and I was shocked to realise he was almost crying.

I stopped being angry with him, and gulped. 'Stella

swore an oath, Seth. She's broken it to come and get me. What'll happen to her?'

'Nothing will happen to her.' He still didn't look at me, I noticed. 'Don't listen to that mumbo-jumbo, Finn. Jinxes, curses, shite. Don't think about it. It can drive you mad.'

'Damn her.' Tears stung my eyes. 'I won't even have Jed.'

'You'll have your mother, so don't you dare damn her.' He put down his whetstone at last to look up at me. 'Jed would go back if he could have his. Don't you understand that she loves you?' He scraped his fingers through his regrown hair. 'Finn, if you ever choose to come back here, you'll need to do it without hating yourself and her. You need to learn to forgive each other. And,' he added sharply before I could interrupt, 'you need to forgive your clann.'

I couldn't. I couldn't help it. I remembered his body jerking, the shock of pain gouged over and over into his face. As for the sickening sound of the lash, I'd never get it out of my head. I couldn't imagine how much it had hurt him. Their Captain, their friend, the brother of the man they claimed to love. Oh, the clann did my head in. All of them. Even him.

I glared into his eyes. 'I will never forgive them. *Never.*'

'Quite,' he said, and I knew I'd blown any chance I might have had. 'Finn, you hate them and you have to go. It's dangerous for you and the clann if you stay. Besides, I'm one of them, understand?'

'All right. Don't lecture me.'

'Sorry. I'm kind of upset myself.' Standing, he slung an arm round my shoulders. 'Go and see the world, Finn. Get over all this. I see that damn silly raven's back, so take him with you. He likes it over there.' Frowning, he used his fingertips to turn my face so that he could see my eyes. He took a breath. 'Oh. I see. Faramach didn't . . . he didn't come to Brokentor.'

Mind-reader. I gave him a quick smile of relief and gratitude.

'School won't be so bad.' He grinned. 'Your last year. And I don't think Shania will trouble you again.'

I said, 'Conal was so mad about that.'

'I was kind of proud of you. Don't do it again, though,' he added quickly as I lifted my eyebrows in surprise. 'Look, be alone if you have to. It's not bad. Me, I like it.'

That figured. 'I'll miss you and Jed,' I said miserably. 'It's going to be years.'

'It's not so long.' He gave me half a grin and released me. 'It's not a punishment, Finn. It's a breathing space. Oh, and before you go? We have a job to do, you and me.'

The beach was winter-desolate. Its fringes of harsh grass were iced with frost and patched with snow, and the sea was grey and angry, lashing the bay. The black horse paced, hooves thudding into the hard sand, nostrils flaring red. At the far end of the bay it backed onto its haunches, flailing the air, then galloped the length of the surf again, stopping just short of trampling Seth.

Grinning, he stroked its face, and it shoved its muzzle into his palm, breath snorting and smoking through bared teeth. Seth hefted Conal's silver-traced bridle in his other hand, and green light sparked in the black depths of its eye.

'I'm sorry to see you go, *each-uisge*. But go.'

Turning, he flung the bridle in a huge arc. The straps swung wildly in midair, but it was carried far into the waves. For long seconds, it was visible in the trough between two swells; then it sank.

The black horse screamed. Without a backward glance, it went into the sea at a flying canter, plunging through the windblown waves. When it was beyond its depth, it swam, powerful neck driving through the water like the prow of a ship. It crested three massive waves; then a fourth broke over it, and it did not reappear. I watched till my eyes watered, but it was gone.

I went to Seth's side and hugged my chest, the wind fanning my hair across my face. Unexpected tears burned. The wake still haunted me: the drums, the eerie music with its racing beat, Seth's rough beautiful voice singing in a language I didn't understand.

'He wasn't meant to die,' said Seth, staring out to sea. 'That was my job too.'

'Oh, quit doing that.' I shoved my windblown hair out of my eyes. 'Want to give yourself a break for once?'

He laughed. 'Ach, Finn. You'll love your clann, I promise you. Kate is thwarted for now. We have the Bloodstone. We don't know what Rory can do, but neither does she, and she'll have years of sleepless nights. Whether you or I believe in prophecies doesn't matter: she does, and she'll be afraid of us for a long time. So you can get the last of her out of your head.'

'Aye.' My smile was sceptical. 'Like you have.'

Wordless, he looked towards the dun. Jed was scrambling and sliding down the dunes, and Rory was pelting across the hard sand like a small bullet, straight for Seth. The man fell to his knees and let Rory collide with his chest, then staggered to his feet and swung him up onto his shoulders. He still flinched a little, but I decided not to mention it.

'Time's up,' he told me. Steadying Rory's balance, he laid an arm across Jed's shoulders. 'Don't worry, I won't let Jed cut himself. And we'll be here when you get back. I promise.'

'You'd better be.' I went into their arms.

Rory's stubby fingers were entangled in my hair, and in the moment it took to disengage him, a tear escaped. Seth brushed it away with his thumb as my mother rode to my side.

'Her name's Reultan,' he whispered in my ear.

Stella sat bareback on a white horse, four Sithe riders waiting at a diplomatic distance. As Seth gave me a boost onto the horse, I grinned at my mother.

Raising an eyebrow, Stella gave Seth a curious glance. 'Thank you,' she told him coolly.

He smiled at her.

Stella stroked her horse's neck, and I noticed her fingers were trembling. 'I'll send my bridle back with the escort. Please return it to the sea.'

'Of course.'

'I'll never come back here, Seth, you know that.'

Stella made a heroic effort at a genuine smile. 'But come and see Finn whenever you like.'

She turned her horse and dug her heels into its sides. It sprang forward into a gallop, making her silky black hair banner back in the wind as the escort fell in behind us. My arms tightened around her waist, feeling Stella's heartbeat racing with the rhythm of the hooves. *Reultan,* I thought. Star; Stella. Maybe she couldn't altogether let go of the Sithe in her.

My mother's mind was a crazy mess of relief and unbearable sadness, and I realised it broke her heart to leave this place again, and for the last time. She was doing the wrong thing, and she was breaking more hearts than her own, but she was doing it to protect me. Because she actually did love me. And that was a kind of homecoming too.

Closing my eyes against the northern wind, I smiled, and I didn't look back. In my head I could still see them anyway. Jed and Rory and Seth, and a wild winter sea, and grey-bellied waves already obliterating the hoofprints in the sand.

About the Author

Gillian Philip was born in Glasgow but has spent much of her life in Aberdeen, Barbados, and a beautiful valley near Dallas (not that one; the very small rural one). Before turning to full-time writing, she worked as a barmaid, theater usherette, record store assistant, radio presenter, typesetter, hotel wrangler, secretary, political assistant, and Celtic-Caribbean singer.

She has been nominated for a Carnegie Medal and a David Gemmell Legend Award, and short-listed for many prizes including the Royal Mail Scottish Book Award. Her favorite genres are fantasy and crime (her novels include *Bad Faith*, *Crossing the Line*, and *The Opposite of Amber*), and she has written as one of the Erin Hunters (*Survivors*) and as Gabriella Poole (*Darke Academy*).

She lives in the northeast Highlands of Scotland with husband Ian, twins Jamie and Lucy, Cluny the Labrador, Milo the Papillon, Otto the half-Papillon (guess how that happened), Buffy the Slayer Hamster, psycho cats The Ghost and The Darkness, chickens Mapp and Lucia, and umpteen nervous fish. She is not getting any more pets. No way.

Turn the page for a sneak peek at the exciting
third installment of Gillian Philip's
Rebel Angels series.

WOLFSBANE

*Available from Tom Doherty Associates
in July 2014*

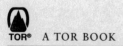

TOR® A TOR BOOK

RORY

So all I had to do was tame the kelpie.

Any self-respecting Sithe could master a water horse, or so my father never tired of telling me. If he could do it, anyone could do it. And he was a good bit younger than me when he bonded with his blue roan. And as my late but sainted Uncle Conal (who I don't even remember) once said, *there's nothing like it.* (I may not remember him, but I'm limitlessly familiar with everything he ever said.)

Anyway, truly, I didn't see what the problem was. Neither did my father.

Perhaps that was the problem.

Seth was in one of those high moods of his, happy and hyper-confident. Who ever said kelpies were easy? Not even him, not before today.

Still, maybe it was the weather, but his mood was infectious. The two of us rode out from the dun across a moor gilded with dew and spangled with spider-webs and misty sunlight. The hills in the distance

looked too ephemeral to be real, but I knew that as
the sun rose higher the day would be diamond-hot.
My father hadn't wiped the grin off his face since he
dragged me out of bed before dawn. And dawn came
bloody early at this time of year.

'Language,' he said absently.

I gave him a half-hearted scowl, and blocked my
mind. He laughed.

'I hope you're not expecting too much,' I told him.

'Course not.'

Yes, he was. He always did.

The little loch was in its summer mood, innocuous
and enticing, looking smaller than it truly was because
of the thick growth of reeds and grasses blurring its
edges. Seth rode his horse in up to its fetlocks, let the
reins fall loose on its neck. He'd left the blue roan behind; no point provoking the kelpie with one of its
own kind, he said. The bay gelding he'd brought in its
place looked none too happy about being expendable.
It tossed its head, pawing the water nervously.

Seth patted its neck, murmuring to it absently as
he watched the rippling surface. 'Go on, then, Rory.
Get on with it.'

My own horse didn't want to go as close to the
water and I didn't blame it. I slid from its back and
hooked its reins over a broken stump, then waded
into the shallows. The water wasn't even that cold. A
moorhen appeared out of the reeds, cocked its red
face-shield at me, then vanished without urgency
into a clump of bulrushes.

'I don't think it's around,' I said.

'Not yet, it isn't.' There was an edge of impatience in his voice. 'Call it.'

I dropped my block, focused, let my mind sink under the silver glittering skin of the loch. The song in my head was familiar enough; I'd learned straight from my father's brain the way to sing in silence to a water horse, and I'd practised last night in the stillness of the dun till I almost hypnotised myself.

Seth leaned forward on his horse, and I realised he was holding his breath.

The surface trembled, stirred. The marsh birds stopped singing. I knew what to expect, but when the creature's head breached the water I still stumbled back.

It was all muscle, gloss and savagery. Its jaws were open, ears laid back, its grey mane matted with weed. Loch-water cascaded from its arched neck and its forelock as it twisted its head to stare at me with eyes as black and impenetrable as a shark's.

We looked at each other for an infinite moment, and then it lurched up and forward, squealing and plunging into the shallows, its hooves sending spray exploding upwards. When it was hock-deep, it halted, glaring.

At least my father couldn't interfere. He was too busy swearing at the bay gelding, which was backing and snorting with fear. By the time he'd calmed it, the kelpie was so close to me I could feel its hot jetting breath on my cheek. It pulled back its lips, grazed its teeth along my hair.

I thought my heart was going to stop.

'Keep calling it,' Seth barked. 'Don't let it in your head yet.'

That was easy enough; almost automatic, so long as he would quit distracting me. In fact I doubted I was ever going to get the song out of my brain. Of course, just keeping the kelpie at a mental distance wouldn't stop it killing me. If it felt that way inclined.

I raised a trembling hand to the crest of its neck. Its mane was silk in my fingers; hard to imagine it could lock tight and hold me. Inside my head the song had become a dull constant chant, embedded enough to let me concentrate on the creature, the feel of it. Oh gods, the warmth and power beneath that cloud-white skin. For the first time this wasn't something I was doing for my father; for the first time I really, truly ached for this horse.

I closed my fist round its mane, close to its withers. I shifted my weight to spring.

It jerked aside, violently. Then it screamed and slammed its head into my chest. The breath was knocked out of me and lights exploded behind my eyelids, but I staggered and kept my footing, and rebalanced myself in time to see it lunge, teeth bared.

I threw myself flat onto the sodden ground, felt its hooves hit the water on either side of my head, drenching me as it bolted. I didn't see it plunge back into the loch, but I heard the gigantic splash, and the panicked clatter of waterfowl.

I leaned on my elbows, mired in my father's silence as much as in the muddy water. I did not want to raise my head. Ever.

After an endless wordless time, he blew out a breath.

'Well,' he said. 'I suppose it had just eaten. Luckily.'

There were things my brother had told me about the hideous, perilous otherworld beyond the Veil. Honestly, I sometimes wondered how it would be to live there. I sometimes dreamed of a place where they called social services if your parents sent you to school with the wrong kind of gloves.

I pushed myself up out of the bog and brushed off pond-muck as well as I could. 'Sorry,' I muttered.

'Don't worry,' he said shortly, pulling his horse's head round. 'Obviously untameable.'

'I thought there was no such thing,' I snapped.

'*Obviously* there *is*.'

What he meant was, if his son couldn't tame it, nobody could. And I'd have liked to tame it, to prove him wrong, but I knew I was never going to. And this time, as I hauled myself onto my horse's back, I made sure my block was just perfect; not because I was afraid of Seth knowing I feared failure, but because I didn't want him to know how much his disappointment was going to matter to me.

It's not that I was unduly afraid of kelpies; I was used to the blue roan, after all. I could ride the blue roan alone, without my father there. Frankly, that pissed him off. I shouldn't have been able to do it, but then there were a lot of things I shouldn't have been able to do. It didn't stop me doing them.

Except that the one thing I really wanted to do, the one thing that would have sent me soaring in my father's estimation, was the one thing I couldn't do. I glared resentfully at the loch and wiped mud off my face.

'Listen,' he said at last, as our horses ambled back towards the dun. 'Forget about it. It doesn't matter. It's not as if it's compulsory.'

'If it wasn't,' I pointed out coldly, 'you wouldn't have said that three times.'

'Jesus, Rory. I won't try and make you feel better, then.'

'I don't need you to make me feel better.' Liar. If I could never be the fighter he was, at least I could have been his equal on a kelpie. Or not, it seemed.

'We're not in a frigging competition. You're my son, not my sparring partner.'

My face burned. 'You weren't meant to hear that. Butt out.'

'So raise a better block.'

I did. 'Just let me come alone next time. It's you that puts me off.'

I didn't look at him for a bit, because he hadn't replied. I didn't want to know how much that last barb had hurt him. Not that he'd think it showed.

'Forget that,' he bit out at last. 'You know fine why you don't get to wander about on your own.'

'I'm fourteen years old. When are you planning to let me grow up?'

'When you start acting it? Hey!'

I'd put my heels to the grey's flanks and I was already way ahead of him by the time he could think about coming after me. As it happened, he didn't. I was heading for the dun and he knew it; and he probably wanted time away from me, just as much as I needed to get away from him. All he did was yell a warning after me.

'You can't tame your own, *doesn't mean you're going near mine.*'

Fine.

Let's see how far he'd go to stop me.